George McHenry

The Cotton Trade

its bearing upon the prosperity of Great Britain and commerce of the American republics, considered in connection with the system of Negro slavery in the Confederate States

George McHenry

The Cotton Trade
*its bearing upon the prosperity of Great Britain and commerce of the American republics,
considered in connection with the system of Negro slavery in the Confederate States*

ISBN/EAN: 9783337409982

Printed in Europe, USA, Canada, Australia, Japan

Cover: Foto ©Andreas Hilbeck / pixelio.de

More available books at **www.hansebooks.com**

THE COTTON TRADE:

ITS BEARING UPON THE PROSPERITY OF GREAT BRITAIN AND COMMERCE OF THE AMERICAN REPUBLICS

CONSIDERED IN CONNECTION WITH THE SYSTEM OF

NEGRO SLAVERY

IN

THE CONFEDERATE STATES.

BY

GEORGE M^CHENRY.

'The resolutions of the States who favoured Abolition were adopted entirely with the view of obtaining additional political power, and imposed on the South the strongest obligation to rise in self-defence. It was a fraternal feeling which induced the Southern States to make common cause with the North in the war of the Revolution. The South had no especial cause of complaint ; it was flourishing by its trade with Great Britain ; but it was actuated by that feeling and principle, to take up arms ; and now, was she to be asked to give up her domestic institutions ? The South asked for no new guarantees, no new security ; but she desired that the Constitution should be preserved from violation.' *Speech of* JEFFERSON DAVIS, *United States Senate, July* 12, 1848.

LONDON:

SAUNDERS, OTLEY, & CO., 66 BROOK STREET, W.

1863.

CONTENTS.

CONTENTS.

CHAPTER VIII.

CHAPTER IX.

CHAPTER X.

CHAPTER XI.

CHAPTER XII.

WILLIAM H. GREGORY, ESQ., M.P.

My DEAR SIR,—I have written some papers on the cotton trade, which, with these remarks addressed to yourself, I propose publishing collectively. I discuss at length several matters in connection with American affairs that have not before, I believe, been fully considered.

During the last twenty-eight weary months—weary enough to all Confederate Americans in Europe—I have been more and more convinced, that the long train of calamities which have occurred within that time might have been averted, but for the opposition on the part of the British ministry and Radical members of Parliament to the motion which you, on March 4, 1861, gave notice of your intention to bring forward in favour of the recognition of the Southern Confederacy, then composed of the seven cotton States. Some time—a week or more—before my departure from America, on the 30th of that month, intelligence had been received in the Northern States of your proposition, which, coupled with the somewhat pacific tone of President Lincoln's inaugural message delivered on the same day, gave assurance to the public mind that the dissolution of the Federal Union would be accomplished in as peaceable a manner as was the case at its formation seventy-two years before, when eleven of the thirteen States 'seceded' from the 'Articles of Confederation.' Confidence in such a happy issue was likewise felt, from the fact that the commissioners appointed by the Confederate States* 'for the settlement of all questions of disagreement between the two governments upon principles of right, justice, equity, and good faith,' had reached Washington on March 5, but at the request of Mr. Seward, through ' a friendly mediator,' did nothing more than give formal notice of their arrival, in order to allow time for the new administration to become fairly organised. What happened subsequently is thus related by President Davis in his message of April 30, 1861 :—

It was not until the 12th of the month that they officially addressed the Secretary of State, informing him of their arrival, and stating, in the language of their instructions, their wish to make to the Government of the United States overtures for the opening of negotiations, assuring the Government of the United States that the President, Congress, and people of the Confederate States desired a peaceful solution of these great questions; that it was neither their interest nor their wish to make any demand which was not founded on the strictest principles of justice, nor to do any act to injure their late confederates.

* South Carolina seceded from the Union on December 20, 1860, and her first act thereafter was to send commissioners to Washington to make a general settlement with her late political copartners. They arrived at the Federal capital on December 27, and left on January 14, 1861, the President having declined to treat with them. It was not until February that South Carolina united with the other cotton States in forming the Confederacy. In the meanwhile some correspondence had been conducted with a gentleman in London, who replied, upon good authority too, that an ambassador from the State would be received at this court by virtue of the Treaty of 1783. South Carolina did not cede her forts to the general government until 1806, and even then her conditions were, that she was to retain all sovereignty over them, her Legislature expressly reserving that control. So the Washington authorities never had jurisdiction in Charleston Harbour. The Constitution (Article I. Section 8) says :—

' Congress shall have power to exercise exclusive legislation in all
' cases whatsoever, over such district (not exceeding ten miles square) as
' may, by cession of particular States and the acceptance of Congress,
' become the seat of the Government of the United States, and to exercise
' like authority over all places purchased, *by the consent of the Legislature*
' *of the State in which the same shall be,* for the erection of forts, magazines,
' arsenals, dockyards, and other needful buildings.'

To this communication no formal reply was received until April 8. During the interval, the commissioners had consented to waive all questions of form, with the firm resolve to avoid war if possible. They went so far even as to hold, during that long period, unofficial intercourse through an intermediary, whose high position and character inspired the hope of success, and through whom constant assurances were received from the Government of the United States of its peaceful intentions, of its determination to evacuate Fort Sumter; and further, that no measures should be introduced changing the existing status prejudicial to the Confederate States; that, in the event of any change in regard to Fort Pickens, notice would be given to the commissioners.

The crooked path of diplomacy can scarcely furnish an example so wanting in courtesy and candour and directness as the course of the United States Government towards our commissioners in Washington. For proof of this I refer to the annexed documents marked, taken in connection with further facts I now proceed to relate.

Early in April the attention of the whole country was attracted to extraordinary preparations for an extensive military and naval expedition in New York and other Northern ports. These preparations commenced in secrecy for an expedition whose destination was concealed, and only became known when nearly completed, and on April 5, 6, and 7, transports and vessels of war, with troops, munitions, and military supplies, sailed from Northern ports bound southward.

Alarmed by so extraordinary a demonstration, the commissioners requested the delivery of an answer to their official communication, and the reply dated on the 15th of the previous month, from which it appears that during the whole interval, whilst the commissioners were receiving assurances calculated to inspire hope of the success of their mission, the Secretary of State and the President of the United States had already determined to hold no intercourse with them whatever—to refuse even to listen to any proposals they had to make, and had profited by the delay created by their own assurances in order to prepare secretly the means for effective hostile operations.

That these assurances were given has been virtually confessed by the Government of the United States, by its act of sending a messenger to Charleston to give notice of its purpose to use force if opposed in its intention of supplying Fort Sumter.

No more striking proof of the absence of good faith in the Government of the United States towards the Confederacy can be required than is contained in the circumstances which accompanied this notice.

According to the usual course of navigation, the vessels composing the expedition, and designed for the relief of Fort Sumter, might be looked for in Charleston Harbour on April 9. Yet our commissioners in Washington were detained under assurances that notice should be given of any military movement. The notice was not addressed to them, but a messenger was sent to Charleston to give notice to the Governor of South Carolina, and the notice was so given at a late hour on April 8, on the eve of the very day on which the fleet might be expected to arrive.

That this manœuvre failed in its purpose was not the fault of those who controlled it. A heavy tempest delayed the arrival of the expedition, and gave time to the commander of our forces at Charleston to ask and receive instruction from the Government. Even then, under all the provocation incident to the contemptuous refusal to listen to our commissioners, and the treacherous course of the Government of the United States, I was sincerely anxious to avoid the effusion of blood, and directed a proposal to be made to the commander of Fort Sumter, who had avowed himself to be nearly out of provisions, that we would abstain from directing our fire on Fort Sumter if he would promise not to open fire on our forces unless first attacked. This proposal was refused. The conclusion was, that the design of the United States was to place the besieging force at Charleston between the simultaneous fire of the fleet. The fort should, of course, be at once reduced. This order was executed by General Beauregard with skill and success, which were naturally to be expected from the well-known character of that gallant officer; and although the bombardment lasted some thirty-three hours, our flag did not wave over the battered walls until after the appearance of the hostile fleet off Charleston.

Mr. William B. Reed, of Pennsylvania, in 'a paper containing a statement and vindication of certain political opinions,' dated August 14, 1862, thus furnishes an extract from a letter received by him from Judge Campbell, which gives some details of the treachery and baseness of Mr. Seward :—

Then, in the months of March and April 1861, came the interlude, if the word can be so applied, of the negotiations as to Fort Sumter, between the Confederate Commissioners and Mr. Seward. And on this point I feel authorised so far to interrupt my personal narrative as to adduce some unpublished testimony, if for no other reason, in order to do justice to a distant friend. I have said that since these troubles began I have had, with a single exception, no correspondent within the limits of the Confederate States. This exception is the Honourable John A. Campbell, of Alabama, formerly a Justice of the Supreme Court of the United States, whom I hope there is no offence in describing as an eminent jurist, a sound Union man till the policy of the Administration rendered Unionism in the South impossible, and a Christian gentleman. To him, having been honoured by his friendship previously, I wrote urging him to retain his place in the Federal judiciary. On June 5, 1861, he answered my letter, and thus referred to his own patriotic agency in a last and ineffectual effort to keep the peace.

'I suppose you must have seen my letters to Governor Seward in some of the Northern papers. There are some facts connected with them that I am glad to have an opportunity to communicate to you. When I visited Governor Seward, I had not had any communication with General Davis, or any member of the Executive Department of the Montgomery Government. The first knowledge I had of the demand of the Commissioners for recognition, or of Mr. Seward's embarrassment, was derived from Judge Nelson and Mr. Seward. I offered to write to General Davis and ask him to restrain his commissioners. I supposed that Mr. Seward desired to prevent the irritation and complaint that would naturally follow from the rejection of the Commissioners in the South, and the reaction that their expression (*sic*) would have at the North. He informed me that Sumter was to be evacuated, and that Mr. Weed said, " This was a sharp and bitter pang, which he (Weed) was anxious might be spared to them." Mr. Seward authorised me to communicate the fact of the evacuation to Mr. Davis, and the precise object was to induce him to render his commissioners inactive. I did not anticipate having any other interview with Mr. Seward. I supposed that Sumter would be evacuated in the course of a very few days, and without any other action on my part. When upon the second and third interviews with him I found there was to be delay, I conversed with Judge Nelson as to the delicacy of my position, and it was at his suggestion and by his counsel that I agreed to be the " intermediary " until Sumter was evacuated. Neither of us doubted that the fort was to be surrendered or abandoned. The first notice of any other disposition was communicated on April 10. Colonel Lamon, the present Marshal of the district of Columbia, came to Washington with the family of Mr. Lincoln, I believe. He was with him at Washington in some familiar capacity. He visited Charleston in March, obtained access to Sumter, and left the impression on the mind of Governor Pickens that he was the agent of the Government, engaged in making arrangements for its evacuation. In the latter part of March, Governor Pickens sent a telegram to ascertain what had become of Lamon. I bore this to Mr. Seward, and he promised to enquire concerning him. His answer was that the President was concerned at any misconception of Lamon's words or visit, and desired me to converse with him; that Lamon did not visit Charleston for him, and was not commissioned to make any pledge or assurance to bind him. Mr. Seward said Lamon would be at the State Department for me to interrogate him. I declined to converse with Lamon, and recommended that he (Lamon) should himself write to Governor Pickens to explain the matter. I asked Governor Seward about the evacuation of the fort. Without any verbal reply, he wrote: — " The President may desire to supply Sumter, but will not do so without giving notice to

Governor Pickens." Upon reading this, I asked if the President had any design to attempt a supply of Sumter. His reply contained an observation of the President. That I pass. But he said he did not believe any attempt would be made to supply Sumter, and there was no design to reinforce it. I told him if that were the case, I should not employ this language, that it would be interpreted as a design to attempt a supply, and that, if such a thing were believed in Charleston, they would bombard the fort, that they did not regard the surrender of Sumter as open to question, and when they did, they would proceed to extremities. He left the State Department, I remaining there till his return; and, on his return, he wrote these words:— " I am satisfied that the Government will not undertake to supply Sumter without giving notice to Governor Pickens." This excluded the matter of desire, and, with what had taken place, left the impression that if any attempt were made it would be an open, declared, and peaceful offer to supply the fort, which, being resisted by the Carolinians, the fort would be abandoned as a military necessity and to spare the effusion of blood—the odium of resistance and of the evacuation being thrown upon the late Administration and the Confederate States. Had these counsels prevailed—had the policy been marked with candour and moderation—I am not sure that even before this the fruit might have been seen ripening among the States in renewed relations of kindness and goodwill, to be followed ere long by a suitable political and civil union, adequate to the security of both sections at home and abroad. The ideas of union and a common country, as applied to all the States, are *now* simply obsolete.'

This simple and precise narrative, introduced here as having been addressed to me, is, in the light of what has occurred since, a sad revelation, which needs no comment. Neither at home nor abroad does the Administration seem to have known that the best policy is fair play. I answered Judge Campbell's letter soon after its receipt, and, as evidence of my feelings and opinions then, I make an extract from my letter. 'You speak of the united and resolute feeling at the South. Here it is very nearly as unanimous, and I can discern no signs of reaction. There are (I speak of this city) a few gentlemen who hold, as I do, to the doctrine of recognition and peace, but it would do neither us nor you any good to say so. There is a local sentiment which it is not graceful or proper to defy, and minorities must sometimes be silent. What is most painful is to be made conscious of insensibility of those around me to the fearful infractions of the Constitution and conceded law which are daily occurring. Professors of elementary law teach their students that the President may suspend the Habeas Corpus Act. Learned and hitherto patriotic men, admitting the acts of the President to be wrong, justify the outrages on the ground of State necessity. This is worse than the other; and this it is which alarms me as a Northern man and one whose lot must be in the North.

Had the objection to your motion not manifested itself so strongly in the quarters mentioned, and had there been any reasonable prospect of its success, the Washington government would never have been sustained by the American people in its attempt to invade Charleston Harbour, and the 'indignity to the old flag,' as the bombardment of Fort Sumter on April 13 was termed, would have made no more impression on the masses than the similar 'insult' inflicted upon the transport steamer 'Star of the West' a few weeks previously.* Mr. Lincoln, taking advantage of the circumstance, issued his Proclamation on April 15, calling for 75,000 troops 'to defend Washington and recapture Federal property.'

---

* The 'old flag' was adopted several years after independence, and only used for maritime purposes—the battles of the revolution were fought under the ensigns of the thirteen sovereign States. On all the buildings of the commonwealth, the State colours should have been displayed, on those of the city the municipal flag. A great deal of nonsense has been talked and written about the 'Stars and Stripes,' which has been productive of mischief. All 'sensation flags' and 'spread-eagleism' ought to be avoided in future. The popular song, 'The Star-spangled Banner,' had not even a revolutionary origin; it was written by the late Francis S. Key, while confined as a prisoner with a number of other Baltimoreans on board of an English ship off Fort M'Henry, during the last war with Great Britain. The descendants of these gentlemen, each and all, ignore the verses, as well as the flag, now that to 'such base uses have they come at last.'

A large number of 'three months' men' volunteered at once for the protection of the capital, which in fact had never been threatened: not a single Southern soldier was at that time north of South Carolina.* The same Proclamation requested the members of Congress to meet in extra session on July 4. The news of the final withdrawal of your motion, at the request of Lord John Russell, on June 7, having been received in the meanwhile, gave the war party confidence that they could carry out their designs without interference from abroad; and the inflammatory speeches and writings of the republican senators, representatives, and newspaper editors

---

* Among the many falsehoods circulated by the Yankees on both sides of the Atlantic is the charge that the Southerners had, through the Secretary of War, Mr. Floyd, been robbing the Northern arsenals. This was disproved in the report of Mr. Stanton, made to the House of Representatives on February 18, 1861. The testimony furnished by his committee established:—

1. That the Southern States obtained in 1860 less, instead of more, than the quota of arms to which they were entitled by law; and that some of them, North Carolina, Mississippi, and Kentucky, received none whatever, and this simply because they did not ask for them. Mr. Stanton remarked, 'That there are a good deal of rumours and speculations and misapprehensions as to the state of facts in regard to this matter.'

2. That the Government had on hand in the year 1859 500,000 old muskets, which had been condemned 'as unsuitable for public service,' under the Act of March 3, 1825. They were of such a character that, although offered at public and private sale for $2\frac{1}{2}$ each, purchasers could not be obtained at that rate, except for a comparatively small number. On November 30, 1859, Secretary Floyd ordered about one-fifth of the whole number (105,000) to be sent from the Springfield Armoury, where they had accumulated, to five Southern arsenals, 'in proportion to their respective means of proper storage.' This order was carried into effect by the Ordnance Bureau in the usual course of administration. Its date was months before Mr. Lincoln's nomination for the Presidency, and nearly a year before his election.

The Southern States were, in fact, entirely unprepared for the war. They were even too slow in their movements when the conflict began. Fortress Monroe ought to have been seized. And the surrender by Southern naval commanders of the ships of war under their control was an act of doubtful propriety. Those ships belonged to the South as much as to the North, and should have been taken into Confederate ports.

excited the public mind and started the cry of 'On to Richmond'—Virginia, North Carolina, Tennessee, and Arkansas having by that time joined the cotton States. Thus the conflict began, and it has since been carried on by the office-holders, contractors, and other 'shoddy' men of the Northern States, the peaceable inhabitants being deprived of all power, even their right to express the voice of dissent.

Let us examine into this question of recognition, for there seems to be much misunderstanding in reference to the political status of the thirteen sovereign communities, now known as the Confederate States of America; to demand 'recognition' for them is, in truth, only to ask for the fulfillment of treaties already existing. The Yankee assertion, that secession is rebellion, can be proved to be entirely untrue. France, on February 6, 1778, acknowledged the independence of the thirteen American colonies, as so many independent States; this was even before the 'Articles of Confederation' were adopted; the United Netherlands followed her example on October 8, 1782; and Sweden, on April 3, 1783; Great Britain withheld her consent to the separation until September 3, 1783, 'provisional articles' having been signed on November 30, 1782; and Spain, Prussia, and the other powers subsequently recognised the States. Under the treaty of Peace, Virginia, North Carolina, South Carolina, and Georgia, were admitted as members (using the plural) of the family of nations; Kentucky, Tennessee, Alabama, and Mississippi, were included, they then being portions of those States. Louisiana, Missouri, Arkansas, and Florida, afterwards by a clause in the Federal Constitution, became 'free, sovereign, and independent States,' possessed of all the rights of the original States; and Texas, by a resolution presented to the Senate by the Hon. R. J. Walker [see Appendix], in 1837 rose to the dignity of an independent power. France, Holland, and Belgium, likewise acknowledged the independence of Texas in 1839 and Great Britain in 1840. It was not until 1845 that Texas entered the Federal Union.

According to the spirit and letter of the Constitution, and the practice under it, the erection of territories into States is equivalent to a recognition of their independence, and joining the Union signifies nothing more than intrusting their foreign affairs, as a matter of convenience and economy, to the central head.* Upon the admission of a new State, the representatives of the 'Federal agency' at foreign courts become also the ministers for that young power; and, without protest, are received as such. Here, then, are thirteen sovereign States practically recognised by all the leading governments of the world.

John Adams, of Massachusetts, was the first 'commissioner' sent to Europe to represent the thirteen original

* One of the arguments used by the Federalists against the acquisition of the Louisiana territory was that the limits of the Confederation would be too large, and that the States in the South-west, by the force of circumstances, might at some future time separate themselves from those on the Atlantic, after having thinned the latter of a portion of their population. Mr. Jefferson replied to these objections in a letter addressed to Mr. Breckenridge dated August 12, 1803, from which the following is an extract:—

'Besides, if it should become the great interest of those nations to separate from this, if their happiness should depend upon it so strongly as to induce them to go through that convulsion, why should the Atlantic States dread it? But, especially, why should we, their present inhabitants, take side in such a question? . . . The future inhabitants of the Atlantic and Mississippi States will be our sons. We leave them in distinct but bordering establishments. We think we see their happiness in their union, and we wish it. Events may prove it otherwise; and if they see their interest in separation, why should we take side with our Atlantic rather than our Mississippi descendants? It is the elder and the younger son differing. God bless them both, and keep them in union, if it be for their good, but separate them if it be better!'

States ; he was appointed to France in December 1777, and afterwards made Minister Plenipotentiary to Great Britain in 1779, but remained on the continent until after the declaration of Peace. In the meanwhile, Franklin had succeeded him at Paris. Both of these statesmen received their authority from the 'Congress of Delegates' from the respective States, the 'Articles of Confederation' not having been entered into until March 2, 1781, and that 'foreign agency' was dissolved on March 3, 1789. Mr. Adams returned home in 1788, the Government of England having omitted to send a corresponding representative to the States, who, in retaliation for this discourtesy, refused to receive her consuls. Peace had then been established for five years. On April 30, 1789, a new foreign agency under the Constitution was formed by eleven States, there having been in reality no union whatever for the space of fifty-eight days ; but no notice was given to any of the governments with which the States had treaties of these changes : such notice, indeed, was not necessary, the individual commonwealths, as has ever been the case, having *retained* their sovereignty.

There was no representative from the American States in England from the time of Mr. Adams' departure until the arrival in London of Mr. Gouverneur Morris, of New Jersey. Washington, as President of eleven States, requested Mr. Morris, who was in Europe on private business, to wait upon the Duke of Leeds, then Secretary for Foreign Affairs. The following letter was his authority for so doing. It bears a marked contrast to the bombastic, untruthful, and lengthy despatches of Mr. Seward :—

New York: October 13, 1789.

Sir,—It being important to both countries that the treaty of peace between Great Britain and the United States should be observed and performed with perfect and mutual good faith, and that a treaty of commerce should be concluded by them, on principles of reciprocal advantages to both, I wish to be ascertained of the sentiments and intentions of the Court of London on these interesting subjects.

It appears to me most expedient to have these enquiries made informally, by a private agent; and understanding that you will soon be in London, I desire you in that capacity, and on the authority and credit of this letter, to converse with his Britannic Majesty's ministers on these points, viz. whether there be any, and what, objections to now performing those articles in the treaty which remained to be performed on his part, and whether they incline to a treaty of commerce with the United States on any, and what, terms.

This communication ought regularly to be made to you by the Secretary of State; but that office not being at present filled my desire of avoiding delays induces me to make it under my own hand. It is my wish to promote harmony and mutual satisfaction between the two countries; and it would give me great pleasure to find that the result of your agency, in the business now committed to you, will conduce to that end.

I am, &c.
GEO. WASHINGTON.

Gouverneur Morris, Esq.

Can it be doubted that North Carolina and Rhode Island, States remote from each other, which had not then joined the new ' agency,' had a right at that time to likewise send a representative, separately or conjointly? And, on the same principle, are not the States comprising the Southern Confederacy entitled to have ministers at the several European courts? In fact, the Union under the Constitution might have been formed by any *nine* States. Surely the doors of the Foreign Office could not have been closed against the other four?

The non-reception of the Confederate Commissioners by the Governments of the European nations, to whom they have been accredited, is a clear violation of existing treaties, and is, in fact, simply deferring to the whims and ambitious assumption of the Washington Government, which has never been formally recognised by any power on earth, intercourse with it having been merely held as the 'agent' of the respective States. Hence it was that Lord Lyons, about two years ago, remonstrated with Mr. Seward in regard to some violations of the Constitution, the 'power of attorney,' under which authority the Lincoln administration professes to act. Mr. Seward replied that he would not permit any foreign government to thus dictate to him. Surely, in the ordinary walks of life, we all require, in dealing with agents, to know exactly the extent of their powers, and have a right to disregard any acts that do not come within the prescribed limits of their delegated authority. Are the Governments of Europe doing right, then, in thus openly fraternising with a revolutionary Government—that at Washington?— for revolutionary it is, because the Federal Constitution has been completely set aside. It is not necessary to enumerate the violations on the part of Mr. Lincoln, his Cabinet and his Congress, of the Federal compact. They are well known. I will be content to give the following extracts from Mr. Madison's reports of the debates in the convention at Philadelphia, which framed the Constitution, to show that the policy of coercion was twice mooted in that body, and was disapproved of on both occasions :—

Tuesday, May 29, 1787.—Mr. Randolph (Virginia) proposed ' to call forth the force of the Union against any member of the Union failing to fulfil its duty under the articles thereof.'

Thursday, May 31, 1787.—Mr. Madison (Virginia), in reply to the above clause, observed, 'that the more he reflected on the use of force, the more he doubted the practicability, the justice,

and the efficacy of it, when applied to people collectively, and
not individually.   A Union of the States containing such an
ingredient seemed to provide for its own destruction.   The use
of force against a State would look more like a declaration of
war than an infliction of punishment, and would probably be
considered by the party attacked as a dissolution of all previous
compacts by which it might be bound.   He hoped that such a
system would be framed as might render this resource unnecessary, and moved that the clause be postponed.'   This motion
was agreed to *nem. con.*

Friday, June 15, 1787.—Among a series of resolutions offered
by Mr. Patterson (New Jersey) was the following:—'And that
if any State, or any body of men in any State, shall oppose or
prevent the carrying into execution such acts and treaties, the
Federal Executive shall be authorised to call forth the power of
the Confederated States, or so much thereof as shall be necessary
to enforce and compel an obedience to such acts, or an observ-
ance of such treaties.'

Saturday, June 16, 1787.—Mr. Randolph, who seems to have
changed his views on the subject, remarked:—'Coercion he
pronounced to be impracticable, expensive, cruel to individuals.
It tended also to habituate the instruments of it to shed the
blood and riot in the spoils of their fellow-citizens, and consequently train them up for the service of ambition.'

Wednesday, June 20, 1787.—Mr. Mason (Virginia) said:—
' It was acknowledged by Mr. Patterson, that the plan could not
be enforced without military coercion.   Does he consider the
force of this concession ?   The most jarring elements of nature,
fire and water themselves, are not more incompatible than such
a mixture of civil liberty and military execution.   Will the
militia march from one State into another, in order to collect
the arrears of taxes from the delinquent members of the
Republic?   Will they maintain an army for this purpose ?
Will not the citizens of the invaded States assist one another,
till they rise as one man and shake off the Union altogether ?
* * * * He took this occasion to repeat that, notwithstanding
his solicitude to establish a national Government, he never
would agree to abolish the States Governments, or render them
absolutely insignificant.'

Mr. Luther Martin (Maryland) 'agreed with Colonel Mason as to the importance of the States Governments; he would support them at the expense of the general Government, which was instituted for the purpose of that support. * * * * At the separation from the British Empire, the people of America preferred the establishment of themselves into thirteen separate sovereignties, instead of incorporating themselves into one. To these they look up for the security of their lives, liberties, and properties; to these they must look up. The Federal Government they formed to defend the whole against foreign nations in time of war, and to defend the lesser States against the ambition of the larger. They were afraid of granting powers unnecessarily, lest they should defeat the original end of the Union; lest the powers should prove dangerous to the sovereignties of the particular States which the Union was meant to support, and expose the lesser to being swallowed up by the larger. He conceived also that the people of the States, having already vested their powers in their respective legislatures, could not resume them without a dissolution of their governments.'

The question of coercion was then dropped. The only clause in the Constitution giving the Central Government control of the military, to be used except in a foreign war, is contained in Article IV. Section 4, viz.—'The United States shall guarantee to every State in this Union a republican form of Government, and shall protect each of them against invasion; *and on application of the Legislature, or of the Executive* (when the Legislature cannot be convened), against domestic violence.'

Mr. Alexander Hamilton, also a member of the Convention, speaking on this subject, said:—

It has been observed, to coerce States is one of the maddest projects ever devised. A failure of compliance will never be confined to a single State. This being the case, can we suppose it wise to hazard a civil war? Suppose Massachusetts or any large State should refuse, and Congress should attempt to

compel them, would they not have influence to procure assistance, especially from those States which are in the same situation as themselves? What picture does this idea present to our
view? A complying State at war with a non-complying State,
Congress marching the troops of one State into the bosom of
another—this State collecting auxiliaries, and forming, perhaps,
a majority against its Federal head. Here is a nation at war
with itself. Can any reasonable man be well-disposed towards a
Government which makes war and carnage the only means of
supporting itself—a Government that can exist only by the
sword? Every such war must involve the innocent with the
guilty. This single consideration should be sufficient to dispose
any peaceable citizen against such a Government.

The great mass of Northerners of the present generation, especially the middle classes, are very stupid on the
subject of politics, though those of the highest and lowest
strata are, in every sense of the word, much better
citizens. The midway folks, of which such associations
as the New York Chamber of Commerce is composed, are
as conceited as they are ignorant, and have been much
flattered by the ' pot-house ' politicians ; hence the great
decay in public morals in the North. These people, not
regarding the significance of the terms ' Union ' and
' United States,' have imagined the States to be one
country, whereas they are each and all as different as
the nations of Europe, the Constitution being practically
little more than a treaty or alliance between them. The
Governors of the States have the highest prerogatives of
monarchs—the pardoning power; property is held and
crime punished under State laws ; no person can be a
citizen of two States at the same time. Any of the
States can have an established church, as was the case in
Virginia for many years after she acceded to the Constitution ; the clause in that document referring to this subject
merely prohibits Congress from interfering in the matter.

The United States cannot own a foot of soil in any of the States without first obtaining their consent, nor has the Washington Government ever had power to grant to foreigners the right of holding real estate—in short, the 'sovereignty' has always resided in the individual States. Yet the Federal machine—the creature—has assumed to be greater than its principals, as is frequently the case in private life, and for this reason it has ceased to work for the benefit of those who made it.

The words, 'We, the people,' and more 'perfect' union used in the preamble to the Constitution, have been productive of mischief, in consequence of their not having been properly understood by the masses, who have been led astray by designing politicians taking advantage of these expressions without explaining their true intent and meaning. History settles all difficulties on this point. On August 6, 1787, the committee appointed for that purpose reported the first draft of a Constitution. The preamble was in these words:—'We, the people of the States of New Hampshire, Massachusetts, Rhode Island and Providence Plantations, Connecticut, New York, New Jersey, Pennsylvania, Delaware, Maryland, Virginia, North Carolina, South Carolina, and Georgia, do ordain, declare, and establish the following Constitution, for the government of ourselves and our posterity.' On the next day this preamble was unanimously adopted. The draft of the Constitution was discussed, and various alterations made until September 8, 1787, when the following resolution was passed:—'It was moved and seconded to appoint a committee of five, to revise the style of and arrange the articles agreed to by the House; which passed in the affirmative.' This committee had no power to change the *meaning* of any clause

which had been adopted, but were authorised merely to
' revise the style ' and arrange the matter in proper order.
On the 12th of the same month, they made their report.
The preamble read : ' We, *the people of the United States,*
in order to form a more perfect Union, to establish justice,
insure domestic tranquillity, provide for the common
defence, promote the general welfare, and secure the
blessings of liberty to ourselves and our posterity, do
ordain and establish this Constitution for the United
States of America.'   On the next day (September 13)
' it was moved and seconded to proceed to comparing of
the report from the committee of revision, with the articles
that were agreed to by the House, and to them referred
for arrangement, which passed in the affirmative, and the
same was read by paragraphs, compared, and in some
places corrected and amended.'   The only change which
was made in the preamble was striking out the word ' to '
before the words ' establish justice,' and no other change
was made in any of the articles except such as would
make the ' report of the committee of revision correspond
with the article agreed to by the House.'   There is a
perfectly conclusive reason for the change of phraseology
in the preamble, from the States by name, to the more
general expression ' the United States,' and this, too, without supposing that the alteration was meant to convey a
different idea as to the relation of the parties to the Constitution.   The revised draft contained a proviso that the
Constitution should go into operation when adopted and
ratified by *nine* States.   It was, of course, uncertain
whether more than nine States would adopt it or not,
and, if they should not, it would be altogether improper
to name them as parties to the instrument.   As to one
of them, Rhode Island, not being represented in the

Convention, it would have been improper to insert her as a party. Hence it became necessary to adopt a form of expression which would apply to those who should ratify the Constitution, and not to those who might refuse to do so. And it simply means, 'We, the people of those States who have united for that purpose, do ordain,' &c. This construction corresponds with other historical facts, and reconciles the language employed with the circumstances of the case. The word 'people' was both plural and singular at that period; indeed, it was so used up to the year 1847, when the expression 'peoples' was suggested by Kossuth, who, employing the idiom of his native language, when speaking in English, said that the Austrians and Hungarians were two *peoples*.

The Government, under the Articles of Confederation, having only been in existence six years at the time of the framing of the Constitution, it would have been an absurdity to repeat the word 'perpetual' in the latter document, and a term expressing less absolute permanence was inserted—a 'more perfect' union. Now, this language is more qualified in its character. The Government was only to be 'perfect' as long as it lasted. The work of human hands can never be so 'perfect' as to be perpetual;' 'perpetual' motion has not yet been discovered.

Mr. Calhoun, in his work 'On the Constitution and Government of the United States,' thus wrote:—

From all that has been stated, the inference follows, irresistibly, that the Government is a *Federal*, in contradistinction to a national government—a government formed by the States, ordained and established by the States, and for the States—without any participation or agency whatever on the part of the people regarded in the aggregate as forming a nation; that it is throughout, in whole, and in every part, simply and purely Federal—'the Federal Government of these States' as is accurately and concisely expressed by General Washington, the organ of the Convention, in his letter laying it before the old Congress—words carefully selected, and with a full and accurate knowledge of their import. There is, indeed, no such community, *politically* speaking, as the people of the United States, regarded in the light thereof, and as constituting one people or nation. There never has been any such, in any stage of their existence; and, of course, they neither could, nor ever can, exercise any agency, or have any participation, in the formation of our system of government. In all its parts—including the Federal as well as the separate States governments, it emanated from the same source—the people of the several States. The whole, taken together, form a Federal community—a community composed of States united by a political compact, and not a nation composed of individuals united by what is called a social compact.

I shall next proceed to show that it is Federal, in contradistinction to a confederacy.

It differs and agrees, but in opposite respects, with a national government and a confederacy. It differs from the former inasmuch as it has for its basis a confederacy, and not a nation, and agrees with it in being a government; while it agrees with the latter to the extent of having a confederacy for its basis, and differs from it inasmuch as the powers delegated to it are carried into execution by a government, and not by a mere congress of delegates, as is the case in a confederacy. To be more full and explicit, a Federal government, though based on a confederacy, is, to the extent of the powers delegated, as much a government as a national government itself. It possesses, to this extent, all the authorities possessed by the latter, and as fully and perfectly. The case is different with a confederacy; for, although it is sometimes called a *government*, its congress, or council, or the body representing it, by whatever name it may be called, is much more nearly allied to an assembly of diplomatists, convened to deliberate and determine how a league or treaty between their several sovereigns, for certain defined purposes, shall be carried into execution; leaving to the parties themselves to furnish their quota of means, and to cooperate in carrying out what may have been determined on. Such was the character of the congress of our confederacy; and such, substantially, was that of similar bodies in all confederated communities which preceded our present government. Our system is the first that ever substituted a *government* in lieu of such bodies. This, in fact, constitutes its peculiar characteristic. It is new, peculiar, and unprecedented.

In the opinion of many sound lawyers, each one of the Northern States has now a right under the existing treaties to despatch ministers to Europe. The bond of union between them—the Constitution—has been broken by the Lincoln Administration, and they are only held together by the power of a large military force. Mr. Madison, in his inaugural address, declared the duties of the Federal Government to be : ' to support the Constitution, which is the cement of the Union, as well as in its *limitations* as in its authorities ; to respect the rights and authorities reserved to the States, and to the people, as equally incorporated with, and essential to, the success of the general system ; to avoid the slightest interference with the rights of conscience or the functions of religion, so wisely exempted from civil jurisdiction ; in behalf of private and personal rights, and the *freedom of the press,*' &c. &c.

The Lincoln Government is without doubt as revolutionary as that of its neighbours in the South-west — the Mexican States. Indeed, there is a striking similarity between them. The difficulties that have existed in the latter country for the last forty years, have been in a large measure owing to the interference by the central authorities with the rights of the individual States, and the constant effort to form a consolidated power. Now that Napoleon has taken charge of these people, it is to be hoped that ' order will reign in Mexico.'

This brings us to the matter of secession, which is one of the reserved rights of the States, as will be seen by the following preamble and article from the amendments to the Constitution adopted in September 1789 :—

Preamble. The conventions of a number of States having, at the time of their adopting the Constitution, expressed a desire, in order to prevent misconstruction or abuse of its powers, that further declaratory and restrictive clauses should be added; and as extending the ground of public confidence in the Government will best insure the beneficent ends of its institutions, therefore, Resolved, &c.

Article 10. ' The powers not delegated to the United States ' by the Constitution, nor prohibited by it to the States, are ' reserved to the States respectively, or to the people.'

We have the opinion of most of the leading men of America in favour of the right of secession. A few extracts from their speeches and writings may be given in the order of date. In the year 1798, Mr. Jefferson drew up sundry resolutions which passed the Kentucky Legislature, among which will be found the following :—

Resolved, That the several States composing the United States of America, are not united on the principle of unlimited submission to their general government; but that by compact, under the style and title of a Constitution for the United States, and of amendments thereto, they constituted a general government for special purposes, delegated to that government certain definite powers, reserving each State to itself the residuary mass of right to their own self-government ; and that whensoever the general government assumes undelegated powers, its acts are unauthoritative, void, and of no force; that to this compact each State acceded as a State, and is an integral party; that this government, created by this compact, was not made the exclusive or final judge of the extent of the powers delegated to itself, since that would have made its discretion, and not the

Constitution, the measure of its powers; but that, as in all other cases of compact among parties having no common judge, each party has an equal right to judge for itself, as well of infractions, as of the mode and measure of redress.

Resolved, That the Constitution of the United States is a compact between the several States, *as States*, each sovereign State being an integral party to that compact; that, as in other compacts between equal sovereigns who have no common judge, each party has the right to interpret the compact for itself, and is bound by no interpretation but its own; that the general government has no final right, in any of its branches, to interpret the extent of its own powers; that these powers are limited within certain prescribed bounds; and that all acts of the general government, not warranted by its own powers, may properly be nullified by a State within its own boundaries.

The Legislature of Virginia adopted similar resolutions the same year; on their consideration, Mr. Madison from the committee submitted an argument in favour of the doctrines contained in them; he said : —

It appears to your committee to be a plain principle, founded on common sense, illustrated by common practice, and essential to the nature of compacts, that, where resort can be had to no tribunal superior to the authority of the parties, the parties themselves must be the rightful judges, in the last resort, whether the bargain made has been pursued or violated. The Constitution of the United States was formed by the sanction of the States, given by each in its sovereign capacity. It adds to the stability and dignity, as well as the authority, of the Constitution, that it rests on this legitimate and solid foundation. The States, then, being the parties to the constitutional compact, and in their sovereign capacity, it follows, of necessity, that there can be no tribunal above their authority to decide, in the last resort, whether the compact made by them be violated; and consequently that, as parties to it, they must themselves decide, in the last resort, such questions as may be of sufficient magnitude to require their respective interposition.

Mr. Madison concluded his remarks by predicting the

present state of affairs in America with painful and fearful exactness, drawing a picture of the catastrophe yet to come. These are his words :—

If measures can mould Governments, and if an *uncontrolled power of construction is surrendered to those who administer them,* their progress may be easily foreseen and their end easily foretold. A lover of monarchy who opens the treasures of corruption *by distributing emoluments among devoted partisans,* may at the same time be approaching his object, and deluding the people with professions of republicanism. He may confound monarchy and republicanism by the art of definition. He may varnish over the dexterity which ambition never fails to display, with the pliancy of language, the seduction of expediency, or the prejudices of the times. And he may come at length to avow that so extensive a territory as that of the United States can only be governed by the energies of monarchy, that it cannot be defended except by standing armies, and that it cannot be united except by consolidation. Measures have already been adopted which may lead to these consequences. They consist:

In fiscal systems and arrangements, which keep an host of commercial and wealthy individuals embodied and obedient to the mandates of the treasury.

In armies and navies, which will, on the one hand, enlist the tendency of man to pay homage to his fellow-creature who can feed or honour him; and on the other, employ the principle of fear by punishing imaginary insurrections, under the pretext of preventive justice.

In swarms of officers, civil and military, who can inculcate political tenets, tending to consolidation and monarchy, both by indulgences and severities, and can act as spies over the free exercise of human reason.

In restraining the freedom of the press, and *investing the Executive with legislative, executive, and judicial powers* over a numerous body of men.

And, that we may shorten the catalogue, *in establishing, by successive precedents, such a mode of construing the Constitution as will rapidly remove every restraint upon Federal power.*

Let history be consulted; let the man of experience reflect; nay, let the artificers of monarchy be asked what further material they can need for building up their favourite system.

Massachusetts at a very early day advocated secession. Her representatives in Congress in 1789 threatened to break up the Union that had just been formed, if the Federal Capitol were located on the Potomac, and their opposition was only withdrawn upon condition that the Southern members would vote for the assumption of the old war debt of the individual States.* The Yankees are always sharp in money matters. Again, in 1803, in opposing the purchase of the Louisiana territory, they claimed the right to secede, and their State Legislature actually passed a resolution to 'dissolve' their connection with the other States, in the event of a confirmation by the Senate of the treaty with France on that subject. They made a similar difficulty in 1811, upon the erection of the Orleans part of that territory into a State. In 1808 there was a secret plot in Massachusetts, in connection with the other New England States, to withdraw from the Union in consequence of the embargo on all foreign commerce, a retaliatory measure adopted by Congress, against the Berlin and Milan decrees of Napoleon, and Orders in Council of England. Mr. John Quincy Adams, who had favoured the measure, resigned his seat in the Senate, and communicated to the President

---

* In the course of the debate on the selection of a site for the Capitol, September 3, 1789, Mr. Sedgwick, of Massachusetts, said : 'In my view on the principle of population, it is far beyond the centre (alluding to the Potomac), for I do not think it just on this subject to take the constitutional computation. Will any gentleman pretend that men who are merely the subjects of property or wealth should be taken into the estimate? that the slaves of the country should be taken into view in determining the centre of the Government? If they were considerate, gentlemen might as well estimate the black cattle of New England.

the feeling of the Legislature and people of his State. In order to preserve the Union, the Embargo Act was repealed and a Non-intercourse Act substituted, which permitted trade to be carried on with all countries other than those of the belligerents. It was afterwards so modified, that commerce could also be conducted with *them* so soon as their obnoxious measures were removed. Massachusetts, in 1814, again avowed the same principles. The committee of her Legislature, in relation to the war with Great Britain, thus reported :—

We believe that this war, so fertile in calamities and so threatening in consequences, has been waged with the worst possible views, and carried on in the worst possible manner : forming a union of wickedness and weakness which defies, for a parallel, the annals of the world. We believe, also, that its worst effects are yet to come ; that war upon war, tax upon tax, and exaction upon exaction, must be imposed, until the comforts of the present and hopes of the rising generation are destroyed. An impoverished people will be an enslaved people. An army of 60,000 men, become veteran by the time the war is ended, and may become the instrument, as in former times, of destroying even the forms of liberty. It will be as easy to establish a President for life by their arms, as a President for four years by intrigue. We tremble for the liberties of our country. We think it the duty of the present generation to stand between the next and despotism.

The committee had no doubt of the right of the State to resist the enforcement of all unconstitutional laws. They continued :

The power to regulate commerce is abused when employed to destroy it, and a voluntary abuse of power sanctions the right of resistance as much as a direct and palpable usurpation. The sovereignty of the States was reserved to protect the citizens from acts of violence by the United States, as well as for purposes of domestic regulation. We spurn the idea that the free, sovereign, and independent State of Massachusetts is reduced to a mere municipal corporation, without power to protect its people or to defend them from oppression, from whatever quarter it comes. Whenever the national compact is violated, and the citizens of this State oppressed by cruel and unauthorised enactments, this Legislature is bound to interpose its power, and to wrest from the oppressor his victim. This is the spirit of our Union, and thus has it been explained by the very man who now sets at defiance all the principles of his early political life. The question, then, is not a question of power or right, but of time and expediency.

This same Legislature appointed delegates to meet others from Connecticut and Rhode Island, who assembled in convention at Hartford in the first-named State, on December 15, 1814. After reciting various grievances against the central power, the convention declared that :

Though acts of Congress, in violation of the Constitution, were merely void, yet it did not seem to consist with the respect and forbearance due from a Confederated State towards the general government to fly at once upon every infraction to open resistance. The mode and energy of opposition ought rather to conform to the nature of the violation, the intention of its authors, the extent of the injury inflicted by it, the determination manifested to persist in it, and the danger of delay. Yet, in cases of deliberate, dangerous, and palpable infractions of the Constitution affecting the sovereignty of a State and the liberties of the people, it was not only the right, but the duty also, of the State to interpose its authority for their protection. When emergencies occur, either beyond the reach of the judicial tribunals or too pressing to admit of the delay incident to their forms, States which have no common umpire must be their own judges, and execute their own decisions.

At the time the discussion took place in Congress in reference to the admission of Texas, the Legislature of Massachusetts protested against such a policy, declaring that, should the ' annexation ' take place, she would secede from the Union ; and the statute has never been repealed.

On all these six occasions, the Federalists, or Whigs, in Massachusetts were the leading secessionists.*

Here is Pennsylvanian opinion on the same subject. The Hon. William Rawle, one of the ablest members of the Philadelphia bar, wrote as follows, in 1825 :—

The Union is an association of the people of the Republics; its preservation is calculated to depend on the preservation of those Republics. The people of each pledge themselves to preserve that form of government in all. Thus each becomes responsible to the rest that no other form of government shall prevail in it, and all are bound to preserve it in everyone.

But the mere compact, without the power to enforce it, would be of little value. Now, this power can be nowhere so properly lodged as in the Union itself. Hence the term 'guarantee' indicates that the United States are authorised to

---

* Within two months after the formation of the first Union under the Articles of Confederation, and while the revolutionary war was yet pending, the New England States were desirous of 'seceding' therefrom, in consequence of the derangement of the finances, owing to the enormous issues of 'Continental Money.' The disgust and impatience of the people of Massachusetts and New Hampshire (Maine at that time was a portion of the former and Vermont part of the latter State) were so great that they moved for instructions to their delegates in Congress to make overtures for peace with Great Britain. In Connecticut the minds of the people were so directed in that way, that if any influential person had stood forth, and appealed to those who wished to preserve their charter and enjoy immediate peace, he would have been instantly joined by a vast majority of the colony, in a resolve to withdraw from Congress, and oppose what they alleged to be the 'pernicious laws by which they had been so often cheated of their property.' Quietness was only restored by the masses discrediting the 'continental greenbacks,' and on May 7, 1781, they ceased to circulate. On this occasion, as well as the second war with England, the New England States had no moral right to contemplate availing themselves of their privilege of seceding from the other States. They had all entered the conflict together, and it would have been unfair to have left the more Southern States in the lurch. A member of a mercantile firm has no right to withdraw therefrom when his house is in difficulties; 'secession' should only take place when the concern is unembarrassed. The Yankees threw cold water upon the Mexican war, and contributed but very few troops to the service. Even those persons who did aid in the campaign were very unpopular until the successes of the American arms began to be announced. The Puritans were then not slow in taking a share of credit to themselves.

oppose, and, if possible, to prevent, every State in the Union from relinquishing the republican form of government; and, as an auxiliary means, they are expressly authorised and required to employ their force, on the application of the constituted authorities of each State, *to repress domestic violence.* If a faction should attempt to subvert the government of a State for the purpose of destroying its republican form, the paternal power of the Union could be thus called forth to subdue it.

Yet it is not to be understood that its interposition would be justifiable, *if the people of a State should determine to retire from the Union,* whether they adopted another or retained the same form of government; or if they should, with the express intention of seceding, expunge the representative system from their code, and thereby incapacitate themselves from concurring, according to the mode now prescribed, in the choice of certain public officers of the United States.

The principle of representation, although certainly the wisest and best, is not essential to the being of a republic, but to continue a member of the Union it must be preserved, and therefore the guarantee must be so construed. *It depends on the State itself to retain or abolish the principle of representation, because it depends on itself whether it will continue a member of the Union. To deny this right would be inconsistent with the principle on which all our political systems are founded; which is, that the people have in all cases a right to determine how they will be governed.*

This right must be considered as an ingredient in the original composition of the general government, which, though not expressed, was mutually understood; and the doctrine heretofore presented to the reader in regard to the indefeasible nature of personal allegiance, is so far qualified in respect to allegiance to the United States. It was observed that it was competent for a State to make a compact with its citizens, that the reciprocal obligations of protection and allegiance might cease on certain events; and it was further observed, that allegiance would necessarily cease on the dissolution of the society to which it was due. The States, then, may wholly withdraw from the Union, but while they continue they must retain the character of representative Republics.

The secession of a State from the Union depends upon the will of the people of such State. The people alone, as we have already seen, hold the power to alter their constitution. The Constitution of the United States is to a certain extent incorporated with the constitutions of the several States by the act of the people. The State legislatures have only to perform certain organic operations in respect to it. To withdraw from the Union comes not within the general scope of their delegated authority. There must be an express provision to that effect inserted in the State constitutions. This is not at present the case with any of them, and it would perhaps be impolitic to confide it to them. A matter so momentous ought not to be intrusted to those who would have it in their power to exercise it lightly and precipitately upon sudden dissatisfaction or causeless jealousy, perhaps against the interests and the wishes of a majority of their constituents.

But in any manner by which a secession is to take place, nothing is more certain than that the act should be deliberate, clear, and unequivocal. The perspicuity and solemnity of the original obligation require correspondent qualities in its dissolution. The power of the general government cannot be defeated or impaired by an ambiguous or implied secession on the part of the State, although a secession may perhaps be conditional. The people of the State may have some reasons to complain in respect to the acts of the general government; they may, in such cases, invest some of their own officers with the power of negotiation, and may declare an absolute secession in case of their failure. Still, however, the secession must, in such case, be distinctly and peremptorily declared to take place in that event, and in such case—as in the case of an unconditional secession— the previous ligament with the Union would be legitimately and fairly destroyed. But in either case the people is the only motive power.

To withdraw from the Union is a solemn, serious act. Whenever it may appear expedient to the people of a State, it must be manifested in a direct and unequivocal manner. If it is ever done indirectly, the people must refuse to elect representatives, as well as to suffer their Legislature to reappoint senators. The senator whose time has not yet expired must be forbidden to continue in the exercise of his functions.

But without plain decisive measures of this nature, proceeding from the only legitimate source—the people—the United States cannot consider their legislative powers over such States suspended, nor their executive or judicial powers in any way impaired; and they would not be obliged to desist from the collection of revenue within such State.

As to the remaining States among themselves, there is no opening for a doubt.

Secession may reduce the number to the smallest integer admitting combination. They would remain united under the same principles and regulations among themselves that now apply to the whole; for a State cannot be compelled by other States to withdraw from the Union; and, therefore, if two or more determine to remain united, although all the others desert them, nothing can be discovered in the Constitution to prevent it.

These are opinions deliberately expressed, not in reference to any particular suit or any particular action, but the result of the general reflections of a highly educated legal mind as to the Constitution of the United States; and these, too, of a man eminently conservative in his character, and entirely unambitious, who eschewed political life, refused an office of the highest honour under the greatest man our country has ever produced, and belonged to a party that certainly was not indisposed to carry the Federal powers to the utmost extent that the Constitution justified.

Later, in 1832, South Carolina thus expressed herself, when she nullified the protective tariff that had been passed by the Federal Congress :—

That the people of South Carolina will maintain the said ordinance at every hazard, and that they will consider the passage of any Act of Congress, abolishing or closing the ports of said State, or otherwise obstructing the free ingress or egress of vessels to and from the said ports, or any other Act of the Federal Government to coerce the State, shut up her ports, destroy or harass her commerce, or to enforce the said Acts otherwise than through the civil tribunals of the country, as inconsistent with the longer continuance of South Carolina in the Union ; and that the people of the said State will thenceforth hold themselves absolved from all further obligation to maintain or preserve their political connection with the people of the other States, and will forthwith proceed to organise a separate government, and do all other acts and things which sovereign and independent States may of right do.*

Mr. Calhoun, in his work already quoted, writes—

But, according to the fundamental principles of our system, sovereignty resides in the people, and not in the Government ; and if in them, it must be in them, as the people of the several States ; for, politically speaking, there is no other known to the system. It not only resides in them, but resides in its plenitude, unexhausted and unimpaired. If proof be required, it will be found in the fact—which cannot be controverted, so far as the United States are concerned—that the people of the several States, acting in the same capacity and in the same way, in which they ordained and established the Federal Constitution, can, by their concurrent and united voice, change or abolish it, and establish another in its place ; or dissolve the Union, and resolve themselves into separate and disconnected States. A power which can rightfully do all this, must exist in full plenitude, unexhausted and unimpaired ; for no higher act of sovereignty can be conceived. . . . . . They (the States and the United States) stand then, as to the one, in relation of superior to subordinate—the creator to the created. The people of the several States called it into existence, and conferred by it, on the Government, whatever power or authority it possesses. Regarded simply as a constitution, it is as subordinate to them,

* South Carolina did not on this occasion, as is generally supposed, withdraw from the sound position she had taken. It was not until after the tariff on foreign importations was reduced by what is known as 'the Compromise Act' that she rescinded her ordinance of nullification.

as are their respective State constitutions ; and it imposes no more restrictions on the exercise of any of their sovereign rights than they do.   The case, however, is different as to the relations which the people of the several States bear to each other in reference to it.   Having ratified and adopted it by mutual agreement, they stand to it in the relation of parties to a constitutional compact ; and, of course, it is binding between them as a *compact*, and not on or over them as a *constitution*.   Of all compacts that can exist between independent and sovereign communities, it is the most intimate, solemn, and sacred, whether regarded in reference to the closeness of connection, the importance of the objects to be effected, or to the obligations imposed.   Laying aside all intermediate agencies, the people of the several States, each in their sovereign capacity, agreed to unite themselves together in the closest possible connection that could be formed, without merging their respective sovereignties into one common sovereignty,—to establish one common government, for certain specific objects, which, regarding the mutual interest and security of each, and of all, they supposed could be more certainly, safely, and effectually promoted by it, than by their several separate governments ; pledging their faith, in the most solemn manner possible to support the compact thus formed by respecting its provisions, obeying all acts of the government made in conformity with them, and preserving it, as far as in them lay, against all infractions.   But as solemn and sacred as it is, and as high as the obligations may be which it imposes,—still it is but a *compact* and not a *constitution— regarded in reference to the people of the several States in their sovereign capacity.*   To use the language of the constitution itself, it was ordained as a 'constitution *for* the United States,'—not *over* them ; and established, not *over* but ' *between* the States ratifying it :' and hence a State, acting in its sovereign capacity, and in the same manner in which it ratified and adopted the constitution, may be guilty of violating it *as a compact*, but cannot be guilty of violating it as a *law*. . . . . . . That a State, as a party to the constitutional compact, has the right to secede—acting in the same capacity in which it ratified the constitution—cannot, with any show of reason, be denied by anyone who regards the constitution as a compact,—if a power should be inserted by the amending power, which would radically change the character of the constitution, or the nature of the system ; or if the former should fail to fulfill the ends for which it was established. This results necessarily from the nature of a compact, —where the parties to it are sovereign, and, of course, have no higher authority to which to appeal. That the effect of secession would be to place her in the relation of a foreign State to the others, is equally clear. Nor is it less so, that it would make her (not her citizens *individually*,) responsible to them, in that character. All this results, necessarily, from the nature of a compact between sovereign parties.

Further New England testimony in support of the right of secession will be found in Mr. John Quincy Adams' address before the Historical Society of New York, on the occasion of the celebration of the fiftieth anniversary of the adoption of the Federal Constitution, 1839: he said :—

To the people alone is then reserved, as well the *dissolving* as the constituent power; and that power can be exercised by them only under the tie of conscience, binding them to the retributive justice of heaven.

With these qualifications, we may admit the same right to be vested in the people of every State in the Union, with reference to the general government, which was exercised by the people of the United colonies with reference to the supreme head of the British Empire, of which they formed a part; and, under these limitations, have the people of each State in the Union a right to secede from the Confederated Union itself.

Thus stands the right. But the indissoluble link of union between the people of the several States of this confederated nation is, after all, not in the right, but in the heart. If the day should ever come (may heaven avert it !) when the affections of the people of these States shall be alienated from each other —when the fraternal spirit shall give way to cold indifference, or collisions of interest shall fester into hatred—the bands of political association will not long hold together parties no longer attracted by the magnetism of conciliated interests and kindly sympathies; and far better will it be for the people of the *dis united* States to part in friendship from each other, than to be held together by constraint. Then will be the time for reverting to the precedent which occurred at the formation and adoption of the Constitution to form a more perfect Union, by dissolving that which could no longer bind, and to leave the separated parts to be reunited by the law of political gravitation to the centre.

The Congressional records, and other American State papers, are replete with arguments and opinions that have emanated from the ablest minds the country has produced, which strongly endorse the present course of the Southern States. We may, however, pass on, and read what some weaker intellects say upon the subject.

Mr. Abraham Lincoln, as a member from Illinois, said in the Federal House of Representatives on January 12, 1848:

Any people, anywhere, being inclined, and having the power, have a *right to rise up and shake off the existing Government and form a new one that suits them better.* This is a most valuable, a most sacred right—a right which we hope and believe is to liberate the world. Nor is this right confined to cases in which the *whole people* of an existing government may choose to exercise it. *Any portion of such people that can,* may revolutionise and make *their own* of so much of the territory as they inhabit. More than this—*a majority* of *any portion* of such people may revolutionise, putting down a *minority,* intermingled with or near about them, who may oppose their movements. It is a quality of revolution not to go by old lines or old laws, but to break up both, and to make new ones.

It was acting on the principle thus enunciated that Mr. Lincoln 'recognised' what is called 'Western Virginia,' in violation of the 3rd Section of Article IV. of the Constitution, which says, 'New States may be admitted by the Congress into this Union; but no new

State shall be formed or erected within the jurisdiction of any other State; nor any State be formed by the junction of two or more States, or parts of States, without the consent of the Legislatures of the States concerned, as well as of the Congress.'

Mr. Edward Bates, the Attorney-General of the United States, appointed by Mr. Lincoln, and still one of his Cabinet, in the subjoined letter furnishes his opinion in reference to the unconstitutionality of the division of the State of Virginia. Mr. Lincoln seems to disregard even the decision of his own legal advisers.

Attorney-General's Office: August 12, 1861.

HON. A. F. RITCHIE, VIRGINIA CONVENTION, WHEELING.

Sir,—Your letter of the 9th instant was received within this hour, and as you ask an immediate answer, you, of course, will not expect me to go elaborately into the subject.

· I have thought a great deal upon the question of dividing the State of Virginia into two States; and since I came here as a member of the Government I have conversed with a good many, and corresponded with some of the good men of Western Virginia in regard to that matter. In all this intercourse my constant and earnest effort has been to impress upon the minds of those gentlemen the vast importance—not to say necessity—in this terrible crisis of our national affairs, to abstain from the introduction of any new elements of revolution, to avoid, as far as possible, all new and original theories of government; but, on the contrary, in all the insurgent commonwealths, to adhere, as circumstances will allow, to the old constitutional standard of principle and to the traditional habits and thoughts of the people. And I still think that course is dictated by the plainest teachings of prudence.

The formation of a new State out of Western Virginia is an original, independent act of revolution. I do not deny the *power* of revolution (I do not call it *right,* for it is never prescribed—it exists in *force* only, and has and can have no law but the will of the revolutionists). Any attempt to carry it out involves a plain breach of both the constitutions—of Virginia and the nation. And hence it is plain that you cannot take that course without weakening, if not destroying, your claims upon the sympathy and support of the general government, and without disconcerting the plan already adopted both by Virginia and the general government for the reorganisation of the revolted States, and the restoration of the integrity of the Union. That plan I understand to be this: when a State, by its perverted functionaries, has declared itself out of the Union, we avail ourselves of all the sound and loyal elements of the State—all who own allegiance to and claim protection of the constitution— to form a State government, as nearly as may be upon the former model, and claiming to be the very State which has been in part overthrown by the successful rebellion. In this way we establish a constitutional nucleus around which all the shattered elements of the commonwealth may meet and combine, and thus restore the old State to its original integrity.

This I verily thought was the plan adopted at Wheeling, and recognised and acted upon by the general government here. Your convention annulled the revolutionary proceedings at Richmond, both in the convention and general assembly, and your new governor formally demanded of the President the fulfillment of the constitutional guarantee in favour of Virginia —Virginia as known to our fathers and to us. The President admitted the obligation, and promised his best efforts to fulfill it, and the Senate admitted your senators, not as representing a new and nameless State, now for the first time heard of in our history, but as representing 'the good old commonwealth.'

Must all this be undone, and a new and hazardous experiment be ventured upon, at the moment when dangers and difficulties are thickening around us? I hope not; for the sake of the nation and the State, I hope not. I had rejoiced in the movement in Western Virginia as a legal, constitutional, and safe refuge from revolution and anarchy, as at once an example and fit instrument for the restoration of all the revolted States.

I have not time now to discuss the subject in its various bearings. What I have written is written with a running pen, and will need your charitable criticism.

If I had time I think I could give persuasive reasons for

declining to attempt to create a new State at this perilous time. At another time I might be willing to go fully into the question, but now I can say no more.

Most respectfully your obedient servant,

EDW. BATES.

Notwithstanding Mr. Bates gives a correct opinion in opposition to the admission of Western Virginia as a State into the Federal Union, he, like every individual connected with the Lincoln Administration, at home or abroad, cannot write a letter or express a sentiment without indulging in mendacity. There were no 'revolutionary proceedings at Richmond,' as he insinuates. 'Virginia, as known to our fathers and to us,' was the first American colony that adopted a constitution. A convention of delegates elected by her. people assembled on May 15, 1776, for that purpose, and completed their task on June 12 of that year. By the ratification of the Declaration of Independence, July 4, 1776, the colony became a State; and the 'Old Dominion' has, without intermission, continued as an independent sovereignty ever since. Her constitution was amended in 1829 and 1830. Richmond is the capitol of the State; and the Governor and Legislature there represent 'the good old Commonwealth.' The Wheeling Government, to which Mr. Bates alludes, has no authority whatever from the people of Virginia. It is a sham and an imposition, put in force by a few Yankees and their adherents, through the agency and influence of Federal 'greenbacks,' in the western part of the State, and has sent two *bogus* senators to the Northern Congress, who will now be joined by two more of the same character from 'Western' Virginia. In order to illustrate the manner of 'acceding' to and 'seceding' from the Federal Union, the action of Virginia may be cited. Her people, through delegates appointed for that purpose, for such does not come within the scope of the usual legislative power, adopted the following ordinance on June 25, 1788 :—

We, the delegates of the people of Virginia, duly elected in pursuance of a recommendation from the General Assembly, and now met in Convention, having fully and freely investigated and discussed the proceedings of the Federal Convention, and being prepared, as well as the most mature deliberation hath enabled us, to decide thereon, *do*, in the name and in behalf of the people of Virginia, declare and make known that the powers granted under the Constitution, being derived from the people of the United States, *may be resumed by them* whenever the same shall be perverted to their injury or oppression, and that every power not granted thereby remains with them, and at their will; that, therefore, no right of any denomination can be cancelled, abridged, restrained, or modified by Congress, by the Senate, or House of Representatives, acting in any capacity, by the President or any department or officer of the United States, except in those instances in which power is given by the Constitution for those purposes; and that, among other essential rights, the liberty of conscience and of the press cannot be cancelled, abridged, restrained, or modified by any authority of the United States.

The people of Virginia again, through their delegates, met in convention, and passed on April 17, 1861, an ' ordinance to repeal the ratification of the constitution of the United States of America, by the State of Virginia, and to resume all the rights and powers granted under said constitution.'

The people of the State of Virginia, in the ratification of the Constitution of the United States of America, adopted by them in Convention on June 25, in the year of our Lord 1788, having declared that the powers granted under the said Constitution were derived from the people of the United States, and might be resumed whensoever the same should be perverted to their injury and oppression, and the Federal Government having perverted said powers, not only to the injury of the people of Virginia, but to the oppression of the Southern slave-holding States: now, therefore, we, the people of Virginia, do declare and ordain that the ordinance adopted by the people of this State in Convention on June 25, in the year of our Lord 1788, whereby the Constitution of the United States of America was ratified, and all acts of the General Assembly of this State ratifying or adopting amendments to said Constitution, are hereby repealed and abrogated; that the union between the State of Virginia and the other States under the Constitution aforesaid is hereby dissolved; and that the State of Virginia is in the full possession and exercise of all the rights of sovereignty which belong to a free and independent State: and they do further declare that said Constitution of the United States of America is no longer binding on any of the citizens of this State.

This ordinance shall take effect, and be an Act of this day, when ratified by a majority of the votes of the people of this State, cast at a poll to be taken thereon on the fourth Thursday in May next, in pursuance to a schedule hereafter to be enacted.

Done in Convention in the city of Richmond, on the 17th day of April, in the year of our Lord 1861, and in the eighty-fifth year of the Commonwealth of Virginia.

The Convention also passed the following ordinance of adhesion to the Confederate Union :—

We, the delegates of the people of Virginia in Convention assembled, solemnly impressed by the perils which surround the Commonwealth, and appealing to the Searcher of Hearts for the rectitude of our intentions in assuming the grave responsibility of this act, do by this ordinance *adopt and ratify* the Constitution of the Provisional Government of the Confederate States of America, ordained and established at Montgomery, Alabama, on the 8th day of February, 1861: Provided that this ordinance shall cease to have any legal operation or effect, if the people of this Commonwealth, upon the vote directed to be taken on the ordinance of secession passed by this Convention on the 17th day of April, 1861, shall reject the same.

The people of Virginia, on the day appointed, duly

ratified the action of the Convention, and in due course accepted the permanent Constitution of the Confederate States.

Mr. William H. Seward, when urging in the Federal Senate the admission of the territory of California into the Union, as a ' free, sovereign, and independent State,' remarked on March 11, 1850 :

And now it seems to me that the perpetual unity of our empire hangs on the decision of this day and of this hour. California is already a State—a complete and fully appointed State: she never again can be less than that. The question, whether she shall be one of the United States of America, has depended on her and on us. Her election has been made. Our consent alone remains suspended, and that consent must be pronounced now or never. I say now or never. Nor will California abide delay. I do not say that she contemplates independence; but if she does not, it is because she does not anticipate rejection. Will you say that California could not aggrandise herself by separation? Will you say that California has no ability to become independent? Try not the temper or fidelity of California, at least not now—not yet. Cherish her and indulge her until you have extended your settlements to her borders. * * * California would not go alone. Oregon, so intimately allied to her, and, as yet, so loosely attached to us, will go also, and then, at least, the entire Pacific coast would be lost.

These views of Mr. Seward are not at all novel; Mr. John Quincy Adams expressed the same doctrines in the case of Michigan in 1836, declaring that if that territory, which had then formed a State Constitution, was not admitted into the Union, she would have a right to make herself, as in fact she had already done, an independent power.

There is an erroneous impression in Europe in regard to what has been called the ' bullying' propensities of the American people. Whatever blustering there has been in that respect has emanated from the North, not from the South. For instance, the trouble that arose between Great Britain and the United States in 1841 was altogether owing to Mr. Seward, who was then Governor of the State of New York, and to his partisans in and out of Congress. He, on that occasion, refused to accede to the request of the United States Government for the surrender to the English authorities of Alexander M'Leod, a British subject and civil officer, who was arrested and put on his trial before the Circuit Court at Utica, New York, on the charge of murdering Amos Durfree, an American, at the time of the burning of the steamer 'Caroline,' at Fort Schlosser, on December 29, 1837.

The 'Caroline' was a pirate, manned by New York filibusters, which, after committing sundry hostile acts against Canada, retreated to the American side of the river Niagara. It was proved to the satisfaction of the Administration at Washington, who, by its delegated powers under the Constitution, alone had jurisdiction in the case, that the persons who destroyed the 'Caroline' acted under the instructions of the Canadian authorities, and accordingly the affair was adjusted by diplomatic correspondence between the two Governments. Seward, however, was so desirous of creating a difficulty with Great Britain, in order to carry out his favourite scheme of annexing Canada, and thereby making himself popular in the North, that he thus ignored the chief purpose for which the Union was formed—namely, for giving the control of the foreign affairs of the individual States to a central head; and so arrogated to himself a power which the strongest State Rights men never dreamed of claiming.

This disagreement between the State of New York and the Government of the United States, and the threatening aspect of affairs between Great Britain and the United States, in consequence of the conduct of Governor Seward, was disposed of by the acquittal of M'Leod by the jury. The debates in Congress testify that the Southern members energetically opposed the warlike resolutions offered by Mr. Fillmore, one of Seward's satellites, in the House of Representatives.

A second attempt to invade Canada was made by citizens of New York at this period (1841), which Mr. Seward not only failed to repress—as was his duty as chief executive officer of that State—but he actually connived at the proceedings. President Tyler, a Southerner, was therefore obliged to issue the following proclamation (September 25, 1841):—

Whereas it has come to the knowledge of the Government of the United States that sundry secret lodges, clubs, or associations, exist on the Northern frontier; that the members of these lodges are bound together by secret oaths; that they have collected firearms and other military materials, and secreted them in sundry places; and it is their purpose to violate the laws of their country by making military and lawless incursions, when opportunity shall offer, into the territories of a power with which the United States are at peace. And whereas it is known that travelling agitators from both sides of the line visit these lodges, and harangue the members in secret meeting, stimulating them to illegal acts. And whereas the same persons are known to levy contributions on the ignorant and credulous for their own benefit, thus supporting and enriching themselves by the basest means. And whereas the unlawful intentions of the members of these lodges have already been manifested in an attempt to destroy the lives and property of the inhabitants of Chippewa, in Canada, and the public property of the British Government there being. Now, therefore, I, John Tyler, President of the United States, do issue this my proclamation, admonishing all such evil-minded persons of the condign punishment which is certain to overtake them; assuring them that the laws of the United States will be rigorously executed against their illegal acts; and that if, in any lawless incursion into Canada, they fall into the hands of the British authorities, they will not be reclaimed as American citizens, nor any interference made by this Government in their behalf.

I exhort all well-meaning but deluded persons who may have joined these lodges immediately to abandon them, and to have nothing more to do with their secret meetings or unlawful oaths, as they would avoid serious consequences to themselves. And I expect the intelligent and well-disposed members of the community to frown on all these unlawful combinations and illegal proceedings, and to assist the Government in maintaining the peace of the country against the mischievous consequences of the acts of these violators of the law.

It has been charged that, in the cases of the Maine boundary and Oregon disputes, the Southerners desired to make war with England. This is a mistake. Mr. Calhoun, who everyone will admit was the leader of Southern opinion, said in the Senate, when the first topic was under discussion :

So strong, indeed, was his impression, that the dispute could only be settled by a compromise or conventional line, that he remarked to a friend in Jackson's Cabinet that it could only be so determined; and for that purpose some distinguished citizen of Maine should be selected for the special mission to England, and that neither he nor any other Southern man ought to be thought of.

* * * * * *

In deciding the question, it must be borne in mind that it belongs much more to the State of Maine than to the Union. It is, in truth, but the boundary of that State, and makes a part of the boundary of the United States only by being the exterior boundary of one of the States of the Federal Union. It is her sovereignty and soil that are in dispute, except the portion of the latter that still remains in Massachusetts; and it belongs, in the first place, to her and to Massachusetts, as far as her right of soil is involved, to say what their rights and interests are, and what is required to be done. The rest of the Union is bound to defend them in their just claim, and to assent to what they may be willing to consent to in settling the claim in contest, if there should be nothing in it inconsistent with the interest, honour, or safety of the rest of the Union. It is so that the controversy has ever been regarded. It is well known that President Jackson would readily have agreed to the award of the King of Holland, had not Maine objected; and to overcome her objection he was prepared to recommend to Congress to give her, in order to get her consent, one million of acres of the public domain, worth, at the minimum price, a million and a quarter of dollars. The case is now reversed. Maine and Massachusetts have both assented to the stipulations of the treaty, as far as the question of boundary affects their peculiar interest, through commissioners, vested with full powers to represent them; and the question for us to decide is, shall we reject that to which they have assented? Shall the Government, after refusing to agree to the award of the King of Holland, because Maine objected, now reverse its course, and refuse to agree to that to which she and Massachusetts have both assented?

These remarks were made in 1842. In 1846, when the Oregon difficulty was being debated, the same statesman said (March 11):

Having been thus brought, by a line of policy to which I was opposed, to choose between compromise and war, I without hesitation take the former. . . I am opposed to war between the United States and Great Britain. They are the two countries the farthest in advance in the great career of improvement, and of amelioration of the condition of our race. They are, besides, diffusing, by their widely extended commerce, blessings over the whole globe. We have been raised up by Providence for these great and noble purposes, and I trust we shall not fail to fulfill our high destiny. I am especially opposed to war with England at this time, because I hold that it is now to be decided whether we are to exist in future as friends or enemies. War, at this time and for this cause, would decide supremacy. We should hereafter stand in the relation of enemies. It would give birth to a struggle in which one or the other would have to succumb before it terminated, and which in the end would prove ruinous to both. On the contrary, if war can be avoided, powerful causes are now in operation, calculated to cement and secure a lasting—I hope a perpetual—peace between the two countries, by breaking down the barriers which impede their commerce, and thereby uniting them more closely by a vastly enlarged commercial intercourse equally beneficial to both. If we should now succeed in setting the example of free trade between us, it would force all other civilised countries to follow it in the end. The consequences would be to diffuse a prosperity greater and more universal than can well be conceived, and to unite by bonds of mutual interest the people of all countries. But in advocating the cause of free trade, I am actuated not less by the political consequences likely to flow from it, than the advantages to be derived from it in an economical point of view. I regard it in the dispensation of Providence as one of the great means of ushering in the happy period foretold by inspired prophets and poets, when war shall be no more. I am finally opposed to war, because peace is preeminently our policy.

In the House of Representatives, when the same question was under consideration, Mr. W. L. Yancey remarked, on January 4, 1846 :

We should be careful lest prosperity and continued success should blind us to consequences—lest in our pride we fall. Sir, it cannot be treason—it cannot be cowardly—it cannot be unwise—for us calmly and dispassionately to consider our true position in this matter. And I beg of our friends that, if some of us of the South are disposed to put a curb on this hot impetuosity, we shall not be deemed their enemies on this great issue. . . . . I desire to notice these animated attacks on England, these burning appeals to our patriotism, these outbreaks of enthusiastic love for our country, these firm resolves to resist encroachment and insult. But I look around in vain for a point to which to apply all this pent-up ammunition. This is, then, it seems to me, a useless waste of patriotic enthusiasm. . . . . I can well imagine, however, how such a course will operate upon the public mind, how the honest farmer, on reading such furious denunciations of what he is accustomed to think his natural enemy, and of her rapacity, can have his feelings wrought up under the idea that his country is the object of English aggression and overbearance. I much fear that this is the surest way of accounting for the strong popular ferment in relation to this question. . . . . The arguments of the venerable gentleman from Massachusetts (J. Q. Adams) breathe a fierce and energetic war spirit. Truly and well did he himself depict the whole character of this movement, when he illustrated it by citing a celebrated event in history, exclaiming with very great emphasis, 'This is the military way of doing business.'

In a continuation of the debate, on February 6, 1846, Mr. Jefferson Davis, in the course of his speech, said :

He knew not whether he more regretted the time at which this discussion has been introduced, or the manner in which it has been conducted. We were engaged in delicate and highly important negotiations with Mexico, the end of which, he had hoped, would be an adjustment of our boundary on terms the vast advantages of which it would be difficult to estimate. If, sir, by this exciting discussion we shall hereafter find that we have lost the key to the commerce of the Pacific, none who hears me will live long enough to cease from his regrets for the injury our country has sustained. Again, sir, a long peace has served to extend the bonds of commerce throughout the civilised world, drawing nations from remote quarters of the globe into friendly alliance, and that mutual dependence which promised a lasting peace and unshackled commerce. In the East there appeared a rainbow which promised that the waters of national jealousy and proscription were about to recede from the earth, and the spirit of free trade to move over the face thereof. But this, sir, is a hope not so universally cherished in this House as I could desire. We have even been told that one of the advantages to result from war will be emancipation from the manufacturers of Manchester and Birmingham.

I hope, sir, the day is far distant when measures of peace or war will be prompted by sectional or class interests. War, sir, is a dread alternative, and should be the last resort; but when demanded for the maintenance of the honour of the country, or for the security and protection of our citizens against outrage by other governments, I trust we will not sit here for weeks to discuss the propriety, to dwell upon the losses, or paint the horrors of war.

Mr. Chairman, it has been asserted that the people demand action, and we must advance. Whilst, sir, I admit the propriety of looking to and reflecting public opinion, especially upon a question which is viewed as deciding between peace or war, I cannot respond to the opinion, nor consent to govern my conduct by the idea, that the public man who attempts to stem the current of a war excitement must be borne down, sacrificed on the altar of public indignation. Sir, may the day never come when there will be so little of public virtue and patriotic devotion among the representatives of the people that any demagogue who chooses to make violent and unfounded appeals to raise a war clamour in the country will be allowed, unopposed, to mislead the people as to the true questions at issue, and to rule their representatives through their love of place and political timidity !

On the occasion of this Oregon controversy, both parties in the North, the Whig and the Democratic, emulated each other in the race to attain popularity by humiliating England and forcing her to abandon her pretensions. It required the whole strength of the South to keep the country from drifting into a war. Mr. John Quincy Adams, of Massachusetts, headed the extreme party in opposition to the claims of England in the House of Representatives, and speaking before that body advocated the exclusion of European governments from the continent of America, in a manner strikingly in accord with the spirit of his Puritan ancestors, who held ' that the earth was the inheritance of the saints, and that they were the saints.' He had the Holy Scriptures read by the clerk of the House, to prove that God had decreed man to multiply and replenish the earth, and that to His chosen people He had given the heathen for an inheritance, and the uttermost parts of the earth for a possession. This—he argued with a blasphemous application of the Word of God to the purposes of politics, which has never found toleration or imitation outside of New England—this was the title by which the United States might rightfully claim the disputed tract in Oregon. On February 9, 1846, he added:

That same Pope at that time (1493) was in the custom of giving away not only barbarous nations but civilised nations. He dethroned sovereigns, put them under interdict, and excommunicated them from intercourse with all other Christians, and it was submitted to. And now, sir, *the Government of Great Britain—the nation of Great Britain—holds the island of Ireland on no other title.* Three hundred years before that time, Pope Adrian of Rome gave, by that same power, to Henry I. of England, the island of Ireland, and England has held it from that day to this under that title, and no other. That is, no other, unless by *conquest (for it has been in a continued state of rebellion ever since),* and Great Britain has been obliged to conquer it half a dozen times since; and now the question is, whether Ireland shall ever become an independent kingdom. *If we come to a war with Great Britain, she will find enough to do to maintain that island.* * * * * I want the country (Oregon) for our Western pioneers.

About the same time General Lewis Cass, of Michigan, the acknowledged leader of the Democratic party of the North, as ex-President Adams was of the Whigs, thundered forth in the Senate threats of war and conquest against Great Britain. On March 29, 1846, he said:

Let us have no red lines on the map of Oregon, and if war comes, be it so. * * * England might as well attempt to blow up the Rock of Gibraltar with a squib as to attempt to subdue

us. Why the honourable senator from South Carolina fixes upon
ten years for the duration of the war, I know not ; long before
the expiration of that period, if we are not utterly unworthy of
our name and our birthright, we should sweep the British power
from the continent of North America.

The ' blustering ' 'in reference to the San Juan affair a
few years ago was also confined to the North. The difficulty was promptly settled by a Southern Administration.

The charge has likewise been made in some of the Anglo-
Yankee newspapers that Mr. Mason, the accredited representative of the Confederate States to Great Britain, had
hitherto belonged to the ' blustering party.' This assertion is easily disproved. Mr. Mason was not a member
of Congress at the time of any of the disputes with
England, and had, of course, no opportunity of taking part
in the debates. The records of the Federal Legislature,
however, prove that he held anything but hostile feelings
towards this country; as an evidence of this, the case of
the ' Resolute ' may be cited. The following is an extract
from the official report of the proceedings in that matter:—

United States Senate, June 10, 1856. Mr. Foster, of Connecticut, offered the following resolution :—

Resolved, That the committee on commerce be instructed
to enquire into the expediency of authorising the Secretary of
the Treasury to issue a register to the British-built bark ' Resolute,' found derelict near Cumberland inlet, in the Arctic Ocean
by the officers and crew of the American whaling ship ' George
Henry,' of New London, Connecticut, and by said salvors
brought into the port of New London, where she is now lying
—all claim to said vessel by the British Government having
been relinquished to the salvors.

Mr. Mason, of Virginia, in requesting the honourable
senator from Connecticut to withdraw his resolution,
spoke as follows : —

Mr. President,—I saw, as did the whole American people, the fact announced of the recovery of this vessel, and her being brought successfully, and after much danger and peril, within our waters. It occurred to me at the time—and I have been more strongly impressed with it in thinking over the subject since—that the proper disposition of that vessel would be for the Government of the United States to purchase her, and refit her in a proper manner, and send her back to England. She was the property of the English Government, and was one of their public ships, abandoned in an enterprise of discovery in which we have largely participated with them—abandoned from necessity, and accidentally recovered by one of our merchant ships. I had thought that such high national courtesy, which I am gratified to say marks our country certainly with as much distinction as any other in the great family of nations—that national courtesy which does more to preserve the peace of the world even than armed ships themselves—would suggest that, on a suitable occasion, this ship should become the property of the Government, if it can be done on fair and equitable terms, and should be sent back to England in the name of the American people. I would, therefore, suggest to the honourable senator from Connecticut, learning that she has not changed hands, that, unless there be some immediate occasion for this resolution, it would be as well, perhaps, to let it lie over until we can confer on the subject.

Mr. Mason, subsequently, on June 24, 1856, offered a resolution to provide for the purchase and fitting out of the ship and her return to Great Britain, making an appropriation for the expense. His resolution passed the Senate without opposition.

The slavery dispute, although so prominent in American politics, was not the real cause of the dissolution of the Union. The North was desirous of having control of the territories, in order to form them into States, and thus obtain the balance of power in the Federal Congress, so as to impose protective tariffs, against which the South justly protested. The subjoined address, issued by the South Carolina Convention, December 25, 1860, explains this :—

Discontent and contention have moved in the bosom of the Confederacy for the last thirty-five years. During this time, South Carolina has twice called her people together in solemn convention, to take into consideration the aggressions and un-constitutional wrongs perpetrated by the people of the North on the people of the South. These wrongs were submitted to by the people of the South, under the hope and expectation that they would be final. But these hopes and expectations have proved to be void.

The one great evil, from which all the other evils have flowed, is the overthrow of the constitution. The Government is no longer the government of a Confederate Republic, but of a consolidated democracy. It is no longer a free government, but a despotism. The Revolution of 1776 turned upon one great principle—self-government and self-taxation—the criterion of self-government.

The Southern States now stand in the same relation towards the Northern States, *in the vital matter of taxation*, that our ancestors stood toward the people of Great Britain. They are in a minority in Congress. Their representation in Congress is useless to protect them against unjust taxation; *and they are taxed by the people of the North for their benefit*, exactly as the people of Great Britain taxed our ancestors, in the British Parliament, for their benefit. *For the last forty years, the taxes laid by the Congress of the United States, have been laid with a view of subserving the interests of the North.* The people of the South have been taxed by *duties on imports*, not for revenue, but for an object inconsistent with revenue —to promote, by prohibitions, Northern interests in the productions of their mines and manufactures. The people of the Southern States are not only taxed for the benefit of the people of the Northern States, but, after the taxes are collected, three-fourths of them are expended in the North.

In the following pages I enter largely upon the Slavery question, because it is a subject so little understood in Europe, the public mind on this side of the Atlantic

having been poisoned against the South in this respect
by Yankee authors and orators.   The views that I express
are those entertained by the great mass of the people of
my native commonwealth—Pennsylvania—the first State
that abolished slavery.   This was done through the
influence of the Quakers, after the institution ceased to
pay within her limits.   The subjoined is a copy of the
enactment passed in 1780:—

All persons, as well negroes and mulattoes as others, who shall
be born within this State, shall not be deemed and considered
as servants for life or slaves; and all servitude for life, or slavery
of children, in consequence of the slavery of their mothers, in
the case of all children born within this State from and after
the passing of this Act as aforesaid, shall be and hereby is
utterly taken away, extinguished, and for ever abolished: provided, however, children born hereafter of slave mothers are to
be held to servitude until they are twenty-eight years old.

The effect of this statute, which can be repealed at any
time, was very gradual, and slavery was not finally
extinguished within the State until 1845.   The ' Friends'
had held men in bondage for 150 years.   William Penn
was a slave-owner.   The Constitution of Pennsylvania
does not prohibit slavery.   It was upon the demand of
that State, in 1793, for the return of a slave that had
escaped into Maryland, that Washington recommended to
Congress the passage of the Fugitive Slave Law, in order
to conform to the provisions of the Federal Constitution.
Until a very few years back, the votes of Pennsylvania
were always cast with those of her Southern sisters; but
in recent years so many New Englanders have flocked
within her borders, that they, with their natural im-
pudence and acquisitiveness, have taken control of the
affairs of the State, and by frauds and bribery—the
money sent from Massachusetts—they managed in 1860

to place their own candidates in the highest offices. Pennsylvanians—'natives to the manor born'—are now resuming their political duties, and, unless Federal bayonets deprive them of their franchises, will bring about such a change in matters as will astonish the world. The rural districts of the State are all democratic; it is only in the cities of Philadelphia and Pittsburgh, where the Yankees and contractors have congregated, that there is any strong war feeling; and this is the reason for the great apathy that existed at the time of the invasion of General Lee. There has always been much jealousy between New York and Philadelphia; and should Pennsylvania apply for admission, and be received into the Southern Confederacy, the latter city will resume her former position as the centre of finance and chief distributing point on the western continent. Such an accession would give the Confederate States the command of the Delaware river, of the head waters of the Ohio, and a frontage on the lakes, thus cutting the Yankee snake—north-east and north-west—in two, and completely destroying its vitality. That arrangement, coupled with French domination in Mexico, would be a happy event for the peace and prosperity of America.

Pennsylvania, under the guidance of Governor Curtin, has behaved so badly, that I doubt if the South will have anything to do with her. To her credit, however, be it said that, although the Yankee influence within her limits was so great, she, with the exception of New Jersey, is the only Northern State that gave a respectable vote for Mr. Breckinridge, the candidate for the Presidency, who received nearly the unanimous support of the Southern States. Her balloting stood thus:—Lincoln, 268,030. Breckinridge, 178,871. Douglas, 16,765. Bell, 12,776.

The votes of New York, the New England States, and the North-western States, were chiefly cast for Lincoln and Douglas. There can be no stronger evidence of the decay in public virtue effected through Yankee influence than that two such unworthy men should have had bestowed upon them the suffrages of the people, and it is, therefore, time that the present Federal fabric should be destroyed, and something better substituted in its place. Mr. Lincoln, however, is doing the work of ' demolition' with almost electric speed.

In the early portion of this letter, I referred to a violation of treaty stipulations on the part of your Government towards the States now comprising the Southern Confederacy—I mean the treaties of 1783 and 1840. I now desire to call your attention to a more recent agreement that has likewise been disregarded, concerning which the following letters from Mr. Mason to Earl Russell, taken from the Parliamentary publication, ' North America, No. 2, 1863,' will furnish particulars :—

Mr. Mason to Earl Russell. (*Received January 3.*)

24 Upper Seymour Street, Portman Square:
January   , 1863.

My Lord,—In a communication which I had the honour to address to your Lordship, dated on the 7th July ultimo, I said : —

I am instructed by a recent despatch from the Secretary of State for the Confederate States of America, to bring to the attention of your Lordship what would seem to be an addition engrafted by Her Majesty's Government, on the principle of the law of blockade, as established by the Convention of Paris in 1856, and accepted by the Confederate States of America at the invitation of Her Majesty's Government.

The ' addition' to the principle of blockade referred to is stated in my communication to have appeared in a letter from your Lordship to Lord Lyons, of February 15 preceding, then recently laid before Parliament.

I stated further in that communication, quoting from the instructions of the President—

' If such be the interpretation placed by Great Britain on the Treaty of 1856, it is but just that this Government should be so officially informed.'

And after pointing out the force and effect ascribed by the President to this modification of the principle of blockade, to the prejudice of the interests of the Confederate States, my communication to your Lordship proceeded as follows : —

' I have therefore the honour to request, for the information of my Government, that your Lordship will be good enough to solve the doubt entertained by the President of the Confederate States as to the construction placed by the Government of Her Majesty on the text of the Convention of Paris, as accepted by the Government of the Confederate States in the terms hereinbefore cited; that is to say, whether a blockade is to be considered as effective when maintained at an enemy's port, by a force sufficient to create an evident danger of entering or leaving it,' and not alone where sufficient ' really to prevent access.'

To that communication I was honoured only by a reply from the Honourable A. H. Layard, dated at the Foreign Office on July 10, informing me that he was directed by your Lordship to acknowledge its receipt; nor have I since been honoured by any communication from your Lordship furnishing an answer to the specific and important enquiry thus made under instructions from my Government.

On August 4 following, I transmitted to the Secretary of State of the Confederate States a copy of my communication to your Lordship of July 7, together with a copy of the reply of Mr. Layard; and asked for further instructions, made necessary by the silence of the Foreign Office, in regard to the enquiries thus submitted.

I have now, within a few days past, received a despatch from the Secretary of State in reply to mine of 4th of August, the tenour of which I am directed to communicate to your Lordship.

d

I am instructed to say that, from the papers thus submitted, it would appear to the President that the Government of Her Majesty, after having invited the Government of the Confederate States to concur in the adoption of certain principles of international law, and after having obtained its assent, assumed in official despatches to derogate from the principles thus adopted, to the prejudice of the interests and rights of the Confederacy; and that upon being approached, in respectful and temperate terms, with a request for explanation on a matter of such deep concern to the Confederation, that Cabinet refuses a reply.

That Her Majesty's Government can have no just ground for refusing the explanation asked, because of the absence of the recognition of the independence of the Confederate States by the other nations of the world. It was not in the character of a recognised independent nation, but in that of a recognised belligerent, that the two leading powers of Western Europe approached the government of those States with a proposition for the adoption of certain principles of public law, as rules which shall govern the mutual relations between the people of the Confederacy as belligerents, and the nations of Europe as neutrals, during the pending war.

Two of these rules were for the special benefit of Great Britain as one of those neutral powers. It was agreed that her flag should cover enemy's goods, and that her goods should be safe under the enemy's flag. The former of these two rules conceded to her, as a neutral, rights which she had sternly refused when herself a belligerent, with a single temporary waiver thereof in her late war with Russia. To these stipulations in her favour, the Government of the Confederate States will adhere with scrupulous fidelity. On the part of Her Majesty's Government, it was agreed that no blockade should be considered binding unless ' maintained by a force sufficient really to prevent access to the coast of the enemy;' and yet on the first occasion which arose for the application of this, the only stipulation that could be of practical benefit to the Confederate States during the war, Her Majesty's Secretary of State for Foreign Affairs, in an official despatch published to the world, appends a qualification which in effect destroys its whole value,

and when appealed to for an explanation of this apparent breach
of an existing solemn agreement between the neutral and
the belligerent, declines an answer.

In view of these facts, I am instructed by the President to
address to your Lordship, as Her Majesty's Secretary of State for
Foreign Affairs, this formal protest on the part of the Government of the Confederate States against the apparent (if not
executed) purpose of Her Majesty's Government to change or
modify, to the prejudice of the Confederacy, the doctrine in
relation to blockade to which the faith of Her Majesty's Government is, by that of the Confederate States, considered to
be pledged.

I am further instructed to say, that the President abstains
for the present from taking any further action than by his
protest thus presented ; and to accompany it by the expression
of his regret that such painful impressions should be produced
on his mind, by so unexpected a result from the first agreement
or understanding between the Government of the Confederate
States and that of Her Majesty.

I have, &c.,
(Signed)   J. M. MASON.

Mr. Mason to Earl Russell.   (Received February 16.)

24 Upper Seymour Street, Portman Square :
February 16, 1863.

My Lord,—I deem it incumbent on me to ask the attention
of Her Majesty's Government to recent intelligence received
here in regard to the blockade at Galveston, in the State of
Texas, and at Charleston, in the State of South Carolina.

First, as respects Galveston, it appears that the blockading
squadron of the United States was driven off from that port and
harbour by a superior Confederate force, on January 1 last;
one ship of that squadron was captured, the flag-ship destroyed,
and the rest escaped, making their way, it is said, to some point
of the Southern coast occupied by the United States' forces.
Whatever blockade of the port of Galveston, therefore, may
have previously existed, I submit, was effectually raised and
destroyed by the superior forces of the party blockaded.

Again, as respects the port of Charleston : through the

ordinary channel of intelligence, we have information, uncontradicted, that the alleged blockade of that port was, in like manner, raised and destroyed, by a superior Confederate force, at a very early hour on January 31, ultimo; two ships of the blockading squadron having been sunk; a third escaped disabled, and what remained of the squadron afloat was entirely driven off the coast.

I have the honour to submit, therefore, that any alleged pre-existing blockade of the ports aforesaid was terminated at Galveston the 1st day of January last, and at Charleston on the 31st of the same month; a principle clearly stated in a letter I have had the honour to receive from your Lordship, dated on the 10th instant, in the following words:—' The driving off a blockading force, by a superior force, does break a blockade, which must be renewed *de novo*, in the usual form, to be binding upon neutrals;'—a principle uniformly admitted by all text-writers on public law, and established by decisions of Courts of Admiralty.

I am aware that official information of either of these events may not yet have reached the Government of Her Majesty, but the consequences attending the removal of the blockade (whether to be renewed or not) are so important to the commercial interests involved, that I could lose no time in asking that such measures may be taken by Her Majesty's Government in relation thereto as will best tend to the resumption of a commercial intercourse so long placed under restraint.

I avail myself of this occasion to acknowledge the receipt of your Lordship's letter of February 10, instant, to which I shall have the honour of sending a reply in the course of a day or two; and am, &c.,

(Signed)   J. M. MASON.

It may be convenient for statesmen to ignore solemn obligations, to set laws and treaties at defiance, to accede to the monstrous pretensions of the imbecile and tottering Government at Washington, and to make 'precedents' at the expense of a power that they know to be fighting for self-government, and supposed to be labouring under great disadvantages in a war with an enemy better equipped in every way than itself. But the morality or expediency of such a course may well be doubted. I have said, and I have given you evidences of the fact, that the hostility manifested towards England in America has hitherto been confined to the Northern States. I have reason to know, however, that the cold indifference of the British Ministry, and unfriendly disposition occasionally evinced, as well as the strong reluctance they have shown towards according the Southerners their right, is producing a marked change of feeling throughout the Confederacy—a nation that they might have made the most useful ally and warmest friend of this country.

> I am, my dear Sir,
> Very truly and faithfully yours,
> GEO. M^cHENRY.

PAVILION HOTEL, FOLKESTONE:
August 31, 1863.

THE COTTON TRADE.

CHAPTER I.

INTRODUCTION.

EARLY CULTURE AND MANUFACTURE OF COTTON—SLAVERY.

THE warm interest manifested by Europeans in American affairs since the secession of the Southern States from the Federal Union, and the justness with which their various aspects have been appreciated by a large portion of the people of England, induces the publication of a work on a branch of the subject in which Great Britain and the Confederate States have alike the utmost concern, but which has not been so thoroughly discussed in some respects as its importance would seem to warrant—namely, the COTTON TRADE. In presenting the following views, occasion will be taken to consider the question in connection with the system of negro slavery as it is established in the South. The two topics are intimately associated. Cotton production in the American States and cotton manufacturing in the United Kingdom are based upon the 'peculiar institution;' and the great developement of both industries took place, aided by inventions on either side of the Atlantic, just at the period of the suppression of the African slave trade. It will be observed by these reasonings that the writer, while a 'pro-slavery' man, is, like all Confederate Americans, opposed to the traffic of the 'middle passage;' the grounds of the objection thereto being mainly economic — believing that the injudicious philanthropy of the Abolitionists has been a heresy throughout, and of positive injury to the African race wherever their efforts have

B

been felt. The judgment of the civilised world seems now, however, to be receding from the follies, in this respect, of the last generation. While desiring to give credit to the British Government for the liberality displayed in voting twenty millions of pounds sterling to purchase the freedom of the slaves in their West Indian possessions, it is impossible to be blind to the fact that such has proved a mistaken policy in every point of view, nor to forget at the same time that the parliamentary grant, although large, is exceedingly insignificant when compared to the amount which was earned by the English people, with simple interest thereon, up to the period of emancipation, 1834, from their commerce in carrying slaves during the continuance of the trade, 1561 to 1807—246 years—the sum reaching the enormous figures of five hundred millions of pounds sterling. In fact, the African trade was the foundation of the commercial wealth of England, that of India being secondary in date and advantage;* and the cotton manufacturing interest, the result of slave labour, has been of greater consequence than either, as is proved by the tables of population:—

In 1086 † England and Wales had 1,000,000 inhabitants
„ 1570   „   „   4,160,321   „
„ 1600   „   „   4,811,718   „
„ 1630   „   „   5,600,317   „
„ 1670   „   „   5,773,646   „

---

* Sir John Hawkins, the first Englishman who engaged in the African slave trade, was shortly joined by Queen Elizabeth, in 1563. The business was very profitable, and conducted with great spirit—so much so that in the course of time it fell into the hands of wealthy corporations. The gains were so enormous that they formed the foundation of the present credit system, and materially assisted the trade with India, which was started forty years afterwards. The early operations of the East India Company did not much augment the wealth of England; in fact, for many years it was a large exporter of bullion, and the riches of India did not find their way to these islands to any great extent until after the success of Clive in 1756. Money is now truly denominated 'the soil of England,' and interest her 'crops.' That she is indebted to the African slave trade for this boon history abundantly proves; and through the means of her immense commerce, generated chiefly and controlled by her cotton manufactures, her floating capital is made productive.

† The population for 1086 is that of Doomsday-book. The figures for the seventeenth and eighteenth centuries will be found in 'Porter's Progress.'

In 1700 England and Wales had 6,045,008 inhabitants
„ 1750   „   „   6,517,305   „
„ 1770   „   „   7,227,586   „
„ 1790   „   „   8,540,738   „
„ 1801   „   „   9,156,171   „
„ 1851   „   „   18,054,170   „
„ 1861   „   „   20,223,746   „

What more conclusive evidence of the importance of the Southern cotton crops to England can be given than this? The great augmentation in the population, it will be seen, occurred subsequent to the extension of the cotton industry of the kingdom. The population of Scotland within the same period, about sixty years, and for the same reason, nearly doubled.*

Of the four principal materials for human clothing—cotton, silk, wool, and flax—not one is indigenous to Europe; two only, cotton and flax, are native to Africa and America, while all of them belong to Asia. The Hindoos, for a vast unknown period, certainly six or seven centuries before the advent of Christ, had attained great perfection in the art of spinning, weaving, and printing cotton; some of their fabrics were so exquisitely light and beautiful that they have been compared to the gossamer web: they were very costly, and so highly esteemed as to be considered fit to be worn only by princes, while their coarser ' cotton goods' were used generally by the mass of the people. The Egyptians, too, at a very early date, engaged in this species of industry. They did not, however, acquire an eminent degree of excellence in the manufacture; the muslins worn by their luxurious classes were received from India. But the Chinese, in consequence of the abundance of silk, grasses, &c., did not cultivate cotton extensively, or apply it to use until about the year 1280, although it had then been one of their ornamental

* The progress of population in England and Wales for sixty years has been surprisingly regular. In 1801 the whole number of inhabitants was 9,156,171; in 1811, 10,454,529; in 1821, 12,172,664; in 1831, 14,051,986; in 1841, 16,035,198; in 1851, 18,054,170; in 1861, 20,223,746. The rates of increase per cent. during these several decades, beginning with the end of 1801, were 14, 16, 15, 14, 15, 12. The falling off in the last ten years was in consequence of emigration; during that time 2,287,205 persons embarked from the kingdom; of this number, however, one half (1,174,179) were Irish. The population of Scotland on March 10, 1801, was 1,608,420, and on April 8, 1861, 3,062,294, being an increase of 90·32 per cent.

garden plants for more than 600 years : nor have they for over a century grown sufficient for their own wants, relying on India and America for supplying their deficiencies, and oftentimes on England for cotton goods. The Mexicans and Peruvians had also reached great skill in the manufacture of cotton ; and the discoverers of the other portions of America, except the territory now comprising the Confederate States and that north thereof, found the aborigines employing the same material for wearing apparel. The cultivation and manufacture of cotton began in Italy in the eleventh century; it was subsequently introduced into Spain and other parts of Europe where the climate encouraged its growth.

It is a matter of much surprise that the Hindoos, with their imperfect means, should be able to produce such rare fabrics, unrivalled by those of other nations best skilled in mechanism. This is explained by their remarkably fine sense of touch, by their patience and gentleness, and by the hereditary continuance of a particular kind of work through many generations. Their commerce in cotton fabrics was very large from the beginning of the Christian era to the end of the last century. They had for hundreds of years supplied Persia, Arabia, Syria, Egypt, Abyssinia, and all the eastern parts of Africa, together with Europe, with their muslins. Their chief marts were Surat and Calicut, on the west coast of India, and at Masulipatam, Madras, and St. Thomé, on the east coast. At one time the manufacturers of all Europe apprehended ruin by the cheapness and competition of the cotton fabrics of India. In 1698, the Dutch and English East India Companies imported these goods— muslins, chintzes, and calicoes—in such large quantities, that even the woollen manufacturers made a great outcry against their admission, fearing that they would supersede their branch of industry, as well as that of flax. Indeed, the productions of India became so plentiful, that they were complained of as a 'great evil' by a host of pamphleteers ; and in the year 1700 Parliament passed an Act which forbade the importation of Indian silks and printed calicoes for domestic use, either for apparel or furniture, under a penalty of 200*l.* on the seller or wearer, in order to 'avert the ruin of English manufacturers and revive their prosperity.'

Notwithstanding India had held command—almost a monopoly—of the cotton trade for so long a time, and although England was the last country in Europe to enter into the manufacture of cotton goods, it was left for the ingenuity and enterprise of the Anglo-Saxon race, on both sides of the Atlantic, to develope to its present magnitude this great resource provided by nature, which has contributed so much to the comfort and progress of mankind, and been the chief means of rescuing 4,000,000 of Africans from the depths of their original barbarity —christianising and elevating them to a more respectable position than has ever before been attained by men of their race.

The primary importations of cotton into Great Britain were received from the Levant in the early part of the seventeenth century. The 'Treasury of Traffic,' by Lewis Roberts, printed in 1641, states:—

'The towne of Manchester, in Lancashire, must be also ' herein remembered, and worthily for their encouragement ' commended, who buy the yarne of the Irish in great quantity, ' and, weaving it, returne the same again into Ireland to sell. ' Neither doth their industry rest here; for they buy *cotton* ' wool in London that comes first from Cyprus and Smyrna, ' and at home worke the same, and perfect it into fustians, ' vermillions, dimities, and other such stuffes, and then returne ' it to London, where the same is vented and sold, and not ' seldom sent into forrain parts, who have means at far easier ' terms, to provide themselves of the said first materials.'

Mention, however, is made by previous writers, and in Acts of the Legislature passed at a much earlier period,* of 'Manchester cottons,' 'cotton velvets,' 'fustians,' &c.; but it is known that these articles were wholly composed of wool, and had probably been denominated cottons from being prepared in imitation of some of the cotton fabrics imported from India and Italy.

In the first stage of the manufacture of cotton in England, the weavers, who were dispersed in cottages throughout the country, obtained their supplies of the raw materials in the most irregular and uncertain manner, and upon the finishing of their fabrics they carried them to the market towns for sale. About the year 1760 a new system was introduced, which was

---

* In an Act of 5 and 6 Edw. VI. 1552, entitled 'for the true making of *woollen* cloth,' it is ordered 'That all cottons called Manchester, Lancashire, and Cheshire cottons, full wrought for sale, shall be the length,' &c.

the first step towards lessening the cost of production, and caused the 'manufacturer' of those days to become an 'operative.' The Manchester 'merchants' then began to send agents into the rural districts, who employed weavers at wages, furnishing them with linen yarn for the warp and raw cotton for the weft; the families of the 'operatives' assuming the character of 'spinners,' using the common spindle or distaff to turn the latter article into yarn. A second advantage in the reduction of cost was gained in 1764 by the *spinning jenny*—an invention of James Hargreaves, a carpenter at Standhill near Blackburn, Lancashire,* which machine enabled *eight* threads to be spun with the same facility as one, and it was subsequently brought to such perfection that a little girl could work from eighty to *one hundred and twenty spindles.* It was only applicable for the spinning of the weft, being unable to give to the yarn the necessary firmness and hardness required in the warp, which deficiency was soon after supplied by Arkwright's *spinning frame,* and it was not until 1773 that goods were made wholly of cotton,† the flax of Germany and Ireland having anterior thereto provided the warp. These inventions, along with the

---

* Hargreaves also worked as a weaver, and, being aware of the jealousy and ill-will likely to be directed against the author of any mechanical substitute for hand-labour, conducted his trade in secret. By 1767 he had, however, mounted and sold several of his jennies. His invention was for a long while confined to his family, but, becoming known through the indiscretion of one of its female members, the spinsters and their partisans broke into his house in a riotous manner and destroyed the hated rival of their fingers. Thus finding the fruit of his ingenuity, toils, and privations blasted, and the further prosecution of his plans impossible amidst an enraged populace, who even threatened his life, he migrated to Nottingham in 1768, where he found in Mr. Thomas James, a joiner, a partner willing and able to assist him in erecting a small spinning mill upon the jenny principle. He obtained a patent for his invention in 1770. He died in 1778, leaving a decent provision for his wife and children.

† Messrs. Strutt and Need, the partners of Arkwright, were the manufacturers of these goods, and, upon discovering that there was an old law 'for the encouragement of arts,' forbidding that fabrics should be made wholly of cotton, they applied to the Legislature for its repeal, and succeeded after much expense and delay. The following is an account of this Repeal Act, the 14 George III. c. 72 : 'Whereas a new manufacture of stuffs made *entirely* of cotton spun in this kingdom has been lately introduced, and some doubts were expressed whether it was lawful to use it, it was declared by Parliament to be not only a lawful but a laudable manufacture, and therefore permitted to be used, on paying 3*d.* a square yard, when printed, painted, or stained.'

mule jenny of Crompton, 1774, and the *power loom* of Cart-
wright, as well as innumerable other improvements, with the
application of steam power to machinery, and the cultivation of
cotton in the Southern States of America, have been largely
instrumental in placing England on her present proud commercial eminence, and have been the true source of the wonderful prosperity of all the American States.

From the very outset of the settlement of the thirteen
American colonies, they were each and all republics in almost
everything but name, and continued to be governed pretty much
in their original manner until the accession of Abraham Lincoln,
of Illinois, 'rail splitter,' on March 4, 1861. The Crown of Great
Britain, to be sure, retained the veto power, but the people
selected their own legislators, and exercised nearly every other
right of sovereignty; there was no titled nobility or any aristo-
cratic attributes of monarchy—Conservative influences so beneficial and necessary in all the old established countries;* hence,
when the colonists successfully resisted the encroachments of
the mother-country upon their liberties, the 'revolution' made
but little practical change in their political affairs from that
which had before existed. They were well fitted to govern
themselves, which, in truth, was precisely what they had done
from the beginning. Two distinct parties, however, arose
after the cessation of the conflict; one, the Federalists, desired
to consolidate the States, and have a strong central Government; the other, the State Rights men, wished to maintain
the sovereignty of their respective commonwealths. The
latter party, although successful, finally consented, in eleven of
the States, to secede on March 3, 1789, from the 'Articles of
' Confederation' which had been adopted on March 2, 1781,
and unite in creating a more efficient central head, or ' foreign
agency,' which was established under the 'Constitution' that
went into operation on April 30, 1789, and which Lord Brougham
aptly calls a ' treaty between the States ' that are parties thereto.
North Carolina and Rhode Island did not accede to the
new arrangement until some time afterwards (November 21,
1789, and May 29, 1790). This ' treaty ' has been lauded as
being the cause of the prosperity of the American peoples.

* John Locke unsuccessfully attempted to establish titles in Carolina.

That this is a delusion every sound thinker must admit, because the Americans have been governed by State laws, enacted under State constitutions formed long anterior to this boasted ' Union.' It is true that, through the influence of the ' scum of Europe,' that had become naturalised citizens, aided by unprincipled politicians of native growth, it assumed frequently, and in the most arrogant manner, to govern the whole world, but, until the accession of the present Administration at Washington, the hand of Federal power was never felt by an American while at home ; it was only intended to act as a shield and protection to him when abroad. It is also true that, by an assumption of power not delegated to it, the Government under the Constitution has been made the vehicle for benefiting the North to the detriment of the South, by the imposition of protective tariffs upon European manufactures.   The fallacies in reference to the Constitution, which has been absurdly called the ' noblest form of government ever devised by man,' arose from the unexampled prosperity attending the States, by reason of the cultivation of cotton having been commenced on an important scale a few years after their foreign affairs were entrusted to this ' general agency,' which likewise established unrestricted free trade between them. Massachusetts and Rhode Island, while members of the old Union under the ' Articles of Confederation,' had inaugurated a system of protective tariffs, charging duties on merchandise imported from the other States as well as from Europe, in order to encourage their local manufactures.

Cotton was introduced into Virginia as a garden plant in 1621. The precise year in which it began to be grown as a crop in the Southern colonies is not known.   The quantity produced prior to the ' Revolution ' was of very trifling moment ; the unrestricted intercourse with the sister possessions in the West Indies gave large importations to the continent in exchange for provisions shipped thither.   No manufactories were then permitted in America ; such was one of the restraints imposed by the British sovereign when he gave his colonial subjects chartered privileges and other rights to rule themselves.   This restriction did not interfere with the manufacture of ' home-spun ' clothing, which was not much inferior to the ordinary productions of European looms, prior to the improvements in machinery, the better descriptions of which it has been the aim of the free-traders in America to import to this present day. It is thought, however, that the first planting of cotton for use took place in Virginia about the year 1661, at which period there had been an over-production of tobacco, and the colonists were deprived of a market for the whole of their surplus in consequence of the Navigation Act of Charles II.* This directed attention to other crops, cotton included. There is a paper in the historical collections of South Carolina, written and published in England in 1666, entitled, ' A Brief Description of the Province of Caro-lina, on the Coast of Florida,' the object of which was to encourage emigration, and among the inducements it states that

---

* The charters granted to the founders of the settlement of the colony of Virginia distinctly empowered them to carry on a direct intercourse with foreign States ; and they were not slow in availing themselves of this per-mission, for they had, as early as 1620, established tobacco warehouses in Middleburgh and Flushing. The British Government afterwards deprived them of this privilege. It was not until they had surmounted the difficulties and hardships incident to their first establishment, and had begun to increase rapidly in wealth, that their commerce commenced to excite the jealousy of the mother-country. Regulations were, therefore, framed with a view of restricting its freedom. The Act of 1650, passed by the Republican Parlia-ment, laid the first foundations of the monopoly system, by confining the import and export trade of the colonies exclusively to British- or colonial-built ships. But the famous Navigation Act of 1660 (12 Charles II. c. 18) went further. It enacted that certain specified articles, the produce of the colonies, and since well known in commerce by the name of *enumerated* articles, should not be exported directly from the colonies to any foreign country, but that they should be first sent to Britain and then unladen (the words of the Act are *laid upon the shore*), before they could be forwarded to their final destination. Sugar, molasses, ginger, fustic, tobacco, cotton, and indigo were originally enumerated ; and the list was subsequently enlarged by the addition of coffee, hides and skins, iron, coal, lumber, &c. In 1739 the monopoly system was so far relaxed that sugars were permitted to be carried directly from the British plantations to any port or place south of Cape Finisterre. The Act of 1764 provided that no commodity of the growth or manufacture of Europe should be imported into the British plan-tations but such as were laden and put on board in England, Wales, or Berwick-upon-Tweed, and in English-built shipping, whereof the master and two-thirds of the crew were English. In the Charter of Pennsylvania the colonists had been empowered to carry on a direct intercourse with foreign States, but that permission by the general laws was rescinded. It was not until 1803 that Great Britain began to assume a more liberal policy with her dependencies. She has since taken off all restrictions upon commerce.

the lands 'grow indigo, tobacco very good, and *cotton wool.*'
In the same collections Dr. Hewett describes the manner of
cultivating the cotton plant, stating that the colonists did not
consider it of much importance. Peter Purry, a Swiss, the
founder of Purrysburgh in the same colony, memorialised
George I. in 1731, in relation to a certain country, extending
thirty-three degrees on either side of the equator, capable of
producing cotton; he also wrote at the same time from Charleston that '*cotton* and flax thrive admirably.' Cotton was grown
on a limited scale, in the vicinity of Easton in Talbot County,
Maryland, in 1736. Miss Lucas, afterwards Mrs. Pinckney,
of South Carolina, the daughter of the Governor of Antigua, says
in her journal, under date of July 1, 1739, ' Wrote to my father
' to-day on the pains I had taken to bring the indigo, ginger,
' *cotton*, &c. to perfection, and that I had greater hopes for the
' indigo than anything else.' Among the archives of the Department de la Marine et des Colonies at Paris, there is a report on
cotton written in 1760, which speaks of the great advantage
Louisiana might derive from its culture; its introduction from
St. Domingo, the difficulty of separating the seed from the wool,
and suggesting the importation of machinery from the East
Indies for that purpose. Just before the breaking out of the
revolutionary war in 1775, the Congress of South Carolina
recommended its people to raise cotton; and General Delegall,
of that colony, at that time cultivated ' thirty acres of green
seed cotton, near Savannah in Georgia.' In the same year
cotton was grown in St. Mary's County, Maryland, Cape May
County, New Jersey, and Sussex County, Delaware. Mr. Jefferson, in his 'Notes on Virginia' in 1781, alludes to the domestic
economy of making cotton goods in families for their own use.

The cotton seed used, according to some authorities, came from
Manilla, Cyprus, and Malta; others state that it was brought
from Barbadoes. No doubt all varieties were tried. The exports of cotton, prior to the Revolution, consisted of seven bales
in 1748, and ten bales in 1770, but the produce may have been
of island growth.

The attention of the Americans after peace was concluded, in
1783, was turned more towards the cultivation of cotton, not for
export, but for manufacturing purposes. Previous to that event

they relied on obtaining their principal supplies of the raw material from the island colonies, and their best fabrics, as stated above, came from England. There was a disposition to be 'independent' in all things. Mr. Tench Coxe of Philadelphia, who took an active interest in public affairs, in writing in 1785, entertained 'the pleasing conviction that the United ' States in its extensive regions south of Anne Arundel and ' Talbot (Maryland) would certainly become a great cotton ' producing country.' In 1786, Mr. Madison expressed himself in the same manner. These impressions, together with the supply of cotton that had been received at Philadelphia during the Revolution, all of which had not been consumed, induced Mr. Coxe to visit England, in order to purchase machinery, the restrictions upon the use of Arkwright's patent having been removed. He found, however, that the British laws forbade the exportation of machinery. In order to overcome this difficulty, he had complete brass models made, finished, and packed, but they were detected by the Government examining officer, and forfeited. No means then remained to obtain the benefit of the British invention, but to manufacture the machinery in America, and Mr. Samuel Slater, of Belper, Derbyshire, who had been a pupil of Arkwright's, was engaged for that purpose; without patterns or memoranda to assist him in his work, he depended solely on his memory for its accomplishment. Mr. Coxe has been called 'the father of the growth of cotton in America,' and Mr. Slater has been named 'the father of the cotton manufacture in America.' Small as the production of cotton was at that time, not being then considered much more than a garden plant, there seems to have been, with the receipts of that of foreign growth, a surplus. In 1784, eight bales were shipped to Liverpool, and were seized at the Custom House there, as an illicit importation of British colonial produce; they were restored to their consignees so soon as it was discovered that so ' large' a quantity of cotton could be grown on the American continent. Exportations have been continued from that day to this. Neither the embargoes of 1794 and 1808, the Non-intercourse Act that followed, the war of 1812–14, nor the blockade of the Southern ports, nor the sinking of 'stone fleets' at the mouths of harbours, have prevented some American cotton reaching Europe.

Notwithstanding the occurrence at Liverpool in 1784, Mr. Jay, the American Minister at London, ten years later, considered that the cotton grown in the Southern States was not likely to be of much consequence. In the 12th article of the treaty which he negotiated with Great Britain in 1794, cotton was included with molasses, sugar, coffee, and cocoa, as articles which American vessels should not be permitted to carry from the Islands or from the United States to any foreign country. The Senate refused to ratify this provision. Mr. Jay did not regard cotton as an article of regular export; indeed, the United States Tariff Act of July 1, 1789, then in force, called for a duty of three cents per pound on all imported—not for protection, but for revenue. It was at that time thought that American manufacturers would have to depend on other countries for a supply of the raw material. This belief was so general that Congress was petitioned to repeal the duty. In a few years, however, it was ascertained that sufficient cotton could be grown in the South, and the duty became a dead letter. The cultivation of cotton from this period increased rapidly; the improvements in machinery augmenting its use, induced its production, and gave occupation to the plethora of African labour, that was then becoming a serious inconvenience and loss to the people of the South. The negroes had, in fact, multiplied too fast, although all the Southern States had passed laws preventing the ingress of slaves, which the Yankees were smuggling into their borders, from the North as well as from Africa. The British, too, were engaged in the same traffic, though the most stringent measures were adopted from time to time by all the Southern States for its suppression. Not one Northern State ever prohibited the trade. Massachusetts, Rhode Island, and New Hampshire, were extensively engaged in the commerce, until it was interdicted by the General Government, January 1, 1808. It is fortunate for the blacks, as well as the whites, that the cotton business sprang up, for the sons of Africa do not flourish in a state of freedom, and, without the cultivation of the leading staple of commerce, there would not have been sufficient occupation for them. The planters would have preferred to manumit their slaves, which in fact was done in many instances, rather than to be encumbered with idle and superfluous hands. The natural increase of the negroes has more than kept pace with the demand for their labour; it is therefore fortunate that the Southerners prohibited the African slave trade at so early a day. Had they not done so, they would have been overrun with savages; and they now believe that the resumption of that commerce would so alter and vitiate the character of slavery in their States as to render it prejudicial to their interests; hence, there has been engrafted in the Confederate Constitution a special clause that does not exist in the Federal document, placing it out of the power of the Southern Congress to open the traffic, while the Northern Congress has a right to make it legal at any time it may think proper. This was not done to please or conciliate the fanaticism of Europe in reference to slavery, which is altogether distinct from the African slave trade, although frequently confounded therewith, but at the unanimous demand of the people it was thus made a fundamental law of the Southern Union. The slaves in all the States have increased from 697,897 in 1790, to 3,953,760 in 1860. Their value per head is eight or ten times greater now than at the first-named date. Some political economists would argue that these statistics denoted scarcity of this kind of service; the enormous stocks of American cotton and yarns, and goods made therefrom, at all the various markets of the world, when the war in America commenced, and the large quantities of produce now in the South, disprove such a theory. The Southerners have, in their slaves, advantages comparable to a ' patent right,' which would be entirely lost to them were the African slave trade reopened. Cotton cannot be cultivated to advantage in the Confederate States—or in the West Indies— except by forced labour, and African labour can only be properly managed by the controlling influence of the white race. A ' strike ' in the South would imperil an entire cotton crop.

The following pages will, it is to be hoped, prove that the negro in the Confederate States is in his proper sphere of life, and that all attempts to change his present happy condition have not only been an injury to him, but that if the Southern people had swerved from their sound position in the matter, they would have been surrounded by this time by hordes of black barbarians, instead of industrious and useful, well-clad and well-fed labourers, with lighter work and more personal comforts than fall to the lot of any other class of farm hands. While the cruel practices connected with the African slave trade during the latter days of its continuance under British authority, and which have since been emulated by the Yankees, cannot be too strongly condemned, it is only just to say that the slave system established on the continent of America by the English has been not only humane, but civilising in its character. The introduction there of women as well as men has been the means of founding a race far superior to that of the native African. The same cannot be said of the course pursued in the Islands, where nearly all the importations were of the male sex, who were frequently ' worked to death' in order to prevent their becoming a burden and expense in old age upon their masters, who, unlike the slave-owners in the States, have ever been mostly absentees. The coolie system, established to fill up the gap caused by the emancipation of the West Indian negroes, in its practical operations is almost equally iniquitous.

Slavery in the West Indies and on the continent of America has always varied in character. It was the habit of the masters of slave-ships that had a preponderance of males to land their passengers on the Islands, while those that contained a majority of females were discharged on the continent. For many years Nassau, New Providence, was a port of call for slavers; their cargoes were distributed—the males in one direction, the females in another. Negro women and children, for a century and a half, were regularly exported from the Islands to the continent, as remittances to pay for the supply of provisions from Pennsylvania and the other colonies. The reason for this is obvious: there was no employment in the West Indies except for males, and the expense of maintaining women and children there was very great. The very reverse was the case on the continent: the variety of labour introduced from the earliest period gave occupation for both sexes and all ages, and the cheapness of food assisted in the general economy. For these reasons, it has been more profitable to import labour into the West Indies than to raise it. This is evidenced from the fact that, while

1,700,000 slaves were received into the Islands, but a little over
one-third, 660,000, were there at the time of emancipation.
Had they increased at the same rate as those on the continent
of America, it would have taken 500,000,000*l.* to have settled
with their masters ; or, if they had decreased in the States—
only 350,000 having been delivered there—as they did in the
Islands, 4,000,000*l.* would have been ample to have purchased
all the Africans in the South.   There is no such thing, as has
been charged, as ' slave-breeding ' in the Confederate States.
The negroes there ' increase and multiply ' in the same order as
the whites.   The absurdity of this accusation, which has been
principally levelled against Virginia, is most palpable ; the
augmentation in that State is only at the rate of 1 per cent.
per annum against 3 per cent. in the more southern latitudes.
A large number of the wealthy citizens of Virginia own plantations in the South-west, whither they have sent their sons, with
a portion of their servants, just as the Yankees have been
migrating to the North-west.   This has given rise to the
erroneous impression in regard to ' slave-breeding.'   Ireland
might, with equal propriety, be called a ' labour-breeding '
country.   In all the Southern States there are stringent laws
against the introduction of slaves, unless accompanied by their
masters, and even then not for the purpose of sale.   There are
also laws for the protection of negroes, who have their rights as
well as the whites ; in fact, the masters merely own the labour
of their servants, under restrictions established not only by
statutes, but by common sense and force of public opinion.

In the West Indies, negroes were merely articles of merchandise, worked in large numbers upon vast plantations under
the care of agents, their owners mostly residing in England ;
and the great object was to make the yearly income as much as
possible.   The bountiful productions of a generous soil, in a
region of perpetual spring, stimulated avarice to such an extent
that no rest was given to the labourer where none was required
for the land.   An entirely opposite system was inaugurated
upon the continent of America, where the changes in climate
between summer and winter are very great.   The planters there,
unlike the rich West Indian proprietors, were generally men
of moderate means, who had sought a home in the New World.

The negro, purchased from the slave-ship, wielded his axe side by side with his master in felling the forest round his rude house, and was his companion in his wild hunts through the pathless woods. A mutual danger made them defenders of a common home from the red man and the wild beast. The women were employed in spinning flax, and, in the course of time, cotton. The vine, the olive, and the silk-worm were all at one time cultivated, as well as tobacco and breadstuffs; this gave a diversity of occupation for both women and men. It has been the habit of the children of the planter and those of the slaves to hunt, fish, and play together. An almost perfect equality exists between the future master and his future servants. This has made slavery in the Southern States a social institution, not maintained and upheld, as it was in the Islands, solely for profit, but it has become part of a general system, a necessity. The relation between the white and black races has always been patriarchal : they stand towards each other as the protector and the protected.

In point of fact, negroes, when in large numbers, are unfit to be their own masters; they need for their happiness and comfort the controlling care of the white race. An example of their degeneracy in a state of freedom occurred in England several generations ago. About the middle of the last century it was the custom of the fashionable ladies of London to be attended in the streets by slave-pages, who wore brass collars round their necks—a badge of servitude which has never been used in America. These negroes availed themselves of the decision of Lord Mansfield in the Somersett case, 1772, and became freed men. In a short time they were utterly destitute and wandered about the streets; many of them died, and those that remained, 470, were such a nuisance to the people of the metropolis that, through parliamentary aid in 1787, they were sent to Sierra Leone.* The population at that date

---

* These London negroes were the founders of the colony of Sierra Leone; they, however, with a large number of white women of bad character, who were transported to that place at the same time, nearly all died in a very few years. The colony was resettled in 1796 by negroes taken from the Americans during the Revolution, who had resided in the meanwhile in Nova Scotia; their numbers were increased by the ' Maroons,' fugitive and rebellious blacks, captured in the mountains of Jamaica by the aid of blood-

was about 900,000 : if there were an equivalent number of Africans within its limits now, a similar course would have to be pursued in regard to them. This English incident exemplifies the hostile feeling shown towards the African race in the Northern States of America, where, unlike in the South, they are even refused admission into public conveyances. No one acquainted with the negro character can believe him the equal of the white man. The marks of intellect exhibited by Frederick Douglas and others arise from the white blood that is in their veins; but nature puts a stop to the continuance of such mixture, and mulattoes die out in about three generations. The best authority on this question is M. Pruner Bey, who says'—

'The capacity of the negro is limited to imitation. The
'prevailing impulse is for sensuality and rest. No sooner are
'the physical wants satisfied than all effort ceases, and the
'body abandons itself to sexual gratification and rest. The
'family relations are weak; the husband or father is little con-
'cerned. Jealousy has only carnal motives, and the fidelity of
'the woman is secured by mechanical contrivances. Drunken-
'ness, gambling, and ornamentation of the body are the most
'powerful levers in the life of the negro. The whole industry
'is limited to ornaments. Instead of clothing himself, he orna-
'ments his body. Like certain animals, the negro seems
'apathetic under pain. The explosion of passions occur when
'least expected, but are not lasting. The temperament of the
'negro has been called choleric, but it is only so to a certain
'extent. It is a momentary ebullition, followed instantly by

hounds; they were first sent to Lower Canada, but, like those in London and Nova Scotia, became such a nuisance that they had to be removed. One of the libels against the South is, that bloodhounds are used to hunt negroes. This misstatement has gained currency in consequence of the practice in Jamaica, Cuba, and other West India Islands.

Great Britain agreed, by the seventh article of the Treaty of Peace, to return the negroes that had been sent to Nova Scotia, and to compensate the Americans for those transported to the West Indies and there sold into renewed slavery. But she never fulfilled this portion of her agreement. The Treaty of Ghent, December 24, 1814, contained a similar provision; payment, however, was avoided for the negroes deported during the last war until 1827, although the Emperor of Russia, as Umpire, had some years previously decided the case in favour of the claimants in the States.

' perfect apathy.   Life has for the negro no longer any value
' when he cannot supply the physical wants; he never resists
' by increased activity, but prefers to die in a state of apathy,
' or he commits suicide.   The negro has no love for war ; he is
' only driven to it by hunger.   War, from passion or destruc-
' tiveness, is unknown to him.'

Sir Charles Lyell and others contend that the intellectual progress of the negro stops at the age of fourteen. The opinions of these scientific gentlemen, who have made the subject a study, should carry weight with them, and drown out the howling cant and wicked fanaticism of the Abolitionists.

The people of Europe have been greatly deceived as to the true condition of the slaves in the Southern States. Subjected to the supervision of a superior race, they are as much elevated above the position of their ancestors and the present barbarous inhabitants of Africa, in every respect, as they are below the whites. The situation of the slaves differs less from that of the agricultural labourers of some countries in Europe than is generally supposed. As regards morality, and especially the intercourse of the sexes, they present a marked superiority to the free negroes of the Northern States. Notwithstanding the stories of American romance writers, the conjugal obligation is almost universally acknowledged, and every effort is made by the masters to preserve among their slaves the ties of family.

CHAPTER II.

THE PRODUCTION OF THE SOUTH-WESTERN STATES—THE MONOPOLY OF THE BANK OF THE UNITED STATES.

THE production of cotton on the North American continent, north and east of Mexico, beginning in Virginia, was tried in South Carolina, New Jersey, Delaware, and Maryland. The three last States soon abandoned its cultivation; South Carolina continued it; Georgia engaged in its culture in 1791; Tennessee, North Carolina, and Louisiana, in 1811; Alabama and Mississippi, in 1821; Arkansas, in 1826; and, lastly, Florida and Texas. Its cultivation was confined chiefly to the Atlantic States until about the year 1830, when the discovery that the bottom lands of the valley of the Mississippi could grow cotton much cheaper than any yet tried, caused a great speculative excitement in the south-west, and created a corresponding land mania in the north-west, inducing persons to lay out farms and project cities in tracts still covered by primeval woods or inhabited only by the aborigines. Almost every State in the Union became thus infatuated, and plunged itself into debt for the cost of internal improvements to transport this anticipated augmentation of commerce. Large numbers of new banks were incorporated to assist the financial arrangements in 1833, 1834, 1835, and 1836—their capital based principally on the issue of State bonds, in the delusive hope that the quantity of 'money' would be increased. As well might an extra number of flour mills be expected to increase the extent of the wheat crops. Yet charters were hurried through the Legislatures: the greatest wildness ensued. In the space of five or six years the nominal banking capital had risen from $110,000,000 to $378,000,000. Ohio had increased from $1,400,000 to $12,000,000; New York, from $20,000,000 to $37,000,000; Pennsylvania, from $14,000,000 to $56,000,000; and Mississippi, from $1,000,000 to $21,000,000!

These speculations were very much fostered by the Bank of the United States, whose Federal charter expired on March 3, 1836, when its concerns were continued by a new bank of the same name and capital, that had been created by the Legislature of Pennsylvania on the preceding 18th February. The bank engaged in these enterprises in order to obtain popularity in the South, so as to overcome, in the minds of the people, the constitutional objections to its recharter urged by President Jackson. It succeeded in its desires in the Halls of Congress, but the President's veto deprived it of ' national life,' and it had to resort to the State of Pennsylvania for fresh privileges. On the day named the Bill passed the Legislature of that State, and was entitled ' An Act to repeal the State Tax on Real and ' Personal Property, and to continue and extend the improve-
' ments of the State by Railroads and Canals, and to charter a ' State Bank, to be called the Bank of the United States.' The bank, by its acceptance of the charter, came under an obligation to pay, as a bonus to the State, $2,000,000 as soon as required, $500,000 on March 3, 1837, and $2,000,000 in instalments of $100,000 per annum for twenty years; also, to loan the State $6,000,000, payable in 1868, at par if the interest should be 4 per cent., or 10 per cent. premium if the interest was fixed at 5 per cent. In addition to these sums, the bank agreed to subscribe to various railroad and turnpike companies in Pennsylvania to the extent of $675,000; and the charge has been made that some $500,000 or $600,000 were squandered among newspaper editors and members of the Legislature to secure their support to the measure. This sum, it has been alleged, was covered up by the profits on the ' old circulation account.' These items, although costly, enabled the old bank to wind up by merging its affairs into the new concern; its dividends had been large, and the stockholders were tempted to retain their shares. With the vast sums locked up in the form of loans to the new States, the fresh obligations it had just entered into, and the $7,000,000 (made nearly $8,000,000 by overvaluing the assets) of Government stock which it had to pay off, the new institution commenced business with little or no actual capital. It, however, took advantage of a clause in the original charter, which gave it two years

to settle with its stockholders, and in the meanwhile purchased the Federal stock, at the exaggerated value, on a credit of two and three years; it continued making large dividends which it never earned, and availed itself of the accommodation afforded by the reissue of the notes of the old bank, which passed as currency in the distant States of the South and West.* Its nominal capital was large — $35,000,000 —

* The annexed extracts from the messages of Presidents Jackson and Van Buren to Congress give some insight into the manner in which the new bank 'stepped into the shoes' of the old concern.

President Jackson in his eighth annual message, on December 6, 1836, said: — 'The conduct and present condition of that bank, and the 'great amount of capital invested in it by the United States, require your 'careful attention. Its charter expired on the 3rd day of March last, and it 'has now no power but that given in the 21st section, to use "the corporate '" name, style, and capacity, for the purpose of suits for the final settlement '" and liquidation of the affairs and accounts of the corporation, and for the '" sale and disposition of their estate, real, personal, and mixed, but not for '" any other purpose or in any other manner whatsoever, nor for a period ex-'" ceeding two years after the expiration of the said term of incorporation." 'Before the expiration of the charter, the stockholders of the bank obtained 'an Act of incorporation from the Legislature of Pennsylvania, excluding 'only the United States. Instead of proceeding to wind up their concerns, 'and pay over to the United States the amount due on account of the stock 'held by them, the President and directors of the old bank appear to have 'transferred the books, papers, notes, obligations, and most or all of its pro-'perty, to this new corporation, which entered upon business as a continu-'ation of the old concern. Among other acts of questionable validity, the 'notes of the expired corporation are known to have been used as its own, 'and again put in circulation. That the old bank had no right to issue or 'reissue its notes after the expiration of its charter, cannot be denied; and 'that it could not confer any such right on its substitute any more than 'exercise it itself, is very plain. In law and in honesty, the notes of the 'bank in circulation at the expiration of its charter should have been called 'in by public advertisement, paid up as presented, and, together with those 'in hand, cancelled and destroyed. Their reissue is sanctioned by no law, 'and warranted by no necessity. If the United States be responsible in 'their stock for the payment of their notes, their reissue by the new corpo-'ration for their own profit is a fraud upon the Government. If the United 'States is not responsible, then there is no legal responsibility in any quarter, 'and it is a fraud on the country. They are the redeemed notes of a dis-'solved partnership, but, contrary to the wishes of the retiring partner, and 'without his consent, are again reissued and circulated.'

President Van Buren, in his first annual message, on the 4th day of December 1837, said: —

'Just before the banking privileges ceased, its effects were transferred by and its credit, all over the world, almost unlimited. · As a State bank it could not, in its own name, carry on business in other States, New York excepted, where it opened a branch under the general Banking Law of that State. It managed, however, in various ways to avoid this difficulty. For instance, it had become the owner of the bonds of the State of Mississippi, which were issued to form the stock of the Planters' Bank in 1831 and 1833; it also, in 1838, became the proprietor, in a similar manner, of the Mississippi Union Bank, furnishing its whole capital, $5,000,000, excepting $8,000, the organisation of which corporation involved a fraud upon the State, by a supplement smuggled through the Legislature, contrary to law, and which nullified the provisions of its charter, in order to serve the purposes of the Philadelphia institution, and violated the constitution of the State of Mississippi.

The Constitution adopted by the people of the State of Mississippi in 1832 contains the following article:—

‘ No law shall ever be passed to raise a loan of money upon
‘ the credit of the State, or to pledge the faith of the State for
‘ the payment or redemption of any loan or debt, unless such
‘ law be proposed in the Senate or House of Representatives,

‘ the bank to a new institution then recently incorporated, in trust for the
‘ discharge of its debts and the settlement of its affairs.

‘ With this trustee, by authority of Congress, an adjustment was subse-
‘ quently made of the large interest which the Government had in stock of
‘ the institution. The manner in which a trust unexpectedly created upon
‘ the Act granting the charter, and involving such great public interests, had
‘ been executed, would, under any circumstances, be a fit subject of inquiry;
‘ but much more does it deserve your attention when it embraces the re-
‘ demption of obligations to which the authority and credit of the United
‘ States have given value. The two years allowed are now nearly at an end.
‘ It is well understood that the trustee has not redeemed and cancelled the
‘ outstanding notes of the bank, but has reissued and is actually reissuing,
‘ since the 3rd of March, 1836, the notes which have been received by it to
‘ a vast amount.

‘ According to its own official statement, so late as the 1st of October
‘ last, 1837, nineteen months after the banking privileges given by the
‘ charter had expired, it had under its control uncancelled notes of the
‘ late Bank of the United States to the amount of $27,561,866, of which
‘ $6,175,861 were in actual circulation, $1,468,627 at State bank agencies,
‘ and $3,002,390 in transitu; thus showing that upwards of $10,500,000 of
‘ the notes of the old bank were then still kept outstanding.’

' and be agreed to by a majority of the members of each House,
' and entered in their journals, with the yeas and nays taken
' thereon, and be referred to the next succeeding Legislature,
' and published for three months previous to the next regular
' election in three newspapers of the State, and unless a ma-
' jority of each branch of the Legislature so elected after such
' publication, shall agree to and pass such law; and in such
' case the yeas and nays shall be taken and entered on the
' journals of each House: Provided that nothing in this section
' shall be so construed as to prevent the Legislature from nego-
' tiating $1,500,000, and vesting the same in Stock reserved to
' the State by the charter of the Planters' Bank of the State of
' Mississippi.'

The bank had two objects in continuing these transactions:
one, to keep up its credit by a system of ' kiting ;' the other, to
retain, as it were, influence in all the States, until the Whig or
Bank party should attain power, when it hoped to be able to
revert from a State to a Federal charter. Its operations were
intimately connected with the cotton trade, which, with the
India, China, South American, and West Indian trades, conducted by its credits, threw into its coffers large sums of money,
and enabled it to select as agents in Europe the most powerful
and wealthy banking and mercantile houses. The commissions
it was thus enabled to influence to these firms amounted annually
to large sums. Partly with a view to benefit the immediate re-
latives and friends of some of its officers, but, it is believed,
principally to extend its sphere of financial accommodation, it
opened ' a house of its own ' in London and Liverpool.

The cotton planters, who migrated to the south-west from
Virginia and the Carolinas, with gangs of hands from their
paternal estates, entered largely into agricultural operations
through bank aid, which was extended to them from year to
year. The magnificent profits of the first few seasons induced
them to go beyond their depth ; their contemporaries in the
West became solely speculators, and not producers. This state
of affairs, with short crops of cereals, brought about great distress, which culminated in the panic of 1837. The banks of
New Orleans first gave way in March of that year, and by May
every monied institution in the Union had suspended specie

payments; they did not resume until May 1838. In the meantime, on September 22, 1837, the Bank of the United States appointed its cashier, Mr. Samuel Jaudon, to act as its agent, or 'drawing post,' at London, whither he at once proceeded, and commenced business on November 8, 1837. About the same time, Mr. May Humphreys and Mr. Edward Biddle, a son of Mr. Nicholas Biddle, President of the Bank of the United States, started for Liverpool, where they established a commercial house under the firm of Humphreys, Biddle, & Co. The bank made arrangements with Messrs. Bevan and Humphreys of Philadelphia to accept bills drawn upon them by its agents in the South against advances upon consignments of cotton to the Liverpool concern, for which they were reimbursed by the bank at the maturity of the drafts, receiving one-eighth per cent. commission for their trouble and risk. The proceeds of the cotton, or any moneys obtained by the hypothecation of the same, were handed over to Mr. Jaudon, to meet his acceptances of the bills of exchange drawn upon him by the bank. Mr. Jaudon, too, raised large amounts of money by the issue of the post notes of the Bank of the United States, at twelve months' date, which were readily sold in the London market.* The Southern banks, in addition to the capital furnished them by the Bank of the United States, also issued post notes at twelve months' date, payable in New York; the bank itself likewise did the same in every State of the Union, and a large portion of the floating capital of the world was thus made to pass through its channels. These transactions of the 'mammoth,' as it was called, were suddenly brought to a termination by an unsuccessful financial operation. In August 1839, it valued, without any authority whatever, upon Messrs. Hottinguer & Co., Paris, for 6,200,000 francs at 60 days' sight; the proceeds of the bills were remitted in specie to Mr. Jaudon by the same steamer that conveyed them for acceptance. The Paris firm declined to

---

* Nearly all the public loans were at one time negotiated through the Bank of the United States; bank-charter mortgages upon negroes by *name* found ready sale in London, when the anti-slavery furore was at its height. Loans upon American slaves were as 'easy' as the loan to free the blacks in the West Indies.

honour them, when Messrs. Hope & Co. of Amsterdam came forward with their name, at the instance of Mr. Jaudon, who pledged with them sundry State stocks, among them the Mississippis alluded to above, as collateral security. The discredit of the bank by Messrs. Hottinguer & Co. reflected upon it at home : it could sell no more 'accommodation' bills of exchange, and the 'agency' of Mr. Jaudon became valueless for financial purposes. It consequently failed on October 9, 1839, and carried along with it all the banks in Pennsylvania and south of that State. The institutions that were not utterly bankrupt resumed specie payments by March 1842. The New York and New England banks managed to weather the storm throughout.

The securities delivered to Messrs. Hope & Co. had been held by the Bank of the United States for several years, and were sent to London for the purpose of sale. But all State credit was so low at that time that there was no market for them. So depressed was the credit of these State stocks, that scrip to the par value of thirteen millions of dollars was handed to Messrs. Hope & Co., or about thirteen times the amount of their guarantee : Pennsylvanias, Marylands, and the bonds of other wealthy States were included with those of Mississippi.

The news of the disaster to the Bank of the United States reached London on November 7, 1839. 'The Times' of November 9, after commenting on the intelligence, and alluding to the American State securities, among which were those of Mississippi, said that they had never been introduced on the Stock Exchange, or adopted by speculators for time bargains, as the South American and Portuguese stocks had been, and cautioned the public in these words :—' Should ' they consequently become suddenly valueless by breach of ' faith or failure of assets, there can be no gradual decline ' accompanied, as in other cases, by continued fluctuations, but ' the transition will be almost immediate to a mere nominal ' price, at which no business could be done.' There were even some doubts entertained in England at that date as to whether the individual States had any right to borrow money or issue scrip. These doubts elicited an opinion concerning the same from Mr. Daniel Webster, who was then in Europe, and who in an

answer to a letter addressed to him by Messrs. Baring Brothers
& Co., said, under date of London, October 16, 1839 :—

'Your enquiry is, Whether the legislature of one of the States
'has legal and constitutional power to contract loans at home
'and abroad?

'To this I answer that the legislature of a State has such
'power; and how any doubt could have arisen on this point
'it is difficult for me to conceive. Every State is an inde-
'pendent sovereign community, except in so far as certain
'powers which it might otherwise have exercised have been
'conferred on a general government, established under a written
'constitution, and exerting its authority over the people of all
'the States. This general government is a limited government.
'Its powers are specific and enumerated. All powers not con-
'ferred upon it remain with the States, and with the people.
'The State legislatures, on the other hand, possess all usual and
'ordinary powers of government, *subject to any limitation
'which may be imposed by their own constitutions*, and with
'the exception, as I have said, of the operation on those powers
'of the constitution of the United States.

*   *   *   *   *   *

'I have seen a suggestion that State loans must be regarded
'as unconstitutional and illegal, inasmuch as the constitution of
'the United States has declared that no State shall emit bills of
'credit. It is certain that the constitution does contain this
'salutary clause; but what is a bill of credit? It has no
'resemblance whatever to a bond or other security given for
'the payment of money borrowed. The term "bill of credit"
'is familiar in our political history, and its meaning well ascer-
'tained and settled, not only by that history, but by judicial
'interpretation and decisions from the highest source. For the
'purpose of this opinion it may be sufficient to say, that bills
'of credit, the subject of the prohibition in the constitution of
'the United States, were essentially paper money. They were
'paper issues, intended for circulation, and for receipt into the
'Treasury as cash, and were sometimes made a tender in pay-
'ment of debts. To put an end, at once and for ever, to evils
'of the sort and to dangers from this source, the constitution
'of the United States has declared that no State shall emit

' bills of credit, nor make anything but gold and silver a tender
' in payment of debts, nor pass any law which shall impair the
' obligation of contracts. All this, however, proves, not that
' States cannot contract debts, but that, when contracted, they
' must pay them in coin, according to the stipulation.'

The London journals of the latter part of 1839 were filled
with articles on the affairs of the Bank of the United States.
Mr. Biddle visited Europe after its failure, and, in connection
with Mr. Jaudon, made some arrangements to prevent some of
his acceptances being returned to Philadelphia, in order, as it was
said, to save the damages ; but it was shrewdly suspected that
the creditors were desirous of obtaining some of the stocks in
Mr. Jaudon's hands : and, as part of the history of those days,
the subjoined articles from the City column of ' The Times ' may
be recurred to with interest :—

December 9, 1839.—' It is said in connection with American
' affairs that another loan has been made to Mr. Jaudon, the
' agent of the United States Bank; but another version of the
' rumour is, that the *former* loan, negotiated at the time of the
' dishonour of the Paris bills by Messrs. Hottinguer, which was
' repeatedly announced as completed, is now only disposed of,
' and that its amount is 900,000*l.*, the security being as before a
' deposit of American State stocks.'

December 10, 1839.—' Mr. Jaudon's " loan " transaction,
' adverted to on Saturday, continues to be a standing topic in the
' money market; but some mystery still attaches to the subject,
' which no one seems able to clear up. Messrs. Rothschilds
' have been named as contractors for it, and the total amount is
' stated at 900,000*l.*,* for which they are to issue five per cent.
' debentures at ninety-two, and to hold as collateral security a
' large deposit of Ohio, Indiana, Pennsylvania and Mississippi,
' and other American State stocks. But whether Messrs. Roths-
' childs advance this money as a new transaction, or whether it
' is in part to cover up advances made to take up bills refused by
' Messrs. Hottinguer, or whether it was mixed up with transac-
' tions of a similar kind which were under negotiation some time

---

* ' The Times ' was in error as to the amount of the loan : it was 800,000*l.*
sterling.

' back with Messrs. Hope & Co. of Amsterdam and Messrs. Den-
' nison and Co. of London, and which were repeatedly described
' as being brought to a close, though doubts afterwards arose
' whether they were actually completed, is left totally unex-
' plained. That capitalists who are already deeply embarked in
' American securities should endeavour to protect themselves by
' calling in collateral support of this kind, and giving the name of
' a " loan " to the transaction, will be readily comprehended in
' the money market; but not so readily will it be believed that
' they would enter into new and extensive engagements of the
' nature described, and if one of the contracting parties being at
' the same time an admitted bankrupt estate, a position which no
' deposit of security can alter or modify. These considerations
' are likely to prevent other capitalists from taking any share in
' the transaction until it is more clearly explained.'

December 14, 1839.—' The loan of Messrs. Rothschilds to the
' Bank of the United States has already been mentioned. It is
' announced to-day that a deposit of 22 per cent. will be
' required from subscribers to it, and that the remainder, to
' make up 92*l.*, will be in two instalments of 35*l.* each, payable
' on January 15 and July 15 next. The redemption is fixed at
' 50 per cent. in October 1841, and 50 per cent. in October
' 1842, and as this redemption will be at par, the rate of
' interest paid for the accommodation will be between 11 and
' 12 per cent. When such terms are exacted, it need not be
' enquired what notion the parties themselves entertain of the
' transaction.'

When the ' loan ' taken by Messrs. Rothschilds became due,
the Bank of the United States was hopelessly insolvent, and
could not redeem the collaterals deposited for securing its payment. The parties in interest divided the various State stocks
among themselves, at very low figures, and claimed upon the
assignees of the bank for the difference, which demand, after
some difficulty, was settled by compromise. Messrs. Humphreys and Biddle, finding their ' occupation gone,' closed up
their Liverpool house, and returned to Philadelphia with large
fortunes. Much mystery hung over these cotton transactions
for a long while, and it was not even known that the Bank of
the United States furnished all the funds to conduct the business

by means of its credit, the operations being so covered up by the system of exchanges. The bank for many years anterior to these transactions had been a seller of bills on London, and by continuing to act in that capacity did not excite any suspicion— no one seemed to be aware that it was placed in funds at London by the proceeds or hypothecation of the cotton shipments, instead of, as previously, by sales of Government stocks and produce bills; and, from the fact that the larger portion of the consignments were from the new cotton country, it appeared as if the enterprise of the 'dashing young house' at Liverpool had taken advantage of the new trade. It turned out, however, that nearly all, if not all, the officers of the Bank of the United States were interested in the shipments, which, as far as those made against the crops of 1836 and 1837 were concerned, were successful in consequence of a considerable portion of the latter year's production being withheld from market, and enabling them to divide large profits among themselves. The number of pounds of cotton grown in the entire South in those years was 570,000,000 and 720,000,000 respectively, while the crop of 1838 was only 545,000,000 pounds, which, with the remainder of that of 1837 held over, sold for low prices at Liverpool, notwithstanding the bank managers resorted to every means to keep up the market quotations ; but they had not only the depressing influence of superfluous quantity to contend with, but the commercial world was in a paralysed condition, not having recovered from the panic of 1837. The losses thus made by the officers of the bank outbalanced their profits, and they were compelled to make a compromise with its shareholders, who, as well as many of the directors, had been kept in ignorance of the whole affair, and were very slow to believe it, even when they heard of the wrongdoings charged upon the guilty parties. There is no doubt that the bank was first led astray by its desire to obtain political influence ; then its officers carried on the business as a financial operation, and it was not until afterwards that they became sharers in the profits and the losses. The first intimation the public received of these questionable transactions was through a communication which appeared in the New York 'Evening Post' of August 24, 1839. This was shortly after the shipment of specie, the proceeds of the sales of the bills on Messrs. Hottinguer and Co., to Mr. Jaudon, which created a great commotion in Wall Street, the rate of exchange not warranting the transmission of the precious metals to Europe. The withdrawal of so large a sum, without a legitimate reason, from the vaults of the New York banks, caused much surprise, and Mr. Biddle was charged with wishing to 'break' those institutions; they in turn were charged with being jealous of the power of his bank. Here is the information furnished by the 'Post':—

' BANK OF THE UNITED STATES.

' The merchants of this city and Philadelphia feel the se-
' verity of the times, but are puzzled to know to what cause to
' ascribe it. They are like a blind man in the street struck
' by a brickbat; they feel themselves hurt and bruised, but see
' not the hand that dealt the blow. It seems to them a stale
' and poor fetch after all to ascribe it to the Administration.

' The following statement has been drawn up by a person
' whose situation has given him an opportunity to observe the
' proceedings of the banks which have engaged in the cotton
' monopoly. The extent to which they were concerned in that
' unlucky speculation was already known, but the manner in
' which they had involved themselves in the unfortunate affairs of
' the south-western banks has not before been described. The
' first of these errors led to the second, and both have had the
' effect of disturbing and confounding the natural course of
' trade. No wonder, when these great associations enter upon the
' business of buying and selling merchandise — no wonder that
' the regular merchant, with his comparatively small resources,
' is crushed under their footsteps.

' The winding up of these transactions is yet to come, but it is
' approaching. From all appearances it is likely to be one which
' the community will acquiesce in without regret, and which
' will again leave the field of commerce open to individuals.

' THE PRESENT CRISIS AND ITS CAUSE.

' The disasters which are now grinding the business men in
' this city and Philadelphia have been produced solely by the

' speculations in Wall Street and Chestnut Street, but more
' particularly in the latter, as their operations were on a gigantic
' scale. In 1837 and 1838, Mr. Biddle threw a large amount
' of funds into the South, and invested them in cotton. He
' sent his son, a youth of about twenty years of age, and an
' unsuccessful merchant, May Humphreys, to Liverpool to sell
' this cotton, and to transact a general commission business.
' This mushroom house, though new, and without a knowledge
' either of the business or the people of England, at once ob-
' tained a larger amount of business than William and James
' Brown & Co., the Barings, the Lizardis, or any other of the
' old established and substantial houses of that great commercial
' mart. Early in 1838 it was discovered that the cotton crop
' would be short—that Mr. Biddle held up a large amount of
' the previous crop. In the meantime he, by granting facilities
' to Southern banks, induced them to make advances on cotton,
' and ship a large portion of it to his son's house at Liverpool,
' which would more effectually enable him to control the cotton
' market, and carry out the principle of monopoly which the
' Wall Street bankers had so successfully maintained for three
' or four years in the flour trade. But, as all monopolies must
' be maintained by extending the sphere of their operations,
' Mr. Biddle found it necessary to strengthen the Southern
' banks, which had, as his indirect agents, swindled the planters
' out of the cotton to be sacrificed in Liverpool at their expense,
' while they were compelled to receive depreciated and depre-
' ciating paper for their labour. These banks had lost their
' character, their paper had fallen 28 per cent. below par in the
' summer of 1838, and it was seen at once that they could not
' obtain control of the last crop unless they would resume specie
' payments and raise the value of their paper.

' Under these circumstances, foreign capitalists would have
' flocked to the South and purchased the cotton at a fair price,
' and thus, by throwing it into the Liverpool market, would
' have compelled Mr. Biddle to do the same, or borrow money
' and risk the market another year. Accordingly, Mr. Biddle,
' in August and September 1838, commenced rebuilding the
' Southern banks that had engaged in the cotton trade, and
' he purchased the bonds of others to enable them to go into

' operation, and to continue the cotton monopoly. He and a
' few of his gambling associates in Philadelphia, principally the
' officers of the Girard Bank, commenced the purchase of State
' and Bank bonds; and in one week they invested about
' $10,000,000 in the State of Mississippi. $5,000,000 of this
' money on credit were distributed among four insolvent banks
' at a nominal interest of 7 per cent., to be repaid in three
' annual instalments. These banks were the Commercial and
' Railroad Bank of Vicksburg, the Planters', the Agricultural
' and Commercial Bank of Nachez; the former has again sus-
' pended, and it is believed that not one of them can now pay
' the interest, much less the first instalment, which, we believe,
' is due about this time.

' Besides, the Agricultural and the Planters' Bank of Nachez
' owe the Federal Government nearly $1,000,000; and the Go-
' vernment owe it to the people to force its collection, and to that
' extent, at least, abridge the power of the unprincipled specu-
' lation. In purchasing the bonds of these banks, Mr. Biddle
' and his compeers had other strong personal inducements.
' They had purchased an immense amount of their notes at
' 28 per cent. discount, and by the operation were enabled to
' use it at par.

' The other $5,000,000 were invested in Mississippi State
' bonds, to establish the Union Bank at Jackson; and in one
' month this new institution was flooding the country with post
' notes, and was found also in the cotton trade advancing $60
' a bale. By thus holding back the crop, Mr. Biddle might be
' enabled to realise a large profit on the crop of 1837 and 1838,
' which he had purchased, and in the meantime the planters of
' the South would be left to bear the whole of the loss from a
' falling market, after the monopoly had become too heavy for
' the credit system and the gambling system to sustain it any
' longer. Well, this Union Bank is now prostrate, though not
' a year in operation, and commencing with $5,000,000 of
' capital; its paper will now sell for 75 cents on the dollar, even
' when bearing 5 per cent. interest.

' The bonds on which the bank was established are now remain-
' ing unsold in the vaults of the bank in Chestnut Street' [they
had been remitted to Mr. Jaudon, in London, which was the

same thing, as they were still in his hands], 'and if put into the market would not bring 20 cents on the dollar.' [The United States Bank had purchased them on credit, and, before the second payment was made upon them, the Governor of Mississippi proclaimed the fraud that had been practised upon the State, and cautioned all persons against negotiating them; but Mr. Biddle did not heed his advice, but continued his payments to the Union Bank. In fact, it was simply paying out of one pocket into the other—robbing Peter to pay Paul.]

' In Arkansas, Alabama, Georgia, and New Orleans, the same ' system was resorted to; and now we have its glorious results ' in Philadelphia and New York. The bankers and speculators ' have been disappointed in not getting returns from their ' Southern coadjutors; the action of the great " mammoth " ' (United States Bank) in England has forced cotton into ' market, and reduced its price from the monopoly standard; ' and to make up the money to keep the Girard Bank, the ' United States Bank of Pennsylvania, and the speculating con- ' cerns of Wall Street, from again suspending, the honest dealer ' and the regular merchant are compelled to throw their paper ' into market, and sacrifice from 2 to $2\frac{1}{2}$ per cent. per month to ' maintain their credit and carry on their business.'

The warning contained in this communication was not heeded by the people of Philadelphia; on the contrary, they condemned every man that said aught against the Bank of the United States. The presidents and directors of the other banks of Philadelphia were, in fact, so stupid and blinded that they came to the rescue of the 'mammoth,' after its bills had been dishonoured in Paris, and not only loaned it money, but concluded to suspend specie payments with it on October 9, 1839. The utter insolvency of the Bank of the United States was thus covered up for many months. So wanting are many of the bank presidents in America in the knowledge of the ordinary principles of finance, that they have several times all 'suspended' in order to shield from view the rottenness of one of their number. As well might all the merchants in London fail when one concern happens to be unable to meet its engagements. On that occasion all the banks were compelled by legislative enactment to resume specie payments on January 15, 1841 ; they did so, but again failed on February 4. The 'mammoth' then went into liquidation; the other banks did not recur to gold and silver for over a year. Though the conduct of Mr. Biddle has been so severely criticised, and so many injurious aspersions cast upon his character, he morally was not so guilty as the disastrous results of his policy and commercial operations would indicate. Being in effect the sole manager of the institution for a long series of years, he appears to have lost sight of the fact that he was only the agent for others, and responsible to them for the use of the funds entrusted to his care. The flatterers and sycophants who encouraged this delusion of a too prosperous man were his most bitter enemies and vilifiers when he fell. At one time, it was almost 'treason' and 'disloyalty' to even hint at or question the illegality or immorality of the transactions of the bank; the Democrats of those days were nearly as much persecuted because they were anti-bank men as their successors at the present period are for their political faith. Nor would the masses believe that it was the bank that assisted in bringing about the commercial distress that existed from 1837 to 1840, but they charged it upon President Jackson's opposition to the recharter of the 'national' institution. Surely the new bank was national enough, for it extended its sphere of usefulness (?) all over the Union, and assisted the Whigs or Bank party in the election of Harrison and Tyler in 1840. Fortunately for the country, President Harrison died after being in office only one month; this made John Tyler President, whose chief acts were to veto two Bank bills that had been passed by Congress at a special session called for that purpose by his predecessor. Mr. Tyler, although a Whig, was an anti-bank man, and his name was, therefore, placed on the ticket with that of Harrison, to give it strength, and prevent too much opposition from those who held that the Federal Government had no more right to grant a charter for a bank than to engage in any other species of finance or commerce—no such power having been delegated to it by the States.

Since Mr. Biddle's day, the presidents of the Philadelphia banks, except in a few cases, have not been remarkable for their ability, but rather for their want of it. They have had the weakness to furnish funds to the Lincoln administration for the purpose of carrying on the crusade against the South — moneys which had been entrusted to them by their stockholders to be employed for legitimate business purposes. This, in its practical effects, is much worse than Mr. Biddle's operations; for they, by their unauthorised and improper course, have brought irretrievable ruin and disgrace upon the country; while the evils inflicted by the former, though widespread and carrying misery to many a hearth, were felt only by individuals. The presidents of the Philadelphia banks had it in their power to stay the hands of those of New York and Boston.

Nor is this all: the monied institutions of the three cities have been deceiving the people. It is said that they have a standing arrangement with the Federal Secretary of the Treasury to keep down the volume of greenback currency, by taking the 5·20 loan at 80 cents on the dollar, they receiving the benefit of any sales that may be made to the public through the United States subscription agency. In other words, all Mr. Chase's financial arrangements are now made through these banks, who thus receive what is equivalent to a commission of 20 per cent. on each transaction; and for this they allow him the use of the specie in their vaults to 'bear' the gold market. The result will be, that the Government and the banks will break up, or rather break down, together, and the ruined stockholders and outraged communities will take their vengeance upon the guilty parties.

The politicians of the old Federal party, and their successors, the Whigs and Republicans, have ever had a desire for a national bank; in this they have always been opposed by a large majority of the Democrats, on the ground of the inutility and unconstitutionality of the measure. Its advocates base their arguments upon the success of the Bank of England as the fiscal agent of the British Government, without making allowance for the difference in political institutions or in geographical extent of the two countries. The 'respectable old lady' in Threadneedle Street might as well extend her sphere of operations to Canada and Australia, as for a bank in the American States to control the currency and regulate exchanges throughout their entire space. The two banks chartered by Congress—the first in 1791, the second in 1816—never accomplished what was expected of.them: the latter concern became, with the decay in public morals, a most corrupt corporation ; the Pennsylvanian charter was a mere continuation of the Federal grant.   The circulation of the banks of the individual States was always much larger than that of the Bank of the United States.   It took some time for the business of the country to become settled after the two wars with Great Britain ; and the operations of each bank created by Congress beginning at a favourable period, the cause of the restoration of mercantile credit was ascribed to those institutions on both occasions.

The Federals have fallen into another error in attributing the success of the revolutionary struggle to financial facilities afforded by the Bank of North America at Philadelphia, which institution was chartered by the Congress of the Confederation in 1781 ; the proposition for its organisation having originated in a resolution of May 26, 1781, founded on a suggestion of the Superintendent of Finance, which was carried into execution by an ordinance of December 31, 1781, entitled, ' An Ordinance to ' Incorporate the Subscribers to the Bank of North America ; ' and it commenced business on January 7, 1782, eighty days after the surrender of Yorktown, which was the decisive event of the struggle.   It is, therefore, folly to say that the bank contributed in any degree to the success of the cause in which the Americans were then engaged.   The truth is, that the bank received great pecuniary aid from the Government by means of the credit conferred by its charter ; and how history has been so warped it is difficult to comprehend.   The bank was a sort of close corporation, used to serve the selfish ends of some speculators who managed its affairs.   It continued in existence only a few years, when it was succeeded by another bank of the same title, chartered by the State of Pennsylvania, but endowed with dissimilar powers, the directors of which institution have had the hardihood at this late day to make the subjoined misstatement :—

' Bank of North America, Philadelphia: July 28, 1862.

' At a meeting of the directors this day, the following preamble and resolution were adopted unanimously :—

' Whereas this bank was instituted in 1781 to aid the colonies
' in the struggle for their independence ; and whereas it has ever
' since prospered under the Government it assisted in creating;
' and whereas (in carrying out the policy of making contribu-
' tions to such objects only as are in its legitimate sphere) the
' stability of the Government is most essential to the interests
' of the stockholders : It is therefore

' Resolved, that the sum of ($5,000) five thousand dollars be
' contributed by the bank, and disposed of in such manner as
' the president may deem most expedient, to assist the Govern-
' ment in maintaining its integrity.

' Extract from the Minutes.

'THOMAS SMITH, *President.*

'J. Hockley, *Secretary.*'

The bank, chartered by Congress, never ' contributed' a penny
to the Federal Government for any purpose whatever. It did
not assist in ' creating' either the Federal or State Governments, and its successor has not ' ever since prospered;' it has
failed several times, and does not at present pay its debts. Nor
did it meet its liabilities at the time of the passage of the above
resolution. Surely appropriating its stockholders' money, or
that of its creditors, towards prosecuting the atrocious war
against the South, cannot be ' carrying out the policy of making
contributions to such objects only as are in its *legitimate*
sphere.'

From the beginning of 1780 until the close of the war, specie
was very plentiful in the States. The large expenditures
of the English and French forces found their way into the
interior. The foreign loans, too, were paid in hard money;
and the Havannah trade, clandestinely conducted during hostilities, occasioned a large influx of silver dollars. In fact,
the operations of the war caused such a drain of the precious
metals from Europe, that the Bank of England was brought
into jeopardy, and the Caisse d'Escompte at Paris actually suspended in 1783.

A remarkable hallucination in reference to a national debt
has likewise been prevalent in the Northern States. Many
persons have believed that such was desirable, in order to

' cement the Union,' again holding out the example of England in order to strengthen their arguments, without making any discrimination as to causes or consequences. The enormous wealth thrown into the lap of England by the African and Indian trades enabled the Government to carry on successfully the wars in which it was engaged; the money having been spent mostly at home, the nation became, as it were, the trustee for the capital, and thus originated the Consolidated Fund. Under the operation of the laws of entail and primogeniture, this arrangement has answered admirably well in Great Britain. In the American States, however, where each generation, with a few exceptions, has entire control of the principal of its property, and is not restricted to the income as in England, it is right, and in accordance with the spirit of the institutions of the country, that it should pay its own expenses in full, and not entail a burthen on those that come after it.

CHAPTER III.

THE MISSISSIPPI UNION BANK BONDS.

THE question of the repudiation of the Mississippi bonds handed to Messrs. Hope & Co. as collateral security by Mr. Jaudon having been much misunderstood, it will be appropriate here to present a copy of the correspondence between that house and Governor McNutt, which, with the details of the transactions of the Bank of the United States furnished in the previous chapter, will throw some light on the affair, and, it is to be hoped, rectify the misapprehensions in reference thereto that have for so long a time taken possession of the public mind. When Messrs. Hope & Co. received these bonds they were tainted with repudiation. The agency of the Bank of the United States in London, which was continued until its directors made an assignment, in the autumn of 1841, had paid the interest on them from the time they passed out of its hands in the latter part of 1839 up to November 1840, the amount being credited against the principal of the loan contracted with Mr. Jaudon by the Messrs. Rothschilds :—

To the Governor of the State of Mississippi.

The undersigned, as trustees for the holders of debentures of the Bank of the United States of Philadelphia, on deposit of American State stocks, and amongst others of a considerable amount of bonds of the State of Mississippi, bearing five per cent. interest, issued through the Union Bank of Mississippi, and made payable at the agency of the United States Bank of Pennsylvania, in London, the principal in 1850 and 1858, and the dividends semi-annually in May and November, having been refused payment of the interest due the 1st of this month on said bonds, are compelled to address themselves to the government of the State of Mississippi ; and from their confidence in the faith of that government, they feel convinced that the simple mentioning the fact of the non-payment will be a sufficient stimulus for the government of the State of Mississippi to take immediate measures for the payment of the interest now due and which will further successively become due on those bonds, and to prevent irregularities or demur, so prejudicial to the interest of American credit in general, and to that of the State of Mississippi in particular.

HOPE & Co.

Amsterdam: May 22, 1841.

Executive Department, City of Jackson: July 13, 1841.

GENTLEMEN,—I have received your letter, dated Amsterdam, May 22, 1841, post-marked Washington city, June 21, 1841, and bearing the official frank of the Honourable Daniel Webster, Secretary of State of the United States. I have duly considered the contents thereof. Those bonds were not sold in accordance with the constitution and laws of this State; they were delivered by me as *escrows,* to be sold at not less than their *par value,* and for cash, as the statute of this State required. The charter of the Mississippi Union Bank prescribes not only the substance but the form of the bonds ; and provides that they shall be in the sum of two thousand dollars each, 'which sum the said ' State of Mississippi promises to pay *in current money* of the ' United States,' to the order of the bank, with interest at the rate of five per cent. per annum, payable half-yearly at the place named in the indorsement of the bonds. The Act further provides that 'said bonds shall not be sold under their par ' value.' The bonds having been delivered to the managers of the bank to be sold on certain conditions, the State cannot be bound for their redemption, unless the terms prescribed were complied with in the sale. The constitution of this State expressly provides that ' no law shall ever be passed to raise a ' loan of money upon the credit of the State, or to pledge the ' faith of the State for the payment or redemption of any loan or ' debt, unless such law be proposed in the Senate or House of ' Representatives, and be agreed to by a majority of the members ' of each House and entered on their journals, with the yeas and ' nays taken thereon, and be referred to the next succeeding

' legislature, and published for three months previous to the next
' regular election in three newspapers of this State, and unless
' a majority of each branch of the legislature so elected after
' such publication shall agree to and pass such law, and in such
' case the yeas and nays shall be taken and entered on the journals
' of each House : Provided that nothing in this section shall be
' so construed as to prevent the legislature from negotiating a
' further loan of one and a half millions of dollars, and vesting
' the same in stock reserved to the State by the charter of the
' Planters' Bank of the State of Mississippi.'

Five millions of State bonds, dated June 5, 6, 7, 8, and 9,
1838, were sold by the commissioners appointed by the Mississippi Union Bank to N. Biddle, Esq., on August 18, 1838, for
5,000,000 dollars lawful money of the United States, payable in
five equal instalments of 1,000,000 dollars each, on November
1, 1838, and on the 1st days of January, March, May, and
July, 1839, and made ' payable at the agency of the Bank of the
' United States, in London, in *sterling* money of *Great Britain*,
' at the rate of four shillings and sixpence to the dollar, with in-
' terest payable semi-annually at the same place and rate.'   No
authority was ever given by an act of the legislature of this
State to change the currency in which said bonds were made
payable.   By selling the bonds on a credit, and changing them
from dollars, current money of the United States, to pounds
sterling of Great Britain, the following sums were lost :—

Interest on five millions State bonds, from June 7, 1838, to November 1, 1838	$100,000	00
Interest on four millions, 2 months	33,338	38
Interest on three millions, 2 months. . . . . -	24,999	96
Interest on two millions, 2 months	16,666	64
Interest on one million, 2 months	8,333	32
	$183,338	30

Difference between five millions dollars, principal of State bonds, in current money of the United States and sterling money of Great Britain, at four shillings and sixpence to the dollar	$478,750	00
Difference of interest on $1,250,000 of State bonds, payable in twelve years, between current money of the United States and pounds sterling of Great Britain, at four shillings and sixpence to the dollar . . .	59,625	00
Carry forward	721,713	30

Brought forward   .   721,713   30

Difference of interest on $3,750,000 of State bonds, payable in twenty years, between current money of the United States and pounds sterling of Great Britain, at four shillings and sixpence to the dollar   .   .   .   363,038   00

$1,084,751   30

From the above statement it will be perceived that 183,338 dollars and 30 cents were lost by selling the 5,000,000 dollars of bonds on a credit, and paying interest thereon from their respective dates; and the further sum of 901,343 dollars was lost by changing the bonds from dollars current money of the United States, to pounds sterling of Great Britain. These two items amount to the enormous sum of 1,084,781 dollars and 30 cents. Surely such a sale cannot be binding on the State of Mississippi. The faith of this State was pledged for the payment of those bonds only on one condition, that they were not sold at less than their par value. The State expected the full amount of those bonds to be paid into the vaults of the Mississippi Union Bank. If the full amount had been received, and the currency in which they were made payable not have been changed, the bank would have been better enabled to indemnify the State.

It appears that the bonds were endorsed in blank by the officers of the bank, and delivered to the commissioners charged with the sale. Neither their power of attorney nor letter of instructions authorised those gentlemen to fill up said endorsement by making the bonds and coupons payable in pounds sterling of Great Britain at the rate of four shillings and sixpence to the dollar. If such a change had been made on the face of the bonds after their execution and delivery to the bank, the parties making the alteration would have been guilty of forgery, and could have been immured in the penitentiary for the offence. It will be no answer to the argument to allege that the endorsement could only bind the Mississippi Union Bank. That institution has undertaken to pay both the principal and interest of the bonds. If the bank is compelled to pay the $1,084,784 30c. for the loss sustained by the credit sale of the bonds and the change in the currency in which they were made payable, her means will be reduced that amount, and the risk of the State thus greatly increased. The State was willing to entrust her credit to the bank on the conditions prescribed in the charter. The faith of this government has never been pledged for the illegal and fraudulent sale of those bonds.

This is a constitutional government, and all its officers take an oath to support the constitution of the State, and faithfully to discharge the duties of their respective offices. Her chief magistrate is required to take care that the laws be faithfully executed. He would be recreant to his trust and violate his official oath were he to suffer the laws of the land to be trampled upon and the constitution disregarded.

The contract for the sale of the State bonds shows that the statutes of the State in relation to the bonds were made a part of the contract. The purchaser was well aware of the conditions on which they were issued, and knew that the purchase was neither sanctioned by the constitution and laws of this State nor of Pennsylvania. The contract was guaranteed by the Bank of the United States. The whole of the purchase-money was paid by that institution. The name of Mr. Biddle was merely used in the contract as a *device* to get round that clause in the charter of the Bank of the United States which prohibits her from dealing in State stocks. The currency in which the bonds were made payable was changed from dollars to pounds sterling to give a false colouring to the transaction, and make it appear that the bonds were sold at par value. The principle is universal, that fraud vitiates all contracts. The commercial law of this State relative to negotiable paper is different from that of most other countries. The transfer of bonds and notes does not prevent the drawer from setting up any defence against an innocent purchaser which could be more available against the original payee.

The State, therefore, denies all obligation to pay the bonds held in trust by you, for the following reasons :—

1st. The bonds were sold on a credit.

2nd. The currency in which the bonds were made payable was changed from current money of the United States to pounds sterling of Great Britain, at the rate of four shillings and sixpence to the dollar.

3rd. The contract of the sale was fraudulent.

4th. The Bank of the United States was not authorised to make the purchase.

5th. The bonds were sold at less than their par value, in violation of the charter of the bank.

The money paid for those bonds did not come into the State Treasury. The officers of this government had no control over its disbursement. The bonds were disposed of in August 1838 by collusion and fraud, in violation of the constitution and laws of this State. The Mississippi Union Bank and the Bank of the United States were parties to this unlawful transaction. You have the endorsement of both of these institutions, and to them you must look for payment. *This State never will pay the five millions of dollars of State bonds issued in June 1838, or any portion of the interest due, or to become due, thereon.*

When I ascertained, in January 1839, the terms on which the bonds had been sold, I communicated the same by message to the Legislature, and denounced the sale as illegal. At that time only two millions of dollars had been paid on the bonds by the Bank of the United States. By a proclamation I subsequently issued the sale of the second five millions of dollars of State bonds delivered to the Mississippi Union Bank was prevented; I absolutely refused to execute the last five and a half millions of dollars of State bonds demanded by that institution. These decisive measures prevented the illegal disposal of ten and a half millions of dollars of State bonds, and will convince you that the government of this State never has countenanced and cannot be made responsible for the fraudulent acts of the Mississippi Union Bank.

I have forwarded to your address the journals of the legislature of this State for the years 1840 and 1841. It will afford me much pleasure to forward you such other documents as you may desire. I am anxious that the bondholders should be possessed of all the facts in relation to the issuance and disposal of the bonds held by them. Your great experience in commercial affairs no doubt has made you familiar with the principle that parties contract with reference to the law, and that, in a constitutional and free government, every act of a public functionary is merely an exercise of delegated power entrusted to him by

the people for a specific purpose, and that his acts are the
acts of the people only while within the powers conferred upon
him.

I am, gentlemen, very respectfully,
Your obedient servant,
A. G. McNUTT.

Messrs. Hope & Co., Amsterdam, Holland.

Governor McNutt, in replying to Messrs. Hope & Co., seems
to have overlooked the fact that the Mississippi Union Bank was
established under a 'supplement' to the original Act, which
nullified the terms of the charter, and therefore violated the
provisions of the constitution of the State of Mississippi.

Some eight or nine years after this correspondence took place
the following statement was furnished :—

' The law which established the Mississippi Union Bank
' originated in the House of Representatives at the biennial
' session of the Legislature in 1836 ; at the adjourned session, in
' 1837, it was passed and approved by the Governor, " so far as
' " the action of this Legislature is concerned." At the next
' regular biennial session, in 1838, the bill again passed, received
' the sanction of the Governor, and became a law on the 5th of
' February, 1838. Ten days thereafter, a bill passed the Legis-
' lature, and was approved by the Governor, which was entitled
' " An Act supplementary to an Act to incorporate the sub-
' " scribers to the Mississippi Union Bank." It was under this
' supplemental act, which had not been submitted to the people,
' and which had not been enacted by two successive legislatures,
' that the bonds were issued, and the Union Bank came into
' existence. So far from these bonds having been issued by the
' authority conferred in the original charter of the Union Bank,
' this supplemental act repealed the power of the Governor to
' issue the bonds, according to the provisions and for the pur-
' pose of the original law. If the people had agreed that the
' Legislature might pledge the faith of the State, in the manner.
' and for the object which its discretion might select, the con-
' ditions being changed would not affect the constitutional
' question ; but if the conditions constituted an essential part
' of the grant, those conditions could not be repealed without
' carrying the grant with them. The grant, connected with

' other and incompatible conditions, would be a new and distinct
' proposition. To show that such is the case in relation to the
' Union Bank bonds, I will compare the original law, which,
' after much deliberation and a reference to the people, passed
' two successive legislatures, with the supplemental act, the
' hasty creation of one.

' The original law authorised the establishment of the Missis-
' sippi Union Bank, with a capital of fifteen millions five
' hundred thousand dollars, "to be obtained by the directors of
' " the institution."

' It provided for books of subscription to be opened, divided
' the stock into small shares, and directed that none but owners
' of real estate and citizens of the State should be stockholders.
' Thus it was expected " to secure the loan of said fifteen
' " millions five hundred thousand dollars," the capital stock of
' the bank.

' It further provided, " That, in order to facilitate the said
' " Union Bank for the said loan of fifteen millions five
' " hundred thousand dollars, the faith of this State be and is
' " hereby pledged, both for the security of the capital and
' " interest; and that seven thousand five hundred bonds of
' " two thousand dollars each," &c., " shall be signed by the
' " Governor of the State to the order of the Union Bank,
' " countersigned," &c.

' After guarding, with great care, against the allowance of
' more stock to any subscriber than was amply secured by
' mortgage, and requiring that each stockholder should " pay in
' " cash," whenever required by the directors, ten per cent. upon
' his stock, it further provided, " That after the closing of the
' " books, and when it shall appear that at least five hundred
' " thousand dollars shall have been subscribed and paid in on
' " the original stock of the capital of said bank, the said
' " institution shall go into immediate operation."

' It further provided, that when a board of directors, with a
' president, should be organised, that the same should be notified
' to the Governor of the State, " who will thereupon execute to
' " the said bank, from time to time, bonds in amount propor-
' " tioned to the sums subscribed, and secured to the satisfaction
' " of the directors, as required by the charter, until the whole

' " amount of fifteen millions five hundred thousand dollars
' " shall be furnished in bonds, as hereinbefore provided for."

' The supplemental act provided, " That as soon as the books
' " of subscription for stock in the said Mississippi Union Bank
' " are opened, the Governor of this State is hereby authorised
' " and required to subscribe for, in behalf of this State, fifty
' " thousand shares of the stock of the original capital of the
' " said bank; the same to be paid for out of the proceeds of
' " the State bonds, to be executed to the said bank as already
' " provided for in the said charter."

' Under this supplemental act the bonds were issued. Will
' any candid intelligent mind fail to perceive that it was not by
' the authority of the original law, but in violation of its most
' important provisions, and in direct contravention to the pro-
' hibition of the constitution which I have quoted? By the law
' which received, in the constitutional mode, the assent of the
' people, the faith of the State was to be pledged to facilitate a
' loan to the Union Bank; by the supplemental act, bonds of
' the State were to be issued in payment for bank stock. By
' the original law, the State was to be secured by bonds and
' mortgages on real and personal estate before any liability
' should be incurred; by the supplement, the State was to
' become liable for five millions of dollars, without any security
' whatever, unless the stock for which she became a subscriber
' be so considered.

' The Legislature was authorised to pledge the faith of the
' State for a specific purpose, and under certain enumerated
' conditions. Could the authority so given be used for a totally
' different purpose, and without the fulfillment of the con-
' ditions? If not, then the supplemental act, and the bonds
' issued under it, impose no legal obligation upon the State.
' As an independent act, by which the faith of the State was to
' be pledged, it was necessary that this supplement should be
' passed by the Legislature—the yeas and nays entered on the
' journal—then be referred to the people by publication in
' three newspapers of the State, and be again passed by the
' next succeeding Legislature, before it could become a law.
' These constitutional requirements were not complied with, and
' therefore we have held that the supplemental act, so far as

' it assumed to pledge the faith of the State, was, from the
' beginning, constitutionally void.'

It was bad enough in the officers of the Bank of the United
States to part with the bonds, even as collateral security, after
the notification of Governor McNutt; but it is 'passing strange'
that Messrs. Hope & Co., and their constituents, the Messrs.
Rothschilds and others, should likewise transfer them to innocent (?) holders. But these 'innocent holders,' as the dates
make manifest, were aware of their worthlessness at the time
they received them. The real sufferers were the stockholders
of the Bank of the United States at Philadelphia, whose own
agents had committed the fraud.

The persons who received the Union Bank bonds made largely
by the transaction; the other American State stocks held by
them having risen rapidly in value, sold for more in the market
than the amount of the original debt. The par figures of the
State securities lodged in the hands of Hope & Co. against the
loan of £800,000 amounted to $14,450,506$\frac{16}{100}$

' The Times' of December 4, 1839, publishes a statement of
the affairs of the Bank of the United States, furnished to the
Legislature of Pennsylvania the preceding January. Among
the list of assets is the item 'Mississippi bonds, $7,000,000.'
As the Union Bank bonds amounted to but $5,000,000, it
follows that the sum was made up by the $2,000,000 issued
to the Planters' Bank, which institution was likewise intimately
connected with Mr. Biddle's bank and the cotton transactions.
Since the date mentioned there has not been a market for
these bonds. It is quite clear, therefore, that the stockholders
of the Bank of the United States—the 'widows and orphans'
of Philadelphia—were also the actual losers by this transaction.

CHAPTER IV.

THE PRESENT STATE OF THE TRADE—THE GROWTH OF COTTON IN THE WORLD.

IN addition to the very large stocks of cotton and cotton goods, at the various consuming points in the early part of 1861, the exclusion of 8,000,000 of customers from European and North American markets, by reason of the blockade of the Southern ports, has made the retention of the crops of the Confederate States less inconvenient to the outer world than would otherwise have been the case. The people of the South have, since May 1, 1861, depended almost entirely on the production of their own mills for all descriptions of ' dry goods,' and have used their leading staple for almost every conceivable purpose. The quantity which they have thus disposed of, up to September 1 next, will be equivalent to at least 1,500,000 bales. The following estimate may, therefore, be received as approximating very nearly to the amount of cotton that may be expected on hand at the commencement of the next commercial year :—

Crop of 1860 *remaining over on September* 1, 1861.

		Bales
At the Ports, including 300 bales new crop	. . . .	37,574
In the interior towns.	. . . .	6,200
On the plantations	. . . .	25,000
		68,774

	Bales	
Crop of 1861	3,500,000	
,, 1862	1,000,000	
,, 1863	800,000	
		5,300,000
		5,368,774

	Bales	
Destroyed and damaged equal to . . .	1,350,000	
Exported, eluded the blockade and taken by the Yankees	150,000	
Consumed	1,500,000	
		3,000,000

Estimated stock in the Confederacy on September 1, 1863	.	2,368,774

Of this quantity, however, it is not likely (assuming the advent of peace this summer) that more than 1,500,000 bales can be sent to market prior to the close of the shipping season in 1864, in consequence of the absence of the proper inland transportation facilities, the operations of the war having so deranged the steamboat, railroad, and wagon communications, that very many months must elapse before they can be restored to their former efficiency. 700,000 bales, at least, will be required for consumption in the American States, North and South, leaving 800,000 bales for exportation to foreign countries, against 3,127,568 bales shipped during the season which closed August 31, 1861, and which were distributed as follows :—

	Bales
Great Britain	2,175,225
France	578,063
North of Europe	216,250
Other Foreign Ports	158,030
	3,127,568

(These figures do not include that consumed in the Northern States, which will in future be classed as ' Foreign Ports.')

The average annual consumption of American cotton, on both sides of the Atlantic, for the ten years preceding the discovery of gold in California and Australia, was about 2,400,000 bales ; since that epoch 3,000,000 bales have been required ; and it is probable that the impetus that will be given to commerce by the recurrence of peace may cause the demand in the next decade to increase to 3,500,000 bales. The crops from 1851 to 1857, inclusive, averaged 3,090,943 bales each year, or just equal to the wants of the world, while those of 1858, 1859, and 1860, yielded an average of 4,059,112 bales per annum, showing an excess of 3,000,000 bales at the breaking out of the war, most of which had been converted into manufactured goods, there having been an increase within those three years in the spinning force of Europe and America of about thirty per cent., which gave a fictitious, not an actual, consumption to the extra production. This was evidenced by the enormous quantities of ' dry goods ' at all the chief markets, particularly those of India and China, the large profits on a few small invoices that reached their ports at the close of the wars in which they had been engaged having stimulated excessive shipments thereto, which business acted favourably for a time upon the home trade, and for a while increased the exports, but subsequently lessened them, as far as *quantity* was concerned, although the *value*, according to the Board of Trade tables, was not so greatly diminished, the enhanced price keeping up the amount. With this exception, nothing whatever happened to augment the demand; in fact, the commercial panic that occurred in the latter part of 1857, if it effected any change, caused considerable economy in the use of cotton goods for the several succeeding years. In ordinary times there is always two years' supply of cottons in the crude and manufactured state at the consuming points; at the fall of Fort Sumter there was a sufficiency for three years' requirements. And hence European, as well as American, statesmen, who were unfamiliar with the details of the trade, made an error in thinking that the war would at once bring about a cotton famine. Articles of commerce that are used for food are rarely carried over the year of their growth, owing to their perishable nature, while the materials for clothing—cotton, wool, silk, flax, &c.—can, either in their raw or finished condition, be kept for an indefinite time without deterioration in quality. Capital thus becomes invested in them, and stocks accumulate. When money is 'easy,' cotton is firm; when money is 'tight,' cotton is weak. Short crops of wheat will at once create an additional demand for foreign grain; but not so with cotton or other products of a like character, which of course are depreciated in value by a breadstuffs scarcity causing large sums of money to be sent abroad to purchase, or rather to meet the drafts valued against the importations of grain. The idea now entertained by many of these statesmen, ' that the world having got along pretty well ' so far without the usual supply of American cottons coming to ' hand, indicates that other nations are not so dependent on the ' Confederate States as was supposed,' is equally fallacious. Only a portion of the three years has transpired; yet cotton is selling at Liverpool at ' three prices,' or famine rates. What, then, must be its value a few months hence? Surely the warehouses will not be permitted to be exhausted of the raw material and manufactured article before an effort be made to obtain the

1,000,000 bales that could be afforded by the Cotton States within the next twelve months, and which is not much over one-third of a supply for all Europe, even when there are the usual stocks of cotton and cotton fabrics, and allowing for the quantities received from other quarters. Nor could prices, in the event of that number of bales coming to hand, recede much, if at all, as a large portion of the cotton, and of which the earliest shipments would be composed, is already mortgaged to the holders of the Confederate loans, who, it is expected, will not be very pressing sellers. In addition, the breaking or the abolishing of the blockade would at once give Great Britain 8,000,000 more customers for her textile fabrics, as well as other manufactures, than she has at the present time, without lessening the portion of cotton, 700,000 bales, above mentioned as the consumption in the American States; 150,000 or 200,000 bales are always required in the South, and the operation of the almost prohibitory Federal tariff will draw into the Northern States, at the lowest estimate, 600,000 bales of the raw material. It is difficult, however, to perceive what the North will have to exchange for this vast amount of produce when the South purchases direct from Europe. But the North must have the cotton to clothe the people. The consumption of cotton in the American States with the old and more moderate tariff, was, in the last year of the Union, 843,740 bales. Under the most favourable circumstances no cotton of any moment can be received in Europe from America before next November; and, allowing two months for its fabrication, the demand for goods during the whole of the current year will have to be met from the present scanty stocks, the limited quantities of cotton that may be shipped, and the trifling amount that will be imported from other quarters.

The usual importations of cotton into Great Britain are 80 per cent. of American, and 20 per cent. of other sorts; but, as the exports from hence to the continent are principally of 'other sorts,' there remains 85 per cent. of American, to make what are known as British fabrics, of which, up to the present time, there has been an adequate reserve. After two years of 'agitation' on the subject, an increased supply of the raw material beyond what is induced by high quotations, does not reach these shores from other countries, and even that which has been despatched will not more than compensate, as will be discovered, for the great waste of cotton for war purposes in the Federal States. It hardly remains to be tested whether these 'outside' productions will ever take the place of American cottons; they may answer very well for certain kinds of goods manufactured for the home demand : but it must be remembered that the great export trade of England is in other descriptions of fabrics. 'A silk purse cannot be made out of a sow's ear;' no more can India ever be capable of superseding the Southern States of America in quality of cotton, to say nothing of price. And the same remark applies to Algeria, and other localities where cotton cultivation has been tried over and over again in vain, unless, by some freak of nature, the peculiar climate— influenced by the Gulf-stream, and other advantages possessed by the States for the culture of their principal staple (among which is their excellent system of slavery, which if discontinued would ruin them, and England too)—be transferred to those countries, as well as the return commerce and general ramifications of trade upon which exchanges depend, and which ever tend to lessen the cost of raw materials at the points when they are needed. The truth is, that the more American cotton manufactured in England, the greater will be the necessity for Surat cotton, and the less American cotton that is passed through British looms (the present is an exceptional period), the smaller will be the quantity of Surat taken. And, in the event of the total cessation of the American cotton trade, India might begin to resume her former occupation of supplying the world with cotton goods, or, what is more likely, her system of labour would become so shipwrecked and deranged as to interfere with her prosperity and entail great loss upon the people of this country, who have invested their capital largely in that part of the globe. Her people are not idlers, and they have various occupations other than that of raising cotton. The general trade of India is steadily on the increase, as will be observed by the following table, which clearly demonstrates that the British commerce with that region is indirectly assisted through the agency of American cottons :—

*Statement of Exports of principal products from India for the
years 1850–51 and 1860–61.*

		1850-51	1860-61
Cotton	. . . . .	£3,474,789	£7,342,167
Grain	. . . . .	752,205	3,350,877
Drugs	. . . . .	19,502	45,239
Coffee	. . . . .	100,509	337,436
Jute	. . . . .	196,936	409,372
Saltpetre	. . . . .	375,632	661,772
Raw Silk	. . . . .	619,319	1,036,728
Seeds	. . . . .	339,514	1,785,527
Wool	. . . . .	68,335	478,188
Tea	. . . . .	*nil*	151,982
Gross Merchandise	. .	£5,946,831	£15,599,288

To the minds of many persons, it is quite clear that the
people of England must consent to abandon the cotton trade,
or again turn their eyes westward for supplies. An argument
has recently been brought forward, however, that Great Britain
might be better off without the industrial pursuits of Lancashire and other districts having similar occupations, or, at least,
that their advantage to the country has been greatly exaggerated ; and this theory its advocates attempt to substan-
tiate by referring to the large Governmental 'returns' since
the trade became diminished. They omit to take into consideration that the people of this country held three years'
supply of American cotton, and goods and yarns made therefrom, at home and abroad, which had been 'laid in' at a rate of
under sevenpence per pound, and that for the last two years that
accumulation has been 'dealt out' to meet the demand at unprecedented profits: thus constituting an equivalent to a most
gigantic monopoly. It will be remembered that in April, May,
and June, 1861, many of the exporters of Manchester goods
were compelled to suspend payment by reason of their inability
to dispose of their shipments except at ruinous sacrifices, while
others were on the verge of bankruptcy; the 'time' granted
by the creditors of the houses that had failed gave them an
opportunity to take advantage of the rise in prices, and they
sold out at handsome profits. They thereby were not only able

to resume payment, but found themselves in possession of a large surplus; whereas, had the Southern crop of 1861—3,500,000 bales—been let loose, such a further reduction in the value of their merchandise would have ensued as to have caused their hopeless downfall, and a universal distress, of a different character from that which is existing, would have prevailed in all the manufacturing districts, sensibly affecting the whole commercial and financial interests of the kingdom. John Bull has, in fact, the past twenty-four months, been receiving extra large earnings from his manufacturing horse, fed upon the old supply of provender; but the animal cannot continue to work much longer for his master unless a new feed-bill be contracted. The millions of pounds sterling that have been expended in England and Scotland for war supplies, and which cannot be considered a permanent trade, have also assisted in augmenting the 'returns.' Freer trade with France has, likewise, added to the general favourable result.

This statement of the quantity of cotton in the South has been made up from the most reliable sources of information; and, although the figures presented are smaller than any hitherto published, it in no manner diminishes the resources of the Confederate States—on the contrary, it augments their wealth, as 2,300,000 bales will, at the larger price and lesser expenditure, net more money to the planters than would the proceeds of double that quantity, the more particularly so now, from the reason that, when the Southern crops do come forward, they will, for the first time in the history of the trade, meet a demand for manufactured goods which must necessarily be for very many months far in advance of the supply of the raw material. It will take three or four years of large crops before the quotations can again resume anything like their former level. Besides the great and healthy demand for goods and yarns that must certainly spring up after a restoration of peace, the warehouses will again begin to call for their accustomed stocks. The capital withdrawn from the cotton trade since the beginning of the war, and the profits earned by the rise in prices, have been the means of founding many joint-stock banks and financial associations; and as these funds are not intended to remain in the vaults of those institutions, they will eventually pass through the 'new sieves' only to reach their old and natural channels. In short, the capital released from the cotton trade in consequence of the American war, with the profits on the stocks of the raw material, goods, and yarns on hand at the commencement of hostilities, added to the beneficial action of freer trade with France, and the American demand for war supplies, have kept the British money market 'easy' during the last two years, notwithstanding thirty millions sterling has been paid for grain within that time, beyond the usual cost to the country for food, to say nothing of the large amount of foreign loans placed in Lombard Street.

The whole cotton question, after all, depends upon the production of the American States. That grown in India, China, Brazil, Turkey, Egypt, &c., it is hardly worth while to consider, for each and all of those countries import more cotton in the shape of goods and yarns than they export of the raw material, thereby showing that they do not raise enough for their own wants. The crops of America have more than compensated for their deficiencies, and enabled their peoples to apply themselves to other pursuits. If the trade was in its usual state of vigour, there would be in the hands of all classes between the planter and consumer throughout the globe, on the 1st of September, 1863, two years' supply of cotton and cotton goods—equivalent to 6,000,000 bales—besides the crop for another year's demand —3,000,000 bales—in readiness to come forward, making a total of 9,000,000 bales of American cotton. The reader can easily estimate how small a proportion of that quantity will be in existence at that date, and make his calculations accordingly.

Allusion has already been made to the fact, that cotton shipments from India had increased somewhat in consequence of the high prices ruling in Europe. It may be remarked that the extra quantity does not more than balance the portions of the excessive productions of America in 1858, 1859, and 1860, which had reached that country in the manufactured state, as it will be remembered that British exports had been continued on a moderate scale to India, in anticipation of a rise in quotations, and in order to avoid sales at home—the value of goods not responding at once to that of the raw material. Even in

1862, the shipments thither in weight of goods and yarns, allowing for waste in the manufacture, were equivalent to the importations thence of cotton in 1859, and not far short of those of 1860. Of course, high prices in England will induce exports of cotton from India, and lessen the stocks there until they are reduced to a *minimum* point, which result may not be far distant. It must not be forgotten that India, unlike the Southern Confederacy, is a manufacturing country as well as a producing country, and consequently has always been in the habit of keeping stocks on hand, while the South has had no occasion to do so, but has ever parted with her entire crops as rapidly as they could be carried to market.

Some very exaggerated ideas exist in reference to the extent of cotton grown in India. In a letter from Manchester published in 'The Times' on July 7, 1862, will be found the following remarks:—'Your correspondent " an old Indian " endorses my statement that India annually produces 6,000,000 bales of cotton, and quotes Dr. J. Forbes Watson as his authority, than whom no one is more competent to form an opinion ; and yet in the face of this the merchants of Bombay state that they will not be able to furnish us with a quantity equal to what they sent us last year, viz. 986,290 bales. What, then, becomes of the other 5,000,000 bales ? ' The answer is that the vast population of India requires the remainder, whatever it may be, for clothing purposes, notwithstanding their large importation of British manufactures. It is not possible, however, that over one-third the quantity named is grown in India, as will be seen by the subjoined estimate of the entire consumption of the world. Cotton is not cultivated for amusement in India, or anywhere else, but for use ; and the erroneous statements in reference thereto have, no doubt, been caused by the recent augmented exports, the high prices attracting the old stocks from the interior. Few persons take into consideration that India is frequently very short of food, and never has a surplus. In 1840, about half a million of her inhabitants perished from starvation and its attendant diseases ; the same was the case in 1861, and nearly every year there is a partial famine. India, unlike America, has no wide extent of fertile country with great rivers, affording a natural means of conveying the produce to the consuming points.* The truth is that the vast emigration from Europe to the American States has been the cause, indirectly, of the extraordinary increase in their cotton crops, the agricultural labour of the West having thus supplied the East, thereby releasing a certain portion of the plantation labour of the South for the production of cotton, which would otherwise have been engaged in raising food. This is strikingly manifested by the enormous cotton yield of 1859 : in that year, the low prices for grain in the North-west induced the people of the South to purchase largely from that section of country. Indeed, while some of the Southern States were exporting their grain and provisions to the North, others were receiving supplies from the West. The food-resources of the South, notwithstanding the smaller population, are, however, greater than those of the North and West combined.†

* Since this was written, a pamphlet has appeared from Mr. Samuel Smith, a Liverpool gentleman, who has just returned from India, on page 12 of which will be found the subjoined remarks :—

'Cotton in most parts of India is cultivated in rotation with other crops, and is seldom looked upon as the mainstay of the ryot, but only as a subordinate product. The great staple of cultivation everywhere is breadstuffs in some shape or another. The holdings of the ryots are extremely small, and it has been the custom from time immemorial for each individual to raise sufficient food for his own family. In addition to this, he may grow a little plot of cotton yielding on the average one or two bales. But the ryot will not neglect the raising of food for the sake of cotton, however high its price may be. No surplus stocks of grain are available to meet an emergency of this kind ; the internal commerce of India is still in the crudest possible shape ; no such thing exists as large districts devoted to special branches of agriculture, and drawing their supplies of food from others : the rule, speaking generally, all over India is for each locality to raise its own supplies of food, and for each separate cultivator to do the same for himself. So true is this that, if the grain crops fail in any one region, a famine ensues, and people perish by thousands, even though the rest of India is unaffected. During the famine in the North-west provinces two years ago, half a million of people are said to have died from starvation, while in most of India the crops were not deficient ; but so wretched were the means of internal communication, and so little was the trade in breadstuffs organised, that supplies could not be thrown into the famished districts in time to avert this awful calamity. It is not, then, to be wondered that the natives are reluctant to diminish their food crops in order to turn their land into cotton.'

† See article on Wheat trade, p. 133.

Consumption of Cotton in Machine Goods, 1860.

	Population	Pounds
France, 4 lbs. per head	37,000,000	148,000,000
Great Britain and Ireland, 9 lbs. per head .	29,000,000	261,000,000
Rest of Europe, average 1 lb. per head . .	210,000,000	210,000,000
Asia, including islands; Australia, including islands; Polynesia and Egypt, 1 lb. per hd.	770,000,000	770,000,000
Federal and Confederate States, 12 lbs. per hd.	31,000,000	372,000,000
Rest of America, 1 lb. per head . . .	39,000,000	39,000,000
	1,116,000,000	1,800,000,000

The average consumption in Europe is given: In Turkey and Germany 3 lbs. per head are used, but in many places there is none whatever; in fact, out of the 1,116,000,000 of people, only 600,000,000 wear cotton.

Add that manufactured by hand, and stocks held over in various places in the world, exclusive of the interior of Africa 600,000,000

Total . . 2,400,000,000

Contributed by the following countries:—

	Pounds
Brazil	36,000,000
West Indies	8,000,000
Egypt	34,000,000
Rest of Africa	35,000,000
India	450,000,000
Rest of Asia	130,000,000
Mexico and South America, except Brazil .	57,000,000
Confederate States	1,650,000,000
	2,400,000,000

An examination concerning the kinds of wearing apparel, as well as general habits of the various nations, and taking into consideration their climate, will show that this statement is as near exactness as it is possible to reach.* It will be seen that the Confederate States in 1860 supplied more

* Mr. Smith says: 'It still appears to me probable that the native consumption of cotton in India could never have exceeded one million of bales, and the total amount grown never equalled two millions. It may be added further, in explanation of this opinion, that the amount of clothing used by the population of India is incredibly small according to the European standard; vast numbers of the people wear nothing but a narrow strip of calico round their loins and a turban on their head, and the great majority of the little children all over the country go perfectly naked.'

than two-thirds the quantity of cotton, and over three-fourths that which entered the arena of commerce. In all the statements of the stocks of cotton emanating from mercantile sources, and otherwise furnished, no allowance is ever made for the portion on hand in the manufactured state, and it is for this reason that many errors as to the course of the markets have been committed. The proper manner of giving correct information on the subject is to reduce the goods to pounds weight, allowing for the loss in the fabrication, just on the same principle that the statistics of breadstuffs—wheat and flour—are presented to the reader as so many bushels or quarters of grain.

The statement is verified by the quantity of cotton used by the manufactures in Europe and America, namely, 1,800,000,000 pounds. The American manufacturers return the gross weight of the bales, the bagging of which is about equal to the number of pounds of machine goods made in other parts of the world, not enumerated in the following table :—

Cotton Manufactures of Europe and America, 1860.

	No. of factories	Hands employed	Spindles	Pounds of cotton used
Great Britain .	3,046	650,000	21,000,000	990,000,000
France . .	2,600	274,830	5,500,000	140,000,000
Switzerland .	132	51,908	1,112,303	30,000,000
Zollverein . .	208	110,190	2,018,536	65,000,000
Austria . .	99	32,010	655,000	25,000,000
Belgium . .	28	28,000	510,000	31,000,000
Lombardy . .	33	29,000	140,000	10,000,000
Sardinia . .	17	14,000	210,000	17,000,000
Russia . .	55	60,000	1,100,000	65,281,000
United States .	90	101,000	6,000,000	426,719,000
	6,308	1,350,938	38,245,839	1,800,000,000

The following is an estimate, in millions of pounds at the dates named, of the

Growth of Cotton in the World.

	1791	1801	1811	1821	1831	1841	1851	1861
Brazil . .	22	36	35	32	38	30	40	36
W. Indies .	12	10	12	10	9	8	3	6
Egypt. .	—	—	1	6	18	25	30	34
Rest of Africa	45	46	44	40	36	34	34	35
India . .	130	160	170	175	180	185	210	450
Rest of Asia	190	160	146	135	115	110	120	132
Mexico and S. America, except Brazil	68	56	57	44	35	35	40	57
Elsewhere .	—	15	11	8	4	13	15	100
S. States .	2	48	80	180	385	654	990	1,650
	469	531	556	630	820	1,094	1,482	2,500

Average production and consumption of Cotton which entered into the Channels of Commerce 1825 to 1860 (in bales).

	Production in bales per annum	Consumption in bales per annum
Average, 1825 to 1830 . . .	1,431,000	1,387,000
„ 1830 to 1835 . . .	1,800,000	1,900,000
„ 1835 to 1840 . . .	2,319,000	2,443,000
„ 1840 to 1845 . . .	3,061,000	2,914,000
„ 1845 to 1850 . . .	3,591,000	3,316,000
„ 1850 to 1855 . . .	4,248,000	4,000,000
„ 1855 to 1860 . . .	5,000,000	4,700,000
	21,450,000	20,750,000

Deduct consumption 20,750,000

Overplus . . . . . . 700,000 × 5 = 3,500,000 bales,
a large part of which had been converted into goods and yarns.

In 1825, the stocks of cotton and cotton goods and yarns in existence must have been equivalent to about 4,000,000 bales, which added to the above overplus, 3,500,000 bales, makes 7,500,000 bales; the unconsumed portion of the crops of 1861 amounted no doubt to 1,500,000 bales, making a grand excess of about 9,000,000 bales of the raw material and manufactured articles on hand at the breaking out of the American war, not including that which never appears in the markets, some of which, as already explained, has been attracted from the interior of India by high quotations. With the small crops in the Southern States in 1862 and 1863, and the large portion of their crop of 1861 destroyed and wasted, there must necessarily be at the present time a much less amount of cotton in the world in every shape, taking into consideration the consuming population, than at any period since the trade was established.

A perusal of the foregoing tables cannot fail to satisfy the most sceptical reader that it is useless to rely on India as a locality to occupy the place of the American States in the production of cotton. In order to accomplish such a result, the climate, the system of labour, the whole course of trade, would have to be revolutionised. As to the superior cheapness of Hindoo labour, which is so often urged in favour of the opposite idea, it may be stated that one well-fed negro slave comfortably cared for—and the African is unfit for service in any other condition than that of bondage—managed by the intelligence of the American planters, will do more effectual work, with greater ease to himself, than five uncertain Hindoos, with their poor diet, and still poorer agricultural skill, independent of the extreme vicissitudes of their parching climate. The negro flourishes in the Cotton States of America; the climate agrees with him, and he with the climate — in fact, he is the happiest ' labourer ' on the face of the globe, and in the best condition of any of his race since the days of Noah.

In the calculation made concerning the consumption of cotton, about two pounds per head for the aggregate population have been allowed for that used in the interior of Asia, South America, and Mexico. This will be found a high average, as that in Europe, with the exception of Great Britain, Ireland, and France, is but one pound per head, and in this average is included three pounds per head for that used in Turkey and Germany, which are the next largest cotton-consuming countries on this side of the Atlantic. In many places no cotton whatever is worn. As the vast sums of money now flowing back to India develope the resources of that country under the careful management and control of the British race, the demand for English manufactured goods will greatly augment, and furnish occupation for the increased slave-labour of the South. A market for the handiwork of Britain may in time be opened up with the interior of Africa, which will also take off a greater number of pounds weight in goods than it can possibly supply in the raw material. But the idea entertained by some imaginative persons, that Africa can be made to render Manchester independent of the South, is altogether fallacious. In the tables no estimate has been given of the quantity of cotton produced in the interior of that country; when so much doubt exists as to the extent of its population, it would be impossible to make a calculation of that of production. Its population has been variously estimated at from 60,000,000 to 200,000,000. Its growth of cotton, from the known *habits* of the people, must be very limited, and probably not equal to the quantity of *wool*, which serves as a protection to the head of the negro from the vertical rays of the sun of his own burning climate. It is not supposed that the expansive custom of crinoline has been introduced into Africa, but certain it is that the 'ladies' indulge more in the use of cotton than the 'gentlemen.' Dr. Livingstone, under date of May 12, 1859, thus writes upon the subject, but he does not throw much ' light ' upon so *dark* a matter : —

' Cotton is cultivated largely, and the further we went the
' crop appeared to be of the greater importance. The women
' alone were well clothed with the produce, the men being
  content with goat-skins and cloth made of bark of certain
' trees. Everyone spins and weaves cotton. Even chiefs may
' be seen with the spindle and bag, which serves as a distaff.
' The process of manufacturing is one of the most rude that can
' be conceived. The cotton goes through five processes with
' the fingers before it comes to the loom. Time is no value.
' They possess two varieties of the plant. One, indigenous,
' yields cotton more like wool than that of other countries. It
' is strong and feels rough in the hand. The other variety is
' from imported seed, yielding a cotton that renders it unne-
' cessary to furnish the people with American seed. · A point in
' the culture worth noticing is, the time of planting has been
' selected, so that the plants remain in the ground during
' winter, and five months or so after sowing they come to
' maturity, before the rains begin, or insects come forth to
' damage the crop.'

The terms ' larger ' and ' greater,' used by Dr. Livingstone, are very indefinite expressions, when applied to an area of such vast extent as Africa, particularly when its population requires but little clothing; and if it were possible that the savage inhabitants of that country could so far compose their intestine strifes, and so organise a system of labour for the cultivation of the land, as to be able to raise and export a sufficient quantity of cotton to affect the trade in any appreciable degree, the inevitable result would be a demand on their part for manufactured goods which would greatly outstrip their production of the raw material. This is evidenced by the experience in the trade with India and South America. The demand for British manufactured cotton goods, which have to be made chiefly out of American cotton, is always augmented by the developement of the resources of new districts of country.

The Yankee charge, that the Southerners had placed an embargo on the exportation of cotton, is false. The Confederate Congress, while interdicting an overland traffic with the enemy, have given every facility to neutral commerce. Had the export of cotton been prohibited, there would not have been a single bale of the American staple in Europe for many months past. In spite of the illegal and vexatious blockade, the importations from Charleston and other ports have been four or five times greater than are the present stocks of American cotton in warehouse on this side of the Atlantic. These shipments, with the quantity previously on hand, have been the chief means of keeping the mills in partial operation, and have paid for the supplies sent to the South. It cannot, however, be expected that this business will continue, since the seceded States are growing daily more independent of all kinds of European manufactures. The Confederate Government may, therefore, through political considerations, be shortly induced to close their ports, except for the outlet of the produce hypothecated for the redemption of the 3,000,000l. loan contracted in Europe.

CHAPTER V.

BRITISH OPINIONS ON THE COTTON QUESTION PRIOR TO THE DISSOLUTION OF THE AMERICAN UNION.

NOTWITHSTANDING the importance of the subject, comparatively little has been said recently in reference to the cotton question. It may, therefore, be well to take a retrospective glance at the views entertained in reference to the cotton supply before the disruption in the American States. The following is a report of the proceedings in the House of Lords, on January 27, 1860.

'Lord Brougham, in rising to move, according to notice, for 'returns, relating to the importation of cotton, said he under-'stood there would be no objection on the part of the Govern-'ment to granting them. He thought it would be most satis-'factory to all to know, that since the repeal of the duty on 'cotton there had been such an enormous increase in the im-'portation of cotton, from 63,000,000 lbs. to 1,024,000,000 lbs., 'an increase of sixteenfold, and the importations from the 'United States alone had risen from 23,000,000 lbs. to '830,000,000 lbs., or an increase of thirty-twofold. This 'enormous increase in the importation of cotton—so advan-'tageous to our manufacturers and the community generally—'had been accomplished at the trifling cost of 500,000*l.*, which 'was the amount of the duty on cotton previous to its re-'mission. He hoped the fact would be an encouragement to 'us to repeal duties, without any regard to what was called the 'reciprocity system, but to repeal them simply because we 'wished to get rid of the burden imposed upon us by those 'duties. There were now no less than 480 articles upon which 'excise or customs duties were levied, to the great discomfort 'of trade, and the injury of those who dealt in those articles, 'while the total product to the revenue was under 1,000,000*l.* ; 'indeed, he believed it was only about 630,000*l.* He rejoiced 'in the benefits which had resulted to the people of the United

' States from our repeal of the duty on raw cotton; but it
' should not be forgotten that some of our own colonies pre-
' sented great facilities for the growth of cotton, and he hoped
' that in British Guiana, Jamaica, and in Africa, every en-
' couragement would be afforded by the Government to the
' cultivation of this most important material. Above all, he
' trusted that a trade in cotton would be opened up on the
' coast of Africa, in the districts explored by Dr. Livingstone,
' for upon the high land of that country cotton to any amount,
' and of the best quality, might, with a slight encouragement,
' be raised. He was told that a capital of 20,000*l.* judiciously
' directed there, would be sufficient to secure this very great
' advantage; and he did hope that if it were inexpedient for
' the Government to interfere in such matters, his wealthy
' friends at Manchester and Liverpool would lend a hand to raise
' that sum of money.'

After much vituperation against the Southern States Lord
Brougham was followed by the Bishop of Oxford, who said: —

' That he had heard with the greatest satisfaction what had
' fallen from the noble lord. It was quite true that it was not
' the custom of the British Government to engage in direct
' speculations to promote the trade in any article, but, with
' regard to the growth of cotton, the British Government had
' rendered great assistance—namely, by making the highways of
' the great continent of Africa, the rivers, accessible to English
' merchants, so that cotton might be cultivated on each side of
' them, and the traders have a safe passage up and down. The
' difficulty which was experienced in other countries of obtain-
' ing free labour to produce cotton did not exist in Africa, where
' there was an abundant native population, whose cultivation of
' cotton would be attended with the additional advantage of in-
' troducing a wholesome and lawful commerce, which would
' absolutely destroy the slave trade; for the only way by which
' that trade could be ultimately destroyed was by *teaching the*
' *African chiefs that the employment of their dependent people*
' *in the production of the raw material of cotton, would be*
' *more advantageous than the selling them into slavery for*
' *transportation to other parts of the world.* He, therefore,
' earnestly trusted that the attention of the Government would

' be directed to the maintenance and even to the increase of
' efforts for opening the great rivers in Africa, especially the
' Zambesi, the opening of which he believed the Government
' was about to aid, and the Niger, which for years the Govern-
' ment had assisted in opening. (Hear, hear.)'

Lord Overstone believed 'that a question of more importance
' than that relating to the extension of the source for the supply
' of the raw material of cotton could not be brought under the
' consideration of the Legislature. (Hear, hear.)   He had, there-
' fore, heard with satisfaction the statement of the noble duke,
' that the attention of the Government was directed to this sub-
' ject, and that every encouragement consistent with sound
' principles would be afforded to extend the supply of cotton.
' (Hear, hear.) The noble and learned lord had stated that
' within a short period the importation of cotton had multiplied
' thirty-twofold in this country ; and when their lordships con-
' sidered how extensive was the demand for cotton goods
' throughout the world, they would at once perceive that it was
' a serious matter to have for the supply of the raw material
' only a single source, liable to be affected by the uncertainties
' of climate, to say nothing of the obstacles which any unfor-
' tunate state of political relations might raise up in the way of
' our merchants applying to that source. (Hear, hear.) He
' trusted that no efforts would be omitted by the people of this
' country to promote every rational enterprise for the supply of
' cotton in every quarter where it could be obtained, and that
' all the encouragement which the Government could legiti-
' mately give would be afforded.'

Mr. Kettell, in commenting on this debate, truly remarks :
' The coolness with which the Bishop of Oxford states that
' cotton could be made by " free labour " if the " African chiefs
' " would *employ their dependent people*," is amusing. If,
' instead of selling the man, or eating him, he compelled him
' to grow cotton, the Bishop, it appears, would be satisfied with
' the progress of freedom. The discussion was narrowed down
' to the hopes that Africa might grow cotton. If we reflect
' that the supply of other materials for clothing increases much
' less than cotton, the importance of the question will appear to
' be greater.' The five chief materials for human clothing are

hemp, flax, silk, wool, and cotton. These have been imported into England as follows :—

Imports of Raw Materials for Textile Fabrics into Great Britain.

	Hemp	Flax	Silk	Wool	Total four articles	Cotton
	lbs.	lbs.	lbs.	lbs.	lbs.	lbs.
1835 .	72,352,200	81,916,100	4,027,649	41,718,514	160,014,463	326,407,692
1840 .	82,971,700	139,301,600	3,860,980	50,002,976	276,137,256	531,197,817
1845 .	103,416,400	159,562,300	4,866,528	76,813,855	344,258,785	721,979,953
1850 .	119,462,100	204,928,900	5,411,934	74,326,778	404,137,912	714,502,600
1855 .	136,270,912	145,511,437	7,548,659	99,300,446	388,631,454	891,751,962
1856 .	142,613,525	189,792,112	8,236,685	116,211,392	456,863,714	1,023,886,304
1857 .	169,004,562	209,953,125	12,718,867	129,749,898	521,456,452	969,318,896
1858 .	184,316,000	144,439,332	6,635,845	127,216,973	462,608,150	1,076,519,800
1859 .	237,485,584	160,388,144	10,248,358	133,284,634	541,406,720	1,225,999,072
1860 .	177,499,840	164,058,720	9,402,982	148,396,577	499,358,119	1,390,938,752
1861 .	187,459,664	149,372,048	8,835,255	147,172,841	492,839,808	1,256,984,736
1862 .	210,513,072	201,415,202	10,434,350	171,943,472	594,306,696	523,973,296

Lord Brougham and Lord Overstone overlooked the fact, that in order to cultivate cotton successfully not only a suitable climate is required, but that the directing hand and system of the white race, which is unobtainable in Africa, is also absolutely indispensable; as to the ' uncertainties of climate ' in the Southern States, adverted to by the latter nobleman, for the purpose of urging the importance of obtaining supplies elsewhere, that argument completely falls to the ground upon an examination of the tables of the cotton crops of the Confederacy.* These crops have ever been ample—in fact, of recent years more than sufficient—for the supply of every demand. The only vicissitudes to which they are liable are occasional frosts, which but partially lessen the yield, and never spread over the entire cotton region. Freed labour would not answer in those States; but, in a philanthropic point of view, the really unprejudiced and thoughtful European can have no trouble in selecting the South as his best source of supply, even if Nature gave him the choice of any other.

' The Times,' in alluding to the debate in the House of Lords, makes the following remarks :—

' The importation of cotton into this country has, since the ' import duty was abolished, increased sixteenfold. Having ' been 63,000,000 pounds, it is now 1,000,000,000 pounds.

---

* See table of Cotton Crops, p. 100.

' This is one of those giant facts which stand head and shoulders
' higher than the crowd—so high and so broad that we can
' neither overlook it nor affect not to see it. It proves the
' existence of a thousand smaller facts that must stand under
' its shadow. It tells of sixteen times as many mills, sixteen
' times as many English families living by working those mills,
' sixteen times as much profit derived from sixteen times as
' much capital engaged in this manufacture. It carries after it
' sequences of increased quantity of freights and insurances,
' and necessities for sixteen times the amount of customers to
' consume, to our profit, the immense amount of produce we
' are turning out. There are not many such facts as these,
' arising in the quiet routine of industrial history. It is so
' large and so steady that we can steer our national policy by it;
' it is so important to us, that we should be reduced to embar-
' rassment if it were suddenly to disappear. It teaches us to
' persevere in a policy which has produced so wonderful a result;
' its beneficent operation makes it essential to us to deal care-
' fully with it now that we have got it. Some years ago an
' island arose in the Mediterranean, and we were all discussing
' it, and quarrelling about it, and keeping up a brisk fire of
' diplomatic notes over it, when one fine morning the disgusted
' island suddenly went down again, and ships sent out to survey
' it sailed over the site it had occupied. We must not do any-
' thing to disgust this huge lump of profitable work which has
' suddenly risen among us. We are inclined to look at it with
' a respectful and superstitious tenderness, rather as a gambler
' does upon a run of luck at cards, hoping it may last for ever.'
' Lord Brougham and the veterans of the old Anti-Slavery
' Society do not, we fear, share our delight at this great increase
' in the employment of our home population. Their minds are
' still seared by those horrible stories which were burnt in upon
' them in their youth, when England was not only a slave-owning,
' but even a slave-trading state. Their remorse is so great, that
' the ghost of a black man is always before them. They are
' benevolent and excellent people; but if a black man happened
' to have broken his shin, and a white man were in danger of
' drowning, we much fear that a real anti-slavery zealot would
' bind up the black man's leg before he would draw the white

' man out of the water. It is not an inconsistency, therefore,
' that while we see only cause of congratulation in this
' wonderful increase of trade, Lord Brougham sees in it the
' exaggeration of an evil he never ceases to deplore. We, and
' such as we, who are content to look upon society as Provi-
' dence allows it to exist—to mend it when we can, but not to
' distress ourselves immoderately for evils which are not of our
' creation—we see only the free and intelligent English families
' who thrive upon the wages which these cotton bales produced.
' Lord Brougham sees only the black labourers who, on the
' other side of the Atlantic, pick the cotton pods in slavery.
' Lord Brougham deplores that in this tremendous importation
' of a thousand million of pounds of cotton the lion's share of
' the profit goes to the United States, and has been produced by
' slave labour. Instead of twenty-three millions, the United
' States now send us eight hundred and thirty millions, and this
' is all cultivated by slaves. It is very sad that this should be
' so, but we do not see our way to a remedy. There seems to
' be rather a chance of its becoming worse. If France, who is
' already moving onwards in a restless, purblind state, should
' open her eyes wide, should give herself fair play by accepting
' our coals, iron, and machinery, and, under the stimulus of a
' wholesome competition, should take to manufacturing upon a
' large scale, then these three millions will not be enough.
' France will be competing with us in the foreign cotton
' markets, stimulating still further the produce of Georgia and
' South Carolina. The jump which the consumption of cotton
' has just made is but a single leap, which may be repeated
' indefinitely. There are a thousand millions of mankind upon
' the globe, all of whom can be most comfortably clad in
' cotton. Every year new tribes and new nations are added
' to the category of cotton wearers. There is every reason to
' believe that the supply of this universal necessity will for
' many years yet to come fail to keep pace with the demand;
' and, in the interest of that large class of our countrymen to
' whom cotton is bread, we must continue to hope that the
' United States will be able to supply us in years to come with
' twice as much as we bought of them in years past.

' " Let us raise up another cotton market," say the anti-

' slavery people. So say we all. We know very well that the
' possibility of growing cotton is not confined to the New
' World. The plains of Bengal grew cotton before Columbus
' was born; and we, with our mechanical advantages, can
' actually afford to take the Bengal cotton from the growers
' and send it back to them in yards and pieces cheaper than
' they can make it up. So, also, thousands of square miles in
' China are covered by the cotton plant; and some day we may,
' perhaps, repeat the same process there. Africa, too, promises
' us cotton. Dr. Livingstone found a country in which the
' growth was indigenous, and where the chiefs were very
' anxious to be taught how to cultivate it for a European
' market. There is no lack of lands and climate where cotton
' can be produced. It is said of gold, that no substance is more
' widely diffused and more omnipresent, but unfortunately
' it is diffused under conditions which make it seldom pos-
' sible to win it with a profit. So it is of cotton. The condi-
' tions under which it becomes available for our markets are
' not often present in the wild cotton which our travellers dis-
' cover; nor are they to be immediately supplied. Remember
' the efforts which the French have made to produce cotton in
' Algeria, the enormous prizes they offered, the prices at which
' they bought up all the produce, the care with which fabrics
' were prepared from their cottons at Rouen and exhibited at
' the Paris exhibition, and then note the miserable result after
' so many years of artificial protection. It will come eventu
' ally; as the cotton wants of the world press heavily, and more
' heavily, it must come. We shall have cotton from India,
' from China, and from Africa. We would advocate every means
' within reasonable limits to quicken the developement. We
' would not even ask whether to introduce cotton culture upon
' a large scale into Africa would be to secure that African
' cotton would not be raised by slave-labour. But even Lord
' Brougham would not ask us to believe that there is any proxi-
' mate hope that the free cotton raised in Africa will, within
' any reasonable time, drive out of culture the slave-grown
' cotton of America. If this be so, of what use can it be to
' make irritating speeches in the House of Lords against a state
' of things by which we are content to profit? Lord Brougham

' and Lord Grey are not men of such illogical minds as to be
' incapable of understanding that it is the demands of the
' English manufacturers which stimulate the produce of slave-
' grown American cotton. They are neither of them, we appre-
' hend, so reckless or so wicked as to wish to close our factories
' and throw some millions of our manufacturing population out
' of bread. Why, then, these inconsequent and these irritating
' denunciations? Let us create new fields of produce if we can;
' but, meanwhile, it is neither just nor dignified to buy this raw
' material from the Americans, and to revile them for produc-
' ing it.'

This excellent leader was written before Mr. Lincoln was even
thought of for the Presidency, and therefore had no reference
to the present state of affairs in America; and while it is true
and forcible in so many points, it errs in somewhat loosely
expressing a hope that the Southern States will cultivate
' twice as much ' in future as in years past. No doubt this
will be the case in time—improvement is constant in the cultivation of cotton, the increase in the negroes is steady and
gradual, and meets the requirements of the planter; but it would
be as great folly to produce too much cotton, as to mine too
much coal or iron—to construct too many ships and railways.

' The Times ' also errs in stating that India takes back the
identical cotton that she sends after it has passed through
British looms. This is not so. Before she will again touch it, it
must be mixed with eighty-five per cent. of the growth of the
Southern States of America. Cotton is a sort of generic name
for the chief staple of commerce, but there is as great a variety
of it as there are of jewels. Some countries give rubies, others
diamonds, and the different precious stones are obtained from
corners of the earth remote from each other. All the rubies in
existence thrown upon the London market for sale would not
cause diamonds to be discarded; on the contrary, rubies would, in
mercantile parlance, become a ' drug: ' so it is with cotton. Without American cottons it is likely that those of India would become
a ' drug,' because they need the ' setting ' of the transatlantic
produce. Nor in any case can India, or China, or Africa, supply
the place of American cotton, even if they could grow the same
quality at the same price. The populations of those countries

are large, and although their territories are great, and their peoples, in a great measure, agricultural, they never have a superabundance of food.   In fact, they are often very short of provisions.   The case of India in this respect has already been adverted to.   In the year 1780 there was a famine in China; it was of such a magnitude that the cultivation of cotton was interdicted in some districts of country for a year or two, that the people might devote their labour to producing food.   Since that time the Chinese have never raised enough cotton for their own wants.*   If they were to abandon the cultivation of tea, they might turn their labour to cotton.   It is better, however, for them, and the whole world, that they should have the 'monopoly' of tea, that the Southerners should retain their 'monopoly' of cotton, and that the Hindoos should hold the 'monopoly' of indigo, and other produce particularly assigned to them by nature;   and that Great Britain, the great distributer, banker, and manufacturer, should keep those monopolies which she has enjoyed for the last sixty years, but which would be lost to her by the destruction of the industrial system of the Confederate States, who alone have an abundance of labour suited to the cultivation of cotton.

Had the torrents of invective and abuse heaped upon the people of the Southern States of America by European and Northern Abolitionists been allowed to influence them to emancipate the slaves, their productive lands would now have been an idle waste, and the condition of the negroes would have been even worse than that of those in the West Indies, in consequence of their greater numbers.   And where would have been the manufacturing strength of Great Britain?   The English cotton business rose up with the American crops, and displaced the monopoly for 'goods' enjoyed for eighteen hundred years or more by India.   All the British improvements in spinning and weaving would have been rendered nugatory in the absence of the cotton of the South.

* The few invoices of cotton arriving from China in England are quite an exceptional business, induced by high quotations and the large stocks of British manufactured goods, made out of the excessive productions of the Southern States in 1858, 1859, and 1860, remaining unsold in that part of the world.

No other portions of the globe have contributed a sufficient supply in either quality or quantity, nor is there any likelihood that in the absence of the requisite conditions of labour or climate they will be formidable competitors in the future. India, particularly, has had the advantage of British capital, credit, and enterprise, and yet failed to fulfil the sanguine expectations of those who have looked to her to supply all deficiencies, while the South by her own unaided energies has advanced with rapid strides, although the North in the capacity of a useless 'middle man,' through the means of high tariffs, has reduced her profits and drained her of millions of dollars annually. While estimating highly the invention of Eli Whitey, a native of Connecticut, but citizen of Georgia, the *Cotton-gin*, which went into operation in 1793, and to which the prosperity of the South is so frequently attributed, it may be remarked that other nations have also had the opportunity of its use, but failed to turn it to such good account. It has been used in India and elsewhere, but no other part of the world has successfully competed with the Southern States, who still retain their so-called 'monopoly' of cotton. In all the discussions that have taken place in reference to the cotton question, no allusion has been made to the fact that the British Tariff Act of 1787* placed a duty on the importations of that staple from the American States of 9*s.* 4*d.* per cwt., while that which was grown in the British possessions was admitted free of any charge. The tariff of 1819 raised the tax on foreign cotton to 9*s.* 7½*d.* per cwt., and on colonial produce to 7*s.* per cwt. The Act of 1834 fixed the rate on the former at 2*s.* 11*d.* per cwt., and on the latter of 4*d.* per cwt. Notwithstanding these differential duties against the Southern States, and with Great Britain too as their principal customer, they have steadily advanced in the cultivation of cotton. It has, therefore, been a great error to attribute the increase of the American cotton crops to the repeal of the British tariff in 1845; and it is absurd to say that it was the competition of the States that caused the decline in the production in the West Indies. The falling off in the importations from thence from 10,000,000 lbs.

* Prior to 1787, the year that Mr. Pitt's Consolidation Act was passed, the tariff was always composed of numerous charges and percentages, added from time to time to some ancient first duty.

in 1822 down to 300,000 or 400,000 lbs. should be ascribed to
the true reason—the emancipation of the negro slaves. The
subjoined extract from 'The Times' furnishes an excellent com-
mentary upon the mistaken enthusiasm of the emancipationists
for negro liberty.

That journal, after twenty-five years' experience, in 1859,
makes some graphic remarks upon the subject. In fact, it is a
'confession' from the chief labourer in the cause of emancipation. The Abolitionists cannot accuse the *Thunderer* of having
had 'southern proclivities' at the time the article appeared.

'There is no blinking the truth. Years of bitter experience;
'years of hope deferred; of self-devotion unrequited; of
'poverty; of humiliation; of prayers unanswered; of suffer-
'ings derided; of insults unresented; of contumely patiently
'endured; have convinced us of the truth. It must be spoken
'out loudly and energetically, despite the wild mockings of
'"howling cant!" The freed West India slave will not till the
'soil for wages; the freed son of the ex-slave is as obstinate as
'his sire. He will not cultivate lands which he has not bought
'for his own. Yams, mangoes, and plantains—those satisfy his
'wants; he cares not for yours. Cotton, sugar, coffee, and
'tobacco, he cares but little for. And what matters it to him
'that the Englishman has sunk his thousands and tens of
'thousands on mills, machinery, and plants, which now totter on
'the languishing estate that for years has only returned beggary
'and debt? He eats his yams, and sniggers at "Buckra."

'We know not why this should be so, but it is so. The negro
'has been bought with a price — the price of English taxation
'and English toil. He has been redeemed from bondage by
'the sweat and travail of some millions of hard-working Eng-
'lishmen. Twenty millions of pounds sterling — one hundred
'millions of dollars — have been distilled from the brains and
'muscles of the free English labourer, of every degree, to fashion
'the West India negro into a "free, independent labourer."
'Free and independent enough he has become, God knows,
'but labourer he is not, and, so far as we can see, never will
'be. He will sing hymns and quote texts, but honest steady
'industry he not only detests, but despises. We wish to
'Heaven that some people in England — neither Government

‘ people, nor parsons, nor clergymen, but some just-minded,
‘ honest-hearted, and clear-sighted man—would go out to some
‘ of the islands (say Jamaica, Dominica, or Antigua)—not for a
‘ month, or three months, but for a year, would watch the pre-
‘ cious *protégé* of English philanthropy, the freed negro, in his
‘ daily habits; would watch him as he lazily plants his little
‘ squatting; would see him as he proudly rejects agricultural
‘ or domestic service, or accepts it, only at wages ludicrously
‘ disproportionate to the value of his work. We wish, too,
‘ they would watch him while, with a hide thicker than a hippo-
‘ potamus, and a body to which fervid heat is a comfort rather
‘ than an annoyance, he droningly lounges over the prescribed
‘ task, over which the intrepid Englishman, uninured to the
‘ burning sun, consumes his impatient energy, and too often
‘ sacrifices his life. We wish they would go out and view the
‘ negro in all the blazonry of his idleness, his pride, his ingrati-
‘ tude, contemptuously sneering at the industry of that race
‘ which made him free, and then come home and teach that
‘ memorable lesson of their experience to the fanatics who have
‘ perverted him into what he is.’

CHAPTER VI.

REMARKS ON THE SPEECHES OF MR. BRIGHT—FREE AND SLAVE
LABOUR.

LORD BROUGHAM and the other eminent advocates of emancipation no longer appear at Exeter Hall, now that the councils of that establishment are monopolised by a violent and radical party, who, in their zeal for the negro, pay very little respect to justice, reason, or common sense; and, in order to enlist the sympathies of the public in their designs, do not scruple to resort to every species of misrepresentation.

Among these 'nobodies' are to be found two prominent names—Cobden and Bright—the apostles in former days of peace and free trade. It is strange, indeed, that they should now set aside their old doctrines to become the representatives of a war and high-tariff party in America. There seem, however, to be no bounds to their fanaticism, and they seek to impress the minds of the credulous with the idea that voluntary industry alone can develope the cotton culture in an adequate degree to meet the demands of manufacturers. 'The Times,' in its issue of June 17, 1863, said —

' Whatever may be the faults of the Southern social system,
' there can be no doubt that it has been wonderfully adapted to
' that end for which Mr. Bright says it is unfit—the growth of a
' particular staple. If it had not been for Southern planters,
' it is quite certain that there would have been no cotton
' manufacture to speak of in England, no Stockports and
' Staleybridges, perhaps no Cobdens and Brights.'

Mr. Bright, in his speeches at the London Tavern on June 16, and in the House of Commons, June 30; 1863, stated that only one-fourth part of the slave labour of the Confederate States was engaged in the cultivation of cotton; that the remaining three-fourths were employed in raising rice, sugar, tobacco, and other agricultural staples; that the increase in the slaves was two and a half per cent. (2½%) per annum; that 60,000 square miles of land were suited for growing cotton; that in the absence of hands only 10,000 square miles were devoted to that purpose; and that the annual augmentation, therefore, could not materially exceed 150,000 bales. It is certain that only one-fourth part of the slave population of the entire South is directly engaged in the production of cotton; but Mr. Bright might have stated that fact more intelligibly. The total number of slaves in all the American States and territories, according to the census of 1860, was 3,953,760. The ten cotton-growing States, however, contained but 3,030,245; of these about one-third, the best male hands, were cultivators of that staple, and the other two-thirds, less the men and women who were too old and the children who were too young, were employed in other kinds of agriculture, in mechanical pursuits and as house servants. The growth of cotton averages about four bales to each negro solely occupied in raising it, and the product is about 350 lbs. to the acre. Mr. Bright is correct in saying that a comparatively limited extent of soil is under cotton cultivation, but his figures are not accurate. The area of the ten cotton-growing States, North Carolina, South Carolina, Georgia, Florida, Tennessee, Arkansas, Alabama, Mississippi, Louisiana, and Texas, is 666,196 square miles, or 426,365,440 acres. The crop of 1859, the largest ever made, did not occupy over 7,000,000 *acres*. Of course all the land in the States named is not suited for growing cotton; each year, however, as the clearings are opened, adds to the number of cotton fields. Mr. Bright is entirely in error in intimating that the wants of the world are equivalent to an extension of double the quantity produced, and that ' there was not labour enough in the Southern States' to supply the demand.

By considering a series of years it is very easy to ascertain what are the requirements of mankind. The American crops averaged as follows :—

	Number of Years	Bales per annum
From 1821—1830	10	686,025
1831—1840	10	1,427,607
1841—1850	10	2,189,475
1851—1857	7	3,090,943
1858—1860	3	4,059,112*

* The census of 1860 thus records the growth of cotton for the year previous in bales of 400 lbs. :—

The quotations for American cotton within the same period were : —

	Cents
For the five years ending 1825	$10\frac{12}{100}$
1830	$10\frac{44}{100}$
1835	$12\frac{24}{100}$
1840	$12\frac{25}{100}$
1845	$7\frac{05}{100}$
1850	$8\frac{35}{100}$
1855	$9\frac{38}{100}$
1860	$11\frac{25}{100}$

The advance in value between 1850 and 1860 was caused by the discovery of gold in California and Australia, creating a redundancy of the currency ; but the price of cotton had reached its height, was on the wane at the time of the fall of Fort Sumter, in consequence of over-production, and the decline was checked by the subsequent occurrences.   The great rise since that event has been owing to the retention of the crop of 1861, the small planting of 1862 and 1863, and the large quantity destroyed to prevent its falling into the hands of the enemy.

It is not to the interest of the Southern people to grow more cotton than is needed.   There is, however, practically no limit to their facilities for production.   They have, even Mr. Bright admits, plenty of land, and if they thought proper they could

Illinois	6
Missouri	100
Kentucky	4,092
Virginia	12,727
Florida	63,322
North Carolina	145,514
Tennessee	227,450
South Carolina	353,413
Arkansas	367,485
Texas	405,100
Georgia	701,840
Louisiana	722,218
Alabama	997,978
Mississippi	1,195,699
	5,196,944

The four first named States cannot properly be classed as cotton-growing States.

readily purchase their provisions from the North-western States, and turn more of their labour on to the cultivation of cotton, doubling or trebling the crop if there was any occasion for such an increase in quantity. No other country has such a granary at hand. The Southerners are too wise to grow more cotton than is wanted, as experience has taught them that their short crops have been as profitable as large ones, bringing higher prices and necessitating less expenditure. Such has been the case in every instance, except that of the crop of 1838, the markets then having been coquetted with by the Bank of the United States. It requires five times more land to grow a pound of cotton in India and China than it does in the South. Asia, as before noticed, has had for a century past great difficulty in raising enough provisions for her teeming population. It is very idle, then, to suppose that America can be superseded by her in the production of cotton.

In 1790, there were 657,047 slaves in the Southern States, or one-fourth too many; they could not be profitably employed, and the value of the best hands sunk to two hundred dollars. Great concern was manifested by statesmen in relation to their increase, when fortunately the cultivation of cotton commenced, and from that year it has regularly advanced, with the augmentation in the number of the negroes. Cotton has merely taken off the surplus blacks, just as emigration has thinned out the plethora of farm labour in Ireland; and it would be as injurious to the South to import negroes from Africa as it would be to the overcrowded districts of Ireland to receive an accession of peasantry from Germany. Mr. Bright's intimations that the Southerners desire to reopen the African slave trade in order to cultivate more cotton, are without any foundation whatever; and it is strange that he should be so illogical as to say so, after alluding to the fact that only about 1,000,000 negroes were employed in its culture. It is supposed from his remarks that he obtains most of his information (?) from Mr. Robert J. Walker, a Federal agent now in England. But he again contradicts himself, and says: ‘I was speaking lately ‘ to a gentleman from Mississippi well acquainted with the facts ‘ of the case, and he told me that he had no doubt whatever ‘ that in ten years there would be freedom in the South, either

' in conjunction with the North, or as an independent State.'
This Mr. Walker was at one time Senator from Mississippi; he
has not, however, resided in that State for many years. His
expressions on the subject of slavery at the present time are
insincere, and at variance with all his former professions. (See
Appendix.)

Had the Southern States been short of labour, they would
long since have followed the example of Great Britain and
France, and engaged in the coolie trade. Or the immense
profit growing out of the ever-increasing demand for their
great staple would have induced the flow of white labour into
that country, if the climate had allowed it, in such volumes as
to overwhelm any antagonistic slave interests; and the only
reason why this result did not ensue is, that the facts are precisely the reverse of those stated by Mr. Bright.

Some of Mr. Bright's misstatements are so palpable as to
be easily detected; the remarks in the preceding pages are
a sufficient answer to many of them. According to his own
estimate, which is no doubt a correct one, the annual increase
in the yield of cotton in the Southern States does not exceed
150,000 bales; this is, without compounding, 1,500,000 bales
every ten years, or far beyond any augmentation in demand
that has ever taken place, and double the actual consumption
of recent years, though it was stimulated by the production
of gold in California and Australia. He, as a cotton manufacturer, should have been aware of this fact. It is patent
to the world that there *has* not only ' been a sufficient supply
' of cotton for the wants of the manufacturers and spinners of
' the world or for the needs of civilisation,' but a superabundance
of that article, or else the European Powers would not have
permitted the illegal blockade to exist for one moment. It is
true that all the slaves in the Confederate States are not engaged in the cultivation of cotton, nor have they been at any
time; only the labour in excess of that which was needed
for other pursuits has been so employed. The removal, however, of such vast numbers of negroes from the Border States
to the Cotton States proper, will throw an additional quantity of
labour into them for that purpose. Very few slaves who had
been producers of cotton have been captured or ' run off ' by the

Yankees, and certainly not a sufficient number to render necessary the reopening of the African slave trade. In the event of so improbable a result to the present conflict in America as the subjugation of the South, and the negroes freed under the Emancipation Proclamation, it will be discovered, in a very short time, that in order to prevent their becoming a nuisance and a burden upon the State, they would have to be re-enslaved, or else exterminated, as the Red Indians have been. In the latter case, the Yankees would renew the importation of slaves from Africa to cultivate the soil, as Europeans are unfit for agricultural labour under the burning sun of southern latitudes. The white population of North America will not endure the presence in their midst of an indolent and inferior race, unless they are possessed of the needful authority to compel their labour and good conduct. The Abolitionists, in asserting that the Southerners desire to reopen the African slave trade, are guilty of a fraud for the purpose of carrying out their fanatical ideas.* The Southerners were the first people to abolish the traffic, and have the least inducement for reopening it. The

* The Constitution of the United States says, Article I. Section 9: '1. The migration or importation of such persons as any of the States now ' existing shall think proper to admit, shall not be prohibited by the Congress ' prior to the year one thousand eight hundred and eight; but a tax or duty ' may be imposed upon such importation, not exceeding ten dollars for each ' person.'

A few months after its adoption a number of amendments were passed, among which is the following:—

'The powers not delegated to the United States by the Constitution, nor ' prohibited by it to the States, are reserved to the States respectively or to the people.' Many able lawyers have contended that Congress was by this clause deprived of the power of interfering with the slave trade; but whether their views are sound or not, it is quite clear that that body can reopen the traffic any time it thinks fit to do so.

The Confederate Constitution prohibits the trade in a most emphatic manner. Article I. Section 9 reads: '1. The importations of negroes of ' the African race from any foreign country other than the slaveholding ' States or territories of the United States of America is hereby forbidden; ' and Congress is required to pass such laws as shall effectually prevent the ' same. 2. Congress shall also have power to prohibit the introduction of ' slaves from any State not a member of, or territory not belonging to, this ' confederacy.'

All the Southern States have laws interdicting the African slave trade.

'New York Times' of June 6, 1863, thus tacitly concedes that the labour of the cotton States has not been much interfered with :—

' SLAVERY IN VIRGINIA.—At the breaking out of the war, there
' were just half a million slaves in Virginia to twice that number
' of white people. A gentleman, a native and resident of Virginia,
' who lives close to the rebel lines, and has had excellent oppor-
' tunities to learn the condition of affairs in that State, assures
' us that at least two-thirds of its slave population have been
' carried from it, or have decamped from it, since the rebellion
' begun. Probably not less than 70,000 or 80,000 have freed
' themselves, or been freed by the advance of our armies; while
' tens of thousands have been sent down to the Carolinas or
' Georgia to save them from the contingencies of war. Beside
' all these, some 20,000 have been taken from their owners, and
' are employed in various services connected with the rebel
' army or the war.

' If these statements even approximate accuracy, it will be
' seen that the negro element is being pretty rapidly eliminated
' from the Old Dominion. There have not been as small a
' number of slaves within her borders for a hundred years past
' as there is now.'

Cotton was introduced as a garden plant into Virginia in 1621 ; the previous year negroes were first landed there, but it was 170 years before the cotton culture began in earnest, and since that time (1790) the surplus negro labour has increased in a full ratio to meet the demand for its cultivation. The negro and the cotton plant seem to be natural allies, and their almost simultaneous introduction into that part of the world now known as the Confederate States of America was a most for-tunate circumstance for both the white and black races. Mr. Bright's theory in reference to the advantage of free African labour is disproved by Mr. Trollope, a gentleman who from personal experience and candid observation is well fitted to speak upon the subject, as will be found by a perusal of the following remarks taken from ' The Times' of January 6, 1860 :—

' Negroes, coolies, and planters — what is the position of
' each, and what are the rights of each ? In England it is too

'much the custom to regard only the first of these. Floods of
'pathetic eloquence and long years of Parliamentary struggling
'have taught us to imagine that the world was made for Sambo,
'and that the sole use of sugar is to sweeten Sambo's existence.
'The negro is, no doubt, a very amusing and very amiable
'fellow, and we ought to wish him well; but he is also a lazy
'animal, without any foresight, and therefore requiring to be
'led and compelled. We must not judge him by ourselves.
'That he is capable of improvement everybody admits, but in
'the meantime he is decidedly inferior — he is but very little
'raised above a mere animal. The negroes know this them-
'selves. They have no idea of country, and no pride of race.
'They despise themselves. They know nothing of Africa, ex-
'cept that it is a term of reproach, and the name which offends
'them most is that of a nigger. So little confidence have they
'in any being who has an admixture of their blood that no negro
'will serve a mulatto when he can serve a European or a white
'creole. In his passion he calls the mulatto a nigger, and pro-
'tests that he is not, never will be, like buckra man. These
'coloured people, too, despise themselves, and in every possible
'way try to deny their African parentage. They talk contemp-
'tuously of the pure blacks, whom they describe as dirty niggers,
'and nasty niggers, and mere niggers.

'He is a very funny sort of animal, and there is something
'interesting in a being so dependent as he is on the sympathy
'of others; but it is evident that he is scarcely fitted to take
'care of himself. He has no care for to-morrow, and it is
'enough if he can strut for a little hour in his finery. His
'virtues and his vices are alike those of momentary impulse.
'Although he is desperately fond of life, yet if he can lie in the
'sun for an hour without pain, he will not drag himself to the
'hospital to be cured of a mortal disease. Although he loves
'his children, he will in his rage use them fearfully. Although
'he delights to hear them praised, he will sell his daughter's
'virtue for a dollar. A little makes him happy, and he is so
'entirely a creature of the present, that nothing can make him
'permanently wretched. Mr. Trollope compares him to a dog
'in his attachments. The dog is faithful to us, and so is the
'negro. In return for our protection, the dogs give us all

‘ their hearts, but it is not given in gratitude; and they abstain
‘ with all their power from injury, but they do not abstain from
‘ judgment. The master may use either his dog or his negro
‘ ever so cruelly — yet neither has any anger against him when
‘ the pain is over. If a stranger should save either from such
‘ ill usage, there would be no thankfulness after the moment.
‘ Affection and fidelity are things of custom with him. As for
‘ the negro’s religion, our author has little faith in it. The
‘ negroes, he says, much prefer to belong to a Baptist congre-
‘ gation, or to a so-called Wesleyan body, because then an ex-
‘ citement is allowed to them which is denied in the Church of
‘ England. They sing, they halloo, they scream, they have
‘ their revivals, they talk of their “ dear broders ” and “ dear
‘ sisters,” and “ in their ecstatic howlings get some fun for their
‘ money.”

‘ A servile race, peculiarly fitted by nature for the hardest
‘ physical work in a burning climate, the negro has no desire
‘ for property strong enough to induce him to labour with
‘ sustained power. He lives from hand to mouth. In order
‘ that he may have his dinner, and some small finery, he will
‘ work a little, but after that he is content to lie in the sun.
‘ This, in Jamaica, he can very easily do, for emancipation and
‘ free trade have combined to throw enormous tracts of land
‘ out of cultivation, and on these the negro squats, getting all
‘ he wants with very little trouble, and sinking in the most
‘ resolute fashion back to the savage state. Lying under his
‘ cotton-tree, he refuses to work after ten o’clock in the morning.
‘ “ No, tankee, massa, me tired now; me no want more money.”
‘ Or, by way of variety, he may say, “ No; workee no more;
‘ “ money no ’nuff; workee no pay.” And so the planter must
‘ see his canes foul with weeds because he cannot prevail on
‘ Sambo to earn a second shilling by going into the cane-fields.
‘ He calls him a lazy nigger, and threatens him with starvation.
‘ The answer is, “ No, massa; no starve now; God sent plenty
‘ “ yam.” These yams, be it observed, on which Sambo relies,
‘ and on the strength of which he declines to work, are grown
‘ on the planter’s own ground, and probably planted at his
‘ expense, and Mr. Trollope suggests an enquiry into the
‘ feelings of an English farmer if our labourers were to refuse

' work on the plea that there is plenty of potatoes and bacon to
' be had — the potatoes and bacon being the produce of the
' farmer's own fields.   There lies the shiny, oily, odorous negro
' under his mango-tree, eating the luscious fruit in the sun.
' "He sends his black urchin up for a bread-fruit, and, behold,"
' says Mr. Trollope, " the family table is spread.   He pierces a
' " cocoa-nut, and lo ! there is his beverage.   He lies on the
' " ground, surrounded by oranges, bananas, and pine-apples.
' " Why should he work ? "   Let Sambo himself reply: " No,
' " massa, me weak in me belly; me no workee to-day; me
' " no like workee just 'em little moment."

' The evil which thus cruelly embarrasses the planters is
' chiefly felt in Jamaica, and in some of the smaller islands,
' Granada, Dominica, and St. Lucia, where the negro has the
' chance of squatting.   The negro imagined that his emancipa-
' tion was to be an emancipation, not merely from slavery, but
' from work ; and British philanthropy proposes to protect him
' in his laziness from the competition of the coolies.

' As far as Jamaica is concerned, what is there to tempt the
' Englishman?   It is a fact that half the sugar estates, and
' more than half the coffee plantations, have gone back into a
' state of bush ; and a great portion of those who are now grow-
' ing canes in Jamaica are persons who have lately bought the
' estates " for the value of the copper in the sugar-boilers, and
' of the metal in the rum-stills."   The Anti-Slavery Society
' will scarcely believe in the poverty and ruin of the planter,
' because they hear wonderful accounts of his hospitality.
' " We send word to the people at home that we are very poor,"
' say the planters.   " They don't believe us, and send out
' " somebody to see.   For this somebody we kill the fatted
' " calf and bring out a bottle or two of our best.   He goes home
' " and reports that these Jamaica planters are princes, who swim
' " in claret and champagne."   The planter accordingly makes
' the complaint : " This is rather hard, seeing that our common
' " fare is salt fish and rum and water."   Mr. Trollope advised the
' planters to produce their ordinary fare on such occasions ; but
' the reply was, " Yes, and then we should get it on the other
' " cheek—we should be abused for our stinginess.   No Jamaica
' " man could stand that." '

It is a remarkable fact that Toussaint l'Ouverture, the only black who has ever displayed any of the characteristics of original genius, acknowledged that his countrymen would neither till the ground nor work for a livelihood unless under compulsion. This extraordinary negro, having headed the horrible insurrection and massacres of St. Domingo, and driven the French from the island, established an iron despotism, so complete that no individual was exempt from its operation. Seeing that the fertile lands, deserted by planters and labourers, would soon become an idle waste, he adopted the violent remedy of obliging all the negroes—who had imagined that freedom was to bring them immunity from toil as well as civil liberty—to return to the plantations and other employments, and placed over them harder taskmasters than they had ever known under the dominion of the whites.

The idea of working for pay never entered into black nature. Mungo Park, long ago, said: 'Hired servants, by which I 'mean persons of free condition, voluntarily working for pay, 'are unknown in Africa;' and no subsequent traveller down to Dr. Livingstone has given a contrary opinion.

In Lewis's 'West Indies,' written seventeen years before emancipation, it is remarked :—

'As to free blacks, they are almost uniformly lazy and im-
'provident; most of them half-starved, and only anxious to live
'from hand to mouth. Some lounge about the highways with
'pedlar boxes stocked with various worthless baubles; others
'keep miserable stalls, provided with rancid butter, damaged
'salt pork, and other such articles; and these they are always
'willing to exchange for stolen rum and sugar, which they
'secretly tempt the negroes to pilfer from their proprietors:
'but few of them ever endeavour to earn their livelihood
'creditably. Even those who profess to be tailors, carpenters,
'or coopers, are, for the most part, careless, drunken, and dis-
'sipated, and never take pains sufficient to learn any dexterity
'in their trade. *As to a free negro hiring himself out for
'plantation labour, no instance of such a thing was ever
'known in Jamaica;* and probably no price, however great,
'would be considered by them as a sufficient temptation.'

Captain Hamilton, in his examination as a witness before

a select committee of Parliament, stated that Jamaica had become '*a desert*;' and being asked if he thought the term '*desert*' was quite applicable to the state of things there, replied: 'I should say, peculiarly applicable, *without any ex-* '*aggeration.*'

In a memorial addressed by the Council and Assembly of Jamaica to the Queen, dated February 19, 1852, after alluding to the distressed condition of the island, and the probable complete abandonment of the sugar culture throughout the British Antilles, unless a remedy were provided, the moral deterioration of the inhabitants of the island is thus noticed: —

'In conclusion, we would humbly entreat the consideration 'of Your Majesty to the moral effects which must be produced 'in the lower classes of the population of this island, by the 'general abandonment of property and withdrawal of capital, 'now unhappily in progress. Convinced that in granting 'freedom to the British slave it never was intended to allow 'him to sink into a state of barbarism and uncivilisation, we 'still feel it our humble duty to assure Your Majesty that the '*downward progress of the agricultural resources of the* '*colony has been already accompanied by a retrogression in* '*moral conduct on the part of the lower classes*; and we are 'assured that this retrogression must and will, for obvious 'reasons, keep pace with the destruction of property, and the 'consequent expulsion from the colony of all whom necessity 'may not compel to residence—events that must speedily occur, 'unless Your Majesty should be pleased graciously to receive 'our petition, and obtain from the Imperial Parliament efficient 'aid, ere ruin and desolation shall have taken the place of pros- 'perity and cultivation, and religion and morality shall have 'been superseded by barbarism and superstition.'

Since the late riots in New York, Mr. Bright has been silent on the 'nigger question.' But how can he, a 'peace man,' with any semblance of honesty applaud Mr. Lincoln for his Emancipation Proclamation, when he must have seen the following circular from Mr. Seward, addressed to all the diplomatic and consular agents of the United States in Europe? —

'Department of State, Washington: Sept. 22, 1862.

' GENTLEMEN,—You will receive by the mail which will carry
' you this despatch evidence which will convince you that the
' aggressive movement of the rebels against the States remain-
' ing faithful to the Union is arrested; and that the forces of
' the Union, strengthened and reanimated, are again ready to
' undertake a campaign on a vast scale. If you consult the
' newspapers, you will easily perceive that the financial re-
' sources of the insurrection decline rapidly, and that the means
' of raising troops have been exhausted.

' On the other side, you will see that the financial situation
' of the country is good, and that the call for fresh troops, with-
' out which the material force of the nation would be seriously
' crippled, is being promptly responded to. I have already
' informed our representatives abroad of the approach of a
' change in the social organisation of the rebel States. This
' change continues to make itself each day more and more
' apparent. *In the opinion of the President, the moment has*
' *come to place the great fact more clearly before the people of*
' *the rebel States, and to make them understand that if these*
' *States persist in imposing upon the country the choice be-*
' *tween the dissolution of this Government, at once necessary*
' *and beneficial, and the abolition of slavery, it is the Union*
' *and not slavery that must be maintained and saved.* With
' this object the President is about to publish a proclamation, in
' which he announces that slavery will no longer be recognised
' in any of the States which shall be in rebellion on January 1
' next. While all the good and wise men of all countries will
' recognise this measure as a *just and proper military act,*
' intended to deliver the country from a terrible civil war, they
' will recognise at the same time the moderation and magna-
' nimity with which the Government proceeds in a matter so
' solemn and important.

' I am, gentlemen, your obedient servant,
' WILLIAM H. SEWARD.'

Mr. Seward, who has been gasconading about 'the tradi-
' tional policy of the American people,' pays very little respect to
the actions of his predecessors.

In the war of 1812, the American troops burned Newark, Long Point, and St. David's in Canada. The first adjoined Fort George, and its destruction was defended by the officer who ordered it, on the ground that it became necessary in military operations there. The act, however, was disavowed by the United States Government, Mr. Madison being President at the time, and Mr. Monroe his Secretary of State. The burning at Long Point was unauthorised, and the conduct of the officer subjected to the investigation of a military tribunal. For the burning of St. David's, committed by stragglers, the officer who commanded in that quarter was dismissed without a trial for not preventing it.

Mr. Monroe, in a letter to Admiral Cochrane, said, ' No sooner ' were the United States compelled to go to war against Great ' Britain, than they resolved to wage it in a manner most con- ' sonant to the principles of humanity, and to those friendly ' relations which it was desirable to preserve between the two ' nations after the restoration of peace.'

The war with Mexico, too, was conducted in a humane spirit; and General Halleck, before he became tinctured with Seward- ism, in his treatise on International Law and the Laws of War, observed : ' It is sometimes alleged, in excuse for such conduct, ' that the general is unable to restrain his troops: but in the ' eye of the law there is no excuse; for he who cannot preserve ' order in his army has no right to command it.'

When the wicked Emancipation Proclamation was resolved upon, Mr. Lincoln seems to have ignored the fact that in the discussion with Great Britain, growing out of the first article of the Treaty of Ghent, the American Government had committed itself in the strongest and most pointed manner in opposition to such a policy. Mr. John Quincy Adams, of Massachusetts, in his despatch to Mr. Rush, of Pennsylvania, then minister to the Court of St. James, under date of July 7, 1820, said, in italics: ' The principle is that the emancipation of enemies' ' slaves is not among the acts of civilised warfare;' and in his letter of October 18, 1820, to Mr. Middleton, of South Carolina, the American minister at St. Petersburg, he wrote: ' The right of putting to death all prisoners in cold blood, ' and without special cause, might as well be pretended to be

' a law of war, or the right to use poisoned weapons, or to
' assassinate.'

The ' rail-splitter ' President pays very slight respect even to
the most worthy precedents; he seems to have forgotten —
probably he never knew—that Napoleon, although solicited in
his Russian campaign, by deputations from villages, to proclaim
liberty to the serfs, had refused to resort to a measure which,
as he said to the Senate of France, would have devoted many
families to death.

Fortunately for the negro race and the world generally, Mr.
Lincoln has not had the power of putting his Proclamation in
force except in a few instances.

After such evidences of the devotion of the negroes towards
their masters as has been given to the world by the circumstances connected with the war in America, it is really time
that such men as Mr. Bright and his ' reverend ' satellites should
stop their crusade against the institution of slavery in the Confederate States. Even President Lincoln admits that the freed
negroes will not work—that they will ' do nothing but eat, eat.'
And why should these ignorant philanthropists (?) applaud him
for his emancipation scheme, when he boldly declares that it
was promulgated only as a ' military necessity?' Nor is there
any excuse whatever for Mr. Bright's blunders in regard to the
cotton question. He said in the House of Commons on June 30
that he knew ' a little about cotton,' and that, ' professedly,' he
had been all his life ' connected with the cotton trade.' He is,
then, either so blinded by fanaticism that he cannot see the
truth, or he has made wilful misrepresentations to serve his
political purposes.

CHAPTER VII.

THE IMPORTANCE OF AMERICAN COTTON—THE POLITICAL HERESIES OF SEWARD AND LINCOLN.

The cotton question, although so simple in its character, is generally imperfectly understood. This is evidenced by speeches in Parliament, and many articles that have appeared in the public prints. It would seem that persons unfamiliar with the trade have regarded all descriptions of cotton as available for the purposes of British industry. This mistake will be made apparent should the conflict in America continue another year. The importance of the product of the Southern States has yet to be fully appreciated. The King of Commerce is temporarily dethroned, but he will rise again in all his majesty and power. The cleverest exposition of the matter was given a few years ago by Mr. J. B. Smith, the member for Stockport. The following is his text:—

' Everyone seems adequately impressed with the desirableness,
' not to say the necessity, of multiplying to the utmost possible
' extent the sources whence we derive the supply of ·this raw
' material of our greatest national manufacture. But one branch
' of the question, though a most essential one, appears to have
' been nearly overlooked. We need not only a large supply and a
' cheap supply, *but a supply of a peculiar kind and quality.*

' For practical purposes, and to facilitate the comprehension
' of the subject by non-professional readers, we may state in
' general terms that the cotton required for the trade of Great
' Britain may be classified into three divisions—the long staple,
' the medium staple, and the short staple.

' 1. The long staple, or long-fibre cotton, is used for making
' the warp, as it is technically called, i.e. the longitudinal
' threads of the woven tissue. Those threads, when of the finer
' sorts—for all numbers, say above 50's—must be made of long-

' staple cotton ; for numbers below 50's they may be made of
' it, and would be so made were it as cheap as the lower quali-
' ties of the raw material. No other quality of cotton is strong
' enough or long enough either to spin into the higher and finer
' numbers or to sustain the tension and friction to which the
' threads are exposed in the loom.

' 2. The medium-staple cotton, on the contrary, is used partly
' for the lower numbers of the warp (and as such enters largely
' into the production of the vast quantities of " cotton yarn "
' and sewing thread exported), but mainly for the weft, or trans-
' verse threads of the woven tissue. It is softer and silkier than
' the quality spoken of above, makes a fuller and rounder
' thread, and fills up the fabric better. The long-staple article
' is never used for this purpose, and could not, however cheap,
' be so used with advantage; it is ordinarily too harsh. For the
' warp, strength and length of fibre is required; for the weft,
' softness and fullness. Now, as the lower numbers of " yarn "
' require a far larger amount of raw cotton for their production
' than the higher, and constitute the chief portion (in weight)
' both of our export and consumption, and as, moreover, every
' yard of calico or cotton-woven fabric, technically called cloth,
' is composed of from two to five times as much weft as warp, it
' is obvious that we need a far larger supply of this peculiar
' character of cotton, the medium staple, than of any other.

' 3. The short-staple cotton is used almost exclusively for
' weft (except a little taken for candle-wicks), or for the very
' lowest numbers of warp, say 10's and under. But it is
' different in character from the second description, as well as
' shorter in fibre; it is drier, fuzzier—more like rough wool;
' and it cannot be substituted for it without impoverishing the
' nature of the cloth, and making it, especially after washing or
' bleaching, look thinner and more meagre; and for the same
' reason it can only be blended with it with much caution, and
' in very moderate proportions. But its colour is usually good,
' and its comparative cheapness its great recommendation.

' It will be seen, therefore, that while we require for the pur-
' poses of our manufacture a limited quantity of the first and
' third qualities of raw cotton, we need and can consume an
' almost unlimited supply of the second quality. In this fact

' lies our real difficulty; for, while several quarters of the world
' supply the first sort, and India could supply enormous quanti-
' ties of the third sort, the United States of America alone have
' hitherto produced the second and most necessary kind.

' 1. The finest long cotton in the world is called the "Sea
' Island." It is grown on the low-lying lands and small islands
' on the coast of Georgia. The quantity is small, and the price
' very high. It is used mostly for muslin thread, and the very
' finest numbers of yarn—say 100's and upwards; and price, in
' fact, is of little moment to the manufacturers who purchase it.
' It usually sells at about two shillings per pound. A quality
' much resembling it, and almost if not quite as good, has been
' grown, as a sample article, in Australia. But of this denomi-
' nation of cotton the consumption is very small. Another
' species—long, strong, fine, and yellowish—is grown in Egypt,
' and imported in considerable quantities. An inferior quality
—coarse, harsh, bright in colour, but strong—is imported
' from Brazil, and a very small quantity from the West Indies.
' Doubtless if the price were adequate, and the demand here
' very great and steady, the supply from many of these quarters
' might be largely augmented. But it is not of this sort that
' we need any considerable increase, nor could we afford the
' price which probably alone would remunerate the grower.

' 2. Our great consumption and demand is for the soft, white,
' silky, moderately long cotton of America—the quality usually
' called " Uplands," " Bowed Georgia," and " New Orleans."
' This used to be sold at prices varying from 3d. to 6d. per
' pound (it is now from 6d. to 8d.); it can be consumed in any
' quantity, for it is available not only for weft, but for warp,
' except for the finer numbers. We need and consume nine
' bags of this cotton for one bag of all other qualities put
' together.

' 3. It is the insufficient supply, or the higher price of this
' cotton, that has driven our manufacturers upon the short-
' stapled native article of India, called Surat. If the price of
' the two were equal, scarcely a bag of Surat would be employed.
' When the price of American cotton rises, owing to an inade-
' quate supply, that of East India cotton follows it at a con-
' siderable interval—the usual ratio being two to three—and

'the import of the latter is greatly stimulated. It is always
'grown in India in large quantities, and with improved means
'of communication, and more careful preparation, might be
'supplied in time in indefinite and probably ample quantities.
'But it is the quality that is in fault, and, as far as the past is a
'guide, it would seem incurably in fault. Many attempts to
'amend the character of this cotton have been made. American
'planters and American "Saw gins" have been sent over, and
'American seed has been planted; and the result has been a
'sensible amelioration in cleanliness and colour, and some slight
'increase in length of fibre, but scarcely any change in specific
'character. The dry, fuzzy, woolly characteristics remain.
'Sometimes the first year's samples nearly resemble the Ame-
'rican article, but the resemblance never becomes permanent.
'Hitherto (we believe we are correct in stating), either from
'the peculiarity of the soil or of the climate, or, as some say,
'from adulteration by the air-borne pollen of the inferior native
'plant, the improved and altered character of the cotton has
'never been kept up.

'We are far from saying that this difficulty may not be over-
'come, and American cotton be naturalised in our East Indian
'possessions; but certainly the results of our past efforts have
'not been of favourable augury. So far as our own observation
'and experience have gone, only from the other parts of the
'world have we seen samples of cotton analogous in character
'to that of the United States, and equally available for our
'purposes: one of these was the west coast of Africa, where,
'we understand, there is a considerable native growth, which
'doubtless our commerce might encourage and increase; the
'other is the opposite side of the continent, where Port Natal
'has exported some very hopeful samples, soft and silky, but
'not clean nor of a very good colour, but still decidedly Ame-
'rican in quality.

'The point we have to bear in mind, then, is this: our de-
'sideratum is not simply more cotton, but more cotton of the
'same character and price as that now imported from the States.
'If India were to send us 2,000,000 bales of Surat cotton per
'annum, the desideratum would not be supplied, and our
'perilous problem would be still unsolved. We should be
'almost as dependent on American as ever.'

Mr. Smith in these very excellent and luminous remarks, which were addressed to the Society of Arts some months before the secession of the Confederate States from the Federal Union, and when a non-supply of cotton was imminent, although unfelt or even unsuspected, has erred in two particulars. He says: ' It is always grown in India in large quantities, and, ' with improved means of communication and more careful ' preparation, might be supplied in time in indefinite and ' *probably* ample quantities.' After two years' experience it is found that cotton does not come forward in ' ample ' quantities. Undoubtedly the importations are greater than formerly, but this is owing to high quotations attracting the large surplus stock that happened to be on hand, much of which is mere rubbish. Nor would *it* have been exported to this country if the India markets had not been overcrowded with British dry goods, manufactured out of the usual proportion of American cotton, the produce of the excessive crops of 1858, 1859, and 1860, which caused an accumulation in all parts of the world, equivalent to a year's consumption in addition to the ordinary stocks. It is a mistake to suppose that the interior of India is one vast cotton plantation. That country never had, for the reasons given, so large a surplus as at the time of the breaking out of the American war; and, with everything in favour of a large exporting trade, has fallen far short of what was expected of her. In 1861, Mr. Bazley, who is not disposed to underrate the resources of India, said that for every additional 2,000,000 bales, which would not be much more than equivalent in the number of pounds to 1,500,000 of American, it would require 5,000,000 of bullocks to draw the cotton from the interior, besides 1,000,000 attendants. Even if the cotton was there, where are the bullocks and where are the attendants? Mr. Smith further states, in alluding to the inferior quality of India cotton : ' We are far from saying that this difficulty may ' not be overcome, and American cotton naturalised in our East ' Indian possessions.' In this he omits to take into consideration the laws of climate, that no species of legislation can alter. The people of the Confederate States, who are the most intelligent cotton planters in the world, and who have studied this as well as every other branch of the subject most thoroughly, have never seen reason to fear rivalry from any quarter whatever.

Notwithstanding the leading journal of Europe commenced very early to point out the dependence of other countries upon the cotton productions of the Southern States, the public mind does not seem yet to comprehend fully this highly important subject. Some excuse may be given for this want of knowledge, when it has been found that the people of the Northern States of America, with the exception of the city of New York— Boston is too fanatical, and Philadelphia too stupid — were so ignorant as to the true cause of their advancement that they considered the South of little moment, and that the Constitution was the source of their increasing wealth. Just as if any species of legislation created commercial prosperity! The absence of legislation is frequently beneficial. The Northern States, to be sure, have reaped a temporary advantage, by protective tariffs, enacted through the instrumentality of the ' Union,' but not by any authority granted by the Constitution. But where will they be after the war is over? Factories they will have, but no raw materials; railways and canals, but no inland commerce; ships, but no cargoes. The Constitution, as intended by its founders, and as interpreted by the Southerners, was a useful treaty, embodying the principles of free trade between the States, and, except for revenue purposes, with the rest of the world. The Yankees, however, with their desire to interfere with their neighbours' business, have perverted the meaning of the document to suit their own purposes. At the time of its adoption in 1789, there were but 67,201 negroes — 40,370 slaves, and 26,831 free—in the Northern States, against 690,162 negroes—657,527 slaves, and 32,635 free—in the Southern States. Yet Mr. Seward,. in speaking at Rochester on October 25, 1858, said that the encroachments of the South were such that the whole Union must become all free or all slave; thus ignoring historic facts, and failing to make allowance for difference in climate and productions. No wonder that the Southern people declined being ruled by such a madman or political trickster. Here are his words :—

' It is an irrepressible conflict between opposing and enduring ' forces, and it means that the United States must and will,

‘ sooner or later, become either entirely a slave-holding nation
‘ or entirely a free-labour nation.’

Mr. Seward, finding that he had then gone too far, and in his
desire to obtain the nomination for the Presidency, temporarily
changed his tactics, and said in the Senate of the United States
on February 29, 1860:

‘ The whole sovereignty upon domestic concerns within the
‘ Union is divided between us by unmistakeable boundaries;
‘ . . . . you have your fifteen distinct parts, we eighteen
‘ parts, equally distinct. Each must be maintained in order
‘ that the whole may be preserved.’

The people of the South never attempted to interfere with
the domestic concerns of their neighbours of the North—
they merely desired to be let alone.

Mr. Lincoln, on February 27, 1860, which was prior to his
nomination for the Presidency, and just two days before Mr.
Seward’s speech in the Senate, made the following remarks
while on a visit to New York :—

‘ Perhaps you will say the Supreme Court has decided the
‘ constitutional question in your favour (Southern);—not quite
‘ so. But waiving the lawyer’s distinction between *dictum* and
‘ decision, the courts have decided the question for you in a sort
‘ of a way. The courts have substantially said, “ It is your
‘ “ constitutional right to take slaves into the Federal terri-
‘ “ tories, and to hold them there as property.” When I say
‘ that the decision was made in a sort of a way, I mean that it
‘ was made in a divided court, by a bare majority of the judges,
‘ and they not quite agreeing with one another in the reasons
‘ for making it; that it is so made, as that its avowed supporters
‘ disagree with one another about its meaning; and that it was
‘ mainly based upon a mistaken statement of facts — the state-
‘ ment in the opinion that the right of property in a slave is
‘ distinctly and expressly affirmed in the Constitution. An in-
‘ spection of the Constitution will show that the right of property
‘ in a slave is not distinctly and expressly affirmed in it. Bear
‘ in mind that the judges do not pledge their judicial opinion
‘ that such a right is implicitly affirmed in the Constitution,
‘ but they pledge their veracity that it is distinctly and ex-
‘ pressly affirmed there—“ distinctly,” that is, not mingled with

' anything else — " expressly," that is, in words meaning just
' that without the aid of any inference, and susceptible of no
' other meaning.   If they had only pledged their judicial opinion
' that such right is affirmed in the instrument by implication,
' it would be open to others to show that neither the word
' " slave " nor " slavery " is to be found in the Constitution ;
' nor the word " property " even, in any connection with the
' language alluding to the things slave or slavery ; and that
' wherever, in an instrument, the slave is alluded to, he is called
' a " person," and wherever his master's legal right in relation
' to him is alluded to, it is spoken of as " service, or labour
' " due " as a " debt," payable in service or labour.   Also, it
' would be open to show, by contemporaneous history, that the
' mode of alluding to slaves and slavery, instead of speaking of
' them, was employed on purpose to exclude from the Constitu-
' tion the idea that there could be no property in man.'

This confused and untruthful speech of the man elected by
the Republican party as their President probably occasioned
the remarks of Mr. Seward, made so shortly afterwards.   Mr.
Lincoln, however, in his inaugural address on March 4, 1861,
admitted that slavery was recognised by the Constitution, and
that he had no right to interfere with it.*   He said : ' I have no
purpose, directly or indirectly, to interfere with the institution of
slavery in the States where it exists.   I believe I have no lawful
right to do so ; and I have no inclination to do so.'

The Federal Government has no right to meddle with slavery
in the States or in the territories farther than to protect it.   It
was a mistaken policy that induced any of the States to pass
enactments of abolition, as such only created a politico-geographical line that otherwise would not have existed, and did
not emancipate a single slave.   The New England States are

---

* An extract from the opinion of Chief Justice Taney in the case referred
to by Mr. Lincoln will be found on reference to the Appendix.   Associate
Justices Catron of Tennessee, Wayne of Georgia, Grier of Pennsylvania, and
Nelson of New York, concurred in the decision.   Associate Justices
McLean of Ohio and Curtis of Massachusetts dissented.   The arguments of
the former were simply those of a political speech, their author being
desirous of becoming a candidate for the Presidency, while those of the
latter were merely law quibbles—what might be called a ' fence ' opinion.

less to blame in this respect than is generally supposed. Maine, New Hampshire, Vermont, and Massachusetts have never passed any laws on the subject. The 'institution' ceased to pay, and most of their slaves were sent South ; the same was the case in the other States. The Acts of Rhode Island, Connecticut, New York, New Jersey, and Pennsylvania, did not in the slightest degree hasten the disappearance of slavery from the North.

The late Sir George Cornewall Lewis gave his opinion concerning the differences between the States. In a private letter written in 1856 he said —

' Dana's lecture on Sumner is very interesting. It illustrates ' the relations of the North and South, and their feelings to one ' another. People here speak of the outrage on Sumner as a ' proof of the brutal manners of the Americans, and of their ' low morality. TO ME IT SEEMS THE FIRST BLOW IN A CIVIL WAR. ' IT BETOKENS THE ADVENT OF A STATE OF THINGS IN WHICH ' POLITICAL DIFFERENCES CANNOT BE SETTLED BY ARGUMENT, AND ' CAN ONLY BE SETTLED BY FORCE. *If half England was in* ' *favour of a measure which involved the confiscation of the* ' *property of the other half, my belief is that an English* ' *Brooks would be equally applauded.* If Peel had proposed ' a law which, instead of reducing rents, had annihilated them— ' instead of being attacked by a man of words like Disraeli, he ' would probably have been attacked with physical arguments ' by some man of blows. I SEE NO SOLUTION OF THE POLITICAL ' DIFFERENCES OF THE UNITED STATES, BUT THE SEPARATION OF THE ' SLAVE AND FREE STATES INTO DISTINCT POLITICAL COMMUNITIES. ' If I was a citizen of a Northern State, I should wish it. I ' should equally wish it if I was a citizen of a Southern State.'

Neither Seward nor Lincoln, nor any of their followers, are sincere in their remarks on the negro question. One of their representatives, Mr. Thurlow Weed, while in Europe last year, admitted this. He said: ' There has been for thirty years in ' America "an irrepressible conflict" between slavery and free- ' dom, limited, however, in the North, to a small minority of its ' citizens, moved by philanthropic or *political impulses or* ' *objects.* The great majority of Northern people, recognising ' their constitutional obligations, abstained from interference ' with slavery.'

After the black republican party, by corruption and fraud, succeeded in electing their candidates, they were willing to give the South additional guarantees. Even Mr. Charles Francis Adams, the minister in London from the remnant of the United States, endeavoured to retain the Southern States by holding out pro-slavery measures, as the following extracts from ' The New York Herald ' of January 28, 1861, will show : —

' The propositions of Mr. Adams, of Massachusetts, in the
' committee of thirty-three, contain a stronger element for the
' settlement of the vexed question of slavery than the majority
' of the people seem to understand. When discussing his pro-
' positions, as a general thing, reference is only made to the
' admission of New Mexico as a State, with or without slavery,
' as her people may elect. . . . . The great argument
' adduced in favour of the admission of New Mexico as a State
' under the present (Buchanan's) administration, is, that it
' removes so much territory from being subject to the doctrines
' of the Chicago platform under the Lincoln administration, and
' to that extent removes a great difficulty in the pathway of
' Mr. Lincoln. But this is not the vital proposition made by
' Mr. Adams. The one which strikes at the evil complained of
' by slaveholders is squarely met in the first proposition made
' by Mr. Adams to amend the Constitution by inserting the
' following article, after it has been adopted by three-fourths of
' the legislatures of the several States, viz.—

' " No amendment of this Constitution having for its objects
' " any interference with the relation between their citizens and
' " those (slaves) described in Section II. of the fourth article
' " of the ' Constitution,' or other persons, shall originate with
' " any State that does not recognise that relation within its
' " own limits, or shall be valid without the consent of every one
' " of the States composing the Union." *

* Article IV. Section 2 reads —

' 1. The citizen of each State shall be entitled to all privileges and im-
' munities of citizens in the several States.

' 2. A person charged in any State with treason, felony, or other crime, who
' shall flee from justice and be found in another State, shall, on demand of

' This proposition of Mr. Adams not only removes that fear at
' once, but, together with the New Mexico proposition, also
' removes the nigger question from the politics of the country,
' and will bring peace to a distracted people.'

One of Mr. Adams's abolition constituents entered his protest
against the proposed amendment, which elicited the following
reply, dated Washington, January 7, 1861.

' DEAR SIR,— I have received your letter, and have read it
' with respectful attention. Nothing pleases me better than the
' frank expression of opinion. I deal in it myself, and expect
' it from others. But you may remember that I have always
' claimed for myself the right to judge what I ought to do in
' public affairs, though others whom I greatly respect do not
' quite agree with me. But for this quality I should have
' remained where I was sixteen years ago. I am so unfortunate
' as to believe that I have offered no compromise, or any con-
' cession which is not already granted in the Chicago platform
' or in the National Statute Book. If you can show me that I
' have, I will admit myself to have been wrong. In the mean-
' time, it may be well to consider that what was rejected by the
' other side could not have been prized much by them as an
' advantage. I say no more at present; but having your
' interests and your principles in my keeping, I shall endeavour
' to prove to you in the long run that you may have been hasty
' in your opinion.

' I am very truly your friend,

' C. F. ADAMS.'

It will be observed that Mr. Adams places his party
' platform ' on a level with the Constitution and laws of his
country.

Mr. Thomas Corwin, now Mr. Lincoln's minister to Mexico,
offered the following resolution as a substitute for that of

' the executive authority of the State from which he fled, be delivered up,
' to be removed to the State having jurisdiction of the crime.

' 3. No person, held to service or labour in one State under the laws
' thereof, escaping into another, shall in consequence of any such law or
' regulation therein, be discharged from such service or labour; but shall
' be delivered up on claim of the party to whom such service or labour may
' be due.'

Mr. Adams; it covered the same ground, was passed by both Houses of Congress, and approved March 3, 1861 :—

' That no amendment shall be made to the Constitution ' which will authorise or give Congress power to abolish or ' interfere within any State with the domestic institutions ' thereof, including that of persons held to labour or servitude ' by the laws of said State.'

The resolution was unanimously adopted, Mr. Seward, of course, voting for it.

Yet, after these pro-slavery amendments to the Constitution, Mr. Seward and Mr. Adams affect to be Abolitionists.   Here is their latest appearance in the English newspapers :—

' Legation of the United States : London, Aug. 22.

' Sir,—The President of the United States having received ' at the hands of the Rev. Drs. Massie and Rylance the address ' of the meeting recently held at the Free-trade Hall, Man- ' chester, I have now the honour, under instructions from ' Washington, to forward to you the accompanying letter, in ' reply, from the Secretary of State.

' I have the honour to be, Sir, your obedient servant,

' CHARLES FRANCIS ADAMS.

' Thomas Bayley Potter, Esq., &c.'

' Department of State, Washington : July 25.

' Sir,—I have had the honour to receive from the Rev. Dr. ' Massie and the Rev. Dr. Rylance your address in the name of ' a large public meeting, which was recently held at the Free- ' trade Hall, in Manchester, to the President of the United ' States, together with papers which constitute the accompani- ' ments of that communication.   These papers have been sub- ' mitted to the President of the United States, and I am ' charged by him to inform you that he has read them with the ' most lively satisfaction, and with a profound sense of the obli- ' gation which the reverend religious pastors in France and the ' reverend religious pastors in Great Britain have laid upon the ' world by their correspondence with each other, and their ' common address to the Christian ministers and pastors through- ' out the United States.   The proceedings of the meeting at ' Free-trade Hall, and its address to the President, touchingly

' and admirably harmonise with the sentiments which pervade
' the correspondence before mentioned.

' The parties in these proceedings will readily understand
' that the attempted revolution in the United States sensibly
' affects this Government, and American society itself, in many
' ways which it has not fallen within the province of those
' parties to examine. While the interests thus naturally, and
' not improperly, overlooked in Europe furnish the strongest
' possible motives to the people of the United States for sup-
' pressing the insurrection and maintaining the Constitutional
' Government received at the hands of their fathers, the Pre-
' sident readily accepts and avows, as an additional and irre-
' sistible motive, the suggestion made by the friends of our
' country in Europe, that the success of the insurrection
' would result in the establishment, for the first time in the
' history of the human race, of a State based upon the ex-
' clusive foundations of African slavery.

' I have the honour to be, Sir, your very obedient servant,

' WILLIAM H. SEWARD.

' Thomas Bayley Potter, Esq., Manchester, England.'

It is sheer nonsense in Mr. Seward to say ' that the success
' of the insurrection (i. e. secession) would result in the estab-
' lishment, for the first time in the history of the human race, of
' a State based upon the exclusive foundations of African
' slavery.' As to slavery, there is not a particle of difference
between the old Federal and new Confederate Constitutions, as
adjudicated by the Supreme Court. The Southern Constitution,
to be sure, provides that the master shall have the right of
transit with his slave through any of the States, while there is
no such express provision in the Federal Constitution. But it
is an implied right, however, repeatedly decided as such by the
highest tribunal in America, and likewise as an international
right by the verdict of the English Court in the case of Grace.
The express provisions in both Constitutions in reference to
slavery are as follows, viz. :—

1. Representation and direct taxes shall be apportioned among
the several States according to numbers, to be ascertained by
adding to the whites three-fifths of the slaves.

2. In the Federal Constitution there is no prohibition of the African slave trade; but after 1808 Congress had the power to abolish it, if it saw proper. In the Confederate Constitution there is an absolute prohibition of that trade; and a further provision, giving Congress a discretionary power to prohibit the introduction of slaves from the United States.

3. In each Constitution are provisions to render up fugitive slaves to masters, and to use the military power to suppress all attempts at rebellion by the slaves.

The simple truth is that both Constitutions embrace the same fundamental principle, namely, the supremacy of the white over the black race. Mr. Seward's representations to the contrary are nothing less than hypocrisy and an attempt to deceive the European public in regard to this matter. Here are his own words, delivered in the Senate Chamber on March 11, 1850, in contravention of his present statements: —

' The population of the United States consists of natives of
' *Caucasian origin*, and exotics of the same derivation. The
' native mass readily assimilates to itself and absorbs the exotic,
' and *these* constitute one homogeneous people. The African
' race, bond and free, and the aborigines, savage and civilised,
' being incapable of such assimilation and absorption, remain
' distinct, and, owing to their peculiar condition, constitute
' inferior masses, and may be regarded as accidental if not
' disturbing political forces.'

This is a clear confession that the maxim set forth in the Declaration of Independence, ' that all men are created equal,' referred only to the white race, who alone framed and adopted the constitutions of all the States, as well as that of the United States. And it is also an admission that the negro, although ' a man,' is not ' a brother.' But Mr. Seward is guilty of an absurd blunder when in his ethnological display he seeks to place the Indian upon the same level with the negro. The ' aborigines ' of America, unlike the natives of Africa, are capable of high mental culture, and are not debarred from political privileges in either section of the late Union.

CHAPTER VIII.

THE AMERICAN COTTON CROPS—'SOUTHERN WEALTH AND NORTHERN PROFITS.'

THE extension of the trade in cotton has been the most wonderful circumstance in the history of commerce, and it is very clear that it has been mainly owing to the cultivation on the Western continent. While the moist climate of the British Isles is so well suited for its manufacture by machinery, the peculiar soil and atmosphere of the Southern States is the best adapted for its culture. The subjoined table gives a statement of the number of pounds of cotton yielded by those States from the earliest period, the average annual price, the value, and the quantity exported each year:—

Year	Crop in lbs.	Price	Value	Exported	Value of Exports
		cts.	$	lbs.	$
1748				80	
1754				100	
1770				100	
1784				1,085	
1785	*5,000,000		2,000,000	140	9,000
1786				70	
1787				1,500	
1788				6,000	
1789				10,000	
1790	1,500,000	30	450,000	1,200	3,600
1791	2,000,000	29	580,000	25,000	8,000
1792	3,000,000	26	780,000	200,000	52,000
1793	5,000,000	35	1,750,000	143,000	50,000
1794	8,000,000	45	3,500,000	1,167,000	500,000
1795	8,000,000	33	2,640,000	6,000,000	2,000,000
1796	10,000,000	33	3,300,000	6,000,000	2,000,000
1797	11,000,000	32	3,520,000	3,500,000	1,000,000
1798	15,000,000	33	4,950,000	9,000,000	3,000,000
1799	20,000,000	45	9,000,000	9,000,000	4,000,000
1800	35,000,000	35	8,750,000	17,000,000	5,000,000
1801	48,000,000	44	21,120,000	20,000,000	9,000,000
1802	55,000,000	22	12,100,000	27,000,000	5,000,000
1803	60,000,000	21	12,600,000	41,000,000	8,000,000
1804	65,000,000	24	15,600,000	38,000,000	8,000,000
1805	70,000,000	26	18,200,000	40,000,000	9,000,000
1806	80,000,000	25	20,000,000	37,000,000	8,000,000
1807	80,000,000	24	19,200,000	66,000,000	14,000,000
1808	75,000,000	17	12,750,000	12,000,000	2,000,000
1809	82,000,000	17	13,940,000	53,000,000	8,000,000
	738,500,000		186,730,000	386,055,275	88,622,600

* Estimate from 1748 to 1789.

Year	Crop in lbs.	Price	Value	Exported	Value of Exports
		cts.	$	lbs.	$
	738,500,000		186,730,000	386,055,275	88,622,600
1810	85,000,000	17	14,450,000	93,000,000	15,000,000
1811	80,000,000	15½	12,400,000	62,000,000	9,000,000
1812	75,000,000	9½	7,125,000	29,000,000	3,000,000
1813	75,000,000	10¼	7,520,000	19,000,000	2,000,000
1814	70,000,000	8¼	5,620,000	17,000,000	2,000,000
1815	100,000,000	20	20,000,000	83,000,000	17,000,000
1816	124,000,000	30	37,200,000	81,000,000	24,000,000
1817	130,000,000	24	31,200,000	95,000,000	24,000,000
1818	125,000,000	30	37,500,000	92,000,000	31,000,000
1819	167,000,000	25	41,750,000	88,000,000	21,000,000
1820	160,000,000	17	27,200,000	127,000,000	22,000,000
1821	180,000,000	16	28,800,000	124,893,405	20,000,000
1822	210,000,000	19	39,900,000	144,675,095	24,000,000
1823	185,000,000	14	25,900,000	173,723,270	23,000,000
1824	215,000,000	15	32,250,000	142,389,063	22,000,000
1825	225,000,000	16	36,000,000	176,449,907	29,000,000
1826	250,000,000	13	32,500,000	204,535,415	25,000,000
1827	270,000,000	14	37,800,000	294,310,115	29,000,000
1828	325,000,000	11	35,750,000	210,590,463	22,000,000
1829	365,000,000	10	36,500,000	264,837,186	26,000,000
1830	350,000,000	9	31,500,000	298,459,102	30,000,000
1831	385,000,000	9	34,650,000	276,979,784	25,000,000
1832	390,000,000	9	35,100,000	322,215,122	32,000,000
1833	445,000,000	11	48,950,000	324,698,604	36,000,000
1834	460,000,000	12	55,200,000	384,717,907	49,000,000
1835	550,000,000	16	88,000,000	387,358,992	65,000,000
1836	570,000,000	16	91,200,000	423,631,307	71,000,000
1837	720,000,000	14	100,800,000	444,211,537	63,000,000
1838	545,000,000	10	54,500,000	595,952,297	62,000,000
1839	870,000,000	14	121,800,000	413,624,212	61,000,000
1840	654,000,000	8	52,320,000	743,941,061	64,000,000
1841	673,000,000	10	67,300,000	530,204,100	54,000,000
1842	942,000,000	8	76,360,000	584,717,017	48,000,000
1843	812,000,000	6	48,720,000	792,297,106	49,000,000
1844	958,000,000	8	76,640,000	663,633,455	55,000,000
1845	840,000 000	6	50,400,000	872,905,996	52,000,000
1846	711,000,000	8	56,880,000	547,558,055	43,000,000
1847	940,000,000	10	94,000,000	527,219,958	53,000,000
1848	1,100,000,000	7½	80,000,000	814,274,431	62,000,000
1849	860,000,000	6½	55,900,000	1,026,602,269	66,000,000
1850	990,000,000	11	108,900,000	635,381,604	72,000,000
1851	1,300,000,000	11	143,000,000	927,237,089	112,000,000
1852	1,400,000,000	8	112,000,000	1,093,230,639	88,000,000
1853	1,300,000,000	9	117,000,000	1,111,510,370	109,000,000
1854	1,200,000,000	8¾	105,000,000	987,833,106	94,000,000
1855	1,550,000,000	9	139,500,000	1,008,424,601	88,000,000
1856	1,300,000,000	9	117,000,000	1,351,431,701	128,000,000
1857	1,400,000,000	12½	175,000,000	1,048,282,475	132,000,000
1858	1,750,000,000	11¾	199,000,000	1,118,624,012	131,000,000
1859	2,200,000,000	11¾	247,500,000	1,383,802,574	159,000,000
1860	1,650,000,000	11¼	198,000,000	1,490,000,000	178,800,000
	33,969,500,000		3,716,215,000	26,099,419,677	2,810,422,600

The total value of the cotton crops of the Southern States of America, from the earliest period to the dissolution of the Federal Union, allowing for 5,000,000 pounds, the estimated weight of that grown anterior to 1789, amounted to thirty-seven hundred and sixteen millions, two hundred and fifteen thousand dollars ($3,716,215,000), of which twenty-eight hundred and ten millions, four hundred and twenty-two thousand, six hundred dollars ($2,810,422,600) in value, or about three-fourths the whole, was exported to foreign ports, and two-thirds of the remaining one-fourth were sent to the Northern States. These crops formed the basis of a commerce, the aggregate amount of which it is difficult to appraise. Cotton, from the time it leaves the pod until it is converted into paper, goes through a greater number of hands than any other production of the vegetable or animal kingdom. It will be observed that prices of cotton have gradually cheapened, incidental to the usual mercantile fluctuations. The trade has been subjected to several interruptions—the embargo in 1808, followed by the Non-intercourse Act, the war of 1812–14, and the present partial blockade of the Southern ports. On these occasions prices have, of course, been very high at the consuming points.

The foregoing tables and remarks bring the history of the American cotton trade down to the period of the secession of the Southern States from the Federal Union, which, beginning with the State of South Carolina on December 20, 1860, was followed by the other cotton States in January and February 1861. The shipments of cotton, however, were continued to the close of the season—July; the trade therefore does not show much falling off for that year. The business since then has been confined to the produce reshipped from the North and that which has eluded the blockade.

The rapidity with which the cultivation of cotton increased in the Southern States is truly astonishing. In the beginning of the present century the annual exportation was about 5,000 bales; in 1849 the quantity grown had reached 2,445,793 bales of ginned cotton of 400 lbs. each; in 1859 it had further advanced to 5,196,793 bales, or more than 100 per cent. in ten years. The whole crop is the product of twelve States, but is chiefly obtained from eight of them. Prior to the production

of cotton in the more Southern States, it was moderately cultivated for domestic purposes in North Carolina, Virginia, Maryland, Delaware, and even Southern Illinois. The ocean freights
for many years, earned by Northern ships in transporting cotton,
have averaged over twenty millions of dollars per annum.
When the crops were smaller, the cost of transportation was
higher, the vessels being of more limited capacity.

Among the branches of manufacture in the Northern States,
that of cotton goods holds the first rank, both as to the capital
employed and the value of the product. The Yankees have had
a great advantage in having the raw material so close at hand.
They have not been content with this, but have also demanded
protection under what is called the 'American system,' a term
borrowed by Henry Clay from Napoleon's expression, the
'continental system.'

The total value of cotton goods manufactured in the New
England States in 1859 was $80,301,535, and in the middle
States $26,272,111—an increase of 83·4 per cent. in the
former and 77·7 in the latter since the last decade. The other
States reached a value of $8,564,280, making the whole pro-
duction $115,137,926, against $65,501,687 in 1850 — an
augmentation of 76 per cent. The extension in cotton manufacture was as follows:—Maine and New Jersey, 152 per cent.;
Pennsylvania, 102 per cent.; New Hampshire and Connecticut,
87 per cent.; Massachusetts, 69 per cent.; and Rhode Island,
88 per cent. The value was at the rate of 3\frac{69}{100}$ for each indi-
vidual in all the States, equivalent to 46$\frac{1}{2}$ yards of cloth for
every person, at 8 cts. per yard. The average production in
1850 was but 34$\frac{1}{2}$ yards per head. The increase, therefore, was
about 12 yards per individual, or equal to the entire consumption in 1830. The number of hands employed in the manufactories in 1859 was 45,315 males and 73,605 females—an
increase of 10,020 and 10,944 respectively over 1850. The
average product of an operative was $969, or about 200l.
sterling. The spindles were returned at 5,035,798, against
3,633,693 in 1850—an advance of 1,402,105, or 38·5 per cent.
The cotton manufacturing business of the New England States
was 78·6 per cent. of the whole, Massachusetts alone being 29·3
per cent. The product per spindle was—In Maine, 22\frac{12}{100}$;

Massachusetts, $21\frac{12}{100}$; New Hampshire, $24\frac{87}{100}$; Vermont, $18\frac{13}{100}$; Rhode Island, $16; Connecticut, $16\frac{46}{100}$. The average in the New England States is $20\frac{30}{100}$; in the Middle States, $30\frac{48}{100}$; and all the States together, $22\frac{86}{100}$. The quantity of cotton consumed in the entire Union in 1859 was 364,036,123 lbs.; of this amount the New England States took about two-thirds, one-half of which was used in Massachusetts.

The Yankees by these statements, which are compiled from the last census, have, it will be observed, been killing the goose that has laid their golden egg when they attempted to interfere with the people of the South, who have not only supplied them with the raw material, but who have been their principal customers for all their manufactures.

In dilating upon this subject, the ' Boston Post,' a Democratic paper, said in 1859, when speaking of the trade of the New England States with the South :

'The aggregate value of the merchandise sold to the South 'annually we estimate at some $60,000,000. The basis of the 'estimate is, first, the estimated amount of boots and shoes sold, 'which intelligent merchants place at from $20,000,000 to '$30,000,000, including a limited amount that are manufac-'tured with us and sold in New York. In the next place, we 'know, from merchants in the trade, that the amount of dry 'goods sold South yearly is many millions of dollars, and that 'the amount is second only to that of the sales of boots and 'shoes. In the third place, we learn from careful enquiry and 'from the best sources, that the fish of various kinds sold realise '$3,000,000, or in that neighbourhood. Upwards of $1,000,000 'is received for furniture sold in the South every year. The 'Southern States are a much better market than the Western 'for this article. It is true, since the establishment of branch 'houses in New York, Philadelphia, and other cities, many of 'the goods manufactured in New England have reached the 'South through those houses; but still the commerce of New 'England with the South, and this particular section of the 'country, receives the main advantage of that commerce. And 'what shall we say of New England ship-building, that is so 'greatly sustained by Southern wants? What shall we say of 'that large ocean fleet that, by being the common carriers of

' the South, has brought so large an amount of money into the
' pockets of our merchants ? We will not undertake to estimate
' the value of these interests, supported directly by the South.'
Mr. Kettell, a New Yorker, in commenting upon the above
article, said : ' This estimate of the " Post " for New England
' alone is about half the aggregate that the census indicates as
' the sales of Northern manufactures to the South. The South
' manufactures nearly as much per head of the white popula-
' tion as does the West. Both these sections hold, however, a
' provincial position in relation to the East. As we have seen
' heretofore, the first accumulations of capital in the country
' were at the East from the earnings of navigation and the slave
' trade. These were invested in manufactures, " protected " by
' the tariffs imposed by the Federal Government. The opera-
' tions of these tariffs was to tax the consumers in the South
' and West *pro rata* upon what manufactures they purchased
' from the East, and, by so doing, to increase Eastern capital at
' the expense of those other sections. The articles mostly pro-
' tected, and of which the cost is enhanced to the consumers in
' proportion to the duties, are manufactured at the East to the
' extent of $320,000,000, of which $200,000,000 are sold South
' and West. This gives an annual drain of $50,000,000 from
' the consumers of those sections, as a bonus or protection to
' the capital employed in manufacturing at the North. The
' claim for this protection is based upon the necessity of pro-
' tecting home manufactures against the overwhelming capital
' of England. The manufacturers of the South and West have
' to contend, however, not only against the overwhelming capi-
' tal of New England created in manufactures, but against the
' drain of capital from each locality, caused by the protection to
' Eastern goods. In spite of this disability, as we have seen in
' the tables, the manufactures of those sections increase, and at
' the South faster than at the West. There is another feature
' of this manufacturing industry which deserves attention. It
' is, that one-third of the hands employed at the East are
' females, and the product of their labour is made efficient by
' steam-machinery. If we take the relative numbers employed
' in cotton manufacture in each section in the cotton trade, the
' result is as follows :—

'YEAR ENDING JUNE 1, 1850.

	North	West	South	Total
'Male	27,392	334	5,569	35,295
'Female	53,184	513	8,900	62,661

'YEAR ENDING JUNE 1, 1860.

	North	West	South	Total
'Male	38,984	632	5,664	45,313
'Female	64,698	676	8,231	73,605

'The Northern labour is largely performed by females, and
'this element of labour is supplied by immigration in nearly its
'whole extent, a very large proportion of the females employed
'in the factories being Irish. At the South, female labour is
'taking the same direction with great success.

'If we compare the whole number of persons employed in
'manufactures of all kinds at the South with those so employed
'at the West, as seen in the census tables for 1850, we find at
'the South the number employed is 151,944, or 1 in 41 of
'the white population. At the West the number so employed
'is 122,364, or 1 in 40 of the population. These figures
'give no advantage to the free-labour section, as opposed to the
'slave-labour section. There is here no evidence that the exist-
'ence of slavery is in any degree opposed to the developement
'of white industry. It is only another evidence in corroboration
'of that afforded by the history of the Northern States: the
'theory has been advanced against the extension of slavery into
'the territories that slavery degrades labour and drives out free
'industry. In 1790, the New England and Middle States had
'1,968,455 inhabitants, of which 40,370 were slaves. Did that
'slave labour drive out white labour? or has not the latter ex-
'tinguished the former, and cast adrift the then well-cared-for
'negroes, to starve in little bands on the outskirts of the towns
'and villages, their former happy homes, the wasting monuments
'of the incapacity of a race, and of the selfishness of that
'philanthropy which found a pecuniary relief in conferring the
'blessings of liberty on their henceforth useless servants?'

If there be added to these many advantages the benefits received by the North, in its capacity of importer, banker, commission merchant, and broker, it is not surprising that great
cities grew up and a specious show of wealth has been paraded.
But the truth is, that the natural resources of the American

States lie altogether in the South. Although that section has been thus partially drained, it is quite clear that she is better off this day than the North. Witness the fact that nearly all the bonds of the Southern States, municipalities, and various corporations, including banks and railways, are owned by their people. This is not the case in the North or the West, most of whose railway bonds and State stocks are held in Europe. The Northerners have preferred keeping their capital and that borrowed from Europe (the South has no commercial indebtedness) in an active condition, not content with ordinary interest: much of it is invested in mill property that must necessarily be valueless after the war is over, as their Southern custom is now gone for ever. That great loss, however, has not yet been felt by them, owing to the enormous expenditure for Federal war supplies, which fitted in to fill up the vacuum, as State after State withdrew from the Union. The war, too, with the large European demand for breadstuffs that existed for two years, has given temporary employment for Northern ships that had hitherto been engaged in transporting Southern produce.

Historians will record the Northern crusade against the South as the greatest folly ever committed. President Davis said, in his inaugural message, February 1861 :

‘ An agricultural people, whose chief interest is the export of ‘ a commodity required in every manufacturing country, our ‘ true policy is peace, and the freest trade which our necessities ‘ will permit. It is alike our interest and that of those to whom ‘ we would sell and from whom we would buy, that there should ‘ be the fewest practicable restrictions upon the interchange of ‘ commodities. There can be but little rivalry between ours ‘ and any manufacturing or navigating community, such as the ‘ North-eastern States of the American Union. It must follow, ‘ therefore, that mutual interest would invite goodwill and kind ‘ offices. If, however, passion or lust of dominion should cloud ‘ the judgment or inflame the ambition of those States, we ‘ must prepare to meet the emergency, and maintain by the final ‘ arbitrament of the sword the position which we have assumed ‘ among the nations of the earth.’

As a further evidence of the superiority of the resources of the South over those of the North and West combined, the following figures are taken from the census of 1860:—The population of the non-slaveholding States was 18,907,753; of the slaveholding States, including 3,950,511 slaves, 12,243,293. The assessed value of real and personal property in the North was $6,541,027,619; in the South, $5,465,808,957. The number of acres of improved lands in the North were 88,181,466, and the cash value of the farms, farming implements, and machinery, $4,209,062,835; in the South the acres of improved land were 74,623,055, and the value of the farms and farming implements, $2,675,476,321. The North possessed of horses, asses, and mules, 3,669,239; the South, 3,537,236.

SUMMARY OF MILCH COWS, WORKING OXEN, AND OTHER CATTLE, SHEEP, AND SWINE.

In the North		In the South	
Milch cows . . .	5,235,254	Milch cows . . .	3,428,011
Working oxen . .	1,011,868	Working oxen . .	1,176,286
Other cattle. . .	6,412,200	Other cattle . .	8,187,125
Sheep	15,367,312	Sheep	7,064,116
Swine	11,846,629	Swine	20,651,182
	39,873,263		40,506,720

The value of live stock in the North was $574,525,612
Ditto in the South 524,336,743

FOOD STATISTICS.

Articles	North	South
Wheat . . . . bushels	120,170,315	50,005,712
Rye . . . . . „	16,897,379	4,067,667
Indian corn . . . „	392,756,465	434,938,063
Oats. . . . . „	138,864,580	33,224,515
Barley and buckwheat . „	31,588,149	1,666,516
Rice. . . . . lbs.	4,139	187,136,034
Butter . . . . „	368,646,282	91,026,470
Cheese . . . . „	104,531,095	1,257,557
Irish and sweet potatoes, peas, beans . . . bushels	103,494,753	63,229,982
Sugar (cane) . . . hhds.	283	301,922
Sugar (maple) . . . lbs.	37,186,065	1,677,533
Molasses (cane) . . gallons	66	16,337,017
Molasses (maple) . . „	1,474,155	470,144
Molasses (sorghum) . . „	4,717,125	2,458,917
Hops . . . . lbs.	10,982,296	27,537
Honey in wax . . . „	10,987,926	15,382,905
Wine . . . . gallons	1,427,516	423,303
Value of orchard products and vegetables	$26,894,014	$8,103,216
Value of animals slaughtered . .	$105,669,980	$100,362,075

GENERAL STATISTICS.

Articles	North	South
Clover and other grass seeds . bushels	1,503,050	325,667
Hemp . . . . . tons	40,800	63,680
Flax . . . . . lbs.	2,045,630	1,733,213
Flax seed . . . . . bushels	513,227	98,553
Silk cocoons . . . . lbs.	5,320	1,211
Tobacco . . . . . ,,	58,734,028	370,630,723
Cotton . ginned bales of 400 lbs.	6	5,196,938
Wool	45,247,012	14,685,316

The value of the 'home-made manufactures' in the North was $5,699,727; in the South, $18,526,734. All the naval stores—rosin, tar, pitch, turpentine, &c.—amounting to many millions of dollars annually, were produced in the South. A large portion of the live oak, white oak, and other timber used for the construction of ships in the Northern States, as well as the yellow pine and much of the building material, are of the growth of Southern forests.

In the census, the Northern States are credited with 17,215,952 tons of hay, whilst the produce of that article in the Southern States is set down at 1,857,554 tons. In comparing the resources of the two sections of the late union, this claim is absurd. The South grows more food for cattle than the North, but, thanks to her climate, she is not put to the expense of making her grass into hay for winter keep, except to a very moderate extent.

CHAPTER IX.

THE BRITISH COTTON TRADE—STATISTICS FROM 1697 TO 1863.

THE monopoly enjoyed by India in supplying cotton clothing material and yarns ceased about the beginning of the present century upon the advent of the cotton business with America. It will, therefore, be interesting to review the course of the British cotton trade from the earliest authentic records down to that period.

The Custom House returns give the following figures as the value of raw cotton imported, and manufactured goods exported in the years named :—

Years	Raw cotton imported	Value of goods exported
	lbs.	£
1697	1,979,359	5,915
1701	1,985,868	23,253
1710	715,008	5,698
1720	1,972,805	16,200
1730	1,545,472	13,524
1741	1,645,031	20,709
1751	2,976,610	45,986
1764	3,870,392	200,354

All these cottons were received from the Levant and America. South Carolina contributed within this period 17 bales, viz. in 1748 7 bales and 1754 10 bales—also in 1770 10 bales.

There were imported, from the year 1700 to 1760, considerable quantities of cotton yarn from India, as will be seen by the following table, which shows that during the early part of that period the cotton yarn imported from Hindostan bore a very considerable relation to the whole cotton wool imported from other places into Great Britain. Thus in 1710 the total importation of cotton wool was 715,008 lbs., while in 1707 that of

Indian yarn was 219,879 lbs., and in 1713, 135,546 lbs. The quantities of yarn imported by the Company seem to have suffered extraordinary vicissitudes, ill accordant with the regular course of the home manufactures into which they entered. It is reasonable, therefore, to infer that there must have been in the intervals very large importations of these yarns through the contraband traders, who are known to have supplied the European markets, to a great extent, with the highly prized and then inimitable muslins and calicoes of the Eastern world.

STATEMENT OF THE QUANTITY OF COTTON YARN IMPORTED FROM INDIA IN EACH YEAR FROM 1700 TO 1760.

Year	Quantity		Year	lbs.
1700 1701 1702	The General Books for these years are missing		1731 . . .	20,406
			1732 . . .	46,405
1703 . . .	114,100 lbs.		1733 . . .	70,976
1704 . . .	72,938		1734 . . .	5,924
1705 . . .	39,155		1735 . . .	91,394
1706 . . .	48,120		1736 . . .	40,274
1707 . . .	219,879		1737 . . .	2,083
1708 1709 1710 1711 1712	The General Books for these years do not particularise the goods imported; the Subsidiary Books, from which the information could be supplied, are missing		1738 . . .	3,024
			1739 . . .	8,445
			1740 . . .	3,339
			1741 . . .	20,055
			1742 . . .	11,366
1713 . . .	135,546 lbs.		1743 . . .	9,904
1714 . . .	12,768		1744 . . .	14,593
1715 . . .	nil		1745 . . .	nil
1716 . . .	nil		1746 . . .	nil
1717 . . .	nil		1747 . . .	nil
1718 . . .	37,714		1748 . . .	nil
1719 . . .	nil		1749 . . .	nil
1720 . . .	21,350		1750 . . .	14,112
1721 . . .	50,624		1751 . . .	4,704
1722 . . .	10,800		1752 . . .	336
1723 . . .	24,025		1753 . . .	nil
1724 . . .	21,588		1754 . . .	nil
1725 . . .	5,809		1755 . . .	37,632
1726 . . .	45,300		1756 . . .	6,061
1727 . . .	27,254		1757 . . .	4,357
1728 . . .	11,424		1758 . . .	12,869
1729 . . .	18,816		1759 . . .	4,390
1730 . . .	32,351		1760 . . .	2,814

The trade continued 'steady' at about the figures of 1764 until 1781. The following table exhibits its extent from that date until 1800, and specifies the portion received from the American States.

IMPORTATIONS AND EXPORTATIONS OF RAW COTTON INTO GREAT BRITAIN FROM 1781 TO 1800—20 YEARS—WITH THE QUANTITY RECEIVED FROM THE AMERICAN STATES.

Years	Imported	American portion	Exported
	lbs.	lbs.	lbs.
1781	5,198,798	—	96,778
1782	11,828,039	—	421,229
1783	9,735,663	—	177,626
1784	11,482,083	1,085	201,845
1785	18,400,384	140	407,496
1786*	19,475,020	50	323,153
1787	23,250,268	1,500	1,073,381
1788	20,467,436	6,000	853,146
1789	32,576,023	10,000	297,837
1790	31,447,605	1,200	844,154
1791	28,706,675	25,000	363,442
1792	34,907,497	140,000	1,485,465
1793	19,040,929	90,000	1,171,566
1794	24,358,567	1,000,000	1,349,950
1795	26,401,340	5,500,000	1,193,737
1796	32,126,357	5,500,000	694,962
1797	23,354,371	3,000,000	609,058
1798	31,880,641	8,000,000	601,139
1799	43,379,278	8,000,000	844,671
1800	56,010,732	15,000,000	4,416,610

The foregoing tables exhibit the limited extent of the British cotton trade up to the beginning of the present centennial period. It was not until 1788 that the first importation of raw cotton from India into England took place. Prior to that period, the receipts from thence were in goods and yarns, and it was some years before the shipments became extensive, notwithstanding the efforts of the East India Company to foster the business. The Southern cotton crops, and the great improvements in machinery, completely reversed the current of the commerce; and if the error committed by the British Cabinet and Mr. Jay, the American minister in 1794, had been permitted by a want of foresight on the part

* The sources of supply this year (1786) were as follow:—

		lbs.
British West Indies	. . . . . .	5,550,000
French and Spanish Colonies	. . .	5,430,000
Dutch Colonies	. . . . . .	1,610,000
Portuguese Colonies	. . . . .	1,980,000
Smyrna and Turkey	. . . . .	4,855,020
Southern States	. . . . . .	0,000,050
		19,475,020

of the Senate of the United States to go uncorrected, the developement of the trade might have been much retarded. Until then Great Britain, feeling yet sore on the subject of the 'secession' of the American colonies, was indisposed to increase her commerce with her former subjects, and even at that time, and subsequently, in prohibiting them to trade with the West Indies, entrammeled her mercantile relations with the American States.

It will be observed by the statement below that the cotton trade between the Southern States and Great Britain steadily increased from 1800 to 1820, and this, too, in the face of extending shipments to the Northern States and to the continent of Europe.

The next table gives the extent of the British cotton trade from 1801 to 1820—20 years—noting the portion (estimate) received from the American States:—

Years	Imported	American portion	Exported	Excess of Imports over Exports Consumed
	lbs.	lbs.	lbs.	lbs.
1801	56,004,305	18,500,000	1,860,872	54,203,433
1802	60,345,600	25,000,000	3,730,480	56,615,120
1803	53,812,284	39,500,000	1,561,053	52,251,231
1804	61,867,329	37,000,000	503,171	61,364,158
1805	59,682,406	38,000,000	804,243	58,178,863
1806	58,176,283	36,000,000	651,867	57,524,416
1807	74,925,306	62,000,000	2,176,943	72,248,363
1808	43,605,982	10,000,000	1,644,867	41,961,115
1809	92,812,282	51,000,000	4,351,105	88,461,177
1810	132,488,935	90,000,000	8,787,109	123,701,826
1811	91,576,535	60,000,000	1,266,867	90,309,668
1812	63,025,936	27,500,000	1,740,912	61,285,024
1813	50,000,000	15,000,000	—	50,000,000
1814	73,728,900	16,000,000	19,951,098	53,777,802
1815	96,200,200	80,000,000	3,684,249	92,515,951
1816	97,310,000	80,000,000	10,494,979	86,815,021
1817	126,240,000	93,000,000	9,482,474	116,757,526
1818	173,940,000	90,000,000	11,817,295	162,122,705
1819	137,592,000	85,000,000	4,475,149	133,116,851
1820	147,576,000	125,000,000	14,726,367	132,829,633

The tables (pp. 120, 121) furnish an estimate of the British cotton trade from 1821 to 1860 inclusive—a period of 40 years—with the portions received from the different countries, the quantity exported, and the stock remaining for home consumption on the 31st day of December of each year.

TOTAL IMPORTS AND EXPORTS OF COTTON INTO THE UNITED KINGDOM FROM ALL COUNTRIES,
1821 TO 1840 INCLUSIVE.

Year	From the United States	From the East Indies	From the West Indies	From the Brazils	From all other Countries	Total Import from all parts	Total Quantities Exported	Remaining for Home Consumption
	lbs.	lbs.	lbs.	lbs.	lbs.	lbs.	lbs.	lbs.
1821	93,470,745	8,827,107	7,138,980	19,535,786	3,564,002	132,536,620	14,589,497	117,947,123
1822	101,031,766	4,554,225	10,295,114	24,705,206	2,251,317	142,837,628	18,269,776	124,567,852
1823	142,532,112	14,839,117	7,034,793	23,514,641	3,481,840	191,402,503	9,318,402	182,084,101
1824	92,187,662	16,420,005	6,269,306	24,849,552	9,653,597	149,380,122	13,299,505	136,080,617
1825	139,908,699	20,005,872	8,193,948	33,180,491	26,716,281	228,005,291	18,004,953	210,000,328
1826	130,858,203	20,985,135	4,751,070	9,871,092	11,141,901	177,607,401	24,474,920	153,132,481
1827	216,924,812	20,930,542	7,165,881	20,716,162	6,711,512	272,448,909	18,134,170	254,314,739
1828	151,752,289	32,187,901	5,893,800	29,143,279	8,783,373	227,760,642	17,396,776	210,363,866
1829	157,187,396	24,857,800	4,640,414	28,878,386	7,203,415	222,767,411	30,289,115	192,478,296
1830	210,885,358	12,481,761	3,429,247	33,092,072	4,073,014	263,961,452	8,534,976	255,426,476
1831	219,333,628	25,805,153	2,401,685	31,695,761	9,438,626	288,674,853	22,308,555	266,366,298
1832	219,756,753	35,178,625	2,040,428	20,109,560	9,747,159	286,832,525	18,027,940	268,804,585
1833	237,506,758	32,755,164	2,084,862	28,463,821	2,846,232	303,656,837	17,363,882	286,292,955
1834	269,203,075	32,920,865	2,293,794	19,291,396	3,166,295	326,875,425	24,461,963	302,413,462
1835	284,455,812	41,429,011	1,815,270	21,986,409	11,016,461	363,702,963	32,779,734	330,923,229
1836	289,615,692	75,949,845	1,714,337	27,501,272	12,177,911	406,959,057	31,739,763	375,219,294
1837	320,651,716	51,532,072	1,595,702	20,940,145	12,567,148	407,286,783	39,722,031	367,564,752
1838	431,437,888	40,217,734	1,529,356	24,464,505	10,201,094	507,850,577	30,644,469	477,206,108
1839	311,597,798	47,172,939	1,248,164	16,971,979	12,405,679	389,396,559	38,738,238	350,658,321
1840	487,856,504	77,011,839	866,167	14,779,171	11,974,339	592,488,010	38,673,229	553,814,781
	4,508,154,666	636,062,712	82,402,318	473,690,686	179,121,196	5,882,431,568	466,771,724	5,415,659,664

TOTAL IMPORTS AND EXPORTS OF COTTON INTO THE UNITED KINGDOM FROM ALL COUNTRIES, 1841 TO 1860 INCLUSIVE.

Year	From the United States	From the East Indies	From the West Indies	From the Brazils	From all other Countries	Total Import from all parts	Total Quantities Exported	Remaining for Home Consumption
	lbs.	lbs.	lbs.	lbs.	lbs.	lbs.	lbs.	lbs.
	4,508,154,666	636,062,712	82,402,318	473,690,686	179,121,196	5,882,431,568	466,771,724	5,415,659,664
1841	358,240,964	97,388,153	1,533,197	16,671,348	14,158,693	487,992,355	37,673,552	450,318,803
1842	414,030,779	92,972,609	593,603	15,222,828	8,930,267	531,750,086	45,251,248	486,498,838
1843	574,738,520	65,709,729	1,260,444	18,675,123	12,809,300	673,193,116	39,620,000	633,573,116
1844	517,218,622	88,639,776	1,707,194	21,084,744	17,460,968	646,111,304	47,222,560	598,888,744
1845	626,650,412	58,437,426	1,394,447	20,157,633	15,340,035	721,979,953	42,916,384	679,063,569
1846	401,949,393	34,540,143	1,201,857	14,746,321	15,418,560	467,856,274	65,930,704	401,925,570
1847	364,599,291	83,934,614	793,933	19,966,922	5,412,855	474,707,615	74,954,320	399,753,295
1848	600,247,488	84,101,961	640,437	19,971,378	8,058,897	713,020,161	74,019,792	639,000,369
1849	634,504,050	70,838,515	944,307	30,738,133	18,444,007	755,469,012	98,893,536	656,575,476
1850	493,153,112	118,872,742	228,913	30,299,982	21,022,112	663,576,861	102,469,696	561,107,165
1851	596,638,962	122,626,976	446,529	19,339,104	18,328,178	757,379,749	111,980,400	645,399,349
1852	765,630,544	84,922,432	703,696	26,506,144	52,019,632	929,782,448	111,784,304	817,998,144
1853	658,451,796	181,848,160	350,428	24,190,628	30,437,737	895,278,749	148,569,680	746,709,069
1854	722,151,346	119,836,009	409,110	19,703,000	25,233,084	887,333,149	123,326,112	764,007,037
1855	681,629,424	145,179,216	468,452	24,577,952	39,896,908	891,751,952	124,345,760	767,406,192
1856	780,040,016	180,496,624	462,784	21,830,704	41,056,176	1,023,886,304	146,660,864	877,225,440
1857	654,758,048	250,338,144	1,443,568	29,910,832	32,868,304	969,318,896	131,927,600	837,391,296
1858	833,237,776	132,722,576	367,808	18,617,872	49,396,144	1,034,342,176	149,609,600	884,732,576
1859	961,707,264	192,330,880	592,256	22,478,960	48,879,712	1,225,989,072	175,143,136	1,050,845,936
1860	1,115,890,608	204,141,168	1,050,784	17,286,864	52,569,328	1,390,938,752	250,428,640	1,140,510,112
	17,263,623,081	3,045,940,565	98,996,055	908,667,758	706,862,103	22,024,089,562	2,567,499,782	19,456,589,780

The quantity given as that remaining on hand has been found by deducting the exportations from the importations of cotton. The figures, having passed the scrutiny of the Custom House authorities, may be regarded as much more correct than the brokers' reports of the portion taken for consumption. This method, therefore, gives an accurate account of the cotton manufactured in the United Kingdom, although the quantities opposite the individual years cannot be exact, in consequence of the stocks on hand at the close of each season not being the same.

The last table brings the cotton trade down to December 31, 1860; the quantity received into the United Kingdom from the Southern States in that year was 1,115,890,608 lbs. against 93,470,745 lbs. in 1821—an increase of 1,022,419,863 lbs.; while that from the West Indies declined from 7,138,980 lbs. in 1821 to 1,050,784 lbs. in 1860—a falling off of 6,088,196 lbs.: and the yield of the latter year happened to be exceptionally large — nearly double an ordinary crop. This decline in the growth of cotton in the West Indies was altogether owing to the meddling with slavery by the Abolitionists, which began to embarrass the planters, some years before emancipation actually took place ; but the reduction in the crops of those luxuriant regions was still more marked after it occurred. It will be observed, the receipts from India were enlarged from 8,827,107 lbs. in 1821 to 204,141,168 lbs. in 1860. This does not argue that the actual production of India has increased greatly, but shows that the more American cotton is used in England the greater are the requirements of that of Indian growth—a small proportion of the latter being advantageously consumed in the fabrication of the former. India has been enabled to spare the additional quantity, in consequence of being a large purchaser of British goods and yarn, which enables her to release some of her raw material.

The history of commerce for the last sixty years shows how closely the interests of Great Britain and the Confederate States are allied, and that the Northern States have detracted from the prosperity of both. The earnings of the Yankees out of the staples of the South have, to use Mr. Roebuck's graphic expression, caused them to become an 'upstart nation,' particularly since the revolution in Europe in 1848, which threw into the North and West a very large number of emigrants of the Red Republican type, who have aided the Puritans in abusing England and vilifying the South. And now these vast commissions, brokerages, and profits are being squandered in the futile effort to subdue their benefactors, who have merely desired to throw off the political and mercantile shackles with which they, for so long a time, had been bound.

In order to exhibit the extent of the cotton trade, the business in Europe for 1859, the last year of moderate transactions, is here given *in bales.*

The bales of American cotton have gradually increased from about 215 lbs. to an average of 430 lbs. during the present century. From 1851 to 1858, the net weight of the bales of the several descriptions of cotton have ranged as follows:— American 430 lbs., Egyptian 384 lbs., East Indian 376 lbs., West Indian 201 lbs., and Brazilian 181 lbs.

In 1862, the weight of the bales of cotton received at Liverpool averaged: Uplands, 440 lbs.; Orleans and Mobiles, 452 lbs.; Sea Islands, 338 lbs.; Egyptian, 450 lbs.; East Indian, 380 lbs.; West Indian, 200 lbs.; and Brazilian, 180 lbs.

BALES OF COTTON TAKEN FOR CONSUMPTION IN EUROPE, 1859.

Countries	United States	Brazil	West Indies	East Indies	Egypt	Total
Great Britain . . .	1,907,000	105,000	6,000	177,000	99,000	2,294,000
France	452,000	5,000	17,000	15,000	36,000	525,000
Belgium	38,000	—	1,000	25,000	—	64,000
Holland	62,000	—	3,000	59,000	1,000	125,000
Germany.	146,000	—	5,000	61,000	—	212,000
Trieste	31,000	—	—	14,000	21,000	66,000
Genoa.	41,000	—	—	11,000	1,000	53,000
Spain	109,000	8,000	—	1,000	—	118,000
Surplus of Export— Great Britain . .	94,000	6,000	—	79,000	15,000	194,000
Total delivered . .	2,880,000	124,000	32,000	442,000	173,000	3,051,000
Add consumed in America . . .						849,000
						4,500,000
or 1,800,000,000 lbs.						

Of the 3,651,000 bales delivered for consumption in 1859 the Southern States of America supplied 2,880,000 bales, besides furnishing the Northern States with 730,000 bales, and retaining for their own use 119,000 bales. After reading the following article from the 'London Cotton Supply Reporter' of February 3, 1860, it seems strange that Englishmen should be so little concerned *now* in reference to a supply of cotton, when, long before hostilities commenced in America, they manifested so much uneasiness on the subject.

'Upwards of 500,000 workers are now employed in our 'cotton factories, and it has been estimated that at least '4,000,000 persons in the country are dependent upon the cotton 'trade for subsistence. A century ago Lancashire contained a 'population of only 300,000 persons; it now numbers 2,300,000. 'In the same period of time this enormous increase exceeds 'that on any other equal surface of the globe, and is entirely 'owing to the development of the cotton trade. In 1856 there 'were, in the United Kingdom, 2,210 factories, running '28,000,000 spindles and 209,000 looms, by 97,000 horse- 'power. Since that period a considerable number of new mills 'have been erected, and extensive additions have been made to 'the spinning and weaving machinery of those previously in 'existence.

'The amount of actual capital invested in the cotton trade 'is estimated to be between 60,000,000*l.* and 70,000,000*l.* 'sterling.

'The quantity of cotton imported into this country in 1859 'was 1,181¾ million pounds weight, the value of which at 6*d.* 'per lb. is equal to 30,000,000*l.* sterling. Out of 2,829,110 'bales of cotton imported into Great Britain, America has sup- 'plied us with 2,086,341—that is, 5-7ths of the whole. In 'other words, out of every 7 lbs. imported from all other coun- 'tries into Great Britain, America has supplied 5 lbs. India has 'sent us about 500,000 bales, Egypt about 100,000, South 'America 124,000, and other countries between 8,000,000 and '9,000,000 bales. In 1859 the total value of the exports from 'Great Britain amounted to 130,513,185*l.*, of which 47,020,920*l.* 'consisted of cotton goods and yarns. Thus more than one- 'third, or 1*l.* out of every 3*l.* of our entire exports, consists of

'cotton. Add to this the proportion of cotton which forms
'part of 12,000,000*l*. more exported in the shape of mixed
'woollens, haberdashery, millinery, silks, apparel, and slops.
'Great Britain alone consumes annually 24,000,000*l*. worth of
'cotton goods. Two conclusions, therefore, may safely be drawn
'from the facts and figures now cited: first, that the interests
'of every cotton-worker are bound up with a gigantic trade
'which keeps in motion an enormous mass of capital, and this
'capital, machinery, and labour depend for five-sevenths of its
'employment upon the Slave States of America for prosperity
'and continuance; secondly, that if a war should at any time
'break out between England and America, a general insurrec-
'tion take place among the slaves, disease sweep off those slaves
'by death, or the cotton crop fall short in quantity, whether
'from severe frosts, disease of the plant, or other possible causes,
'our mills would be stopped for want of cotton, employers
'would be ruined, and famine would stalk abroad among the
'hundreds and thousands of workpeople who are at present for-
'tunately well employed.

'Calculate the consequences for yourself. Imagine a dearth
'of cotton, and you may picture the horrors of such a calamity
'from the scenes you may possibly have witnessed when the
'mills have only run on "short time." Count up all the trades
'that are kept going out of the wages of the working classes,
'independent of builders, mechanics, engineers, colliers, &c.,
'employed by the mill-owners. Railways would cease to pay,
'and our ships would lie rotting in their ports, should a scarcity
'of the raw material for manufacture overtake us.'

It has been explained in the preceding pages why many of
the evils anticipated from a dearth of cotton have been avoided
up to the present time. The large stocks of cotton, cotton
goods, and cotton yarns on hand when hostilities commenced,
the unusually extensive trade in breadstuffs since that period,
and the business of supplying both belligerents with the
material of war, have kept back the distress that must yet be
felt unless the American cotton trade be shortly resumed.

The following table shows the course of the trade for the
years 1861 and 1862. In those years a considerable quantity
of cotton was re-shipped to the Federal States of America.

TOTAL IMPORTS AND EXPORTS OF COTTON FROM ALL COUNTRIES.

	American States lbs.	East Indies lbs.	West Indies lbs.
1861 . .	819,500,528	369,040,428	486,304
1862 . .	13,524,224	302,654,528	5,563,370
	833,024,752	761,694,056	6,049,680

	Brazil lbs.	The Mediterranean lbs.	Other Countries lbs.
1861 .	17,290,336	41,479,200	9,187,920
1862 .	23,339,008	65,238,320	23,653,840
	40,629,344	106,717,520	32,841,760

	Total Imported lbs.	Exported lbs.	Excess of Imports lbs.
1861 . .	1,256,984,736	298,287,920	958,696,816
1862 . .	523,973,296	214,714,528	309,258,768
	1,780,958,032	513,002,448	1,267,955,584

The imports of cotton for the six months ending June 30, 1863, were as follows:—American States, 770,112 lbs.; East Indies, 135,049,376 lbs.; Brazil, 13,490,624 lbs.; Egypt, 49,874,832 lbs.; other countries, 39,909,856 lbs. Total, 239,094,800 lbs. The exports were 117,940,256 lbs. Excess of imports, 121,154,544 lbs.

STOCKS OF RAW COTTON OF ALL KINDS IN THE UNITED KINGDOM FROM 1814 TO 1862 INCLUSIVE—DECEMBER 31 OF EACH YEAR.

Year	lbs.	Year	lbs.
1814 . . .	22,272,000	1839 . . .	125,800,000
1815 . . .	22,300,000	1840 . . .	207,000,000
1816 . . .	22,355,000	1841 . . .	216,700,000
1817 . . .	31,034,000	1842 . . .	242,300,000
1818 . . .	85,800,000	1843 . . .	342,000,000
1819 . . .	88,452,000	1844 . . .	390,200,000
1820 . . .	103,458,000	1845 . . .	453,500,000
1821 . . .	106,800,000	1846 . . .	245,400,000
1822 . . .	76,352,000	1847 . . .	184,100,000
1823 . . .	105,875,000	1848 . . .	220,100,000
1824 . . .	64,428,000	1849 . . .	240,300,000
1825 . . .	123,968,000	1850 . . .	231,000,000
1826 . . .	100,548,000	1851 . . .	225,000,000
1827 . . .	134,244,000	1852 . . .	300,000,000
1828 . . .	120,582,000	1853 . . .	304,971,500
1829 . . .	84,966,000	1854 . . .	255,591,600
1830 . . .	95,360,000	1855 . . .	192,642,120
1831 . . .	84,090,000	1856 . . .	137,754,360
1832 . . .	73,560,000	1857 . . .	182,361,530
1833 . . .	94,400,000	1858 . . .	113,959,620
1834 . . .	82,300,000	1859 . . .	197,663,710
1835 . . .	89,600,000	1860 . . .	250,286,605
1836 . . .	116,300,000	1861 . . .	291,674,450
1837 . . .	115,600,000	1862 . . .	100,561,870
1838 . . .	160,900,000		

In 1814, the first year of free trade to India,* the exports of cotton goods amounted to only 818,208 yards, valued at 109,480*l.*, and the shipments of cotton twist to only 8 lbs.—in fact, the business in the latter article amounted to little or nothing until 1822, when 22,200 lbs. were sent thither. The annexed figures will exhibit the increase in commerce with that part of the world.

COTTON EXPORTS FROM ENGLAND TO INDIA, AND IMPORTS FROM THENCE.

Year	Yarn	Calicoes	Weight of Yarns and Goods	Raw Cotton imported from India
	lbs.	Yards	lbs.	lbs.
1835	5,305,212	54,227,084	16,000,000	43,876,820
1841	13,639,562	126,003,400	43,000,000	100,104,510
1845	14,116,237	193,029,703	60,000,000	58,437,426
1857	20,027,859	469,958,011	130,000,000	250,338,144
1858	36,889,583	791,537,041	223,000,000	132,722,576
1859	45,056,189	968,179,390	305,056,189	192,330,880
1860	31,978,364	822,029,210	241,978,364	204,141,168

The year 1857 was, like 1862, an exceptional period for imports of cotton from India. China that year took 121,000,000 yards of cloth. In 1858 91,000,000 lbs. were exported to India in the manufactured state, over the imports of the raw material from thence. The same year the trade with Turkey and Egypt consisted of imports, 38,300,000 lbs.; exports equivalent to 62,000,000 lbs. South America and the West Indies also took more cotton than they sent to the United Kingdom.

Early in 1860, the Chairman of the Manchester Chamber of Commerce, at a meeting of that body, drew the attention of the members to the state of the cotton trade—and this was at a time when the American war was not thought of—to its amazing increase during the previous twelve months, and to the necessity there was for forethought, and an examination of the position they then occupied in regard to the trade. He said :—

'He had made, at some trouble, a calculation of the probable 'exports of cotton goods for the present year. These would very

* On April 14, 1814, the trade to India was opened to private adventure, and the 'monopoly' of the East India Company of course ceased from that date.

' nearly amount to 46,000,000*l.*, which would be nearly an in-
' crease of 3,000,000*l.* on last year, and of 5,000,000*l.* upon the
' year previous. [It will be borne in mind that only a small part
' of the large crop of 1859 had then come forward.] That was
' a startling increase; but on coming to look whence it arose, it
' would be seen that it was due solely to one portion of the
' world—India and China. Looking at the whole state of the
' cotton trade, we *had not yet recovered from the depreciation*
' *before* 1857. If it had not been for the increase in the exports
' to India, the cotton trade would not have stood in as good a
' position as it was previous to the crisis. The cause of the
' great increase in the demand for goods for India arose in the
' amazing increase in the capital sent out to that country, which,
' during the last three years, would not amount to less than
' 60,000,000*l.* We must not consider the present state of the
' cotton trade as the normal one, for unless these loans were
' continued we should not find the increase of exports continue
' to the East. If so, the state of our cotton trade would be
' much changed in twelve months. The exports to India this
' year would amount to upwards of 17,000,000*l.*, and from this
' it would be seen that the proportion of our cotton exports to
' the East was 17,000,000*l.* out of 46,000,000*l.* If our cotton
' trade was to be increased it must probably be with the East,
' and this brought him to the question of the policy of the
' Indian Government. The report stated that they had sent out
' a resolution protesting against any increased duties on manu-
' factures to the East. There was a rumour afloat that these
' duties were to be increased, and if they were, they would
' materially affect our prosperity. Nothing could be more un-
' sound in policy than increased duties on manufactured goods,
' going into a part really of our own country. It was burning
' the candle at both ends, so to speak; taxing ourselves for ex-
' ports from India, and for the imports of the same goods again.'

Setting aside the economic question of tariffs, the people of
India will never have any occasion to send their own cotton to
England to be returned to them in the manufactured state.
They are, however, willing to sell their staple to Europeans, and
to take in return that of America, after it has been converted
into textile fabrics by British looms, for the reason that it is a

different article from that which they produce. On the very same principle, the Southerners find it to their interest to purchase the gunny cloth of India, imported through England and the North, to use as bagging for their cotton. The Americans, too, by their imports of British and other European manufactures, consume a considerable portion of India and other foreign cottons. Trade never works one-sidedly; as the prosperity of India increases, her demand for goods will be still more considerable. Step by step as the exports of cotton from India augment, her demand for dry goods becomes greater.

A correspondent of 'The Times,' on August 27, 1863, alluding to the visionary scheme of the 'African Aid Society' for procuring an adequate supply of cotton from Africa, says:—' The identical passage is incorporated in the pro-
' spectus of a joint-stock company launched last year for
' carrying on a cotton and general trade with the districts in
' question—with what success up to the present time the public
' would no doubt feel gratified to know ; although, as the gen-
' tleman who was appointed its *gérant* honourably distinguished
' himself the other day by an attempt to entrap the captain of
' the steamer Southerner, then at West Hartlepool, into admis-
' sions as to the ownership and destination of that vessel, on
' which•to lodge an information against her to the Government,
' it would seem from this evidence of his occasional leisure that
' the company is not yet in full swing enough to give unlimited
' scope to his activity—unless, indeed, it comes within the com-
' pass of the scheme to clear the cotton market of the risks and
' chances of Southern competition, and this was one expedient for
' that purpose. Be this as it may, it is clear from the cotton
' importation returns just published that, although the experi-
' ment has been for some time in progress, the prospect of obtain-
' ing any important quantity of cotton from West Africa is so far
' a signal failure. . . . . To candid and intelligent minds the
' answer is self-evident — viz., that, from whatever cause it may
' arise, the prospect of any considerable immediate importation
of cotton from West Africa is a sheer delusion.' The receipts thence, Jan. to July 1863, were 625 cwt. against 1,250 cwt. 1862.

The table (pp. 130, 131), gives the exports of cotton manufactures 1820 to 1862 inclusive :—

K

STATEMENT OF THE QUANTITY AND DECLARED VALUE OF BRITISH MANUFACTURED GOODS EXPORTED FROM THE UNITED KINGDOM, DISTINGUISHING THE DESCRIPTION OF GOODS IN EACH YEAR, FROM 1820 TO 1841.

Year	White and Plain Cottons		Printed and Dyed Cottons		Hosiery and Small Wares	Twist and Yarn		Total Declared Value
	Yards	Declared Value	Yards	Declared Value	Declared Value	Pounds	Declared Value	
		£		£	£		£	£
1820	113,682,486	5,451,024	134,688,144	7,742,505	496,580	23,032,325	2,826,639	16,516,748
1821	122,921,692	5,713,722	146,412,002	7,454,243	619,999	21,526,369	2,305,823	16,093,787
1822	151,162,131	6,317,973	150,999,157	7,480,634	722,535	26,595,468	2,697,582	17,218,274
1823	152,184,705	5,884,935	149,631,387	7,095,709	720,014	27,378,986	2,625,946	16,326,604
1824	170,091,384	6,437,817	174,559,749	8,010,432	869,336	33,605,510	3,135,396	18,452,989
1825	158,039,786	6,027,892	178,426,912	8,205,117	919,787	32,641,604	3,206,729	18,359,526
1826	138,159,783	4,477,942	128,897,111	5,388,592	735,497	42,189,661	3,491,338	14,093,369
1827	183,940,186	5,762,576	181,544,618	7,184,459	1,144,552	44,878,774	3,545,578	17,637,165
1828	189,475,956	5,623,802	173,852,475	6,859,447	1,165,763	50,505,751	3,595,405	17,244,417
1829	222,504,344	5,853,625	180,012,152	6,662,623	1,041,885	61,441,251	3,976,874	17,535,006
1830	244,799,032	6,562,397	199,790,466	7,557,373	1,175,153	64,645,342	4,133,741	19,428,664
1831	239,191,261	6,065,478	182,194,032	6,098,035	1,118,672	63,281,440	3,975,019	17,257,204
1832	259,493,096	5,854,924	201,552,407	5,645,706	1,175,003	75,667,150	4,722,759	17,398,392
1833	259,519,864	5,847,840	236,832,232	6,603,220	1,331,317	70,626,161	4,704,024	18,486,401
1834	283,950,158	6,514,173	271,755,651	7,613,179	1,175,219	76,478,468	5,211,015	20,513,586
1835	277,704,525	6,910,506	279,811,176	8,270,925	1,240,284	83,214,198	5,706,589	22,128,304
1836	324,467,179	7,985,349	313,200,448	9,197,818	1,328,525	88,191,046	6,120,366	24,632,058
1837	286,164,256	6,085,789	245,209,407	6,642,200	912,192	103,455,138	6,955,942	20,596,123
1838	363,357,845	7,293,831	326,719,777	8,260,902	1,161,124	114,596,602	7,431,869	24,147,726
1839	380,168,656	7,535,799	351,281,467	8,842,646	1,313,737	105,686,442	6,858,193	24,550,375
1840	433,114,373	7,803,772	357,517,624	8,498,448	1,265,090	118,470,223	7,101,308	24,068,618
1841	421,884,732	7,213,075	329,240,892	7,772,735	1,246,700	123,226,519	7,266,968	23,499,478

STATEMENT OF THE QUANTITY AND DECLARED VALUE OF BRITISH MANUFACTURED GOODS EXPORTED FROM THE UNITED KINGDOM, DISTINGUISHING THE DESCRIPTION OF GOODS IN EACH YEAR, FROM 1842 TO 1862.

Year	White and Plain Cottons		Printed and Dyed Cottons		Hosiery and Small Wares	Twist and Yarn		Total Declared Value
	Yards	Declared Value	Yards	Declared Value	Declared Value	Pounds	Declared Value	
		£		£	£		£	£
1842	435,519,311	6,590,945	298,579,498	6,296,275	1,020,664	137,466,892	7,771,464	21,679,348
1843	562,575,205	8,024,287	356,065,000	7,144,177	1,085,536	140,321,176	7,193,971	23,447,971
1844	623,249,423	9,346,865	403,421,400	8,265,281	1,204,618	138,540,179	6,988,584	25,805,348
1845	678,415,780	9,661,014	413,270,289	8,368,794	1,126,288	135,144,865	6,963,235	26,119,331
1846	697,809,454	9,354,268	367,651,135	7,347,364	1,016,146	161,892,750	9,882,048	25,599,826
1847	541,143,488	8,057,815	401,396,672	8,149,288	1,168,142	120,270,741	5,957,980	23,333,225
1848	657,087,785	7,929,341	445,664,038	7,784,516	1,042,512	135,831,162	5,927,831	22,681,200
1849	795,112,527	9,457,721	542,423,591	9,337,243	1,276,082	149,502,281	6,704,089	26,775,135
1850	772,161,813	9,935,891	586,021,128	10,594,604	1,343,362	131,370,368	6,383,704	28,257,401
1851	965,474,560	11,789,581	577,687,229	10,259,621	1,405,608	143,966,106	6,634,026	30,088,836
1852	953,022,042	11,596,380	571,234,872	10,052,078	1,574,974	145,478,302	6,654,655	29,878,087
1853	936,228,566	12,072,039	658,364,093	11,829,901	1,915,309	147,539,302	6,895,653	32,712,902
1854	1,101,471,222	13,129,155	591,427,900	10,352,351	1,573,021	147,128,498	6,691,330	31,745,857
1855	1,243,517,609	14,527,055	694,216,416	11,596,422	1,455,269	165,493,598	7,200,395	34,779,141
1856	1,221,336,776	14,736,849	813,938,193	13,784,710	1,682,607	181,495,805	8,028,575	38,232,741
1857	1,159,885,575	14,513,325	819,385,205	14,273,321	1,586,185	176,821,338	8,700,589	39,073,420
1858	1,527,184,498	18,527,302	796,954,587	13,514,812	1,379,729	200,016,902	9,579,479	43,001,322
1859	1,699,105,334	21,807,583	863,440,142	15,230,955	1,705,575	192,206,643	9,458,112	48,232,225
1860	1,805,092,537	23,309,437	971,125,890	17,036,905	1,795,163	197,343,655	9,870,875	52,012,380
1861	1,734,585,085	21,913,113	828,873,922	14,211,572	1,455,043	177,848,353	9,292,761	46,872,489
1862	996,681,892	15,203,737	684,691,810	13,356,296	2,009,264	93,236,459	6,203,331	36,772,628

K 2

CHAPTER X.

THE WHEAT TRADE OF GREAT BRITAIN, FRANCE, AND AMERICA—
EXPORTS OF PRODUCE FROM THE STATES.

[This paper on the wheat trade was written about a year ago, and published in 'The Index' on September 18, 1862. There is now no reason to change the views then expressed. The *wants* of Great Britain have not been greater than in ordinary seasons, although the *receipts* of wheat and flour within the twelve months have been nearly as large (equivalent to 8,800,000 quarters) as those during the corresponding period ending in 1862. So, instead of the granaries of the United Kingdom having very limited stocks, as was the case on August 31 of last year, they are at present filled to overflowing, and there is probably on hand a greater quantity of wheat and flour than at any former time. The importations of Indian corn have likewise been excessive, 2,500,000 quarters, one-half of which came from America. The warehouses, in fact, are crowded with all kinds of breadstuffs, and prices in consequence rule very low. The wheat harvest of Great Britain and Ireland is supposed to be the most abundant ever known, and the chances are that less foreign grain will be required during the coming year than at any time since 1845. France has resumed her position as an exporter of wheat and flour, and, with Northern Europe, will be fully able to supply any deficiency that may exist in these islands. The exports from the Federal States from September 1, 1862, to August 31, 1863, will amount to about 3,750,000 quarters of wheat and flour, against 6,000,000 quarters the year previous; and 1,250,000 quarters of Indian corn. The shipments from thence for the coming year must necessarily be very trifling in the absence of an European demand; nor is it likely that the surplus produce of the West can possibly reach the figures of the last three seasons, by reason of the scarcity of hands, the drain of men for the war having so reduced the farm labour of the agricultural sections of the country, that women, as in Germany, but for the first time in America, have been employed to reap the crops. It was the rapid advance in the rate of bills on London that induced the large shipments of cereals to this side of the Atlantic; but the decline in the prices in England, in consequence of the 'glut' of produce, has been greater than the anticipated profits. The fall in the value of gold, caused by Mr. Chase's 'bearing' the market, reducing the quotations for foreign exchange, coupled with dull and drooping accounts received from Europe, has put a check upon this commerce, which has supplied the Northern States since the election of Mr. Lincoln, including the freights and insurances, with very nearly forty millions of pounds sterling. This exceptional trade has, therefore, in a measure, balanced the loss to the Federals, by the absence of the handling of cotton and the other productions of the South; and by putting them in possession of an immense amount of specie funds, the grand crash in their finances, which is now imminent, has thus far been avoided.]

THE course of business in wheat for the past two years is without a parallel in the history of commerce. Under the benign influence of free trade the extraordinary wants of Western Europe have been supplied at moderate prices. The usual annual importations of flour and wheat from all places into Great Britain and Ireland are equivalent to a little under 5,000,000 quarters, but the bad harvest of 1860 necessitated a draft from other countries of 10,000,000 quarters, and the short crops of 1861, with the 1,000,000 quarters exported to the continent early in the season, have demanded about 9,000,000 quarters to be brought from abroad; this latter quantity would have been much increased but for the economy in consumption in the manufacturing districts, and the smaller stocks than usual at present held by the middle men that furnish those neighbourhoods. England began the commercial year with a less amount of old wheat on hand than ever before; the harvest of 1862, however, owing to the additional breadth of land sown with that grain, is, no doubt, over an average; the drain from other countries for the year ending August 31, 1863, will therefore probably not exceed the usual quantity, 5,000,000 quarters. The annual consumption of the British Islands is 22,500,000 quarters, with 3,000,000 quarters taken for seed, making 25,500,000 quarters; the usual production is 20,500,000 quarters, leaving 5,000,000 quarters to be received from other sources. In addition to wheat, the importations of Indian corn are generally about 1,500,000 quarters, but they reached 3,000,000 quarters last year. The population of the United Kingdom is 29,031,298.

Prior to the year 1775 each one of the three divisions of the United Kingdom produced more grain of every kind than was required for its people, oftentimes exporting to foreign parts. After that date a reverse current set in, and the consumption outstripped the quantity grown. The annual deficiency up to 1825 was about 50,000 quarters wheat; in 1835, 750,000 quarters; in 1845, 2,500,000 quarters; in 1851 it had reached 5,000,000 quarters. The average production per acre is twenty-five bushels.

The wheat crops of France, including Savoy and Nice, average 37,000,000 quarters, of which 6,000,000 quarters are retained for seed, 29,500,000 quarters consumed, and 1,500,000 exported. The harvest of the last year (1861), however, was deficient, 6,000,000 quarters being brought from other parts. The growth of this season is said to be much larger than usual, and it is expected that there will be a surplus of 3,000,000 quarters. The cultivation of wheat in recent years has much increased; in 1850, 14,700,000 acres were occupied with that grain; in 1862, 18,000,000 acres. The average production is seventeen bushels to the acre.

France is the largest bread-consuming country in the world; her population is about 37,000,000; besides wheat, she requires 10,000,000 quarters of rye, which is mostly produced from her own soil; also considerable quantities of maize; chesnuts, too, are an important article of food : it is said that 2,000,000 of her inhabitants subsist upon them.

In ordinary years the exportation of wheat from all the American States does not much exceed 1,000,000 quarters, sometimes not over 150,000 quarters ; the exceptions have been for the period ending August 31, 1847, when 3,000,000 quarters were shipped ; for that closing in 1854, 2,000,000 ; in 1856, 2,750,000 ; in 1857, 2,250,000 ; in 1858, 2,000,000 ; in 1861, 5,000,000 ; and in 1862, 6,000,000 quarters. The vast surplus quantity on these occasions can readily be accounted for. For several years prior to the expiration of the Charter of the Bank of the United States in 1836, there had been great speculations in America, so much so that a considerable portion of the inhabitants of the West had become consumers instead of producers ; the consequence was that agricultural pursuits were neglected to such an extent that large importations of grain were made from the Mediterranean in that year to supply the deficiency. The panic of 1837 caused the people to return to their regular occupations as farmers, which enabled the States to meet the slight European demand for cereals that existed in 1839, and was the means of causing an accumulation of wheat for the year 1847, which helped to balance the short crop here in 1846, known as the Irish famine year. With the exception of a moderate business in 1853 and 1854, the wheat trade of America was very trifling; the production being very little beyond the consumption. None of the Northern Atlantic States grew enough for their own wants, and their populations had to be supplied by Virginia and the West. The Russian war intervening cut off the usual supplies from that quarter, and America was called upon for an increased quantity in 1856, at high prices, which stimulated large shipments the following year, with disastrous results, peace having restored the commerce with the North of Europe. The extravagant quotations of 1856 induced much speculation in the West, and gave a fabulous value to land; people rushed to the New States by thousands, and wheat fell from $2\frac{1}{2}$ to 80 cents a bushel; cities that were constructed upon paper were swept from the map; railways partially completed were left unfinished; and the bubble burst in 1857. Large tracts of country were, for this reason, thrown open to the husbandman, who was then joined by the speculators, who were obliged to resume their calling of tillers of the soil. The Southern States at this period, in consequence of the advanced price in cotton, devoted more of their labour to the production of that staple, and purchased a portion of their provisions from their neighbours north of the Ohio; and hence the extraordinary large crops of cotton in 1858, 1859, and 1860. The Western people thus finding a market for their increased yield of cereals, were induced to cultivate grain still more extensively, and their wheat crops, as well as those of Indian corn, were therefore unprecedentedly great in 1860 and 1861; and the anticipated traffic caused the completion of many of the unfinished lines of railway. The dissolution of the Union, however, which took place at this juncture, deprived them of their Southern custom; and had it not been for the short crops of the United Kingdom in those

two years, and in France and other points on the continen.
the latter season, they would have had no market for their
produce ; but the European demand stepped in and relieved
them of 5,000,000 quarters of wheat and flour for the twelve
months ending August 31, 1861, and of 6,000,000 quarters for
the year closing at the same time in 1862. Notwithstanding
the large quantities of breadstuffs taken by the Southern States
in the three last years of the Union, their food resources are
greater, considering the population, than those of all the other
States combined. This is proved by the census figures of 1860.

Although the shipments of wheat for the two seasons closing
August 31, 1861 and 1862, have been so large, they have yielded
little profit to the farmer ; prices have not been high, and the
gross proceeds at the seaboard were eaten up by the heavy expense
of inland transportation, commissions, &c. No inducement has,
therefore, been offered for a continuance of such extensive cultivation. In fact, the land is being worn out : no manures are
used ; and as the agriculturist moves farther West to break
virgin soil, he is subjected to increased expense in getting his
supplies from, and his produce to, market. So the limit of production has not only been reached, but the increased price of
labour, caused by a scarcity of hands, is another obstacle to
the planting of large crops. It must be borne in mind, too,
that the winters in the North-west, where the grain is principally produced, are so severe, that the seed is committed to
the ground in the spring, and not in the autumn, as in most
countries. The seasons of 1860 and 1861 happened to be
unusually early. The harvest of 1862, as far as known, is not as
large as its two immediate predecessors, and with low quotations
on this side of the Atlantic, it cannot be moved forward to the
shipping points at remunerating prices.

The commerce in breadstuffs between the American States
and the West Indian and South American ports has been carried
on with flour made from wheat grown in the Southern States
of Delaware, Maryland, Virginia, Tennessee, Kentucky, and
Missouri, on account of the superiority of the grain ; in fact, the
large cities on the Atlantic have for the same reason also been
fed by the produce of these States.*

* The Philadelphia ‘North American’ of April 1, 1863, a Republican

The average number of quarters of wheat grown in all the American States is computed at 28,000,000, of which 5,000,000 are retained for seed, leaving 21,000,000 quarters for consumption (13,000,000 quarters in the North and 8,000,000 quarters in the South), and 2,000,000 quarters for exportation. The average production per acre does not exceed thirteen bushels.

In the rural districts of America, Indian corn is a leading staple of food ; so is rye. The exportations of the former are very large, and those of the latter are occasionally of considerable moment. The Southern States produced in 1860 55,000,000 quarters of Indian corn, against 50,000,000 quarters grown in the Northern States. The joint population of the North and South .is 31,151,046 — viz. 18,907,753 North, 12,243,293 South.

It will be observed that the United States, unlike Russia, is not naturally a grain-exporting country, and that the business in wheat, the past two years, has been an exception, and not a rule ; that the boast of the Northerners, that ' England cannot get on without her breadstuffs,' is most idle in its character—every intelligent corn merchant being aware that Northern Europe has at all times an almost inexhaustible supply of cereals, should the price be high enough to pay for the inland transportation. The grain crops in the South this year (1862) are very much greater than formerly, in consequence of the hands being employed in that description of agriculture, instead of cotton, tobacco, and sugar.

In the minds of Europeans the South, commercially, has hitherto been associated only with its cotton, tobacco, rice, naval stores, &c., while it should really have been regarded as the great agricultural portion of the United States. Its grain-raising advantages, particularly for winter wheat, are unsurpassed ; possessed of a climate which keeps the meadows always green, and obviates the necessity of providing hay in any considerable

newspaper, confirms this statement as follows :—' We showed last summer, ' from the census tables, that during the decade previous to 1860, the whole ' South had made considerable and somewhat remarkable progress in the ' production of wheat. This was owing to the popularity in our market of ' the Southern varieties of wheat, and the increasing demand for it among ' our millers.'

quantity for the maintenance of cattle in winter, there is practically no limit to its capabilities for producing live stock. This same equability of climate is, moreover, assisted by the steadiness of the most skilled agricultural labour in the world, and hence the great regularity in the increase of the growth of all its productions. The Southerners are not constantly changing their occupations, as has been the habit of the Northerners; but they have ever exhibited the same persevering energy in all their civil affairs that they have shown in their military movements since the struggle against Northern tyranny commenced. A people that is always being led off by speculations, and not content with legitimate employment, is like a man who frequently changes his business—he gains no real wealth—this applies to the North. A nation that pursues the even tenor of its way undisturbed by the visionary schemes of the hour, is comparable to a good merchant, who, although he may be considered somewhat 'slow,' in the end is sure to reap success—this applies to the South.

It has been a mistake to suppose that the Confederate States were dependent upon the North or West for food; a very small portion of their land is employed in the cultivation of the leading staples—cotton, tobacco, sugar, and rice. No country has such self-sustaining power, as has been proved by the experience of the last eighteen months, and no country is capable of giving such benefits to other nations, as will be proved when its ports are opened to the free commerce of the world.

CHAPTER XI.

AMERICAN CURRENCY AND COMMERCE — THE WEST INDIA TRADE — GENERAL REMARKS.

HISTORIANS and nearly all other writers on America have with one accord based their arguments upon the foregone conclusion that the States were indebted to the Constitution for all those advantages, material and political, that until lately they enjoyed as members of the Federal Union. This fallacy originated in the fact that, while the colonies flourished by unrestricted intercourse with the other possessions of Great Britain, a marked decline was visible in their prosperity after their establishment as States, by reason of their exclusion from trade with the islands. This decline, however, was attributed to 'want of strength' in the Articles of Confederation. Surely, when under those Articles, the States succeeded in bringing the revolutionary war to a successful issue in the face of almost insurmountable difficulties, they might, if fairly tested and amended, have been made to answer the purposes of a peace establishment. In truth, the conflict with the parent country had been carried on for six years by the Continental Congress, composed of delegates from the thirteen colonies. It was not until March 2, 1781, less than eight months previous to the decisive event at Yorktown (October 19, 1781), that the 'Confederation' was formed. The merits of the 'Union' then, as since under the Constitution, have been unreasonably over-estimated. The 'United 'States' have never had a 'name,' and there was no occasion even to give the Confederacy a 'local habitation.' It was a false step to dedicate any particular spot for the capital of a league of States; it would have been far better to have preserved the archives and held the sessions of Congress in some old-established city. Great trouble arose in reference to the 'location' at the very outset of the operation of the Constitution, and recent events prove very clearly that the possession of neutral territory alone gives strength and force to the Lincoln Administration.* Let the Confederates once seize the capital and destroy the vipers' nest, and the backbone of tyranny in America will be broken. Washington politics and Washington society have been degenerating for years, under the influence of Northern spoilsmen, who have gone thither to attain their own selfish ends. The hotels have been crowded with 'lobby men' from New York and New England; it became one of the most disreputable cities in the world, with a population that gambled away the prosperity of the sovereign States and the very life of the Government. The conservative influences of commerce, the arts, sciences, and manufactures, were much needed to give a tone of sobriety and responsibility to the place. It certainly was a great mistake to make the Federal seat of Government of so much importance. Why should a league of States have jurisdiction anywhere, except on the ocean — the highway of nations? The laws of the respective States protect life and property. And how unjust it has been that in a Republic the citizens of the District of Columbia were deprived of a representation in Congress, or a voice in the selection of President. A resident of Washington, no matter how great his qualifications, could not be a senator or member of the House of Representatives, or President or Vice-President, as persons

* During the sitting of the Congress of the Confederation at Philadelphia in 1783, that body was insulted by some riotous troops who had not been paid. The authorities of Pennsylvania were so timid that they failed to repress the outbreak, when the representatives of the States removed to Princeton, New Jersey. While at that place, the question of a permanent residence with jurisdiction for the 'Government' was raised, and excited a good deal of local feeling; one party was in favour of the Delaware, another the Potomac; Maryland offered to cede Annapolis; New York volunteered Kingston on the Hudson. The Philadelphians apologised for their dereliction of duty, and invited Congress back to their city. It was finally agreed that two Federal capitals should be erected, at which the sessions of Congress should be alternately held, one near the Falls of the Delaware, the other near the Falls of the Potomac. In the following year commissioners were appointed to lay out a Federal city near the Falls of the Delaware, and $100,000 was voted for the purpose of erecting public buildings. A resolution was passed that it was inexpedient to build more than one capital city at that time. Nothing, however, was done in the matter until after the adoption of the Constitution.

holding those offices must by law be domiciled in the States. There has been something radically wrong in the arrangement from the beginning to the end.   It evoked an overestimate of the importance that should be attached to the Union, and there is no doubt that the moral effect produced thereby has caused the people of the North to enter upon that career of madness and cruelty that brings down on them the condemnation of the civilised world.   The following graphic and truthful description of the course of affairs at Washington was given some time ago by the 'Times' :—

'What, may we ask, did Congress meet for at Washington? 'Did these senators and representatives do anything for the 'people who sent them to the Federal capital?   Did they im- 'prove the laws of the States?   Did they make railroads or 'canals, or perform any of the usual duties of legislation?   No; 'they merely took their seats to listen to, to join in, acrimonious 'disputes on the everlasting subject of slavery.   To talk about 'slavery, to abuse each other, defy each other, bludgeon each 'other about slavery, was the whole occupation of the Federal 'Congress.   To this one question every other was made subser- 'vient.   Whether a duty was imposed, or a new State admitted, 'the interests of the two rival sections were pitted against each 'other as if they had been hostile States making a treaty of 'peace instead of component parts of the same nation.   How, 'then, can it be said by Mr. Seward that society on the Ame- 'rican continent could encounter no reverse so disastrous as the 'division of the American Union?   To us, on the contrary, it 'seems that the Union has been long ago divided, that the pro- 'phecy of Jefferson has been fulfilled, and that the coincidence 'of a geographical line with a division of interests and institu- 'tions have long since made North and South two nations.   The 'withdrawal from the same Confederacy is only the formal re- 'cognition of this diversity.   What, indeed, does it amount to? 'Merely that the two sections of the Union will not commit to 'the same authority the management of their post-office, their 'mint, and their national defences.   In every other respect they 'will remain the same.   As each State legislated for itself be- 'fore, so it will now.   As each determined for itself the question 'of freedom or slavery within its borders, so it will now.   Why

'should Virginia go to war with New York, or South Carolina
'with Massachusetts, simply because they do not send delegates
'to quarrel in the same dreary capital?   Under a Constitution
'which had become an anachronism, and which could never be
'modified, the situation of the Federal States had become in-
'tolerable.   A mischievous Union has bred the war now raging.
'The best hope of permanent peace is a final separation.'

The Americans did not wish at first a separation from
England.   They merely desired to resist taxation sought to
be imposed upon them by an assembly in which they were
unrepresented, and to withstand an assumption of authority on the part of King and Parliament that they held to
be antagonistic to the first principles of British freedom.
They had repelled by moral force the encroachments upon
their liberties in the matter of the Stamp Act in 1765, and
had hoped for equal success in obtaining a repeal of the
indirect taxes that were subsequently attempted to be levied
upon them by duties on importations; they were even content
to abstain from luxuries—to do without tea, in order to avoid
a difficulty with the parent country: but they could not have
it 'forced down their throats,' and thus the 'rebellion' was
inaugurated at Boston on December 14, 1773.   'Coercion'
was commenced at the battle of Lexington, April 19, 1775,
although the other colonies had, prior to that time, agreed
to come to the rescue of Massachusetts—the Virginians declaring that 'an attack upon one colony was an attack upon all.'
Even after this the American subjects of the English king had
little wish to make themselves independent 'citizens.'

In the Continental Congress held at Philadelphia, Franklin,
on July 12, 1775, presented a plan for 'Articles of Confederation
and *Perpetual* Union,' which was the groundwork for those
finally adopted on March 1, 1781.   Article 13 said:—

'13th. Any and every colony from Great Britain upon the
'continent of North America not at present engaged in our
'association, may, upon application and joining the said associa-
'tion, be received into the Confederation — viz. Quebec, St.
'John's, Nova Scotia, Bermudas, and the East and West
'Floridas, and shall thereupon be entitled to all the advantages
'of our Union, mutual assistance, and commerce.

' These Articles shall be proposed to the several provincial
' conventions or assemblies, to be by them considered; and if
' approved, they are advised to empower their delegates to agree
' and ratify the same in the ensuing Congress; after which *the
' Union thereby established is to continue firm till the terms of
' reconciliation proposed in the petition of the last Congress to
' the King are agreed to; till the acts since made, restraining
' the American colonies and fisheries, are repealed; till repa-
' ration is made for the injury done to Boston by shutting up
' its port; for burning Charleston; and for the expense of this
' unjust war; and till all the British troops are withdrawn
' from America. On the arrival of these events, the colonies
' are to return to their former connection and friendship with
' Great Britain; but on failure thereof, this Confederation is
' to be perpetual.'*

It was not until nearly a year afterwards, July 4, 1776, that
the Declaration of Independence was approved by Congress, and
promulgated to the world.

The revolution terminated by the Treaty of Peace, 1783,*
although politically successful, inflicted a great blow upon the
commercial prosperity, internal and external, of the American
people, especially as regarded the Northern States, which enjoyed
but a limited outlet for their surplus produce, after being deprived of what had previously formed a great source of profit—
that business which had enabled them to meet their balances
in Europe—their unobstructed trade with the British West
Indies. The loss was of course felt by the agricultural and
other classes as well as the mercantile interests, who, in order
to ' protect' themselves, inaugurated a system of tariffs and tonnage dues, which in turn embarrassed their relations equally with
the Southern States and foreign countries, and, consequently,
prejudiced themselves in a corresponding degree. Nor was
there any direct intercourse with the Spanish- and Portuguese-

---

* On March 4, 1782, the House of Commons passed a resolution in
favour of peace. Provisional articles were signed by the British and
American Ambassadors at Paris on November 30, 1782. The armistice
declaring a cessation of hostilities was dated at Versailles, January 20, 1783.
Peace was proclaimed by Congress on April 11, 1783. The definite treaty
was signed at Paris on September 3, 1783.

American colonies. The commodities in mutual demand between the States and the possessions of those two kingdoms had to be first exchanged at a port of the dominant power, and afterwards transported under its flag to the subject country. The Congress of the Confederation, although entrusted with all diplomatic affairs of the States, had no power to regulate commerce between them, or with other nations. Their mercantile intercourse with all parts of the world was, therefore, seriously trammelled.

So early as 1781 a member of the Continental Congress proposed that the States should give that body power to levy duties on imports for purposes of revenue, say 5 per cent., to be continued until the payment of the existing debt; but the plan was rejected. It was also suggested that Congress should have the regulating of the commerce between the States, but that was likewise negatived. After the adoption of the Articles of Confederation, similar projects were entertained, with proposed limitations of twenty-five years; but in 1783 they shared the fate of their predecessors. Again, in 1784, the subject was under consideration. The following extracts are from a report of a committee presented on April 30 of that year:—

' Already has Great Britain adopted regulations destructive
' of our commerce with her West India Islands. There was reason
' to expect that measures so unequal, and so little calculated to
' promote mercantile intercourse, would not be persevered in by
' an enlightened nation. But their measures are growing into a
' system. It would be the duty of Congress, as it is their wish,
' to meet the attempts of Great Britain with similar restrictions
' upon her commerce; but their powers on this head are not
' explicit, and the propositions made by the legislatures of the
' several States render it necessary to take the general sense of
' the Union on this subject.

' Unless the United States in Congress assembled shall be
' vested with powers competent to the protection of commerce,
' they can never command reciprocal advantages in trade; and
' without them our foreign commerce must decline, and eventu-
' ally be annihilated. Hence it is necessary that the States
' should be explicit, and fix on some effectual mode by which
' foreign commerce not founded on principles of equality may
' be restrained.'

The committee then proposed that the States should give the Central Government control of their foreign commerce for a period of fifteen years. But the States refused to concur in the proposition. The condition of affairs in the North became worse every year. The farmers were behind-hand in their taxes, and harassed for payment by the courts. In Massachusetts there was an open rebellion in 1786, and the laws were set at defiance, The Union was considered to involve a useless expense. Congress having failed in every other effort to obtain authority over commerce — inter-State as well as foreign — by appealing directly to the States for such power, concluded to call a general Convention; and, on February 21, 1787, by a majority of one — it voted by *States* — passed the following preamble and resolution:—

' Whereas, there is a provision, in the Articles of Confedera-
'tion and Perpetual Union, for making alterations therein, by
'the assent of a Congress of the United States and of the
' Legislatures of the several States, and whereas experience has
' evinced that there are defects in the present Confederation—
' as a means to the remedy of which several of the States, and
' particularly of the State of New York, by express instruction
' to their delegates in Congress, have suggested a Convention for
' the purpose expressed in the following resolution, and such
' Convention appearing to be the most probable means of
' establishing, in the States, a firm national Government—

' *Resolved*, That, in the opinion of Congress, it is expedient
' that, on the second Monday of May next, a convention of dele-
' gates, who shall have been appointed by the several States, be
' held in Philadelphia, for the *sole* and *express* purpose of
' *revising the Articles of Confederation* and reporting to Con-
' gress, and the several legislatures, such *alterations* and *pro-
' visions therein* as shall render the *Federal Constitution*
' adequate to the exigencies of the Government and the preser-
' vation of *the Union.*'

In accordance with this resolution delegates were appointed : they met at Philadelphia, May 14, 1787, but the Convention was not organised until May 25, when a quorum of States — seven — were represented. The Constitution was adopted on September 17, 1787, when the Convention adjourned. It concludes with the words, 'Done in Convention, by the *unanimous* consent of *the States* present.' This clause is somewhat ambiguous, and has led to a mistaken impression that the Constitution received the assent of every member of the Convention.* Colonel Hamilton was the only signer from New York; his colleagues, declaring that they had no authority to overthrow the Articles of Confederation, withdrew from the deliberations; and Mr. Randolph and Colonel Mason of Virginia, and Mr. Gerry of Massachusetts, refused to subscribe their names to the instrument. Nor did the Constitution receive the signatures of the following delegates who attended the Convention:—Caleb Strong of Massachusetts, Oliver Ellsworth of Connecticut, William C. Houston of New Jersey, John Francis Mercer and Luther Martin of Maryland, George Wythe and James McClurg of Virginia, Alexander Martin and William R. Davie of North Carolina, and William Pierce and William Houston of Georgia. Patrick Henry of Virginia refused even to countenance the proceedings.

A large number of the delegates to the Convention were Federalists—a term applied to those who desired to consolidate the States and absorb their authority in a strong central government. Though sincerely and patriotically intended, their policy was a mistaken one, and opposed to the feeling of the people of each State, who were, for many reasons, averse to abandoning their position as sovereign communities. It was impossible to make one nation out of thirteen distinct States, differing widely in the character and feelings of their inhabitants, and whose climates and productions rendered their interests incompatible as homogeneous parts of a single empire. The Federalists made no allowance for extent of territory, or increase in population consequent on the rapid influx of emigrants from Europe. Nor, it must be remembered, had the cultivation of cotton as a crop commenced at that time: this has since caused the Southern States to diverge more and more widely in character,

---

* Mr.'Madison, in his reports of the 'Debates in the Federal Convention,' admits that this clause was a 'trick.' He says: 'This ambiguous form had been drawn up by Mr. Gouverneur Morris, in order to gain the dissenting members, and put into the hands of Dr. Franklin, that it might have the better chance of success.'

habits, and social organisation from the North; they have become relatively less mercantile than previous to the revolution. New England, New York, New Jersey, and Pennsylvania, on the other hand, having but little outlet for their surplus produce, declined as agricultural States; their inhabitants were, therefore, encouraged to exert their energies in commerce, in mining, and in the manufacture of that staple which the South from that time so abundantly supplied. The North-west was then un-settled; and the entire domain beyond· the Mississippi was under the jurisdiction of Spain. The 'foreign element,' in-stead of being diffused among the States, as was the case while colonies, has, since Independence, been confined nearly altogether to the North. Statesmen should have foreseen, at least, some of these changes; but one of the great parties of the day was blind to the teachings of history, and could not, therefore, view the future. The Federalists enthusias-tically supported the principles to which they were attached; the 'State Rights' men held to theirs with equal tenacity. The result was that, while the former could not accomplish their object, they took advantage of the necessities of the States for free commercial intercourse, and through this in-fluence succeeded in investing the new Federal head with more powers than were necessary to supply the deficiencies of the Articles of Confederation; these have been the means of creating confusion in the public mind as to the true purport and importance of the general government, and an indirect cause of the present disastrous condition of affairs in America. The great error consisted in *abolishing,* instead of simply *amending,* the Articles of Confederation. In fact, the members of the Convention who voted for the Constitution became nothing less than a body of secessionists; they created what might be called a peaceable revolution, for they disregarded their instructions from the respective States, which were merely to *revise* the Articles of Confederation, the 13th Section of which provides that—

' Every State shall abide by the determination of the United ' States in Congress assembled, on all questions which by this ' Confederation are submitted to them. And the Articles of ' this Confederation shall be inviolably observed by *every State,*

'and *the Union shall be perpetual; nor shall any alteration*
'*at any time hereafter be made* in any of them; unless
'such alteration be agreed to in a Congress of the United
'States, and be afterwards *confirmed by the legislatures of*
'*every State.*'

Yet, in spite of this emphatic and unmistakeable language,
the 'Articles' were abrogated by a portion of the States, and
the 'Constitution' adopted in their stead, containing the following clause:—

'The ratification of the *Conventions* of *nine States* shall be
'*sufficient* for the establishment of this Constitution, *between*
'*the States so ratifying the same.*'

No provision was made for arranging with the dissentient
States for the payment of the public debt, the division of the
public property, or in reference to the 'Crown lands' ceded by
Virginia and other States to the 'Confederation' for the benefit
of *all* the States. This was in violation of a solemn compact.
The rights of four sovereign States which might have refused
to concur were deliberately set aside. The Articles of Confederation, unlike the Constitution, did not reserve for the States,
or imply the right of secession.

The old Congress, too (without any authority under the
'Articles,' which gave them power), so soon as nine States had
acceded to the Constitution, agreed to adjourn on March 3,
1789, and called a new Congress of the members from
those States, which, after much debate, had been cajoled into
confirming the action of the 'Secessionists' of 1787, to
meet on March 4. No quorum, however, of Representatives was present until April 1, or of Senators until the
6th. Washington was not notified of his election as President
until the 14th, and his inauguration did not take place until
April 30, when the operation of the government 'under the
Constitution of the United States of America' commenced.
The Executive and Legislative branches being installed, dated
from that day their power of making laws, and appointing all
the officers necessary to constitute the Judiciary as well as the
Executive departments, with subordinate officers both civil and
military. From March 3 to April 30, no 'union' whatever
existed, and during that period of fifty-eight days each State

might, if so minded, have sent separate ambassadors to the several European Courts.

New York did not unite with the 'Secessionists' on that occasion until after Washington had been elected President. North Carolina did not accede to the arrangement until November 21, 1789, while Rhode Island withheld her assent until May 29, 1790. Washington postponed his Cabinet appointments until September 1789. Mr. Jefferson, to whom he confided the portfolio of the foreign department, was appointed while absent in Europe, and although he returned in November 1789, he did not assume the duties of his office till March 1790.

It so happened that the French Revolution broke out during the very throes of the organisation of the general government under the Constitution. This placed in the hands of the Americans a large share of the carrying trade of the world, and revived their drooping commerce. Such a business was, of course, temporary; but so long as it lasted gave great prosperity to the States. About the same time cotton cultivation was commenced on an extensive scale, and, as has been shown in the preceding pages, soon became a paramount and lasting staple and article of export.

COLONIAL CURRENCY.

The first settlers of a country do not require a great deal of money for a medium of exchange. Trade can be carried on by barter. The coin brought by emigrants generally returns to the parent country for supplies. Such was the condition of the financial affairs of the colonists in Virginia at a very early day. Their Governor, Argall, in 1618, ordered ' that all goods should ' be sold at an advance of 25 per cent., and tobacco taken in ' payment at 3s. per lb., and not more or less, on the penalty of ' three years' servitude to the colony.' In 1623 the ' council ' fixed a scale of exchange between specie and tobacco. Canary, Malaga, Alicant, Muscadel, and Bastard wines were rated at 6s. in specie, or 9s. in tobacco per gallon. Sherry, sack, and aqua-vitæ, at 4s. in specie, or 4s. 6d. in tobacco. Cider and beer-vinegar, at 2s. in specie, or 3s. in tobacco. Newfoundland fish, 2l. in specie, or 3l. 10s. in tobacco per cwt. English meal sold at 10s., and Indian corn at 8s. per bushel. The price of labour was also fixed. The colonists were generally without families, and, in order to supply this deficiency, the London Virginia Company sent over, in 1620, 90 girls, 'young and uncorrupt,' and 60 more the following year. The price of a wife at first was 100 pounds of tobacco, but, 'becoming scarce,' advanced to 150 pounds, the debt so incurred taking precedence of all other claims. In 1641 the General Court of Massachusetts 'made orders about payment of debts, settling corn at the usual 'price, and making it payable for all debts which should arise 'after a time prefixed.' Two years afterwards the same Court ordered 'that Wampompeag should pass current in the payment 'of debts to the amount of 40s., the white at eight a penny, the 'black at four a penny, except at county rates.' This was an article of traffic with the Indians, and did not answer as a legal tender. The measure was, however, in accordance with the orders of 1633, declaring 'that artificers, such as carpenters and 'masons, should not receive more than 2s. a day, and propor- 'tionately, and that merchants should not advance more than 'fourpence in the shilling' above what their goods cost in England. Rice was a legal tender in the Carolinas, and tobacco and maize in Maryland. An unsuccessful attempt was made in Pennsylvania, in 1700, to use 'domestic products' for the same purpose.

There was very little necessity for barter after the year 1640. A clandestine commerce with the Spanish Main, and a trade that had sprung up with the West Indies, caused silver dollars to become very plentiful. The balances, however, being in favour of Great Britain, much of the specie was transmitted in settlement. This excited the jealousy of the colonists, and they attempted by legislative action to prevent the precious metals leaving their shores. Virginia, in 1645, altered the value of the dollar piece, worth four shillings and sixpence sterling, to six shillings, as the measure of currency. The New England colonies did the same. In Pennsylvania, New Jersey, Delaware, and Maryland it was fixed at seven shillings and sixpence; New York and North Carolina rated it at eight shillings; and in South Carolina and Georgia it passed for five shillings. Thus although all accounts were kept in pounds, shillings, and pence, 100l. of money of Great Britain was equal in Virginia and New England to 133⅓*l.*; in Pennsylvania, New Jersey, Maryland, and Delaware, to 166⅔*l.*; in New York and North Carolina, to 177⅛; in South Carolina and Georgia, to 103½*l.** Changing the value of the silver dollar did not have the desired effect, and bills on London have been calculated from that day to this on the basis of its real value, four shillings and sixpence sterling, or four dollars forty cents, and forty-four mills to the pound, without any regard to the currency of the colonies, or that established by the States in 1791. A mint was organised in Boston in 1652 for coining change—shillings, sixpences, and threepenny pieces; it continued its operations until 1682, the abundance of small Spanish coins rendering it unnecessary after that period. Maryland likewise erected a mint for the same purpose in 1662; it lasted about twenty years.

So remunerative was the trade with the West Indies, that in 1698, only sixteen years after the settlement of Pennsylvania, silver was more plentiful in that colony than in England.

Paper money was first issued by Massachusetts in 1690 to pay some clamorous troops who had returned from Quebec, the Government not having made any provision for that purpose, thinking that sufficient treasure would have been wrested from the French. The notes were of all denominations, from 2s. to 10*l.* As long as the bills were moderate in amount, silver continued to be the standard of value. After a second expedition to Canada in 1711, further issues were made, when an inflation commenced; and, in order to satisfy the cry of ' scarcity of money,' silver having entirely disappeared by 1713, the Government of the colony in 1714 emitted 50,000*l.*, and again, in 1716, 100,000*l.* The 5s. notes of 1690 were then worth only 8*d.* in specie. In 1702 an ounce of silver was worth 6s. 8*d.*; in 1749 it was worth 50s. Under the vicious currency

---

* In the Island colonies the same changes were made, viz.—

	Sterling Currency		Dollar Currency		
	£	£	$	s.	d.
Jamaica	100	= 140	1	= 6	8
Barbadoes	100	= 135	1	= 6	3
Windward Islands (except Barbadoes)	100	= 175	1	= 8	3
Leeward Islands . . .	100	= 200	1	= 9	0

the trade of the province declined, and all persons with fixed incomes and salaries were ruined. In 1721 the Governor recommended some measures for preventing the depreciation, but the Assembly idiotically passed a bill for the issue of another 100,000*l.*, which contained a clause prohibiting the buying or selling of silver at any higher rate than that fixed by Acts of Parliament. New Hampshire followed the example of Massachusetts in reference to paper-money; but the amount in circulation at any one time was never very great—only 12,000*l.* were outstanding in 1742. Rhode Island first issued paper-money in 1710, to pay its proportion of the expenses incurred in the expedition against Nova Scotia, and then for the ordinary expenses of Government. Emissions were subsequently made for loans — a system of banking — to its inhabitants. In 1739 the entire sum had reached 399,300*l.* Connecticut, in 1709, met its expenses by paper-money; the notes, however, were soon cancelled by taxes. Other issues were made for various purposes, all of which amounted to 155,000*l.* in 1739. A charter was granted by this colony in 1733 to a society in New London, to circulate 'bills of credit,' but they did not obtain currency among the people, and the Government was induced to create a medium of exchange to the extent of 50,000*l.*

By 1733 there was general mercantile distress throughout New England. The currency, although large, was outstripped by the inflation. Massachusetts and New Hampshire were prevented by royal instructions from issuing any more 'bills of credit.' Rhode Island and Connecticut were under no such restraint, and flooded their neighbours with their notes. The merchants of Boston, too, formed a company, a sort of bank, which circulated 100,000*l.* of bills payable in ten years in silver, at 19*s.* per ounce; but silver rising to 27*s.*, the bills disappeared: they were hoarded. When the 'grand crash' came in 1749, the bills of Massachusetts in the hands of her people amounted to 2,200,000*l.* Exchange on London at eleven for one was the lowest price that had been quoted for several years. In order to redeem the outstanding issues, the colony agreed to compound with her creditors at that rate by paying out 180,000*l.* in silver that had been received from England, as a reimbursement for expenses incurred in obtaining Cape

Breton. This redeemed 1,980,000*l.*, and the remainder was provided for by a special tax. Silver of sterling alloy was then fixed at 6*s.* 8*d.* the ounce, if in bullion, or dollars at 6*s.* each. Massachusetts, however, again issued paper-money.

In 1706 New York commenced her issues of paper-money, for paying the expenses of the colony. Three years afterwards 13,000*l.* of 'public bills' were disbursed, as its share of the cost of the expedition to Canada; they originally bore interest, and did not, as was intended, answer for currency. To prevent hoarding —used as an investment—the interest was repudiated in 1710, when 10,000*l.* more were put in circulation.* Again, in 1714, 2,080*l.* were issued for Government expenditure, payable in twenty years, to be redeemed by an excise on liquors, and in 1717, an addition of 16,607*l.* was made, to be cancelled by duty on wines and rums for seventeen years. These emissions were connived at by the home boards of council, trade, and plantations, and, being made without the royal approbation, established a precedent, which was subsequently taken advantage of. The cost of fortifications, in 1734, was paid by paper issues to the extent of 12,000*l.*, these to be liquidated by an excise on imports prior to 1746; they were followed by an increase of 48,300*l.* in 1738, 40,000*l.* of which were loaned to the people, redeemable in 1750. This redundancy of the currency caused exchange on London to rise to seventy per cent., and silver to 9*s.* 3*d.* per ounce. 15,000*l.* of the issues of 1714 and 1717 remaining in circulation in 1739, it was deemed expedient to extend the excise for fifteen years.

New Jersey, likewise, in 1709, emitted 3,000*l.* of paper-money, as its share of the expenses of the Canadian expedition. In 1711, under pretence of a second invasion, the amount was increased 5,000*l.*, to be gradually redeemed by 1713; but a considerable number of these bills were in circulation as late as

---

* Interest-bearing notes do not answer for currency. The exchequer bills of Great Britain, the treasury notes of the United States, and the more recent emissions of Mr. Chase—the $7\frac{30}{100}$ three years' certificates— have failed to serve that purpose. The last-mentioned class of securities, although the interest was fixed at two cents per day for each hundred dollars, as a matter of convenience to the holders, never passed, as was intended, from hand to hand.

1724. Fresh issues of 40,000*l.* were made that year to cancel the old notes and lend 'money' to the people ; the notes were payable in twelve years, and they were promptly redeemed at maturity. Other notes were issued in 1733, amounting to 20,000*l.*, having sixteen years to run, and a 'loan' was enacted by the Assembly in 1734 for 40,000*l.*, but the bills were not circulated until 1736, in consequence of delay in receiving the royal assent. From that date, New Jersey currency gradually depreciated, and sunk with that of New York, until the emissions of the latter province in 1738, when the bills of the former became sixpence in the pound better, and worth more by one shilling in the pound than those of Pennsylvania. The stability of New Jersey bills, at that period, was owing to their being used as currency in New York and Pennsylvania, while the notes of neither of those colonies circulated in the other.

Pennsylvania, in March 1723, loaned 15,000*l.* in paper-money, taking as security lands or plate ; the bills were a legal tender, and imposed penalties on persons who would value them below specie. 30,000*l.* more were issued in 1724. These bills were to be extinguished by payments of an eighth each year ; and in 1726, the colonists, finding that 6,100*l.* had been thus sunk, obtained an Act for the reissue of the amounts as they were paid in to the Government, and about 30,000*l.* were accordingly kept in circulation for a great length of time. A new issue was made in 1739 on similar terms, which, being beyond the power of the community to absorb, caused exchange to advance from 33 to 75 per cent.

In 1734, the Government of Maryland issued notes to the amount of 90,000*l.*, payable in three periods of fifteen years apart, when exchange advanced from 33 to 150 per cent.

Virginia, as a colony, never had a paper currency.

The Provincial Assembly of Carolina, in 1702, had contracted a debt of 6,000*l.* by the expedition against St. Augustine, Florida, and to discharge the same, bills were issued, to be redeemed in three years by duties laid upon liquors, skins, and furs. The notes passed as specie. The same colony established a bank in 1712 'to defray the cost of the war 'against the Tuscaroras, and to accommodate domestic trade;' 48,000*l.* in bills were loaned out on interest upon landed or personal property, the whole to be sunk in twelve years, at the rate of 4,000*l.* a year. But it does not seem that they were redeemed within that time. Soon after the first emissions, exchange rose, and prices of all goods followed, the first year to 150, the second to 200, per cent. Further large issues were made, on loan to the inhabitants, and for the ordinary expenses of the colony. The British Parliament, in 1729, purchased the proprietary rights of Carolina, and divided the territory into two distinct and separate governments, known afterwards as North and South Carolina. By 1731 the rate of exchange was 700 per cent., at which it continued, with little variation, for forty years. The amount of bills outstanding in 1739 was 250,000*l.* At that date it required eight South Carolina shillings to equal a shilling sterling. Prior to 1739, North Carolina had emitted 40,000*l.* of bills upon loan, and 12,500*l.* for ordinary expenses. In that year exchange was fixed by legislative enactments at ten shillings of the colony for one shilling of Britain.

The currency of Georgia consisted chiefly of 'trustees and old bills sterling.' The funds were allowances by Parliament, and private subscriptions to carry on the settlement.

The whole paper-money system of the thirteen colonies, as well as that of the British possessions in the West Indies, which was equally vicious, was swept away by the passage of an Act of Parliament, in 1763, 'to prevent paper bills of credit 'hereafter to be issued in any of His Majesty's colonies or 'plantations in America from being declared a legal tender in 'payment of money, and to prevent the legal tender of such 'bills as are now subsisting from being prolonged beyond the 'period for calling in and sinking the same.'

COLONIAL COMMERCE.

The foreign commerce of the American colonies, up to the beginning of the eighteenth century, had not become a very important feature in their affairs, as far as amount was concerned. Their West Indian trade, however, not only enabled them to avoid indebtedness to England, but absolutely, as will have been observed, supplied them with capital. The following tables exhibit the course of their trade from 1770 up to the period of the Revolution:—

AMERICAN TRADE BEFORE THE REVOLUTION.

Year	NEW ENGLAND		NEW YORK		PENNSYLVANIA		VIRGINIA AND MARYLAND		THE CAROLINAS		GEORGIA	
	Imports	Exports	Imports	Exports	Imports	Exports	Imports	Exports	Imports	Exports	Imports	Exports
	£	£	£	£	£	£	£	£	£	£	£	£
1700	91,918	41,486	49,410	17,567	18,529	4,608	173,481	317,302	11,003	14,058	—	—
1701	86,322	32,656	31,910	18,547	12,002	5,220	199,683	235,738	13,908	16,973	—	—
1702	64,625	37,026	23,991	7,965	9,343	4,145	72,391	274,782	10,460	11,870	—	—
1703	59,608	33,539	17,562	7,471	9,899	5,160	196,713	144,928	12,428	13,197	—	—
1704	74,896	30,823	22,294	10,540	11,819	2,430	60,458	264,112	6,621	14,067	—	—
1705	62,504	22,793	27,902	7,393	7,206	1,309	174,322	116,768	19,788	2,698	—	—
1706	57,050	22,210	31,588	2,849	11,037	4,210	58,015	149,152	4,001	8,652	—	—
1707	120,631	38,793	29,855	14,283	14,365	786	237,901	207,625	10,492	23,311	—	—
1708	115,505	49,635	26,891	10,847	6,723	2,120	79,061	213,493	11,996	10,340	—	—
1709	120,349	29,559	34,577	12,259	5,881	616	80,268	261,068	28,521	20,431	—	—
1710	106,338	31,112	31,475	8,203	8,594	1,277	127,639	188,429	19,613	20,793	—	—
1711	137,421	26,415	28,856	12,193	19,408	38	91,535	373,181	20,406	12,871	—	—
1712	128,105	24,699	18,524	12,466	8,464	1,471	134,583	297,941	20,015	29,394	—	—
1713	120,778	49,904	46,470	14,428	17,037	178	76,304	206,263	23,967	32,448	—	—
1714	121,288	51,541	44,643	29,810	14,927	2,663	128,873	280,470	23,712	31,290	—	—
1715	164,650	66,555	54,629	21,316	17,182	5,461	199,274	174,756	16,631	29,158	—	—
1716	121,156	69,595	52,173	21,971	21,842	5,193	179,595	281,343	27,272	46,287	—	—
1717	132,001	58,898	44,140	24,534	22,505	4,499	215,962	296,884	25,058	41,275	—	—
1718	131,885	61,591	62,906	27,331	22,716	5,588	191,925	316,576	15,841	46,385	—	—
1719	125,317	54,452	56,355	19,596	27,068	6,564	164,630	332,069	19,630	50,373	—	—
	2,142,347	833,282	736,211	301,569	276,547	63,536	2,842,613	4,933,480	341,363	475,871	—	—

AMERICAN TRADE BEFORE THE REVOLUTION.

Year	NEW ENGLAND		NEW YORK		PENNSYLVANIA		VIRGINIA AND MARYLAND		THE CAROLINAS		GEORGIA	
	Imports	Exports	Imports	Exports	Imports	Exports	Imports	Exports	Imports	Exports	Imports	Exports
	£	£	£	£	£	£	£	£	£	£	£	£
1720	128,769	49,206	37,397	16,836	24,531	7,928	110,717	331,482	18,290	62,736	—	—
1721	114,524	50,483	50,754	15,681	21,546	8,037	127,376	357,812	17,703	61,858	—	—
1722	133,722	47,955	57,478	20,118	26,397	6,882	172,754	283,091	34,374	79,650	—	—
1723	176,486	59,339	53,013	27,992	15,992	8,332	123,833	287,907	42,246	78,103	—	—
1724	168,507	69,585	63,020	21,191	30,324	4,057	161,894	277,344	37,839	90,504	—	—
1725	201,768	72,021	70,650	24,976	42,209	11,981	195,884	214,730	39,182	91,942	—	—
1726	200,882	63,816	84,866	38,307	57,634	5,960	185,981	324,767	43,934	93,453	—	—
1727	187,277	75,052	67,452	31,617	31,979	12,823	192,965	421,588	23,254	96,055	—	—
1728	194,590	64,689	81,634	21,141	37,478	15,230	171,092	413,089	33,067	91,175	—	—
1729	161,102	52,512	64,760	15,833	29,799	7,434	108,931	386,174	58,366	113,329	—	—
1730	208,196	54,701	64,356	8,740	48,592	10,582	150,931	346,823	64,785	151,739	—	—
1731	183,467	49,048	66,116	20,756	44,260	12,786	171,278	408,502	71,145	159,771	—	—
1732	216,600	64,095	65,540	9,411	41,698	8,524	148,289	310,799	58,298	126,207	828	—
1733	184,570	61,983	65,417	11,626	40,565	14,776	186,177	403,198	70,466	177,845	1,695	203
1734	146,460	82,252	81,758	15,307	54,392	20,217	172,086	373,090	99,658	120,466	1,921	18
1735	189,125	72,899	80,405	14,155	48,804	21,919	220,381	394,995	117,837	145,348	12,112	3,010
1736	222,158	66,788	86,000	17,944	61,513	20,786	204,794	380,163	101,147	214,083	2,012	—
1737	223,923	63,347	125,833	16,833	56,690	15,198	211,301	492,246	58,986	187,758	5,701	—
1738	203,233	59,116	133,438	16,228	61,450	11,918	258,860	391,814	87,793	141,119	6,496	17
1739	220,378	46,604	106,070	18,459	54,452	8,134	217,200	444,654	94,445	236,192	3,324	233
	3,665,737	1,225,491	1,505,957	383,151	830,305	233,504	3,492,724	7,244,358	1,172,815	2,519,333	34,089	3,481

AMERICAN TRADE BEFORE THE REVOLUTION.

Year	NEW ENGLAND		NEW YORK		PENNSYLVANIA		VIRGINIA AND MARYLAND		THE CAROLINAS		GEORGIA	
	Imports	Exports	Imports	Exports	Imports	Exports	Imports	Exports	Imports	Exports	Imports	Exports
	£	£	£	£	£	£	£	£	£	£	£	£
1740	171,081	72,389	118,777	21,498	56,751	15,048	281,428	341,907	181,821	265,560	3,524	924
1741	198,147	60,052	140,430	21,142	91,010	17,158	248,582	577,109	224,270	236,830	2,553	—
1742	148,899	53,166	167,591	13,536	75,295	8,527	264,186	427,769	127,063	154,607	17,018	1,622
1743	172,461	63,185	134,487	15,067	79,340	9,596	328,195	557,821	111,499	235,136	2,201	2
1744	143,982	50,248	119,920	14,527	62,214	7,446	234,855	402,709	79,141	192,594	769	—
1745	140,463	38,948	54,957	14,083	54,280	10,130	196,799	399,423	86,815	91,847	939	—
1746	209,177	38,612	86,712	8,841	73,699	15,779	282,545	419,371	102,809	76,897	984	—
1747	210,640	41,771	137,984	14,992	82,404	3,832	200,088	492,619	95,529	107,500	24	—
1748	197,682	29,748	143,311	12,358	75,330	12,363	252,624	494,852	160,172	167,305	1,314	—
1749	238,286.	39,999	265,773	23,413	238,637	14,944	323,600	434,618	164,085	120,499	5	51
1750	343,659	48,455	267,130	35,632	217,713	28,191	349,419	508,939	134,037	191,607	2,125	1,942
1751	305,974	63,287	248,941	42,363	190,917	23,870	247,027	460,085	138,244	245,491	2,065	355
1752	273,340	74,313	194,030	40,648	201,666	29,978	325,151	569,453	150,777	288,264	3,163	1,526
1753	345,527	83,395	277,864	40,553	245,644	38,527	356,776	632,575	213,009	164,634	14,128	3,057
1754	329,433	66,538	127,497	26,663	244,647	30,649	323,513	573,435	149,215	307,238	1,974	3,236
1755	341,796	59,533	151,071	28,055	144,456	32,336	285,157	489,668	189,887	325,525	2,630	4,437
1756	384,371	47,359	250,425	24,073	200,169	20,001	334,897	337,759	181,780	222,915	536	7,155
1757	363,404	27,556	353,311	19,168	168,426	14,190	426,687	418,881	213,949	130,889	2,571	—
1758	465,694	30,204	356,555	14,260	260,953	21,383	438,471	454,362	181,002	150,511	10,212	—
	4,984,016	988,758	3,696,766	430,872	2,763,551	354,038	5,700,000	8,993,445	2,885,104	3,675,849	68,825	24,307

AMERICAN TRADE BEFORE THE REVOLUTION.

Year	NEW ENGLAND		NEW YORK		PENNSYLVANIA		VIRGINIA AND MARYLAND		THE CAROLINAS		GEORGIA	
	Imports	Exports	Imports	Exports	Imports	Exports	Imports	Exports	Imports	Exports	Imports	Exports
	£	£	£	£	£	£	£	£	£	£	£	£
1759	527,067	25,985	630,785	21,684	498,161	22,404	459,007	357,228	215,255	206,534	15,178	6,074
1760	599,647	37,802	480,106	21,125	707,998	22,754	605,882	504,451	218,131	162,769	—	12,198
1761	334,225	46,225	289,570	48,648	204,067	39,170	545,350	455,083	254,587	253,002	24,279	5,764
1762	247,385	41,733	288,046	58,882	206,199	38,091	418,599	415,709	194,170	181,695	23,761	6,522
1763	258,854	74,815	238,560	52,998	284,152	38,228	555,391	642,294	250,132	282,366	44,908	14,469
1764	456,765	88,157	515,416	53,697	436,191	36,258	515,192	559,508	305,808	341,727	18,338	31,325
1765	451,299	145,819	382,349	54,959	363,368	25,148	383,224	505,671	334,709	385,918	29,165	34,183
1766	409,642	141,733	330,829	67,020	327,314	26,851	372,548	461,693	296,733	293,587	67,268	53,074
1767	406,081	128,207	417,957	61,422	371,830	37,641	437,628	437,926	244,093	395,027	23,334	35,856
1768	419,797	148,375	482,930	87,115	432,107	59,404	475,984	406,048	289,868	508,108	56,562	42,402
1769	207,992	129,353	74,918	73,466	199,906	26,111	488,362	361,892	306,600	587,114	58,340	82,270
1770	394,451	148,011	475,991	69,882	134,881	28,109	717,782	435,094	146,273	278,907	56,193	55,532
1771	1,420,119	150,381	653,621	95,875	728,744	31,615	920,326	577,848	409,169	420,311	70,493	63,810
1772	824,830	126,265	343,970	82,707	507,909	29,133	793,910	528,404	449,610	425,923	92,406	66,083
1773	527,055	124,624	289,214	76,246	426,448	36,652	328,904	589,803	344,859	456,513	62,932	85,391
1774	562,476	112,248	437,937	80,008	625,652	69,611	528,738	612,030	378,116	432,302	57,518	67,647
1775	71,625	116,588	1,228	187,018	1,366	175,962	1,921	758,356	6,245	579,349	113,777	103,477
1776	55,050	762	—	2,318	365	1,421	—	73,226	—	13,668	—	12,569
	8,174,360	1,787,083	6,433,427	1,195,070	6,456,658	744,563	8,548,748	8,682,264	4,644,358	6,204,820	814,452	778,646

The foregoing tables show the imports of the Northern colonies, for the first period, 1700 to 1719, to be 3,155,105*l.*, against those of the Southern colonies, 3,184,076*l.*, or nearly equal in amount, while the exports of the former were only 1,198,387*l.*, against the latter of 5,409,351*l.* The figures for the second period, 1720 to 1739, were imports North, 6,001,999*l*; South, 4,699,628*l.* The exports were 1,842,146*l.*, and 9,767,172*l.* respectively. In the third period, 1740 to 1758, the import account stands, North, 11,144,433 ; South, 8,653,349*l.* ; and the export returns, 1,773,668*l.* for the one, and 12,693,601*l.* for the other. The fourth and last colonial period records the Northern imports at 21,064,445*l.*, and the Southern at 14,007,558*l.* ; the exports at 3,726,716*l.*, and 15,665,730*l.* The total Northern imports reached 41,665,882*l.*, against the Southern of 30,544,611*l.*, while the exports aggregated as follows : Northern, 8,540,917*l.* ; Southern, 43,535,854*l.* The imports of the whole thirteen colonies thus amounted to 72,210,493*l.*, and the exports to 52,076,771*l.* The shipments from the colony of Delaware are included with those of Pennsylvania, and the produce of East and West Jersey was forwarded by way of New York and Philadelphia. There appears a balance against the Northern colonies of 33,124,965*l.*, and a balance in favour of the Southern colonies of 12,991,243*l.*, leaving a net deficiency of 20,133,722*l.* The indebtedness of the North was settled by the sale of negroes to the South : most of the blacks were purchased in Africa and the West Indies, but some were 'bred' at home — the increase in the coloured population of New England, New York, New Jersey, and Pennsylvania, thus finding a profitable outlet. The money received for the negroes was invested in Southern bills of exchange, drawn on Europe, against the shipments of tobacco, rice, and other produce. These bills, along with the specie received from the West Indies — the value of the merchandise sent to the islands being always greater than that imported from thence — enabled the Northerners to pay the balances due by them to their correspondents in Europe. It will be observed that, in a colonial condition, the South carried on a more direct trade with Europe than she has since done as States. Cotton cultivation, however, led her to abandon commerce in a great measure and take to planting.

As an example of the foreign trade of the colonies, statistics concerning the business of the year 1764 are presented:—

	Imported from England		Exported to England	
New England . .	£459,765		£88,157	
New York . . .	515,416		53,097	
Pennsylvania . .	435,101		36,258	
Total . . .		£1,410,372		£168,112
Virginia and Maryland .	£515,192		£559,408	
Carolina . . .	305,808		341,727	
Georgia . . .	18,388		31,325	
Total . .		£839,388		£932,460
Grand total . . .		£2,249,760		£1,100,572

The fact is, the Northern colonies at that time, and ever since as States, had very little to export that was suited for the English market. In their earlier days they had furs and skins, and other rude articles of a newly settled country; but as civilisation progressed, those commodities of course disappeared, and their only surplus produce for which there was a demand on this side of the Atlantic was tobacco, then grown in their own neighbourhood, but of course to a much more limited extent than in Maryland or Virginia; flax-seed; fish, sold to the Catholic countries of the continent; and occasionally breadstuffs. The islands relieved them of their inferior fish, for slave consumption, as well as beef, pork, butter, poultry, maize, flour, cider, apples, cabbages, onions, horses, mules, &c. The commerce of the Northern colonies with Europe and the West Indies stood thus (in dollars) in 1764 :—

	Exported to	Imported from
New England	$407,314	$340,339
New York	118,524	113,046
New Jersey	2,531	1,990
Pennsylvania	382,644	194,841
	$911,013	$650,216

The exports of the Southerners always paid for more than they imported. Their trade prior to Independence being direct, the real state of their balances can be more readily approximated. They, as well as the Northerners, earned largely by freights and the sale of vessels in Europe. The outward shipments being much more bulky than the receipts of manufactured goods, enabled

them to dispose of some of their ships after their cargoes
were discharged in foreign ports.   In addition to purchases of
negroes from the Northern colonists, the Southerners bought
from the English slave-traders Africans to the value of many
millions of dollars.

Franklin explained the course of business carried on at that
time.   As a representative from Pennsylvania, he was examined
before a committee of the House of Commons on this subject,
on January 28, 1765, when the following questions and answers
were given:—

'What may be the amount of one year's imports into Penn-
'sylvania from Britain?—I have been informed that our
'merchants compute the imports from Britain to be above
'500,000*l.*

'What may be the amount of produce of your province
'exported to Britain?—It must be small, as we produce little
'that is wanted in Britain.   I suppose it cannot exceed 40,000*l.*

'How, then, do you pay the balance?—The balance is paid by
'our produce carried to the West Indies, and sold in our own
'(British) islands, or to the French, Spaniards, Danes, and
'Dutch; by the same carried to other colonies in North Ame-
'rica, as to New England, Nova Scotia, Newfoundland, Carolina,
'and Georgia; by the same carried to different parts of Europe,
'as Spain, Portugal, and Italy; in all which places we receive
'either money, bills of exchange, or commodities that suit for
'remittance to Britain, which, together with all the profits on
'the industry of our merchants and mariners arising in those
'circuitous voyages, and the freights made by their ships, centre
'finally in Britain, to discharge the balance, and pay for British
'manufactures continually used in the province, or sold to
'foreigners by our traders.'

AMERICAN CURRENCY SUBSEQUENT TO INDEPENDENCE.

The first emissions of 'continental notes' by the 'Congress
of Delegates' was under an Act passed June 23, 1775; the
bills, however, bore the date of the meeting of that body,
May 10, 1775.   This currency professed to be redeemable in
silver dollars, and circulated throughout the colonies, in accordance with the values established by them, as already noticed.

The issues were as follow :—

						Dollars	
1775 and 1776	.	.	.	.	.	20,064,464	66-90ths
1777	.	.	.	.	.	26,426,333	1-90
1778	.	.	.	.	.	66,965,269	34-90
1779	.	.	.	.	.	149,703,856	77-90
1780	.	.	.	.	.	82,908,320	47-90
1781	.	.	.	.	.	11,408,095	
					357,476,541	45-90

Until the amount exceeded $9,000,000., the notes passed at their nominal value, and kept near par until January 1779, when the depreciation was rapid throughout the whole of that year, there being a redundancy of the currency. It then and subsequently required the number of paper dollars specified in the subjoined table, compiled from the books of the principal merchants at Philadelphia, to exchange for the Spanish pillar dollar, worth 4s. 6d. sterling silver money :—

	1777	1778	1779	1780	1781
January . .	$1\frac{1}{4}$	4	7, 8, 9	40, 45	100
February .	$1\frac{1}{2}$	5	10	45, 55	100, 120
March . .	2	5	10, 11	60, 65	120, 135
April . .	$2\frac{1}{4}$	6	$12\frac{1}{2}$, 16, 14, 22	60	135, 200
May . .	$2\frac{1}{2}$	5	22, 24	60	200, 500
June . .	$2\frac{1}{2}$	4	22, 20, 18	60	
July . .	3	4	18, 19, 20	60, 65	
August .	3	5	20	65, 75	
September .	3	5	20, 28	75	
October . .	3	5	30	75, 80	
November .	3	6	32, 45	80, 100	
December .	4	6	45, 38	100	

On January 11, 1776, five months after the issue was made, and six months before independence was declared, Congress resolved that 'whosoever shall refuse to receive in payment ' continental bills should be declared and treated as an enemy ' to his country; and be precluded from intercourse with its ' inhabitants,' that is, outlawed, which is the severest penalty, except life and limb, known to the law. 'This principle was ' continued in practice for five years, and appeared in all shapes ' and forms; i. e. in tender acts, in limitation of prices, in sin-

' ful and threatening declarations; in penal laws, with dreadful
' and ruinous punishments, and in every other way that could
' be devised, and all executed with a relentless severity by the
' highest authority then in being, viz. by Congress, by assemblies,
' and by conventions of States, whose powers in those days were
' nearly sovereign, and even by military force.'

In 1779 these notes were made a legal tender, but this, as
will be seen, did not augment their value. On March 17,
1780, the amount had increased so much that Congress, in
order to lessen the 'volume of currency,' called in the emissions
of 1777 and 1778 ($93,391,602$\frac{3}{8}\frac{6}{0}$) at 40 for 1, or only 2½ per
cent. for fresh issues, and accordingly there was cancelled of
that sum $82,819,432, by other bills of credit amounting to
$891,236$\frac{8}{1}\frac{0}{0}\frac{0}{0}$ in 1780, and $1,176,249 in 1781. This made
matters worse. Specie or barter then began to be used in
settlement of transactions, although laws had been passed regulating the price of goods for paper-money, and by May 7, 1781,
continental notes ceased to be of any value. So worthless had
this currency become at that date, and so great the discontent
consequent upon its depreciation, that manifestations of impatience and disaffection became frequent. In Philadelphia a
large body of the inhabitants paraded the streets, with paper
dollars in their hats by way of cockades, displaying colours,
with a dog tarred, and, instead of the usual ornament of
feathers, his back was covered with continental money. This
procession, immediately under the eyes of the rulers of
the revolted provinces, in solemn session at the State House
assembled, was directly followed by the jailer, who refused
accepting the bills in purchase of a glass of rum, and afterwards
by the traders of the city, who shut up their shops, declining
to sell any more goods but for gold or silver. It was declared
also by the popular voice, that if the opposition to Great
Britain was not in future carried on by solid money instead of
paper bills, all further resistance were in vain, and must be
given up. A letter dated August 19, 1780, thus alludes to the
state of financial affairs:—'Ten thousand pounds Pennsylvania
' currency *was* worth 6,000*l*. sterling; 10,000*l*. continental
' money *is* worth 100*l*. The difference makes a loss of 5,900*l*.
' sterling, being as sixty to one. This was the exchange at

‘ Philadelphia in June last, and, as they had not then heard of
‘ Gates’ defeat, it must be now lower. Actions commenced for
‘ considerable sums by creditors have been obliged to be with-
‘ drawn, or a non-suit suffered; a lawyer of eminence not
‘ opening his mouth in a trial of consequence under a fee of
‘ 1,000l., though the legal fee is about forty; and the debt, if
‘ recovered, being paid in continental money, dollar for dollar,
‘ worth now but a penny, the difference between a penny and 4s.
‘ 6d. sterling is lost to the receiver. The Congress having called
‘ in the former emissions, $40 for one, and giving that *one* in
‘ paper, cuts off every hope of redemption. The freight of a
‘ hogshead of tobacco is 300l., or one hogshead for the carriage
‘ of another. Instead of the creditor pursuing the debtor with
‘ an arrest, the debtor pursues the creditor with a tender of
‘ continental money, and forces the bond out of his hand.
‘ Hence it appears what the best fortunes are reduced to; an
‘ unpleasing reflection it must be; for time, which lightens all
‘ other losses, aggravates the loss of fortune. Every day we
‘ feel it more, because we stand more in want of the conveni-
‘ ences we have been used to. On the other hand, new fortunes
‘ are made on the ruin of old ones. War, which keeps the
‘ spirits in motion, has diffused a taste for gaiety and dissipation.
‘ The French resident minister at Philadelphia gives a rout
‘ twice a week to the ladies of that city, amongst whom French
‘ hairdressers, milliners, and dancers are all the *ton*. The Vir-
‘ ginia jig has given place to the cotillion and *Minuet de la*
‘ *Cour*. Congress has fallen into general contempt, for its want
‘ of credit and power; the army is absolute, and has declared
‘ it will not submit to a peace made by Congress; the people
‘ grumble, but are obliged to surrender one piece of furniture
‘ after another to pay their State taxes.’ So long as the continental notes retained a market quotation, they changed hands
frequently, and at 200 for 1 speculators became large purchasers; they were finally sold at 1,000 to 1. Some compulsory
measures upon the people being put in force in regard to them,
as well as to State bills, by the Executive Council of Pennsylvania, caused their complete overthrow.

None of these continental notes have ever been redeemed,
with the exception of $151,740$\frac{45}{100}$, paid by the State of Penn-

sylvania to the General Government, on March 3, 1792, in settlement for the purchase of about 200,000 acres of land, north of the line of 42° N. on Lake Erie, which forms the peculiar north-west corner of that State as seen in the map.

The several States during the war also emitted bills of credit, in accordance with their respective currencies. They had merely a local circulation. The second bank established in America was the 'Bank of Pennsylvania,' opened at Philadelphia July 17, 1780, with a capital of 300,000*l*. Its special object was to supply the American army with provisions; but it was of little use, and lingered in its operations until its stock was merged into that of the Bank of North America, which institution commenced business the following year. Specie became very plentiful in 1781, in consequence of the large expenditure of the British and French forces finding their way into the interior, as well as a profitable commerce that was conducted with the Havannah.

Within a year after the Articles of Confederation had been adopted—1782—the attention of Congress was called to the subject of the currency, great inconvenience being felt by reason of the 'measures of value' being so unlike in the several States. The matter was considered under the authority of Article IX., which reads: 'The United States in Con-
'gress assembled shall also have the sole and exclusive
'right and power of regulating the alloy and value of coin
'struck by their own authority, or by that of the respective
'States, fixing the standard of weights and measures through-
'out the United States.' Mr. Morris, of New Jersey, pro-
posed a money unit of 1·1,440 of a dollar, which was the worth of the penny of every State. Mr. Jefferson objected to Mr. Morris's plan—suggested the dollar as a unit, and the other coins so regulated in relation to it as to be conformable to the decimal arithmetic. After much discussion this latter method was adopted. In 1785 the comparative value of gold to silver was estimated at 15 to 1; the change from the weight of the original Spanish dollar to the Federal dollar made the pound sterling worth four dollars and eighty cents, or 8 per cent. premium on the par of four dollars, forty-four cents, forty-four mills. No mint, however, was established until shortly after the

adoption of the Constitution.* In 1834 gold was debased, in order, as the politicians vainly supposed, to keep it from being exported, when the premium rose to 9 per cent., or $4 84 cents and eighty-four mills to the average sovereign. The act of Congress of March 3, 1853, reduced the weight, but not the fineness of the silver coins; this was done in consequence of their being worth more as bullion on account of the large quantity of gold received from California and Australia, causing silver to appreciate in value. At the beginning of the present century the production was in the proportion of about one ounce of gold to forty-six ounces of silver. When the mines of California were opened, it had probably changed to one ounce of gold to less than four ounces of silver. The alterations, therefore, in the standard weight of the silver coins were rendered absolutely necessary. Previous to 1853, American silver was issued from the Mint at $1,16 4-11 cents per ounce; the half dollar is now fourteen and a quarter grains lighter, and the smaller coins in proportion.

Mr. Chase's ' greenbacks' resemble bank bills, and ' promise,' on their face, to pay gold and silver on demand. Yet, on their back, in colours typifying the *verdancy* of the holders, they nullify that obligation. The Confederate issues, unlike those of the Federal Government, have never been made a legal tender; they are payable ' six months after the treaty of ' peace with the United States.' ·

The Confederate States would find much convenience in an assimilation of the values of their currency to British coinage, which can readily be done, without abandoning the decimal system. Let their principal gold piece be a ' Sun'—Eagles should be dispensed with, as well as Stars and Stripes—and the dollar might be one-fifth its value; the smaller pieces, the subdivisions of the dollar. Specie is an article of merchandise in America at the present time, and the change can, therefore, be readily made without confusion or interfering with the business of the people. An international ' clearing house' might be established for the precious metals, which would save the frequent loss by recoinage, on the occasion of exports and imports; and

* See Report of Alexander Hamilton, Secretary of the Treasury, January 28, 1791, ' on the establishment of a Mint.'

the 'shaves' to which travellers have always been subjected in
selling foreign money, would be altogether avoided. The 'Na-
'poleon' might be equivalent to four American dollars, or one-
fifth less than a British sovereign. The ancient habit of
calculating exchange on London at $4 44 cents and forty mills
to the pound sterling, or 4s. 6d. to the dollar, should be discontinued. A sovereign being worth $4\frac{85}{100}$ in American gold,
9 per cent. premium becomes actual par.

COMMERCE OF THE AMERICAN STATES DURING THE ARTICLES OF CONFEDERATION.

The foreign commerce of the States was of necessity almost
entirely suspended during the Revolution. The subjoined
table, made up from the records of the British Custom House,
will show the extent of the trade between that period and the
first year of the Union under the Constitution.

Years	Imports from Britain	Exports to Britain
	£	£
1784	3,679,467	749,345
1785	2,308,023	893,594
1786	1,603,465	443,119
1787	2,009,111	893,637
1788	1,886,142	1,023,784
1789	2,525,298	1,050,198
1790	3,431,778	1,191,071
	17,443,284	6,244,748

The exports in these seven years, which were chiefly of
Southern produce, amounted to not much more than one-third
the imports. The trade to the Continent was limited, but
assisted, with the specie that had accumulated during the revolution, to settle the balances due to England. The importing
States took advantage of their situation, and levied duties on
foreign goods for their own benefit, at the expense of the other
States. The loss of the West Indian trade was severely felt by
New England, New York, and Pennsylvania; it divested them
of an outlet for their surplus produce which was unsuited for
the European markets. Pitt made an unsuccessful effort, in
1783, to open the colonial ports to the Americans. .Mr.

Jefferson, in a letter addressed to the Marquis de la Fayette, dated Paris, July 17, 1786, thus commented on the prostration of American commerce posterior to the separation from Great Britain:—'With respect to the West Indian commerce I must 'apprise you that this estimate does not present its present face. 'No materials have enabled us to see how it stands since the 'war. We can only show what it was before that period. New 'regulations have changed our situation there much for the 'worse. This is most sensibly felt in the exports of fish and 'flour. The surplus of the former, which these regulations 'threw back upon us, is forced to Europe, where, by increasing 'the quantity, it lessens the price. The surplus of the latter is 'sunk; and to what other objects this portion of industry is turned 'or turning, I am not able to discover. The imports, too, of 'sugar and coffee are thrown under great difficulties. These 'increase the price, and being articles of food for the poorer 'classes (as you may be sensible on observing the quantities 'consumed), a small increase of prices places them above the 'reach of this class, which, being numerous, must occasion a 'great diminution of consumption. It remains to be seen whether 'the American will endeavour to baffle these new restrictions 'in order to indulge his habits, or will adapt his habits to other 'objects which may furnish employment to the surplus of in- 'dustry formerly occupied in raising that bread which no longer 'finds a vent in the West India market. If, instead of either of 'these measures, he should resolve to come to Europe for coffee 'and sugar, he must lessen, equivalently, his consumption of 'some other European articles, in order to pay for his coffee and 'sugar—the bread which he formerly paid for them in the West 'Indies not being demanded in the European market. In fact, 'the catalogue of imports offers several articles more dispensable 'than coffee or sugar. Of all these subjects the committee and 'yourself are the most competent judges. To you, therefore, I 'trust them, with every wish for their improvement.'

COMMERCE WITH THE BRITISH COLONIES.

In the treaty made with Mr. Jay in 1794, the British agreed to the following clause : 'Provided always, that the said American 'vessels do carry and land their cargoes in the United States

'only, it being expressly agreed and declared that during the
'continuance of this Article the United States will prohibit and
'restrain the carrying of any molasses, sugar, coffee, cocoa, or
'*cotton** in American vessels, either from His Majesty's islands,
'or from the United States, to any part of the world except the
'United States, reasonable sea stores excepted.' The Senate
refused to ratify this provision of the treaty, in the hope of obtaining better terms. In 1802, the British proposed a mutual
abolition of all discriminating duties between the two countries;
but Congress declined to concur in the arrangement. They,
however, threw open their West Indian ports to American ships
after the Berlin and Milan decrees were issued, in order to obtain supplies. The 'Convention' of 1815 equalised the tonnage
duties between the British home ports and those of the States,
but did not arrange for those of the colonies, which were soon
closed to vessels of the United States. Congress, in retaliation,
first laid a duty on all British vessels coming from the West
Indies, and in 1818 excluded them altogether. The people of
the islands complained bitterly of this; they were often short of
provisions and frequently received American flour *viâ* Liverpool,
an expensive and circuitous route.† Parliament in 1822 took
off the interdiction as far as some of the ports were concerned,
and permitted the entrance of vessels of all countries that gave
reciprocal advantages. Congress then rescinded its act of prohibition, still, however, continuing the discriminating duties.

---

* Mr. Jay was not so much to blame for allowing what now appears to
be so curious a stipulation as the exclusion of cotton shipments in American
vessels from the States. At that date, 1794, cotton had just begun to be
an article of export. Mr. Hamilton, the Secretary of the Treasury, in his
report of December 5, 1791, said (in speaking of cotton): 'Not being, like
'hemp, a universal production of the country, it affords less assurance of an
'adequate internal supply; but the chief objection arises from the doubts
'which are entertained concerning the quality of the national cotton. It
'is alleged that the fibre of it is considerably shorter and weaker than that
'of some other places; and it has been observed, as a general rule, that the
'nearer the place of growth to the equator, the better the quality of
'cotton.'

† The non-intercourse with the States was oftentimes very annoying to
the West Indians. A report of the Committee of the Assembly of Jamaica
states that between 1783 and 1787, 15,000 negroes perished through famine,
occasioned by hurricanes. The same was the case at Dominica in 1817.

The British imposed countervailing charges. In 1825 they removed all restrictions, on condition that their commerce and navigation should be put on a footing with the most favoured nations, by those that had no colonies. Congress was unwilling to grant such a favour, and the ports were again closed to the ships of both powers. An effort was made by the Americans for the renewal of the commerce in 1827. Mr. Gallatin, the United States' minister at London, in his despatch of September 11 of that year, remarked :—

'Mr. Huskisson said it was the intention of the British 'Government to consider the intercourse of the British colonies 'as being exclusively under its control, and any relaxation from 'the colonial system as an indulgence to be granted on such 'terms as might suit the policy of Great Britain at the time it 'was granted. I said every question of *right* had, on this 'occasion, been waived on the part of the United States, the 'only object of the present enquiry being to ascertain whether, 'as a matter of mutual convenience, the intercourse might not 'be opened in a manner satisfactory to both countries. He '(Mr. H.) said that it had appeared as if America had enter-'tained the opinion that the British West Indies could not exist 'without her supplies, and that she might, therefore, compel ' Great Britain to open the intercourse on any terms she pleased. 'I disclaimed any such belief or intention on the part of the ' United States. But it appeared to me—and I intimated it, 'indeed, to Mr. Huskisson—that he was acting rather under ' the influence of irritated feelings, on account of past events, ' than with a view to the mutual interests of both parties.'

Mr. Gallatin was succeeded at London by Mr. James Barbour, who was likewise unsuccessful in his application to the British Government for a restoration of the West Indian commerce. Mr. John Quincy Adams was President at the time; he complained to Congress of the obstinacy of England. President Jackson came into office on March 4, 1829, and Congress, through his influence, the following year passed an Act which was considered at the time to be highly favourable to British navigation, inasmuch as all American ports were to be opened, while it was only required of the English that they should give access to their ' free ' ports. The vessels of both countries were allowed to carry the productions of either, but not the merchandise of other nations, to and from the islands. The English, in acceding to the American proposition, however, charged higher duties on American produce imported direct into the islands than through their North American colonies. Under this arrangement many cargoes were first sent to the north coast, and then re-shipped to the West Indies. President Jackson, by proclamation dated October 5, 1830, announced the West Indian ports to be open; and they have so continued to this day without interruption. All restrictions were afterwards taken off by the Act of Parliament of 1849. That commerce, which had been so beneficial to the northern colonies for over a century, was, with a few intermissions, lost to them as States for forty-seven years.

THE FRENCH REVOLUTION.

In the meanwhile—the very year of the organisation of the second Union under the Constitution—the French Revolution broke out. The American States, preserving their neutrality, became the common carriers for all nations, and conducted, in a great measure, the commerce of their colonies. There was a sudden transition from the insolvency and ruin that seemed pending over the American people, to an era of unprecedented prosperity. Never in the history of the world was there a more rapid increase in trade. Every other art and pursuit seemed eager to send its votaries to 'go down to the sea in ships and do business in great 'waters.' The capital of all countries flowed into this channel. Pennsylvania and the other Northern States shared more largely the benefits arising out of the European troubles than their neighbours of the South. Enormous importations were made from China and India into Philadelphia for re-exportation to the European markets. Despite the many captures of American ships for alleged violations of the various orders and decrees of the belligerent powers, the fortunes reaped by the merchants, in point of number, were beyond all precedent, and have never since been rivalled. The cities grew rapidly in population and wealth, and the capital earned was employed in seeking new sources of emolument. Hence the great outcry in the North when the embargo of 1808 was enacted, as such put an end to the lucrative employment of American tonnage. This, with the war with England that so soon followed, diverted the profits accruing from commerce to be invested in manufactures. During all this time the cultivation of cotton was expanding, and long ere the conflict at Waterloo the Southern States had, besides supplying the North with the raw material, become the largest cotton exporters in the world.

The next table exhibits the course of the commerce after

THE ADOPTION OF THE FEDERAL CONSTITUTION.

STATEMENT OF THE DEBT OF THE UNITED STATES, THE TOTAL VALUE OF IMPORTS AND EXPORTS, AND THE TOTAL TONNAGE, EACH YEAR, FOR THIRTY-ONE YEARS, FROM 1790 TO 1820.

Years	Debt	Imports	Exports	Tonnage
	$	$	$	
1790-91	75,463,476	52,200,000	39,217,197	502,146
1792	77,227,924	31,500,000	20,753,098	564,457
1793	80,352,634	31,100,000	26,109,572	520,764
1794	78,427,405	34,600,000	33,026,233	628,618
1795	80,747,587	69,756,268	47,989,472	747,965
1796	83,762,172	81,436,164	67,064,097	831,900
1797	82,064,479	75,379,406	56,850,206	876,913
1798	79,228,529	68,551,700	61,527,097	898,328
1799	78,408,669	79,068,148	78,665,522	939,400
1800	82,976,294	91,252,768	70,971,780	972,492
1801	83,038,050	111,363,511	94,115,925	947,577
1802	80,712,632	76,333,333	72,483,160	892,104
1803	77,054,686	64,666,666	55,800,033	949,172
1804	86,427,120	85,000,000	77,699,074	1,042,404
1805	82,312,150	120,600,000	95,566,021	1,140,369
1806	75,723,270	129,410,000	101,536,963	1,208,716
1807	69,218,398	138,500,000	108,343,150	1,268,548
1808	65,196,317	56,990,000	22,430,960	1,242,596
1809	57,023,192	59,400,000	52,203,233	1,350,281
1810	53,173,217	85,400,000	66,757,970	1,424,784
1811	48,005,587	53,400,000	61,316,833	1,232,502
1812	45,209,737	77,030,000	38,527,236	1,269,997
1813	55,962,827	22,005,000	27,855,997	1,166,629
1814	81,487,846	12,965,000	6,927,441	1,159,210
1815	99,833,660	113,041,274	52,557,753	1,368,128
1816	127,334,933	147,103,000	81,920,452	1,372,219
1817	123,491,965	99,250,000	87,671,569	1,399,912
1818	103,466,633	121,750,000	93,281,133	1,225,185
1819	95,529,648	87,125,000	70,142,521	1,260,751
1820	91,015,566	74,450,000	69,691,669	1,280,167
		2,350,627,238	1,839,003,367	

In the above table the exports, as compared with the imports, exhibit a deficiency of $511,623,871. Included in the former were foreign goods to the amount of nearly $700,000,000, which were cleared at their cost price, whereas the enormous profits on them, as well as on the shipments of domestic produce during the wars in Europe, should be placed to the credit of the country. The carrying trade, as before remarked, was very remunerative within this period. A large amount of unclaimed property was received from St. Domingo by Girard and others at the time of the insurrection. And very many West Indians and Europeans of wealth migrated to the States with their available fortunes, and invested the same in Bank and other Stocks.

STATEMENT OF THE DEBT OF THE UNITED STATES, THE TOTAL VALUE OF IMPORTS AND EXPORTS, EXCLUSIVE OF SPECIE, AND THE TOTAL TONNAGE EACH YEAR, FROM 1821 TO 1847—TWENTY-SEVEN YEARS.

Years	Debt	Imports	Exports	Tonnage
	$	$	$	
1821	89,987,427	62,585,724	64,974,382	1,208,958
1822	93,546,676	82,241,541	72,160,281	1,324,699
1823	90,875,877	77,579,267	74,699,030	1,336,566
1824	90,269,777	80,549,007	75,986,657	1,389,163
1825	83,788,432	96,340,075	99,535,388	1,423,112
1826	81,054,059	84,974,477	77,595,322	1,534,191
1827	73,987,357	79,484,068	82,324,827	1,620,608
1828	67,475,043	88,509,824	72,264,686	1,741,392
1829	58,421,413	74,492,527	72,358,671	1,260,798
1830	48,565,406	70,876,920	73,849,508	1,191,776
1831	39,123,191	103,191,124	81,310,583	1,267,847
1832	24,322,235	101,029,266	87,176,943	1,439,450
1833	7,001,032	108,118,311	90,140,433	1,606,151
1834	4,760,082	126,521,332	104,336,973	1,758,907
1835	351,289	149,895,742	121,693,577	1,824,940
1836	291,089	189,980,305	128,663,040	1,822,103
1837	1,878,223	140,989,217	117,419,376	1,806,084
1838	4,857,660	113,717,404	108,486,616	1,995,640
1839	11,983,737	162,092,132	121,028,416	2,096,479
1840	5,125,077	107,141,519	132,085,946	2,180,764
1841	6,737,398	127,946,177	121,851,803	2,130,744
1842	15,028,486	100,162,087	104,691,534	2,092,391
1843	27,203,450	64,753,799*	84,346,480*	2,158,603
1844	24,748,188	108,435,035†	111,128,278†	2,280,095
1845	17,093,794	117,254,564†	114,464,606†	2,417,002
1846	16,750,926	121,691,797†	113,488,516†	2,562,084
1847	38,956,623	146,545,638†	158,689,025†	2,839,046
		2,888,098,579	2,606,750,897	

* Only 9 months of 1843.   † For the year ending June 30.

This second table, which includes the imports and exports of specie and bullion, shows an apparent deficit of $221,347,682. This amount was balanced by freights and investments in American securities, and profits on shipments that do not appear in the Government returns. A large and profitable commerce was opened within this period with the new American States that had thrown off the yoke of Spain, as well as with the British possessions. The cotton trade augmented the exports; the reshipments of foreign goods amounted to $508,528,939. The importations of gold and silver coin and bullion between the years 1821 and 1847 exceeded the exportations by $81,188,831, to say nothing of that brought by emigrants.

STATEMENT OF THE DEBT OF THE UNITED STATES, THE TOTAL VALUE OF IMPORTS AND EXPORTS, AND THE TOTAL TONNAGE EACH YEAR, FROM 1848 TO 1861—FOURTEEN YEARS.

Year	Debt	Imports	Exports	Tonnage
	$	$	$	
1848	48,526,379	154,008,028*	154,032,131*	3,154,042
1849	64,704,693	147,851,439*	145,755,820*	3,334,016
1850	64,228,238	178,138,318*	151,898,720*	3,535,454
1851	62,560,395	216,224,932*	218,388,011*	3,772,439
1852	65,131,692	212,945,442*	209,658,366*	4,138,440
1853	67,340,628	267,978,647*	230,976,157*	4,407,010
1854	47,242,206	304,562,381*	278,241,064*	4,802,902
1855	39,969,731	261,468,520*	275,156,846*	5,212,001
1856	30,963,909	314,639,042*	326,964,908*	4,871,652
1857	29,060,386	360,890,141*	362,960,082*	4,940,842
1858	44,910,777	282,613,150*	324,644,421*	5,049,808
1859	58,754,699	338,765,130*	356,789,462*	5,145,038
1860	64,769,703	362,163,941*	400,122,296*	5,353,808
1861	90,867,828	334,350,453*	248,505,454*	5,530,813
		3,737,591,364	3,684,094,338	

This table also includes the gold and silver imported and exported. In the exports are added the reshipments of foreign goods, valued at cost price, $298,621,026.

The total exports from 1848 to 1861 amounted to within $53,497,026 in value of the importations, according to the Custom House returns; but it is not believed that they repre-

* For the year ending June 30.

sent anything like the true figures, in consequence of the foreign invoices having been undervalued, as it is supposed, to the extent of $400,000,000, in order to evade a portion of the high duties imposed upon importations. Should that sum approximate correctness, the deficiency then would be $453,497,026. This balance was outweighed by freights, profits, sales of clipper and other ships, investments by Europeans in American securities, and a large floating indebtedness. Within this last period gold became a regular article of export from the American States. The shipments of all the precious metals in the fourteen years exceeded the receipts from abroad by $365,821,281. It is estimated that the amount of gold and silver coin taken into the American States by immigrants, has been about equal to that brought to Europe by travellers. So the net importations from 1821 to 1847, $81,188,831, deducted from the above figures, leaves the net exports $284,632,450.

The value of the gold and silver bullion and coin in the American States in 1821 was estimated at $25,000,000. The production of the mines of North Carolina, Georgia, Virginia, Kansas, and California has been about $700,000,000, making a total of $725,000,000. Deducting the net exports, $284,632,450, and allowing $65,367,550 for that consumed, it follows that there remained in 1861, $375,000,000 in all the States. Of that quantity a greater proportion, considering the difference in population, was held in the South, the slaves alone being the possessors it is believed of more than $10,000,000. In the Northern States the circulating medium has been chiefly bank notes, but the South, like all agricultural countries, has used coin principally for currency. On January 1, 1860, the last new year's day of the Union, the Southern banks contained $39,033,261 in gold and silver, while those of the Northern States recorded only $44,561,276.

The Southern States have furnished from the very beginning about 80 per cent. of the domestic exports of all the States, excluding the precious metals, and even the Californian contributions are owing, in a great measure, to the large quantities of southern produce sent to the north, being manufactured and forwarded to the Pacific. These crops of cotton, rice, tobacco, sugar, breadstuffs, &c., &c., would of course have been cultivated had the Constitution never been adopted. It was the yield of Southern soil, with the aid of slave labour, that caused the rapid progress of the American people. The 'Great West' has been of little advantage. It is always in debt to the East, and augments the Northern balances in favour of Europe.

Mr. Kettell, writing in the early part of 1860, which was before the large European demand for breadstuffs set in, and which, with fine harvests this year, has almost entirely ceased, said :—'In the last few years of speculative excitement at the 'West, whence such floods of bonds have been sent to New 'York for negotiation, the presence of the proceeds of Southern 'crops lying in the New York banks, and by them used to sus- 'tain the stock market, has been a great aid in the negotiations 'of these Western credits, which were applied to the construc- 'tion of railroads. That large expenditure reflected upon the 'Western trade, producing an unusual demand for goods, which 'disappeared when the railroad expenditures ceased. A very 'considerable portion of the capital created at the South was 'applied to the consumption of Western produce, since the 'thousands of men who were employed in building railroads at 'the West caused a large local demand for that produce on 'one hand, while they increased the demand for goods on the 'other. There has doubtless been a large amount expended for 'railroad construction at the South, but this has not been 'speculative. We shall in a future chapter see that although 'there are as many miles of railroad in operation at the South 'as at the West they have cost hardly more than half the 'money per mile, and their influence in developing local 'resources has been immense. We shall see that more than '20 per cent. of Western railroad obligations is dishonoured, 'while none of the Southern roads have failed to pay. The 'reason is the superior cheapness of the latter. It is also a 'peculiar feature of the Southern roads that their stocks and 'liabilities are nearly all owned at home. The dividends and 'interest do not therefore form a drain upon Southern resources, 'while at the West that drain has reached a very serious extent, 'and must lead to the breaking up of numerous companies. '. . . . . . . The growth of steam tonnage on the Western 'and Southern rivers has been large; but this, as well as the

' sail tonnage, has been much affected by the influence of rail-
' roads, which has directed much produce from the water
' carriage, changing the direction in many cases from down
' stream to across the country, thus benefitting the Northern
' roads by Southern exports. The sugar, cotton, and tobacco of
' the South finds its way to a considerable extent across the
' country into the Western States; and these roads have been
' built in the Western section to a very large extent with
' borrowed money. They have consequently been expensively
' built, far more than those which have been built at the South.
' The aggregate length and cost of railroads has been, at two
' periods, as follows:—

	1853		1860		
	Length	Cost	Length	Cost	Per mile
North . .	7,222	$287,691,587	9,605	$481,874,434	$50,000
West . .	5,535	110,389,337	9,191	365,109,701	40,000
South . .	4,663	91,522,204	9,053	221,857,503	24,100
	17,420	$489,603,128	27,909	$1,008,841,638	

' These returns, for 1853, are from the census, and those for
' 1860 are from the " Boston Railway Times," compiled by an
' eminent engineer. We have then the fact that the South has
' as many miles of railroad as either of the other sections, and
' that they cost per mile less than half the cost of the Northern
' roads, and two-thirds the expense of the Western roads, a fact
' which shows the economy with which the Southern roads were
' built. We now take from " Stow's Railway Annual " the
' railroads delinquent on the interest of the bonds:—

	Companies	Amount
South	3	$2,025,000
North	9	39,000,000
West	21	68,120,000
	33	$109,145,000

' The business of the South has, it appears, paid the cost of
' 9,053 miles of railroad, where the North has been unable to
' do so, and the West has shown still less ability to sustain that

‘ length of road. The capital supplied to the latter section for
‘ construction of the roads came from England and the East,
‘ and was expended in a lavish manner, stimulating business
‘ and speculation, which has fallen through, leaving a disastrous
‘ condition of affairs in all that region. The railroads them-
‘ selves show, in the declining revenues, the fact that they owed
‘ their former prosperity less to the effects of free labour than
‘ to the factitious activity caused by a passing speculation. The
‘ crops of that region are not, like those of the South, in con-
‘ stant and active demand, passing always by the shortest road
‘ to market. They depend for realisation upon short crops
‘ abroad. In ordinary seasons the price will not pay for trans-
‘ portation by rail.’

The New York and Erie, the New York Central, the Philadelphia and Reading, and several other Northern railroad companies are entirely owned in Europe. The quotations of these
securities at the New York and Philadelphia stock boards arise
merely out of speculative transactions. Not a share or a bond is
held for investment in America, and the money required for keeping a certain quantity of the stocks and loans to be thus used is,
in reality, British capital. Ever since the regularity of Atlantic
steam communication the bankers and financiers of Wall Street
have been borrowers from Lombard Street, under a system of
floating indebtedness, conducted through the agency of bills of
exchange at sixty days’ sight. The drafts passing do not as
formerly only represent the value of merchandise; but in the
general ramifications of the money operations the amount of
European acceptances of American bills is probably five or six
times greater than the aggregate commercial transactions. This
business has been a great source of revenue to New York, the
interest charged in Europe being much less than that which is
earned in America by reloaning the borrowed capital. The
stock and bonds of the Pennsylvania and other railroad companies are also largely held in Europe. Up to the year 1820
Philadelphia was the financial centre and most important
commerical port of the Union; but New York having had the
sagacity to increase her trade with the South, took the lead of
the former city, notwithstanding she had the formidable influence of the Bank of the United States in her favour. The

mercantile prosperity of New York was based upon the handling
of the Southern crops.   The Erie Canal was not completed until
October 26, 1827. A great error has, therefore, been committed,
as the dates make manifest, in attributing the advancement of
New York to that undertaking, it being quite clear that she
progressed by and with the augmentation of the cotton trade.
And this fact will be demonstrated when the war expenditure ceases.   Trade's ' proud empire' will then ' haste to swift
decay.'

The Articles of Confederation provided for an army and a
navy, postal arrangements, coinage of money, and trade with
the Indians, as well as diplomatic intercourse with foreign powers.
And it was, as has been observed, for the purpose of bestowing
on a central head the regulation of commerce between the
States and with other nations that the Constitution was adopted.
Until thirty odd years ago that document was read and understood by the people of both sections of the late Union in the
spirit of its authors; but since that time the Northerners, for
their own selfish objects, have construed it with a latitude un-
warranted by its text and evident meaning, and in contempt of
the interpretation of contemporaneous writers.   In this they
were supported by a few ambitious politicians in the South who
wished to gain their favour.   The false construction of the
Constitution was brought about mainly by the fact that a large
portion of the capital which had accrued from commerce during
the European wars had been attracted to manufactures, in consequence of the demand for goods that existed pending the
second conflict with Great Britain, when the States were deprived of their customary supplies from abroad.   At the commencement of the war the Federal debt was $45,209,738 ; at
its conclusion the amount had been increased to $127,334,934.
The country was bare of goods, notwithstanding the encouragement afforded to the New England manufactures by the high
prices for their fabrics that ruled during hostilities, when the
cost of the raw material was lessened by reason of the outward
as well as the inward commerce being in a great measure suspended.   In order to reduce the debt Congress levied very high
duties upon importations, which, while they gave enormous revenues, added a further boon to the interests of New England.

The tariff was foolishly raised in 1824 to please the Yankees, and, as success stimulated cupidity, the 'black tariff' of 1828 marked the growth of abuse. The debt was rapidly lowered.

The people were much alarmed at the principle of protection that had been introduced, when the tariff should have only served the purposes of revenue. A free trade convention of delegates from most of the States was held at Philadelphia on October 1, 1831, when the following resolution was passed:—

'That the present tariff system is unequal in its operation, 'and therefore unjust; that it is oppressive, because it imposes 'burthens on the many for the benefit of the few; unwise and 'impolitic, since its tendency is to disturb the harmony of the 'Union; that it is inconsistent with the principle of free go-'vernment, and at variance with that spirit of justice and mutual 'concession in which the Constitution was conceived and 'adopted; operating unequally and unjustly upon the different 'portions of this Union; having a direct and almost inevitable 'tendency to demoralise our people, and calculated to produce 'discontent among the people of the United States, by a 'numerous and respectable portion of whom it is believed to be 'unconstitutional; and, finally, that its effect is to diminish the 'productive resources of the country, and to lessen the amount 'of the necessaries and conveniences of life which are enjoyed 'by our people, and is in many respects infinitely more oppres-'sive upon the poor than upon the rich.'

A tariff convention met at New York on the 26th of the same month, when opposing resolutions were adopted. President Jackson, in 1832, recommended a reduction of duties. Congress acceded; but at the same time retained the principle of protection. A first step had been made in 1820 towards over-riding the Constitution in the matter of the Missouri restriction concerning slavery, which had thus opened the door for further violation of that instrument, notwithstanding the remonstrances of many able and virtuous statesmen. South Carolina, although not fully supported by her sister States of the South, justly protested against this further infringement of the rights of the States, and nullified the Act of Congress. Mr. Calhoun, in the midst of the difficulty, resigned the vice-presidency, and took his seat on the floor of the Senate as a member for South Carolina, and compelled Mr. Clay, who had been catering for Northern influence, to come forward with the 'Compromise Bill' which annulled the Act that had been previously passed, but had not gone into operation. The manufacturers of New England were associated in their efforts to aggrandise themselves at the expense of the South with the speculators in the coal lands of Pennsylvania, which had been opened in 1820, when but 365 tons were sent to market. The quantity had increased to only 34,896 tons in 1825 and 174,734 in 1830. Wood was at that time used as the chief fuel for domestic purposes, and, in order to augment the demand for coal, Pennsylvania thus sold herself to Massachusetts. The general political character of the two States, until 1860, was, however, entirely different: they only voted together when the tariff question was under consideration.

The total quantity of anthracite coal produced in Pennsylvania, as per the census returns of 1860, was 9,397,332 tons, valued at $11,869,574, of which sum only about $2,000,000 can be credited to the 'mineral wealth' of the State, the remainder being consumed in charges and freights paid to inland transportation companies, whose proprietors are mostly foreigners. For such a paltry consideration, for so populous a State, Pennsylvania has ruined her commercial and agricultural position; in fact, a disregard of the enlightened principles of free trade has caused her to recede in material prosperity. She has descended from the proud eminence she once held, and her people are now simply 'hewers of wood (miners of coal) and drawers of water' for New York and New England. Pennsylvania, from her geographical situation, the nature of her real interests, and character of her inhabitants, held what is recognised in Europe as the 'balance of power' among the American States. She has unfortunately thrown her weight in the scale against the South, and must suffer with the general decay that will inevitably take place throughout the North.

Since the adoption of the Federal Constitution twenty-four different tariff bills have been enacted under various pretences. The first, that of 1789, was for revenue and the reduction of the debt; the duties were fixed at 5, 7½, 10, 12½, and 15 per cent. *ad valorem,* and a discrimination of 10 per cent. of the amount of the tax was made in favour of merchandise imported by American vessels. The Act of 1790 was intended as a further provision for the payment of the debt, and that of 1792 for raising means to defend the frontier. In 1794 the duties were increased in some instances to 20 per cent. *ad valorem.* The tariffs of 1795, 1797, and 1800 were of a similar nature. The measure of 1804 was to protect the commerce and seamen of the States against the Barbary powers, and to impose more specific duties. Another bill was passed in 1812 to raise revenue to carry on the war; the duties were doubled in 1816 to pay off the expenses of the same. In 1813 salt was taxed. The tariff of 1824 was intended for protection; many articles of merchandise under it were taxed 50 per cent. The Act of 1828 extended the scale of imposts for the same object; that of 1830 reduced the rate of charges on coffee, tea, cocoa, molasses, and salt, none of which commodities were connected with New England or Pennsylvania, and therefore did not demand protection. The debt being nearly paid off, the tariff of 1832 lowered the duties on some articles, but retained the principle of protection. Coffee and tea were for the first time admitted free. As before remarked, it never went into operation; it gave place to the 'Compromise' bill of 1833, which surrendered the principle of protection, with a gradual lessening of the duties for ten years until they reached 20 per cent. The amount of money in the Treasury had in the meanwhile increased so much that Congress in 1836 resolved to divide $37,468,859$\frac{88}{100}$ among the States in four equal payments on January 1, April 1, July 1, and October 31, 1837, leaving the sum of $5,000,000 on hand. The first three instalments were paid; but the 'great panic' occurring caused the Government to be as needy as the people, and the last amount of $9,367,214$\frac{97}{100}$ was retained. Only $28,101,644$\frac{91}{100}$ were disbursed. The tariff of 1842 was passed by a Whig Congress; it was foolishly high, and was substituted by the more reasonable Act of 1846. In 1856 the imposts were reduced; in 1857 they were raised; and several times since they have been increased. No sooner did the Southern representatives withdraw from Congress than the outrageous Moriff tariff was passed, and the rates of duties have been enlarged subsequently. In fact, if the Yankee manufacturers could obtain their accustomed supply of the raw material from the Southern States, the present Federal laws would, as far as cotton fabrics are concerned, be completely prohibitory.

One of the chief elements among the causes that have produced the dissolution of the Union was this very question of taxing one portion of the States for the purpose of benefiting another. The Abolitionists were never important enough in numbers ('strong-minded women' having no franchise) to control any election without the cooperation of other parties, and failing in their scheme to sever the non-slaveholding from the slaveholding States on the isolated issue of slavery they made common cause with the Protectionists, under the conviction that this new policy would assist eventually in the accomplishment of their designs against the integrity of the Union. The Protectionists, blinded by their pecuniary interests, had not the sagacity to perceive the tendency, or, at least, to see the full significance of the measures into which they were being led. The Northerners, under the 'American system,' had been appropriating to themselves much of the wealth of the South, but finding after the election of Mr. Lincoln that the Southern people were in earnest in regard to their determination long before expressed, of seceding from the Union, and that they could no longer rob them as formerly, they adopted the unconstitutional policy of 'coer-'cion,' and hastened the masses on with the rallying cry of the old watchword of the Jacobins in France's darkest day of blood and tears, '*Fraternité, ou la mort !*'

In order to guard against all future misconstruction, the Confederate Constitution defines much more explicitly than the Federal instrument, upon which it is founded, those powers given to Congress for levying duties upon importations. Article 1, section 8, says :—

The Congress shall have power—

1. 'To lay and collect taxes, duties, imposts, and excises *for* '*revenue necessary* to pay the debts, provide for the common de-'fence and carry on the government of the Confederate States; '*but no bounties shall be granted* from the Treasury, *nor shall* '*any duties or taxes on importations from foreign nations be* '*laid to promote or foster any branch of industry*; and all 'duties, imposts, and excises shall be uniform throughout the 'Confederate States.'

The above article is in exact accordance with the views held by those who framed the Federal Constitution—the Secessionists of 1787—who entertained no notion of protection, but wished to levy duties merely for the purposes of revenue, to meet the ordinary expenditure of the Government, which at that time only amounted to between $3,000,000 and $4,000,000 per annum, and to gradually sink the public debt.

Mr. Jefferson, as Secretary of State, said:—' Instead of em-' barrassing commerce under files of laws, duties, and prohibi-' tions, it should be relieved from all its shackles in all parts of the ' world. Would even a single nation begin with the United States ' this system of free intercourse it would be advisable to begin ' with that nation.'

Why should a Confederacy of States be burdened with a double set of tax-gatherers? The cost of maintaining the general government ought to be assessed among the States. The people would not feel the direct taxes any more than the indirect and more grievous charges imposed upon them by the present system. The expenses of the Union of latter years were about $65,000,000 per annum; those of the individual States were $40,000,000. As the citizens of those States paid both sets of taxes it would have been much better and less costly if the States *as States* had contributed their quota to the general government, and collected the same along with their internal revenues. The very fact of having so many United States' office-holders—and they too nearly all residing in the importing States—prevented the harmonious working of the Federal machine, caused angry debates in Congress, and, with the aid of Abolitionism, has entailed disgrace and ruin upon the country. The people of the Confederate States should as soon as practicable establish unqualified free trade.

The true source of the wealth of the American States has been owing nearly altogether to the productions of the South—the only section of the late Union that is almost free from an European indebtedness. Nor have the Southern States been, as is frequently charged, trading on the borrowed capital of the North. Mr. Kettell proves that the very reverse was the case; he likewise states that the annual earnings of the North out of their connection with the South were as follows:—

Bounties to fisheries	$1,500,000
Customs, disbursed at the North	40,000,000
Profits of manufacturers	30,000,000
,, importers	16,000,000
,, shipping	40,000,000
,, on travellers	60,000,000
,, by schools, colleges, &c.	5,000,000
,, of agents, brokers, &c.	10,000,000
,, on capital drawn from the South	30,000,000

Total Northern drain from Southern sources . $232,500,000

Yet, in spite of these advantages, which the North has possessed, the real and personal property of the Southern States is very much greater per head than that owned by the Northern or Western States. The census of 1860 furnishes the subjoined information in reference to this point :—

REAL ESTATE.

North	$2,744,679,248
South	2,418,306,661
West	1,810,120,140
	$6,973,106,049

PERSONAL PROPERTY.

North	$1,268,189,410
South	3,113,584,041
West	729,780,505
	$5,111,553,956

The property of the South, too, is of a character that, when relieved of Northern commercial shackles, it must necessarily increase in value, while that of the North, with the loss of its mercantile connection with the South, will beyond peradventure decline rapidly. History records how the prosperity of the Northern States ceased after the separation from Great Britain ; and, by a slight taxing of memory, it will be recollected that the secession of the Southern States and the refusal of their people to make purchases to the ordinary amount from the North after the election of President Lincoln, created much distress in the Federal States. Manufacturers were unable to sell their goods, and merchants could not dispose of their wares. The shares in the main lines of railway fell greatly in consequence of the absence of the customary travel, the hotels were almost without guests—many were actually closed, the colleges had but few students, and every evidence existed of the deprivement of what had not been before properly appreciated by the people of the North—the importance to them of their *commercial* relations with the South. And this decay occurred at the time when the Southerners had continued the exportation of their produce; they then had only ceased to be customers, in a lesser degree than formerly, for their supplies. It was not until after the enormous war expenditure of the Washington government that the mock prosperity—the 'Brummagem,' the camel's hair shawl era—appeared. With the cessation of hostilities it will be instantaneously demonstrated that 'all is not *gold* that glitters.' Mr. Chase's financial bubble would have burst many months ago, but for the large amount of specie funds thrown into the Federal States by reason of the extraordinary demand for breadstuffs that existed for three seasons, and which tended, in a measure, to fill up the vacuum created by the loss of the Southern trade. Mr. Chase, too, has had the advantage of monopolising the 'credits' of the North, directly in the matter of currency and indirectly through his contractors. The Southern Secretary of the Treasury has had no such advantages. The people of the Confederate States have ever done business on the cash principle. This is one reason why the quotations for gold in the South are higher than those in the North; another is, that the Confederate Secretary is an honest man, and does not attempt to deceive the people, as Mr. Chase has done, by 'bearing' the market; a third is, that the South is pent up by the blockade, and its transactions with other countries are therefore very limited. So soon, however, as their ports are opened the quantity and value of produce which they will have to spare will be so much greater than what their requirements of European manufactures will be, large as their wants are, that the precious metals will flow into their shores in settlement of the balances. The Southern debt is only one-fourth the amount of the Federal debt, and, with the quotations for bills on London, in the respective States, the figures of the former become inconsiderable when compared to those of the latter. It must not be

forgotten that the North, unlike the South, has hardly anything
to export. Cheese, bacon, apples, wooden clocks, &c., will present
but a sorry show in the future tables of the Federal States.
The statesmen of the South merely desired to sever the political
and commercial shackles that had bound them to the North;
they were willing and anxious for a commercial treaty. Had Mr.
Lincoln permitted the ' wayward sisters' to part in peace, very
little change in the mercantile affairs of the States, except that
unavoidably resulting from the annihilation of the protective
tariff system, would, after the first blush of excitement and
feeling, have ensued. All the ' commercial conventions' that
could have held would have made no impression upon the course
of business. The grooves of trade are so convenient to use
that they are difficult to avoid. This cruel war has, however,
completely severed all ties, broken up all connections, and
established non-intercourse, at least to anything like its former
extent. The South will start fresh in a career of prosperity,
having all the elements of success possessed by an old country,
combined with all the power, strength, and energy, of a newly
established commercial empire.

CHAPTER XII.

THE AFRICAN SLAVE TRADE.—FREE AND SLAVE NEGROES IN THE AMERICAN STATES.

IN the year 1442 some Moorish prisoners captured by the Portuguese obtained their liberty by paying a ransom of ten negro slaves. It is believed that the African slave trade of modern times originated with this transaction. At all events Portugal soon afterwards engaged in the traffic, and was shortly followed by Spain. The Government of the latter country sent the first negroes to the New World, and landed them at Hispaniola in 1501. It conducted the trade until 1516, when the business was placed under control of a company of Genoese merchants. The English did not engage in this commerce until 1561, when Sir John Hawkins fitted out an expedition for the African coast. He, as was the case with the Portuguese and Spaniards, exchanged the manufactures of Europe for negro slaves, the property of barbarous chiefs. After discharging three cargoes at Hispaniola in 1562, he returned to England in the following year. His profits were so large that they were noised about, and a company was quickly formed for the purpose of supplying slaves to the Spanish American colonies, under a charter granted by Queen Elizabeth, who became its largest stockholder. The trade in the course of time grew to be very general, and was carried on by almost every class of speculators; but in 1618 James I. gave to Sir Robert Rich and others the exclusive privilege of conducting it. Through their operations the British American colonies were furnished with black labourers. The first negroes, however, twenty in number, that were received in the American States, unless the Spanish had previously landed them in Florida, were taken to Virginia in 1620 by a Dutch vessel. Another company was organised in 1631, by authority of Charles I. Its business extended so rapidly, and yielded such large returns, that for its defence and accommodation it was found expedient to erect numerous fortifications and warehouses on the coasts of the West Indies.   Charles II., in 1662, gave a monopoly of the trade to an association who were authorised to import into the colonies 3,000 slaves per annum.   Its affairs were placed under the patronage of the Queen Dowager, with the Duke of York at its head.   The King issued a proclamation inviting his subjects to establish themselves in America, and as an encouragement to emigrate tendered a grant of 100 acres of land for each four slaves employed in its cultivation.   Another slave-trading company was chartered in 1672, the King being the chief shareholder.   It continued in operation for many years, and, notwithstanding that the Parliament in 1688 abolished all such privileges, it seized the vessels of private traders, until its powers were again recognised.   The merchants of London found their trade to the slave coast so cramped by the royal monopoly, that they complained bitterly to the House of Commons of their exclusion from so profitable a traffic.   Their remonstrance was effectual, and Parliament enacted, in 1695, 'that for the better ' supply of the plantations, all the subjects of Great Britain should ' have liberty to trade in Africa for negroes, with such *limits* as ' should be prescribed by Parliament!'   In 1698 it was resolved, ' that the trade was highly beneficial and advantageous to the ' kingdom, and to the plantations and colonies thereunto ' belonging.'   The 'limits' prescribed by Parliament were removed in 1708 by the declaration ' that the trade was im- ' portant, and ought to be free and open to all the Queen's ' subjects trading *from* Great Britian.'   Again in 1711 it was enacted that 'this trade ought to be free in a regulated ' company; the plantations ought to be supplied with negroes ' at reasonable rates; a considerable stock was necessary for ' carrying on the trade to the best advantage; and that an export ' of 100,000*l.* at least in merchandise should be annually made ' from Great Britian to Africa.'   A short time prior to the year 1713 a contract had been made between Spain and the Royal Guinea Company of France, which was technically called in those days an 'assiento.'   By the treaty of Utrecht, April 11, 1713, Great Britian obtained a transfer of the agreement to herself. This was considered a great triumph of diplomacy, and the news of its accomplishment was hailed with enthusiasm in England: Queen Anne, in a speech from the throne, boasted of the success then obtained in opening a new market to Englishmen for the trade in slaves. This acquisition was followed in another month by a new contract in form, by which the British Government undertook for the period of thirty years to transport annually at a fixed price 4,800 slaves to the colonies of Spain in America. This gave rise to a question as to the true legal character of the slaves to be thus transported from Africa, and, in accordance with the forms of the British Constitution, the point was submitted to the twelve judges of England, who declared that, ' in pursuance of His Majesty's ' Order in Council, hereunto annexed, we do humbly certify ' our opinion to be that negroes are merchandise.'* Fifteen years afterwards the spirit of false philanthropy began to be developed in Great Britain, and although large numbers of negroes were held and sold daily on the public exchange in London, questions arose concerning the legal right of owners to retain property in slaves in England ; and the principal merchants, alarmed, and fearing an abolition of their lucrative trade, in 1729 referred the matter to Sir Philip Yorke, afterwards Lord Hardwicke, and to Lord Talbot, who were then the Attorney-General and Solicitor-General of the kingdom. The proposition was: ' What are the rights of a British owner of ' a slave in England ?' The two legal functionaries responded by certifying that—' a slave coming from the West Indies ' to England, with or without his master, doth not become free, ' and his master's property in him is not thereby determined ' nor varied, and his master may legally compel him to return ' to the plantations.' This decision caused the slave trade to be conducted with increased vigour. The company established in 1672 presented a claim upon the Government in consequence of the infringement of its franchises by the Act of 1698; and in consideration of the trade having thus been made free to all persons, its shareholders were voted out of the public purse

---

* This was signed by Lord Chief Justice Holt, Judge Pollexfen, and eight other judges.

10,000*l.* per annum for seven years, 1739 to 1746. In 1749 the question of the right of property in slaves again came before Lord Hardwicke, then Lord Chancellor, and by a decision in Chancery he re-affirmed the doctrines advanced by him when Attorney-General. The same year (23rd George II.) Parliament declared ' the slave trade to be very advantageous to Great ' Britain, and necessary for supplying the plantations and ' colonies thereunto belonging with a sufficient number of ' negroes at reasonable rates.' The colony of South Carolina, in 1760, passed an Act prohibiting the further importation of African slaves. The Act was rejected by the Crown, the Governor reprimanded, and a circular was sent to the governors of all the colonies, warning them against presuming to countenance such legislation. In 1765 a similar bill was twice read in the Assembly of Jamaica. The intelligence that this bill was under consideration reached England before its final passage. Instructions were sent out to the royal governor, who, in accordance therewith, forbade any further progress in the measure.

In 1772 Lord Mansfield, under the pressure of fanaticism, subverted the common law of England by deciding that, although slaves brought into Great Britain from the West Indies did not become free, their owners could exercise no authority over them in England: that colonial legislation which recognised the rights of the master did not extend to this country. Lord Mansfield himself, no doubt, felt that this was judicial legislation. The case (Somersett) was repeatedly argued before him, and each time he begged the parties to consent to a compromise. They refused. ' Why,' said he, ' I ' have known six of those cases already, and in five out of the ' six there was a compromise : you had better compromise this ' matter.' But they said, no; that they would stand upon the law. Finally, after holding the case for three terms, he was able to persuade himself to make the decision just adverted to.

In spite of the discountenancing action of the Home Government in 1765, the Assembly of Jamaica, in 1774, passed two bills prohibiting the importation of slaves, when the Earl of Dartmouth, then Secretary of State, wrote to Sir Basil Keith, governor of the colony, that ' their measures had created alarm

' to the merchants of Great Britain engaged in that branch of
' commerce,' and forbade him, ' on pain of removal from his
' government, to assent to such laws.' Finally, when the
revolutionary struggle in America had actually commenced, and
Crown Point and Ticonderoga had been taken possession of by
the ' rebels,' and the first blood had been shed at Lexington, the
same Secretary of State, in answer to the demands of the agent
of the continental colonies, who presented him with a copy of
the ' Bill of Rights' adopted on October 14th, 1774, replied,
' We cannot allow the colonies to check or discourage in any
' degree a traffic so beneficial to the nation.'

Large numbers of Africans were imported into England, and,
as a badge of servitude, wore a collar round their necks, with the
names of their owners engraved thereon. At the time of the
decision in the Somersett case there were about 15,000 negro
slaves in Great Britain. Very few were introduced subsequently.
The negroes, as invariably in climates unsuited to their physical
organisation, rapidly diminished in numbers when no longer
recruited by accessions from abroad. Their extinguishment,
however, was hastened by the loss of accustomed comforts and
restraints, when, taking advantage of Lord Mansfield's decision,
they left the homes and protection of their masters. By 1787
only 470 remained in London. This small remnant, utterly
worthless and demoralised, became such a nuisance in the quarter
where they were congregated, that, through parliamentary aid,
they were transported to Sierra Leone along with some white
women of bad character. Both races, however, soon became
nearly extinct, and the colony was replanted five years later by
the shipment thence of 1,170 blacks from Nova Scotia, who had
been captured from the Americans during the revolutionary war.
Shortly afterwards it received an addition of some rebellious
' maroons,' who had infested the mountains of Jamaica, but
were caught by the assistance of bloodhounds; a cruel and
barbarous practice never resorted to in the continental colonies
of England, nor since they assumed the position of States.
These negroes were first sent out of the island to Lower Canada,
that the loyal slaves might not be corrupted by the example of
their insubordination. Becoming an annoyance to the white
colonists, they were eventually deported to Africa.

The last law regulating the African slave trade was enacted in 1788. About this time the agitation for its repression commenced; but Great Britain did not consent to its abandonment until 1807. The prohibitory bill had been violently opposed for twenty years in Parliament, and it is doubtful if even, at the expiration of that period, it would have been passed had not the traffic ceased to be so remunerative as formerly, in consequence of all the islands having then a superabundance of negro labour. The Act of Congress which had just been passed to take effect on January 1, 1808, also deprived those interested in the slave trade of the market afforded by the American States. In addition, the price of slaves had so greatly declined during the later years of its existence, that the only manner in which the business could be made profitable at all was by disregarding the laws limiting the number of persons to be carried by a single ship according to her size. The practice of overcrowding the vessels with Africans occasioned sickness, and inaugurated the ' horrors of the middle passage.' Previously to this, the commerce was carried on under precisely the same regulations as those with which the emigration from England to America is now conducted. In fact, the old passenger laws of the African trade were the same as those applying to other parts of the world. The repeated violation of these laws, and the circumstances arising therefrom, shocked every feeling of humanity and morality, and thus facilitated the adoption of the interdictory measure that had for so many years ' hung fire ' in Parliament.

Many frauds, too, that had been practised upon underwriters by persons sinking cheap ships, and making false representations regarding the number of negroes on board, likewise tended to accomplish the result. Nor would the anti-slave trade party have been successful at that time had they not ardently avowed their opposition to emancipation. The business was declining, and must in a few years have dwindled down to be of trifling moment without any adverse legislation. The numbers of negroes imported from Africa would not have equalled one-fourth of those who have since been carried into the Spanish islands in an illicit manner. At the outset of the anti-slave trade excitement a committee of Quakers from Philadelphia arrived in London, for the express purpose of influencing the members of Parliament.

Pennsylvania was then an independent State, and her people had no more right to interfere in a question of English policy than have the fanatics of England at the present day to meddle with the internal concerns of the Confederate States. The Quakers, however, were lending their energies to advance a good cause—the abolition of a traffic that, by abuses, had grown to be revolting to every sentiment of humanity; while the fanatical persons and their followers of this time are seeking to take from the African in America his only present hope of progress and civilisation.

England had carried to her own possessions and those of other powers upwards of 4,000,000 of slaves. The males were mostly landed in the islands; the females on the continent of America.

Spain prohibited the African slave trade in 1820, and France in 1831.

Fifty years after Lord Mansfield's decision—twenty years later than the prohibition of the African slave trade, and during the very height of the anti-slavery agitation, 1827—the celebrated case of the slave Grace was brought before Lord Stowell. It was argued that the slave was free because she was carried to England, and boasted, that the atmosphere of this kingdom was too pure to be breathed by a slave. The learned Judge, in reply, said that, after painful and laborious research into historical records, he did not find anything touching the peculiar fitness of the English atmosphere for respiration during the ten centuries that slaves had lived in England. Lord Stowell further remarked :—

' Having adverted to most of the objections that arise to the
' revival of slavery in the colonies, I have first to observe that it
' returns upon the slave by the same title by which it grew up
' originally. It never was in Antigua the creature of *law* but
' of *custom,* which operates with the force of law; and when it is
' cried out that *malus usus abolendus est,* it is first to be
' proved that, even in the consideration of *England,* the use of
' slavery is considered as a *malus usus* in the colonies. Is that
' a *malus usus* which the Court of the King's Privy Council and
' the Courts of Chancery are every day carrying into full effect
' in all considerations of property—in the one by appeal, and
' in the other by original causes—and all this enjoined and

' confirmed by statutes? Still less is it to be considered as a
' *malus usus* in the colonies themselves, when it has been
' incorporated into full life and establishment—where it is the
' system of the State and of every individual in it; and fifty
' years have passed without any authorised condemnation of it
' in *England* as a *malus usus* in the colonies.

' The fact is, that in England, where villenage of both sorts
' went into total decay, we had communication with no other
' country; and therefore it is triumphantly declared, as I have
' before observed, " once a freeman, ever a freeman," there
' being no other country with which we had immediate connec-
' tion which, at the time of suppressing that system, we had
' any occasion to trouble ourselves about. But slavery was a
' very favoured introduction into the colonies; *it was deemed*
' *a great source of the mercantile interest of the country,* and
' was, on that account, largely considered by the mother-country
' as a great source of its wealth and strength. Treaties were
' made on that account, and the colonies compelled to submit
' to those treaties by the authority of this country. This system
' continued entire. Instead of being condemned as *malus usus,*
' *it was regarded as a most eminent source of its riches and*
' *power.* It was at a late period of the last century that it was
' condemned in England as an institution not fit to exist here,
' for reasons peculiar to our own condition; but it has been
' continued in our colonies, favoured and supported by our own
' courts, which have liberally imparted to it their protection
' and encouragement. To such a system, whilst it is supported,
' I rather feel it to be too strong to apply the maxim, *malus*
' *usus abolendus est.* The time may come when this institution
' may fall in the colonies, as other institutions have done in
' other flourishing countries; but I am of opinion it can only
' be affected at the joint expense of both countries, for it is, in
' a peculiar manner, the crime of this country; and I rather
' feel it to be an objection to this species of emancipation, that
' it is intended to be a very cheap measure here, by throwing
' the whole expense upon the country.'

Lord Stowell, who was in correspondence with Judge Story,
of Massachusetts, at the time, sent him a copy of the decision.
The latter Judge, who was possessed of strong anti-slavery feel-

ings and prejudices, was asked to give his views concerning the matter, and in his answer will be found the following words: —

'I have read with great attention your judgment in the 'slave case. Upon the fullest consideration which I have been 'able to give the subject, I entirely concur in your views. If 'I had been called upon to pronounce a judgement in a like 'case, I should have certainly arrived at the same result.'

The emancipation measures of Great Britain were enacted in 1833, to take effect on August 1, 1834, under a system of apprenticeships varying from four to six years; a sum of 20,000,000*l.* was appropriated to compensate the owners for the loss of their property. The number of slaves thus freed was but 660,000, so great had been the mortality among them; 1,700,000 were imported into the British islands, yet a little only over one-third were in existence at that time. The Swedes followed the example of England in 1847, Denmark and France in 1848.

The African slave trade was first prohibited by several of the American colonies, but the Crown of Great Britain in every instance refused to give its assent to the interdiction of the traffic. When the preliminary Continental Congress met in the autumn of 1774, they adopted a 'bill of rights,' in the form of a series of resolutions, among which will be found the following declaration (October 4): —

'That we will neither import nor purchase any slaves im-'ported after the 1st day of December next; after which time we 'will wholly discontinue the slave trade, and will neither be con-'cerned in it ourselves, nor will we hire our vessels, nor sell our 'commodities or manufactures, to those who are engaged in it.'

Again, on April 6, 1776, the Continental Congress passed a similar resolution.

This was the earliest successful legislation against the African slave trade. The traffic was entirely suspended during the revolution. Upon the conclusion of peace in 1783, it was again resumed by the Yankee States, but not by the Southern States. At this juncture, Dr. Franklin, who was the founder and president of the first emancipation society, which was established in Pennsylvania in 1780, remonstrated against the renewal of the trade. In a letter addressed to the

Governor of New Hampshire, the people of which State were
actively engaged in the commerce, Franklin said :—

‘ The Society have heard, with great regret, that a consider-
‘ able part of the slaves who have been sold in the Southern
‘ States since the establishment of peace, have been imported
‘ in vessels fitted out in the State over which your Excellency
‘ presides. From your Excellency's station, they hope your
‘ influence will be exerted, hereafter, to prevent a practice
‘ which is so evidently repugnant to the political principles and
‘ form of government lately adopted by the citizens of the
‘ United States.’

Franklin, in his remarks, should have confined himself to the
truth. The ‘ form of government lately adopted by the citizens
of the United States ’ did *not* forbid the African slave trade.
There is not a word in the ‘ Articles of Confederation,’ adopted
on March 1, 1781, on the subject; nor had the Union under
them any power to interfere with that or any other species of
commerce. At that time, every State, even Massachusetts,
was slave-holding, and four years afterwards the delegates of
that commonwealth in the Convention which framed the Constitution, voted against giving Congress the power to suppress
the traffic in slaves from Africa, or other foreign parts, prior to
1808. In this they were supported by the delegates from New
Hampshire and Connecticut. Rhode Island was unrepresented
in the Convention ; Maine was then a portion of Massachusetts,
and Vermont of New Hampshire. So all the Yankee States
(for Rhode Island was largely engaged in the traffic) were in
favour of keeping open the trade for twenty years. Franklin
himself, on the final vote, agreed to this extension. The clause
securing it is contained in Article 1, Section 9, and reads : —

‘ The immigration or importation of such persons as any of
‘ the States now existing shall think proper to admit, shall not
‘ be prohibited prior to the year 1808, but a tax or duty may be
‘ imposed on such importations not exceeding ten dollars for
‘ each person.’

Virginia and Delaware desired the traffic put an end to at
once; they, in fact, along with Maryland and South Carolina,
had already prohibited it. The latter States, however, did not
consider it a matter to be taken in hand by the General Govern-

ment. The legislation of all the Southern communities, both as colonies and states, for more than 165 years—certainly commencing as far back as 1698—has been distinguished by constant efforts either to embarrass or entirely prohibit the African slave trade. Alone among the nations of Christendom, though fruitlessly against the unanimous policy of the European Governments, they struggled to prevent the increase of slaves from Africa upon the American continent; and never, from that day to this, have they abandoned their determination to exclude the importation of negroes. Not one of the Yankee States has ever enacted laws prohibiting that commerce; nor has Pennsylvania, New York, or New Jersey. The Yankees carried on the business with great vigour, until its prohibition by the Act of Congress of March 2, 1807, which took effect on January 1, 1808. Previous to this, however, Acts had been passed, March 2, 1794, and May 10, 1800, preventing the fitting out of ships in the American States for conducting the slave trade with foreign countries. 350,000 slaves were imported into the American States, viz. up to 1740, 130,000; between that date and 1776, 170,000; from 1783 to 1808, 50,000.

There is a reason for everything, and the expression ' Yankee trick ' is not an exception to this general rule. It is well known that the African slave trade has been carried on principally by the New Englanders, but in the multitude of their new religions, Young Men's Christian Associations, and evangelical (?) haranguings, they have allured the rest of the world into the belief that they were the first people that emancipated their slaves, when the truth is, that they never gave freedom to the African race, and but two of their States— Connecticut and Rhode Island—enacted laws of territorial abolition affecting only unborn generations. Massachusetts, the greatest braggart of them all, has never done anything in the matter; nor has Maine, New Hampshire, nor Vermont.

The erroneous impression in reference to the 'philanthropy' of Massachusetts has been induced by the knowledge that at the time of the adoption of the Federal Constitution in 1789 she was the only State of the thirteen without slaves. By an official census taken in 1754 she possessed 4,896, one-half of whom were over 16 years of age, and their owners were not permitted to manumit them without giving security that they should not become a burden upon the parish; the greater portion were, however, sent to the other colonies, and the advertisements in the Boston newspapers of that date prove that the young negroes were given away during infancy to the neighbouring colonies who would take them as slaves, so that the labour of the mothers might not be lost: hence the first census of the United States, taken in 1790, does not record a single slave; that of 1830 notices the fact of one person being held in bondage, who was probably taken there as a private servant from some other State. The first slave ship fitted out in the English colonies sailed from Boston in 1648.

Maine holds precisely the same position in regard to the negro race as Massachusetts; her people, who had been deserted by the Commissioners appointed to govern them, united themselves with that colony in 1652, but their action was not confirmed by the Crown until 1691, Massachusetts having in the meanwhile purchased the proprietaries right; the political co-partnership continued until March 15, 1820, when Maine was admitted as an independent State into the Federal Union. The census of 1830 records two slaves within her borders.

The laws of Vermont also seem to be silent on the subject of slavery. The political situation of this State had been very singular; she was not represented in the Revolutionary Congress, nor was she recognised as an independent commonwealth by Great Britain. She applied for admission into the Union, but New York and New Hampshire both claimed control over her territory, and it was only upon the threat of her people to place themselves again under the dominion of the British throne that she was permitted to subscribe to the Federal compact on March 4, 1791. The census taken in 1790 reports seventeen slaves within her limits.

The statute books of New Hampshire are equally dumb in reference to emancipation or abolition in any shape; the census acknowledges 158 slaves in 1790, 8 in 1800, 3 in 1830, and 1 in 1840.

Rhode Island adopted a plan of gradual abolition, by declaring that all slaves born in that State after March 1, 1784, should be free. Her census figures stand thus:—952 in 1790,

381 in 1800, 108 in 1810, 48 in 1820, 17 in 1830, and 5 in 1840. In proportion to the size of this State she was very largely engaged in the slave trade, having fifty-four vessels employed in that traffic when the Act of Prohibition took effect, January 1, 1808.

Connecticut passed laws at the same time similar to those of Rhode Island: her slave population was 2,759 in 1790, 951 in 1800, 310 in 1810, 97 in 1820, 25 in 1830, and 17 in 1840.

It must not be forgotten, too, that Massachusetts was the first State to formally recognise 'property in man,' and has never rescinded the code of rights styled 'fundamentals,' adopted as early as 1641, wherein the lawfulness of Indian as well as negro slavery and the African slave trade is approved. African slaves, however, have always been held under common law; they were not stolen by the English from the coast of Africa, as has been alleged, but regularly purchased from their owners in that country when the traffic was as legal as any other branch of commerce. In 1650 Connecticut passed laws causing Indians who failed to make satisfaction for injuries to be seized, ' either ' to serve or to be shipped out and exchanged for negroes, as ' the case will justly bear.' Rhode Island joined in the general habit of the day, with the exception of the town of Providence. The community of the heretical Roger Williams alone placed the services of the black and white races on the same footing.

Having shown the position of the Yankee States in reference to slavery, a sketch of the institution in the other 'Free States' will be next in order.

New York, for the first time, in 1799, passed an Act making free the future issue of her slaves after the males had attained 28, and the females 25 years. Another law was adopted in 1817, declaring them free on the 4th of July, 1827. She held within her borders 21,344 in 1790, 20,343 in 1800, 15,017 in 1810, 10,088 in 1820, 75 in 1830, and 4 in 1840.

In 1784, New Jersey enacted laws for the prospective extinction of slavery—viz.: that all children born after July 4, 1804, should be free. Her slave population was 11,423 in 1790, 12,422 in 1800, 10,851 in 1810, 7,557 in 1820, 2,254 in 1830, 674 in 1840, 236 in 1850, and 18 in 1860.

As early as 1780 Pennsylvania provided for gradual abolition;

all slaves born after that time were to become free at the age of 28 years. Her census stood as follows:—3,737 in 1790, 1,706 in 1800, 795 in 1810, 211 in 1820, 403 in 1830, 64 in 1840. The Constitution of this State, adopted in 1838, does not prohibit slavery; her Legislature can, therefore, make her a slaveholding State at any time.

New York, New Jersey, and Pennsylvania are classed as middle States. In 1626 importations of slaves commenced at New York; the city itself owned shares in a slave ship, advanced money for its outfit, and participated in the profits. The slaves were sold at auction to the highest bidder, and the average price was about $140. The Governor was instructed to use every exertion to promote the sale of negroes. Bancroft, the great Yankee historian, remarks—'that New York is not a 'slave State like South Carolina, is due to climate, and not to ' the superior humanity of its founders.' The slaves constituted one-sixth of the population of the city of New York in 1750. New Jersey was dismembered from New York when New Netherlands was conquered by England in 1664. The next year a bounty of seventy-five acres of land was offered by the proprietaries for the importation of each able-bodied slave. This was, doubtless, done in part to gain favour with the Duke of York, then President of the African Company. The Quakers of Pennsylvania did not entirely eschew the holding of negro slaves. William Penn himself was a slaveholder. He, in 1699, proposed to provide for the 'marriage, religious instruction, ' and kind treatment of slaves;' but the Legislature vouchsafed no response to his recommendation. In 1712, to a general petition for the emancipation of negro slaves by law, the answer of the same body was, 'it is neither just nor convenient to set ' them at liberty.' Slaves, however, were never numerous in Pennsylvania: and as that species of property did not 'pay,' manumissions were frequent. The larger portion were to be found in Philadelphia, one-fourth of the population of which city, in 1750, are supposed to have been of African descent.

The States of Ohio, Indiana, Illinois, Michigan, Wisconsin, and that part of Minnesota east of the Mississippi, were formed out of the north-western territory ceded to the United States, under the Articles of Confederation, in 1784, by the State of

Virginia. In that year Mr. Jefferson submitted to Congress a report for its organisation into five States, with the following proposition: 'That after the year 1800 of the Christian era 'there should be neither slavery nor involuntary servitude in 'any of the said States.' This clause was, however, rejected because it did not provide for the recovery of fugitives from service. In 1787 it was again presented and passed in the following shape: 'There shall be neither slavery nor involuntary 'servitude in the said territory, otherwise than in punishment 'of crimes whereof the parties shall be duly convicted;' and 'that any person escaping into the same, from whom labour 'or service is lawfully claimed in any one of the original States, 'such fugitive may be lawfully reclaimed, and conveyed to the 'person claiming his or her labour or service as aforesaid.' This 'ordinance' was adopted in the month of July during the sitting of Congress at New York. At the same time, the Convention that framed the Federal Constitution, consisting of delegates from twelve States, Rhode Island being unrepresented, was holding its meetings at Philadelphia. Virginia, and not the Northern States, was the cause of the restriction in relation to slavery in the north-western territory, but its climate was hostile to that kind of labour, as events have proved. The States, as independent sovereignties, have a right to hold slaves if they deem proper. Article IV. section 2, of the Constitution, says: 'The citizens of each State shall be entitled to all privi- 'leges and immunities of citizens in the several States.' A 'coloured' person, according to the decision of the Supreme Court, cannot be a citizen of the United States. Ohio had 6 slaves in 1830, and 3 in 1840. Indiana possessed 135 in 1800, 237 in 1810, 190 in 1820, 3 in 1830, and 3 in 1840. Illinois contained 168 in 1810, 917 in 1820, 747 in 1830, 331 in 1840. Michigan held 24 in 1810, and 32 in 1830; and Wisconsin, 11 in 1840. The only other 'Free States' are Iowa and Minnesota, west of the Mississippi—in the former State there were 16 slaves in 1840—and California and Oregon, that never had persons 'held to labour.'

It will thus be seen that the cry of abolition or emancipation by the Northerners is pure hypocrisy. Most of their slaves were sent to the South, and 'philanthropy' in the matter is a perfect myth. It is believed that fifty times as many slaves have been manumitted in the South as in the North.

In the decade, 1850 to 1860, 20,000 slaves were given their freedom, three-fourths of whom went to Canada; others to the North, and some to Liberia. The number of fugitives in 1850 was 1,011, and in 1860, 803. Territorial abolition would no doubt have extended to Delaware and Maryland long since, had it not been for the interference and cant of the Yankees. It was, however, a great mistake to have any legislation whatever in regard to slavery; it would have died out in the States where it was unprofitable; legal tinkering with the matter has only produced irritation, and created a politico-geographical line that otherwise would not have existed, enabling the ' Pharisees ' north of the survey of Charles Mason and Jeremiah Dixon, made in 1764, to settle the boundaries of Delaware, Maryland, and Pennsylvania, to say to the people south of that parallel, ' I am holier than thou.'

In making allusion to the few cases of manumission and emancipation by birth in the North, the late General Cobb, in his admirable work on the ' Law of Slavery,' wrote as follows :—

' The number of negroes emancipated in the United States
' was comparatively small, but the effects do not vary materially
' as to their condition from those already noticed. The fact of
' their limited number, as well as the additional facts that
' previous to their emancipation they were employed but little
' in agricultural pursuits, and that the nature of the agriculture
' of the Northern States of the Union was ill suited to this species
' of labour, protected the prosperity of those States from the
' depressing influences experienced elsewhere from the abolition
' of slavery. That their physical condition does not compare
' favourably with that of the slaves of the South is evident from
' the decennial census of the United States showing a much
' larger increase in the latter than in the former. No surer test
' can be applied.'

He also says : —

' In order to obtain accurate information, I sent a circular to
' the Governors and leading politicians of the non-slaveholding
' States. I received answers as follow :—

' A. *With Reference to the Physical Condition.*

' MAINE.—The condition of the male population varies, but is
' very far below the whites.

' VERMONT.—Their condition and character have great varieties.
' They are not in as good a condition as the whites.

' CONNECTICUT.—Governor Pond says: "The condition of the
" negro population, as a class, is not thrifty, and does not compare
" favourably with the whites. There are many, comparatively
" speaking, who are industrious."

' RHODE ISLAND.—They are, generally, industrious and frugal.

' NEW JERSEY.—Their condition is debased; with few ex-
' ceptions, very poor; generally indolent.

' NEW YORK.—The condition of the negro is diversified —
' some prosperous, some industrious. They have no social
' relations with the whites. Generally on about the same
' level that whites would occupy with the like antecedents.

' PENNSYLVANIA.—I deem the condition of the negro population
' in this State to be that of a degraded class, much deteriorated
' by freedom. They are not industrious.

' INDIANA.—They are not prosperous. The majority of them
' are not doing well. We have sent off thirty or forty this year
' to Liberia, and hope to send off 100 or more next year, and
' finally to get rid of all we have in the State, and do not intend
' to have another negro or mulatto come into the State.

' ILLINOIS.—As a class they are thriftless and idle. Their
' condition far inferior to that of the whites. About the towns
' and cities idle and dissolute, with exceptions. In the rural
' districts many are industrious and prosperous.

' IOWA.—Very few negroes in Iowa. Far above the condition
' of those met with in our eastern cities.

' MICHIGAN.—Tolerably prosperous. Far behind the white
' population.

' B. *With Reference to the Intellectual Condition.*

' MAINE.—Admitted into the public schools with the whites.
' Very far below them in education.

' VERMONT.—Generally able to read and write; a few are
' liberally educated; not like the whites.

' CONNECTICUT.—Fall much below the whites in education.

' RHODE ISLAND.—Some are educated in the district schools.
' Compare well with the whites of their condition.

' NEW JERSEY.—Generally ignorant.   Far below the whites in
' intelligence.

' NEW YORK.—Generally very poorly, or but little educated.

' PENNSYLVANIA.—Not educated.   It is remarkable that almost
' all the decent and respectable negroes we have have been
' household slaves in some Southern State.

' INDIANA.—Not educated.

' ILLINOIS.—Ignorant.

' MICHIGAN.—Not generally educated.   Far below the whites.

' C. *With Reference to the Moral Condition.*

' MAINE.—Far below the whites.

' VERMONT.—Not as good as the whites.

' CONNECTICUT.—Do not compare favourably with the whites.
' They are, with us, an inferior caste; and in morality much
' below the whites.

' NEW JERSEY.—Immoral; vicious animal propensities; drunk-
' enness, theft, and promiscuous sexual intercourse quite common.
' One-fourth of the criminals in the State prison are coloured
' persons, while they constitute only one twenty-fifth of the
' population.

' NEW YORK.—Diversified; some moral.

' PENNSYLVANIA.—Immoral.   I am satisfied, from forty years'
' attention to the subject, that the removal of the wholesome
' restraint of slavery, and the consequent absence of the stimulus
' of the coercion to the labour of that condition, have materially
' affected their condition for the worse.   They exhibit all the
' characteristics of an inferior race, to whose personal comfort,
' happiness, and morality the supervision, restraint, and coercion
' of a superior race seem absolutely necessary.

' INDIANA.—In many instances very immoral.

' ILLINOIS.—Thriftless, idle, ignorant, and vicious.   In towns
' and cities dissolute, with exceptions.

' IOWA.—Of a fair character.

' MICHIGAN.—Tolerably moral.   Far below the whites.

'Notwithstanding the very laboured efforts made for their
'intellectual improvement, taken as a body, they have made no
'advancement. Averse to physical labour, they are equally
'averse to intellectual effort. The young negro acquires
'readily the first rudiments of education, where memory and
'imitation are chiefly brought into action; but for any higher
'effort of reason and judgment he is, as a general rule, utterly
'incapable.

'His moral condition compares unfavourably with that of the
'slave of the South. He seeks the cities and towns, and
'indulges freely in those vices to which his nature inclines him.
'His friends inveigh against "the prejudice of colour," but he
'rises no higher in Mexico, Central America, New Granada, or
'Brazil, where no such prejudice exists. The cause lies deeper:
'in the nature and constitution of the negro race.'

In all the Northern States and territories there were, in
1860, 237,183 free blacks, viz. : —

California	. . .	4,086	New Jersey . . .	25,318
Connecticut	. . .	8,627	New York . . .	49,005
Illinois	. . .	7,628	Ohio . . .	36,673
Indiana	. . .	11,428	Oregon . . .	128
Iowa	. . .	1,069	Pennsylvania . . .	56,849
Kansas	. . .	625	Rhode Island . . .	3,952
Maine	. . .	1,327	Vermont . . .	709
Massachusetts .	. .	9,602	Wisconsin . . .	1,171
Michigan	. . .	6,799	District of Columbia .	11,131
Minnesota	. . .	259	Territories . . .	303
New Hampshire	. .	494		

But now for the Southern States : —
They contained in 1860, 250,787 free blacks, viz. : —

Alabama	. . .	2,690	Mississippi . . .	773
Arkansas	. . .	144	Missouri . . .	3,572
Delaware	. . .	19,829	North Carolina . .	30,463
Florida	. . .	932	South Carolina . .	9,914
Georgia	. . .	3,500	Tennessee . . .	7,300
Kentucky	. . .	10,684	Texas . . .	355
Louisiana	. . .	18,647	Virginia . . .	58,042
Maryland	. . .	83,942		

Delaware possessed 8,887 slaves in 1790, 6,153 in 1800, 4,177
in 1810, 4,509 in 1820, 3,292 in 1830, 2,695 in 1840, 2,290 in
1850, and 1,798 in 1860.

Maryland held 103,036 slaves in 1790, 105,635 in 1800, 111,502 in 1810, 107,397 in 1820, 102,994 in 1830, 89,737 in 1840, 90,368 in 1850, and 87,188 in 1860. She, as well as Delaware, passed laws in 1791 prohibiting the African slave trade, and preventing the ingress of negroes from other States, unless accompanied by their masters, and then not for the purpose of sale.

The Yankees, New-Yorkers, Jerseymen, and Quakers of Pennsylvania, in order to get rid of their slaves, disregarded the laws of Maryland; and in 1797 it was further enacted—

' That it shall not be lawful, from and after the passing of this ' Act, to import or bring into this State, by land or by water, ' any negro, mulatto, or other slave for sale, or to reside within ' this State; and any person brought into the State as a slave, ' contrary to this Act, if a slave before, shall thereupon imme- ' diately cease to be the property of the person or persons so ' importing or bringing such slave within this State, and shall ' be free.'

Exceptions were, however, permitted in favour of persons who came into the State with the *bonâ-fide* intention to become citizens; but even in such cases, the slaves or their mothers were required to be residents of the United States prior to 1794 Finding it very difficult, under the existing laws, to prevent the influx of negroes from the more Northern States, the Legislature in 1809 passed the following Act:—

' That from and after the passing of this Act, if any person or ' persons shall import or bring into this State any free negro or ' mulatto, or any person bound to service for a term of years only, ' and shall sell or otherwise dispose of such free negro, mulatto, ' or person bound to service for a term of years only, as a slave for ' life, or for any longer time than by law such person may be ' bound to service, knowing such negro or mulatto to be free, ' or entitled to freedom at a certain age, every such person or ' persons shall, for every such offence, forfeit and pay the sum of ' $800; and in case of failure to pay, the person or persons so ' offending shall be condemned to work on the public roads for ' a term not exceeding five years.'

The Yankees evaded this enactment, as well as the Federal laws, to such an extent that more stringent measures were adopted. In 1810, the Legislature passed unanimously the following :—

'Every commander of a vessel convicted of wilfully importing
' into this State from any foreign country any slave, and every
' person convicted of bringing into this State, by land or by water,
' any negro or mulatto from any foreign country, with intent to
' dispose of such negro within this State as a slave, the said
' persons so offending shall be sentenced to confinement in the
' penitentiary for a term not less than one year, nor more than
' five years.'

In 1831, the Legislature passed a law totally prohibiting the importation of slaves from even the other States of the Union; but in 1833 it was thought to be oppressive upon the people of the South who wished to reside near the Federal capital, within the jurisdiction of Maryland, and it was, therefore, modified in favour of *bonâ fide* residents. A law was passed in 1839, requiring all persons who came within the State, to make an oath that they did not bring any slaves for the purpose of selling them. All slaves introduced within the limits of the State have to be registered, with their names and full description; the fees for recording the same to be appropriated for the benefit of the African Colonisation Society.

In 1753 the colony of Virginia, conformably to royal orders, enacted that :—

' All persons who have been, or shall be, imported into this
' colony by sea or by land, and were not Christians in their native
' country, except Turks and Moors in amity with His Majesty,
' and such who can prove their being free in England, or any
' other Christian country, before they were shipped for transpor-
' tation hither, shall be accounted slaves, and as such shall be
' bought and sold, notwithstanding a conversion to Christianity
' after their importation.'

Virginia at an early date abolished the African slave trade. Her Constitution, adopted on June 12, 1776, after reciting a series of complaints against the British Sovereign, charges him with ' prompting our negroes to rise in arms among us—
' those very negroes whom, by an inhuman use of his negative,
' he had refused us permission to exclude by law.' Virginia alone, in 1790, contained 293,427 slaves, more than seven

times as many as all the 'Free States' combined. Her white
population exceeded her slaves only 25 per cent. Her soil
and climate were particularly suited for negro labour, but
not to such an extent as the more southern States ; for this
reason there has been a general migration towards the cotton
region. Her slaves numbered 345,796 in 1800, 392,518 in
1810, 425,153 in 1820, 469,757 in 1830, 449,087 in 1840,
472,528 in 1850, and 490,887 in 1860. Virginia also prohibited
the importation of slaves from other States as merchandise.
Here are her laws on the subject, enacted in 1778 :—

'Sec. 1.—For preventing the further importation of slaves
' into this commonwealth be it enacted by General Assembly
' that from and after the passing of this Act no slave or slaves
' shall hereafter be imported by sea or by land, nor shall any
' slave or slaves so imported be sold or bought by any person
' whatever.

'Sec. 2.—Every person hereafter importing slaves into this
' commonwealth contrary to this Act shall forfeit and pay the
' sum of 1,000*l.* for every slave so imported; and every person
' selling or buying any such slaves shall in like manner forfeit and
' pay the sum of 500*l.* for every slave so sold or bought, &c.

'Sec. 3.—That every slave imported into this commonwealth,
' contrary to the true intent and meaning of this Act, shall upon
' such importation become free.

'Sec. 4.—Provided always that this Act shall not be construed
' to extend to those who may incline to remove from any one of
' the United States and become citizens of this State; and
' provided that within ten days after their removal into the same
' they take the following oath before some magistrate of the
' commonwealth :—"I, A B, do swear that my removal to the
' State of Virginia was with no intention to evade the Act for
' preventing the further importation of slaves within the com-
' monwealth; nor have I brought with me, or will cause to be
' brought, any slaves, with an intent of selling them, nor have any
' of the slaves now in my possession been imported from Africa,
' or any of the West India Islands, since the 1st day of November
' 1778 : so help me God." '

A still more stringent law was passed in 1785, viz. :—

'That no persons shall henceforth be slaves within this

' commonwealth, except such as were so on the first day of the
' present session of the Assembly, and the descendants of the
' females of them. Slaves which shall hereafter be brought into
' this commonwealth, and be kept therein one whole year
' together, or so long at different times as shall amount to one
' year, shall be free.'

This law was shortly afterwards amended in order to permit persons from the North who desired to remove to Virginia to bring their servants within the State. Among the slaves thus introduced were a number of mulattoes. They were very nearly white, with straight hair, and no marks of the African race to be seen about their person. A question arose as to whether they were slaves. The Northerners insisted upon their right of property in them either by descent or purchase. In order to determine the matter and enable the owner to prove his claims, the Legislature, in 1785, enacted—

' That every person of whose grandfathers or grandmothers any
' one is, or shall have been a negro, although all his other pro-
' genitors except that descending from the negro shall have been
' white persons, shall be deemed a mulatto; and every such
' person who shall have one-fourth part or more of negro blood,
' shall in like manner be deemed a mulatto.'

The question again arising, the Legislature, in 1786, passed the following law—

' Every person other than a negro, of whose grandfathers or
' grandmothers any one is or shall have been a negro, although
' all his or her other progenitors, except that descending from a
' negro, shall have been white persons, shall be deemed a
' mulatto; and so every such person who shall have one-fourth
' part or more of negro blood shall in like manner be deemed
' a mulatto.'

Although the laws of Virginia were so adverse to the African, as well as the internal slave trade, she had great difficulty in excluding slaves from her limits. The Yankees actually carried on the business (?) of kidnapping free negroes in the Northern States and took them to Virginia and other Southern States for the purpose of sale. To put a stop to these nefarious trans-actions, the Legislature, in 1786, enacted that—

' *Whereas* several evil-disposed persons have seduced or stolen

' the children of black and mulatto free persons, and have
' actually disposed of the persons so seduced or stolen as slaves,
' and punishment adequate to such crimes not being by law
' provided for such offenders:

' *Be it enacted,* that any person who shall hereafter be guilty
' of stealing or selling any free person for a slave, knowing the
' said person so sold to be free, and thereof shall be lawfully
' convicted, the person so convicted *shall suffer death without*
' *the benefit of clergy.*'

In 1792 it was enacted —

' That no persons shall henceforth be slaves within this
' commonwealth, except such as were so on the 17th day of
' October 1785; and the descendants, being slaves, as since
' have been, or hereafter may be brought into this State, or
' held therein pursuant to law.'

The Northerners, by 1806, were pouring their slaves into
Virginia in such numbers, in order to evade the territorial acts
of abolition passed by their own States, that the Legislature was
obliged to pass more stringent measures to prevent the violation
of her laws thus disregarded. The Act of that year says :—

' That if any slave or slaves shall hereafter be brought into
' this commonwealth, and shall either be kept therein one
' whole year or so long, at different times, as shall amount to one
' year, or shall be sold or hired within this commonwealth, in
' every such case the owner shall forfeit all right to such slave
' or slaves, which right shall absolutely vest in the overseers of
' the poor of any county or corporation who shall apprehend
' such forfeited slave or slaves within his jurisdiction, in trust
' for the benefit of the poor of such county or corporation.

' Any person hereafter bringing into this commonwealth
' any slave or slaves, contrary to this act, shall forfeit and pay
' the sum of $400 for every slave so brought in; and every
' person selling, buying, or hiring any such slave or slaves,
' knowing the same to have been brought in contrary to the
' provisions of this Act, shall forfeit and pay the sum of $400 for
' every slave so brought, sold, or hired; which forfeiture shall
' accrue to the use of the commonwealth, to be recovered by
' action of debt or information, in which the defendant shall be
' held to special bail; judgment shall be rendered without

' regard to any exception for want or form, and an attorney's
' fee of twenty dollars shall be taxed in the bill of costs.'

With a view of accommodating actual settlers from the
Northern States, the Legislature, in 1812, enacted—

' That all persons now residing within this commonwealth, or
' who may hereafter remove to the same with a *bonâ fide*
' intention of becoming citizens and inhabitants thereof, who
' now are, or at the time of his, her, or their removal, may be
' the owner or owners of any slave or slaves born in any of the
' United States, or territories thereof, shall be, and they are
' hereby authorised to bring into and hold within this common-
' wealth any such slave or slaves : provided that such owner or
' owners shall, within thirty days after such slave or slaves shall
' have been brought into this commonwealth, exhibit to some
' justice of the peace of the county in which he, she, or they may
' reside, or have removed to, a statement in writing, containing
' the name, age, sex, and description of each and every slave so
' brought in ; and shall, moreover, make oath, or solemn affirma-
' tion before such justice, that the said statement contains a
' true account of the slaves so brought in ; and that the said slave
' or slaves were not brought into this commonwealth for the
' purpose of sale, or with the intent to evade the laws preventing
' the further importation of slaves ; and within sixty days there-
' after return such statement, together with a certificate of said
' oath or affirmation, to the Court of the same county, to be then
' recorded.

' And provided, also, that the said owner or owners shall,
' within three months after any slave or slaves shall have been
' so brought into this commonwealth, export a female slave of the
' age of ten years, and under the age of thirty, for every slave so
' as aforesaid imported, and within the said period, return to the
' Court of said county a statement containing the name, age, and
' description of the slave or slaves so exported, and give satisfac-
' tory evidence to the said Court of the performance of the said
' condition, and make oath that he, she, or they have *bonâ fide*
' performed the same.'

This law disposes of the charge of ' slave-breeding.' The
great object of the Virginians has been for many years to lessen
the number of their slaves.

Although Virginia was the first colony to receive slaves, it does not appear that they increased much for more than a half-century. In 1670 there were only 2,000 within her borders.

The slave population of North Carolina amounted to 100,572 in 1790, 133,296 in 1800, 168,824 in 1810, 205,017 in 1820, 245,601 in 1830, 245,817 in 1840, 288,548 in 1850, and 331,081 in 1860. This State also passed laws for preventing the African slave trade and against the reception of negroes from the Northern States.

Here are two of her laws, the first enacted in 1786, the other in 1795 :—

'That every person who shall introduce into this State any
' slave or slaves after the passing hereof, from any of the
' United States which have passed laws for the liberation of slaves,
' shall, on complaint thereof before any justice of the peace, be
' compelled by such justice of the peace to enter into bond with
' sufficient security in the sum of 50l. current money, for each
' slave, for the removing of such slave or slaves to the State
' from whence such slave or slaves were brought, within three
' months,' &c.

' That from and after the 1st day of April next (1795) it
' shall not be lawful for any person coming into this State with
' an intent to settle or otherwise, from any of the West Indies or
' Bahama Islands, or the settlements on the Southern coasts of
' America, to land any negro or negroes, or people of colour,
' over the age of fifteen years, under the penalty of 100l. for
' each and every slave or person of colour,' &c.

The port of Charleston was so accessible for slave traders, that the Legislature of South Carolina placed many restrictions upon the importation of Africans. An Act, which was passed in 1698, recites that : —

' Whereas the great number of negroes which have of late
' been imported into this colony may endanger the safety there-
' of if speedy measures be not taken, and encouragement given
' for the importation of white servants.'

And requires each planter shall employ one white servant to every six blacks. The Act of 1714 imposes a duty of 2l. upon every slave over twelve years of age imported from Africa, and contains the following preamble :—

' And whereas the number of negroes do extremely increase
' in this province, and through the afflicting providence of God
' the white persons do not proportionably multiply, by reason
' whereof the safety of the said province is greatly endangered :
' for the prevention of which, for the future, &c., &c.'

In 1716 another Act was passed, which offered a bounty to
white persons to settle in the colony.   Its preamble says :—

' Whereas sad experience has taught us that the small number
' of white inhabitants of this province is not sufficient to defend
' the same even against our Indian enemies ; and whereas the
' number of slaves is daily increasing in this province, which
' may likewise endanger the safety thereof, if speedy care be not
' taken to encourage the importation of white servants.'

Again, in 1717, an Act was passed imposing an additional
duty of 40*l.* upon every negro slave ' of any age or condition
' whatsoever, and from any part of the world.'   It will be readily
seen that this law was designed to prohibit altogether the introduction of Africans, without violating the orders of the British
Government, which denied to the colonists the privilege of excluding them by direct legislation.   It certainly acted in this
manner, as will be observed by the preamble to that passed in
1744 ' for the further preventing the spreading of malignant and
' contagious disorders,' which contains the following words :—

' Whereas it hath been found by experience that since the
' importation of negroes and slaves from the coast of Africa into
' this province hath been prohibited, this province in general,
' and Charleston in particular, hath been much more healthy
' than heretofore it hath been,' &c. &c.

These laws failed to accomplish their purpose, and others
were enacted in 1750 and 1751, fixing a tax on slaves, to be
devoted to the encouragement of white servants.   The Act of
1764 imposes an additional duty of 100*l.* on each slave; it
reads :—

' Whereas the importation of negroes, equal in number to
' what have been imported of late years, may prove of the most
' dangerous consequence, in many respects, to this province,
' and the best way to obviate such dangers will be by imposing
' such additional duty upon them as may totally prevent these
' evils.'

Let us now pass from this period of colonial vassalage, and see what was done by the independent sovereignty of South Carolina as a State. In 1787 the Legislature enacted that no negro or other slave shall be imported from Africa, and no slave shall be imported from any other State, unless accompanied by his master. A subsequent Act of the same year declares :—

'That any person importing or bringing into this State a 'negro slave contrary to the Act to regulate the recovery of 'debts, and prohibiting the importation of negroes, shall, besides 'the forfeiture of such negro or slave, be liable to a penalty of '100*l*. in addition to the forfeiture in and by said Act pre- 'scribed.'

The Act of 1788 says : —

'No negro or other slave shall be imported or brought into 'this State, either by land or by water, on or before the 1st of 'January 1793, under the penalty of forfeiting every such slave 'or slaves to any person who will sue or inform for the same; 'and under further penalty of paying 100*l*. to the use of the 'State for every such negro or slave so imported or brought in : 'provided that nothing in this prohibition contained shall 'extend to such slaves as are now the property of citizens of the 'United States, and at the time of passing this Act shall be 'within the limits of the United States.'

In 1792 the law was extended, viz. :—

'That no slave shall be imported into this State from Africa, 'the West India Islands, or any other place beyond the sea, for 'and during the term of two years, commencing from the 1st 'of January 1793.

'That no slave or negro, Indian, Moor, Mulatto, or Mestizo, 'bound to service for a term of years, shall be brought into this 'State, by land or by water, from any of the United States or 'any of the countries bordering thereon, ever hereafter: pro- 'vided, however, actual citizens of the United States shall and 'are hereby permitted to come into this State and settle with 'their slaves.'

In 1794 the prohibition was again extended :—

'That no slave or person of colour, bond or free, shall be 'permitted to be imported, or land, or enter the State from the 'Bahamas or West India Islands, or from any part of the

' continent of America, without the limits of the United States,
' or from any other parts beyond the seas.'

In 1796 the exclusion of negroes was extended to 1799, then to 1801, and further to 1803.

Notwithstanding all the prohibitions and fines, a clandestine trade was carried on through the ports of the Northern States and the interior, very much to the injury of the commerce of Charleston. As a matter of expediency the Legislature at that period opened the ports for the traffic until January 1, 1808, after which date it was determined that no slave should be brought into the State from any part of the world, not even from any of the United States, with the proviso: —

' That it shall and may be lawful to and for any person
' travelling into or through this State to bring into the same
' one or more slaves or free persons of colour, not exceeding two
' as necessary attendants on such person or his or her family,
' and for no other purpose whatsoever; provided, nevertheless,
' to exempt such person from the penalties of this Act, every
' such person shall make an oath before some justice of the
' peace, near to the place where they shall enter the State, that
' such slave or persons of colour is or are his or her necessary
' attendants, and that he or she will not sell or dispose of such
' slave or persons of colour, but will take the same back with
' him or her to his or her usual place of residence.'

Further laws similar to those of Virginia were passed, and in 1803 it was ordered that they ' shall be, and the same are hereby
' declared to be, perpetual laws.' The slaves in South Carolina, by the census, stand 107,094 in 1790, 146,151 in 1800, 196,365 in 1810, 258,475 in 1820, 315,401 in 1830, 327,038 in 1840, 384,984 in 1850, and 402,541 in 1860.

During the four years that South Carolina permitted the importation of slaves, 202 vessels arrived in Charleston harbour, 91 of which belonged to the British, 10 to the French, 88 to the Yankees, and 13 to Southerners. They brought 39,075 negroes, but many of the males were re-shipped to the West Indies, where their value was greater than in the States.

South Carolina requires :—

'That all and every person or persons removing into this
' State, with their slaves, shall immediately on entering the

' State take the following oath before some justice of the
' peace :—

' I, A B, do swear, that my removal into the State of South
' Carolina is with no intention of evading the several laws of this
' State, for preventing the further importation of slaves into this
' State ; nor have I brought with me any slave or slaves with an
' intention of selling them ; nor will I sell or dispose of any slave
' or slaves so brought with me as aforesaid within two years of
' the date hereof ; and it is my intention *bonâ fide* to become
' a resident and citizen of the said State.'

' That each and every slave who shall hereafter be imported
' or brought into this State, except under the limitations pre-
' scribed by this Act, shall be, and each and every one of them are
' hereby declared to be, free, in whosoever hands they may be.'

As late as 1835 the Legislature enacted :—

' That it shall not be lawful for any citizen of this State, or
' other person, to bring into this State, under any pretext what-
' ever, any slave or slaves from any port or place in the West
' Indies, or Mexico, or any part of South America, or from
' Europe, or from any sister State situated north of the Potomac
' river, or city of Washington.'

Georgia prohibited the African slave trade by a clause in her
Constitution adopted in 1798, viz. :—

' There shall be no future importation of slaves into this
' State from Africa, or any foreign place, after the 1st day of
' October next (1798).'

She likewise enacted similar laws to the other States in
reference to the admission of negroes from the North.

The enactment of 1833 says :—

' If any person or persons shall bring, import, or introduce
' into this State, or aid, or assist, or knowingly become concerned
' or interested in bringing, importing, or introducing into this
' State, either by land or by water, or in manner whatever, any
' slave or slaves, each and every such person or persons so
' offending shall be deemed principals in law, and guilty of a
' high misdemeanour, and may be arrested and tried in any
' county in this State in which he, she, or they may be found,
' and, on conviction, shall be punished by a fine not exceeding
' $500 each, for each and every slave so brought, imported, or

'introduced, and imprisonment and labour in the penitentiary
'for any term not less than one year, nor longer than four years:
'provided, however, this Act shall not prohibit actual settlers
'from coming into this State with their slaves from any of the
'other States of the Union.'

Georgia held 29,264 slaves in 1790, 59,404 in 1800, 105,218 in 1810, 149,654 in 1820, 217,331 in 1830, 280,944 in 1840, 381,602 in 1850, and 462,232 in 1860.

Kentucky was formed out of Virginia, and admitted into the Union in 1793. She continued the laws of that State against the African slave trade and the ingress of negroes except as servants. All persons migrating thither with slaves are obliged to take the following oath: —

'I, A B, do swear that my removal to the State of Kentucky
'was with an intention to become a citizen thereof, and that I
'have no slave or slaves, and will bring no slave or slaves with
'intent of selling them.'

In 1790, the District Assembly passed the following law :—

'That no slave shall be imported into this State from any
'foreign country, nor shall any slave who has been imported
'into the United States from any foreign country since the 1st
'day of January 1789, or who may be hereafter imported into
'the United States from any foreign country, be imported into
'the State under the penalty of $300.

'That no slave shall be imported into this State as merchan-
'dise; and any person so offending shall forfeit and pay a fine
'of $300.'

The census states that the territory of Kentucky possessed 11,830 in 1790, 40,343 in 1800, 80,561 in 1810, 126,732 in 1820, 165,213 in 1830, 182,258 in 1840, 210,981 in 1850, and 225,490 in 1860.

Tennessee was formerly a portion of North Carolina, and carried the laws of the parent State with her. The Act of Cession says: — 'Provided that no regulation made, or to be 'made, by Congress shall tend to emancipate slaves.' Her black population was 3,417 in 1790, 13,584 in 1800, 44,535 in 1810, 80,107 in 1820, 141,603 in 1830, 183,059 in 1840, 239,459 in 1850, and 275,784 in 1860.

Alabama has never permitted the African slave trade to be

carried on, and has always refused to admit negroes unless accompanied by their masters, and then not for the purpose of sale.

Here are two of her laws. The statute of 1807 says:—

' That if any person or persons shall be guilty of stealing or
' selling any free person for a slave, knowing the said person so
' sold to be free, and shall be thereof lawfully convicted, the
' person or persons so convicted shall suffer death.'

The statute of 1843 reads :—

' Any slave or slaves brought or imported into this State, con-
' trary to the laws of the United States in such cases made
' and provided, shall be condemned by any supreme court of this
' State within whose jurisdiction the said slave or slaves shall be
' brought or be seized, upon libel filed in the said court, and
' shall be sold by the proper officer of the court, to the highest
' bidder at public auction, for ready money, after advertising
' the time and place of such sale, in some newspaper in this
' State, at least fifteen days previous thereto.'

Alabama had 41,879 slaves in 1820, 117,549 in 1830, 253,532 in 1840, 342,844 in 1850, and 435,132 in 1860.

Mississippi is equally severe in regard to the foreign and internal slave traffic.

In 1822, the Legislature enacted the following law :—

' It shall not be lawful for any person whatsoever to bring into
' this State, or to hold therein, any slave or slaves born or
' resident out of the limits of the United States. Every such
' offender shall forfeit and pay to the State, for the use of the
' Literary Fund, for each slave so brought in, sold, purchased, or
' hired, a fine of $1,000.'

In 1839, the Legislature also enacted :—

' That if any person shall hereafter bring or import any slave
' or slaves into this State, as merchandise, or for the purpose of
' selling or hiring such slave or slaves, or shall be accessory
' thereto, the person or persons so offending shall be deemed
' guilty of a misdemeanour, and on conviction thereof shall be
' fined in the sum of $500, and be imprisoned for a term of not
' less than one nor more than six months, at the discretion of the
' Court, for each and every slave by him brought into this State
' as merchandise, or for sale, or for hire.'

The census of Mississippi records 3,489 slaves in 1800, 17,088 in 1810, 32,814 in 1820, 65,659 in 1830, 195,211 in 1840, 309,878 in 1850, and 436,696 in 1860.

Louisiana passed similar laws, the last of which was enacted in 1825, and reads as follows :—

' No person shall, after June 1, 1826, bring into this State ' any slave with the intent to sell or hire the same, under the ' penalty of being punished by imprisonment not exceeding two ' years, and fined not exceeding $1,000 ; and, moreover, shall ' forfeit said slave or slaves.'

The slaves in Louisiana numbered 34,660 in 1810, 69,064 in 1820, 109,588 in 1830, 168,452 in 1840, 244,809 in 1850, and 332,010 in 1860.

Arkansas imposes the same restrictions concerning the ingress of negroes. She had 1,617 in 1820, 4,576 in 1830, 19,935 in 1840, 47,100 in 1850, and 111,104 in 1860.

Florida likewise followed the example of her sister States. She was ceded by Spain to the United States by the treaty of 1819. Her slave returns are :—15,501 in 1830, 27,717 in 1840, 39,310 in 1850, and 61,753 in 1860.

Missouri has the same regulations in reference to the admission of slaves. Her revised statutes of 1835 declare that—

' Hereafter no person shall bring, or cause to be brought, into ' this State any person, or the descendants of any person, who ' shall have been imported into the United States, or any of the ' territories thereof, in contravention of the laws of the United ' States, and held as slaves, under a penalty of $500 recoverable ' by indictment.'

The slave portion of the census of Missouri stands thus:— 3,011 in 1810, 10,222 in 1820, 25,091 in 1830, 58,240 in 1840, 87,422 in 1850, and 114,965 in 1860.

Texas adopted the same policy in relation to slave immigration. She was admitted into the Union in 1845. The census exhibits 58,161 slaves in 1850, and 180,682 in 1860.

The district of Columbia had 3,244 slaves in 1800, 5,395 in 1810, 6,377 in 1820, 6,119 in 1830, 4,694 in 1840, 3,687 in 1850, and 3,181 in 1860. The territory of Utah had 26 in 1850, and 29 in 1860. Nebraska had 10 in 1860. New Mexico, 24 in 1860. Kansas, 2 in 1860.

The total slave population of all the American States and territories was — 697,897 in 1790, 893,041 in 1800, 1,191,364 in 1810, 1,538,038 in 1820, 2,009,043 in 1830, 2,487,455 in 1840, 3,204,313 in 1850, and 3,953,587 in 1860. Legislation in America has not lessened slavery to any extent; the increase in the several decades from 1790 to 1860 has been tolerably regular, viz. for the ten years ending : —

Year		Percentage
1800	. . . . . .	$27\ \frac{87}{100}$
1810	. . . . . .	$33\ \frac{40}{100}$
1820	. . . . . .	$28\ \frac{78}{100}$
1830	. . . . . .	$30\ \frac{61}{100}$
1840	. . . . . .	$23\ \frac{61}{100}$
1850	. . . . . .	$28\ \frac{82}{100}$
1860	. . . . . .	$23\ \frac{38}{100}$

These figures clearly prove that neither the territorial abolition in one section, nor the territorial extension in the other, has diminished or augmented the ' peculiar institution.'

Of the 697,897 slaves in all the American States in 1790, only 40,850 were in the Northern States. Canada contains about that number of blacks at the present time. The Northern States, in 1790, had 27,109 free negroes; the Southern States, 32,357. The American Colonization Society have sent about 10,000 blacks to Liberia.

The senseless charge of ' slave-breeding' made against the Southerners was started in Europe by Lord Palmerston in 1838, under information (?) received from New England, but was denied and disproved at the time by the then American Minister in London, the Hon. Andrew Stevenson, of Virginia. With the current of opinion, however, running the other way the charge seems to have become stereotyped. There never has been any such occupation as ' slave breeding' in the South; no negro child has ever been brought into the world for the purpose of sale or augmenting the wealth of the planter. The black race ' increase and multiply' in properly organised families, and with as much order as the whites. Although the Africans are naturally very immoral, their propriety of conduct in this particular is remarkable, and exceeds that of any community of negroes in the North. Common sense alone teaches that there is no such thing as 'slave-breeding' in the South, but to make the charge against Virginia and other border States is absurd in the extreme. If such a business were carried on at all it would be conducted in the Gulf States, where the climate is more congenial to the African race, and where their natural increase is nearly 3 per cent. per annum, while in the more northerly States it is only a little rising 1 per cent. The proprietors, with their servants, have been merely moving in a south-westerly direction, and as the latter outnumber the former on all occasions there is a disparity between the white and black population which has given rise to the erroneous impression alluded to.

PROCEEDINGS OF THE CONVENTION THAT FORMED THE CONSTITUTION, IN REFERENCE TO THE AFRICAN SLAVE TRADE.

The minutes of the Convention which met at Philadelphia in 1787 to frame the Federal Constitution give the views of that body in reference to the African slave trade. On August 6th, the committee—three from the North and two from the South—reported a draft containing the following clause :—

' No tax or duty shall be laid by the Legislature (of the United ' States Government) on articles exported from any State ; nor ' on the migration or importation of such persons as the several ' States shall think proper to admit ; nor shall such migration or ' importation be prohibited.'

On August 24, this provision was referred to a special committee of one from each of the eleven States present. Its chairman, Mr. Livingston (New Jersey), offered a substitute, viz. :—

' The migration or importation of such persons as the several ' States now existing shall think proper to admit shall not be ' prohibited by the Legislature (Congress) prior to the year ' 1800 ; but a tax or duty may be imposed on such migration ' or importation at a rate not exceeding the average of the ' duties laid on imports.'

The next day the report was considered, and ' It was moved ' and seconded to amend the report of the committee of eleven, ' entered on the journal on the 24th instant, as follows :—

' To strike out the words, " the year 1800," and insert the words ' " the year 1808," which passed in the affirmative.

' *Yeas.*—New Hampshire, Massachusetts, Connecticut, Mary-
' land, North Carolina, South Carolina, and Georgia, 7.

' *Nays.*—New Jersey, Pennsylvania, Delaware, Virginia, 4.'

After this the following proceedings took place:—

' The importation of *slaves* into such of the States as shall
' permit the same shall not be prohibited by the Legislature of
' the United States until the year 1808.'

' *Yeas.*—Connecticut, Virginia, and Georgia, 3.

' *Nays.*—Massachusetts, Pennsylvania, Delaware, North Caro-
' lina, and South Carolina, 5.

' Maryland delegation was divided.

' On the question to agree to the first part of the report as
amended, namely—

' " The migration or importation of such persons as the several
' " States now existing shall think proper to admit shall not be
' " prohibited by the Legislature prior to the year 1808 : "

' It was passed in the affirmative as follows :—

' *Yeas.*—New Hampshire, Massachusetts, Connecticut, Mary-
' land, North Carolina, South Carolina, and Georgia, 7.

' *Nays.*—New Jersey, Pennsylvania, Delaware and Virginia, 4.'

It has been doubted by many able lawyers whether the clause
in the Federal Constitution giving authority to Congress to
abolish the slave trade, by *implication merely*, was not
nullified by one of the amendments thereto, which says :—' The
' powers not delegated to the United States by the Constitution,
' nor prohibited by it to the States, are reserved to the States
' respectively, or to the people.' The Confederate Constitution,
however, is quite clear upon this subject. It reads : —

' The importation of negroes of the African race from any
' foreign country other than the slaveholding States or territories
' of the United States of America is hereby forbidden; and
' Congress is required to pass such laws as shall effectually
' prevent the same. Congress shall also have power to pro-
' hibit the introduction of slaves from any State not a member
' of, or territory not belonging to, this Confederacy.'

The Federal States can reopen the slave trade at any time by
rescinding the Acts of Congress; the Confederate States have
deprived themselves of such privilege. The natural increase of
negroes in the South is equal to the demand for their labour.

ABOLITIONISM IN AMERICA.

The Quakers, like the Yankees, are given to meddling with other people's affairs, and it was by the indulgence of this propensity that they laid the foundation of the abolition excitement. They did not do so, however, until the system of slave labour in their own neighbourhoods had ceased to be profitable. In Pennsylvania, in North Carolina, and in other colonies, they were slaveholders. One of their ' sect,' George Keith, a Scotchman by birth, once a follower of William Penn, renounced Quakerism, and quarrelled with the ' broad-brimmed courtier.' He declared Quakerism inconsistent with the exercise of political authority, and he preached abolition doctrines in the streets of Philadelphia, stating that negro slavery was antagonistic to the principles of good government. The Quakers persecuted him for promulgating such doctrines, and he was obliged to return to England in 1692. The ' institution ' paid ' at that time in Pennsylvania, and of course it was not deemed improper to hold black men in bondage. Black women and children were ' remitted ' from the West Indies to Philadelphia, to settle balances due to the ' Friends.'

Abolitionism was first mooted in the Federal Congress on February 11, 1790, when a memorial from the Quakers of Pennsylvania, New Jersey, Delaware, Maryland, New York, and Virginia, was presented, praying for the enactment of laws against the further prosecution of the African slave trade. A discussion at once arose, on the abstract question of slavery itself, with respect to the Constitution. Mr. Parker, of Virginia, advocated the reception of the petition, and was pleased to see a desire so promptly manifested to ' ascertain what could be ' done to restrain the nefarious practice.' He was willing to lay a tax of ten dollars per head on all negroes imported, and otherwise unite in any measure that could be devised to discontinue the slave trade, consistent with the terms of the Constitution. Mr. Madison did not conceive that there was any cause for alarm concerning the interference by Congress with slavery in the States. He was opposed to the African slave-trade, so were all the members from the South, but they saw an insidious attempt on the part of the Quakers to engraft abolitionism on

the body politic. Mr. Stone, of Maryland, said: 'It was an
' unfortunate circumstance, that it was the disposition of religious
' sects to imagine that they understood the rights of human
' nature better than all the world besides; and that they would,
' in consequence, be meddling with concerns in which they had
' nothing to do.' Mr. Burke, of South Carolina, remarked, that
' he had a respect for the Quakers, but did not believe they
' had more virtue or religion than other people, nor, perhaps, so
' much, if they were examined to the bottom, notwithstanding
' their outward pretences.' Mr. Jackson, of Georgia, made the
following practical remarks: — ' He would ask those who were
' desirous of freeing the negroes, if they had sufficient funds to
' pay for them? If they had, they should come forward on
' that business with some propriety; but if they had not, they
' should keep themselves quiet, and not interfere with a
' business in which they were not interested. Is the whole
' morality of the United States confined to the Quakers? Are
' they the only people whose feelings are to be consulted on
' this occasion? Is it to them we owe our present happiness?
' Was it they who formed our Constitution? Did they, by their
' arms or contributions, establish our independence? I believe
' they were generally opposed to that measure. But why do
' these men set themselves up in a particular manner against
' slavery? Do they understand the rights of mankind, and the
' disposition of Providence, better than others? If they were
' to consult that Book, which claims our regard, they would
' find that slavery is not only allowed, but commended. Their
' Saviour, who possessed more benevolence and commiseration
' than they pretend to, allowed it; and, if they examine the
' subject, they will find that slavery has been no novel doctrine
' since the days of Cain.' Mr. Sedgwick, of Massachusetts,
' did not believe there would be any considerable number of
' individuals in the South alarmed at the commitment of the
' petition, from a fear that Congress intended to exercise an
' unconstitutional authority, in order to violate their rights.'
Mr. Smith, of South Carolina, was of opinion that 'the me-
' morialists in reality prayed for a violation of the Constitution,
' and their petition "should be rejected as an attempt upon the
' " virtue and patriotism of the house."' Mr. Tucker, from the

same State, 'thought that the least said upon the subject the
' better, particularly as Congress had no power to do anything,
' except to lay a duty of ten dollars upon each person imported ;
' and that was a political consideration not arising from religion
' or morality.   If the Quakers wished to secure the abolition of
' the slave-trade, they should present their petitions to the State
' Legislatures, who alone have the power of forbidding the im-
' portation.' On February 12, 1790, the discussion was resumed
upon the reception of a memorial from Benjamin Franklin, President of the 'Pennsylvanian Society for Promoting the Aboli-
' tion of Slavery, the Relief of Free Negroes unlawfully held in
' Bondage, and the Improvement of the Condition of the African
' Race.' Mr. Tucker, of Virginia, was surprised to see the
petition 'signed by a man who ought to have known the Con-
' stitution better.' A further debate took place on March 23,
1790, when the following resolutions were adopted :—

' That the migration or importation of such persons as any of
' the States now existing shall think proper to admit, cannot be
' prohibited by Congress, prior to the year 1808.'

' That Congress have no authority to interfere in the eman-
' cipation of slaves, or in the treatment of them within any of
' the States ; it remaining with the several States alone to pro-
' vide any regulation therein, which humanity and true policy
' may require.'

On November 26, 1792, an Abolition memorial from
Warner Mifflin, a Quaker, was presented, received by the
House, and laid on the table.   Two days afterwards, Mr.
Steele, of North Carolina, called attention to the matter.
' He was surprised to find this subject started anew by a
' fanatic, who, not content with keeping his own conscience,
' undertook to keep the consciences of other men ; and, in a
manner which he deemed not very decent, had intruded his
opinions upon this House.   Had an application been made to
him to present such a petition he would have avoided a compliance with it.   Gentlemen of the North do not realise the
mischievous consequences which have already resulted from
measures of this kind, and, if a stop were not put to it, the
Southern States would be compelled to apply to the General
' Government for their interference.' Mr. Ames, of Massachusetts,

apologised for having presented the petition, and the House ordered its return to the Quaker.

The following year the Fugitive Slave Law was passed. The negro question was dropped until January 30, 1797, when Mr. Swanwick, of Pennsylvania, presented the petition of four slaves that had escaped into that State from North Carolina. The House declined receiving the petition. On November 30, 1797, Mr. Gallatin, of Pennsylvania, handed in a memorial of the annual meeting of Quakers, relative to the ' oppressed state of ' their African brethren,' particularly those in North Carolina, who, it was alleged, had been manumitted and again reduced to slavery. They furthermore requested the attention of Congress against ' every species of extravagance and dissipation, such as ' gaming, horse racing, cock fighting, shows, plays, and other ' expensive diversions and entertainments.' The reception of the petition was debated at great length, and on February 14, 1798, the House declared the subjects it embraced were exclusively of judicial consequence, and that the parties have leave to withdraw their memorial. The Senate concurred.

The slavery question was renewed January 2, 1799, when Mr. Waln, of Pennsylvania, presented a petition, praying for ' a revision of the laws of the United States relative to the ' slave trade; of the Act relative to fugitives from justice; and ' for the adoption of such measures as should in due time eman- ' cipate the whole of their brethren from their disagreeable ' situation.' Mr. Rutledge, of South Carolina, remarked: ' The ' gentlemen who formerly used to advocate liberty have re- ' treated from their post, and committed the important trust to ' the care of " black patriots; " they tell the House they are in ' slavery; thank God they are! They say they are not repre- ' sented; certainly they are not; and I trust the day will never ' arrive when the Congress of the United States will display a ' parti-coloured assembly. Too much of this new-fangled French ' philosophy of liberty and equality has found its way among ' these gentlemen of our plantations, for which nothing will do ' but liberty.' Mr. Harrison G. Otis, of Massachusetts, said that ' though he owned no slaves, he saw no reason why others ' might not; and that the proprietors of them were the fittest ' persons, and not Congress, to regulate that species of property.'

Mr. Brown, of Rhode Island, argued that 'the petition was but 'the contrivance of a combination of Jacobins, who had troubled 'Congress for many years past, and he feared never would 'cease.' The 'Friends' again intruded themselves with non-success upon the notice of the Federal Legislature on January 21, 1805.

Up to the year 1818 'Abolition proclivities' seemed to be confined pretty much to a section around Philadelphia, wherever Quaker influence extended. It was then taken up by the Yankees as a political weapon to obtain control of the general government. Henry Clay, a Southerner, in order to gain popularity in the North, began a system of compromises, by bargaining away the rights of the South, the result of which was a division of the Louisiana territory, by the establishment of the 'Missouri Line,' which restricted the migration of slavery to 36° 30′ N. lat. This arrangement was clearly a violation of the Constitution, as well as of the Treaty with France in 1803, and was, for those reasons, repealed in 1854. Mr. Clay, although a man of great ability, thus sowed very early the seeds of discord between the States. His 'American system' — high tariffs — also played into the hands of the North, and were equally unconstitutional. He, too, was a warm supporter of a national bank. In fact, all his measures were unsound and impolitic. In his case, it may be truly said, that the 'evil that men do 'lives after them; the good is oft interrèd with their bones.' Mr. Clay, prior to his death, made several strong pro-slavery speeches; he likewise changed his views concerning a tariff and a bank.

THE FUGITIVE SLAVE LAW.

In regard to fugitive slaves, the Constitution of the United States says, in Article IV. section 2, second and third paragraphs:—

'A person charged in any State with treason, felony, or other 'crime, who shall flee from justice and be found in another 'State, shall, on demand of the executive authority of the State 'from which he fled, be delivered up, to be removed to the 'State having jurisdiction of the crime.

' No person held to service or labour in one State, under the
' laws thereof, escaping into another, shall, in consequence
' of any law or regulation, be discharged from such service or
' labour, but shall be delivered up, on claim of the party to
' whom such service or labour may be due.'

In the Convention these clauses were agreed to unanimously.
They stipulate, first; felons, called 'fugitives from justice;'
second, ' apprentices or indentured servants,' or persons ' held
' to service;' and third, slaves or persons ' held to labour.'
These provisions render it incumbent upon all States that are
members of the Union to ' deliver up' any persons of the three
classes, in accordance with the law entitled, ' An Act respect-
' ing fugitives from justice and persons escaping from the
' service of their masters,' approved by President Washington,
February 12, 1793, at whose recommendation it was passed
by Congress, the Senate voting unanimously, the House nearly
so.   Although this Act imposed penalties on all persons who
would obstruct or hinder the arrest of fugitives or conceal them,
it was in the course of time disregarded by many of the Northern
States, who openly ' nullified ' its provisions.*   It therefore
became necessary, in the year 1850, to enact amendments
thereto, in order to protect the Southern States from this
flagrant Yankee violation of the Constitution.   It will be perceived that it was George Washington, and not Mr. Mason, who
was the author of the Fugitive Slave Law.

The Constitution of the Confederate States has a similar
clause, but is much more honest in its expression than its
predecessor.   It says :—

[The second paragraph is identical with that of the Federal
document.]

* No State has a right to remain in the Union and nullify a constitutional
Act of Congress: when she becomes displeased with the provisions of the
Federal compact, she should secede.   The case of South Carolina in 1832
was different from that of the Yankee States: she ignored an unconstitutional Act of the Washington Senate and House of Representatives, as
she had a right to do, and forced the North to alter the tariff.   This matter
of nullification has been much misstated, and not generally understood.
Many cities in America have refused to abide by the action of the State
Legislature, in consequence of those bodies having exceeded the authority
delegated to them.   Counties in England, too, have frequently nullified Acts
of Parliament.

The third recites :—

' No slave or other person held to service or labour in any
' State or territory of the Confederate States, under the laws
' thereof, escaping or lawfully carried into another, shall, in
' consequence of any law or regulation therein, be discharged
' from such service or labour, but shall be delivered up on claim
' of the party to whom such slave belongs, or to whom such
' service or labour may be due.'

Massachusetts, even after the ' compromise of 1850,' passed
the following Act of Nullification (in 1855):—

' No person, while holding any office of honour, trust, or
' emolument under the laws of this commonwealth, shall in
' any capacity issue any warrant or other proof, or grant any
' certificate under or by virtue of an Act of Congress, approved
' the 13th day of February, in the year 1793, entitled, "An
' "Act respecting fugitives from justice, and persons escaping
' "from the service of their masters ;" or under or by virtue of
' an Act of Congress, approved the 18th day of September, 1850,
' entitled, "An Act to amend, and supplementary to an act
' "respecting fugitives from justice, and persons escaping from
' "the service of their masters ;" or shall in any capacity serve
' any such warrant or other process.'

If any officer of the State should comply with the provisions
of the Acts of 1793 and 1850 he is subject to the following
penalty :—

' His office shall be deemed vacant, and he shall for ever
' thereafter be ineligible to hold any office of trust, honour, or
' emolument, under the laws of this commonwealth.'

If a lawyer shall serve on behalf of the owner of the slave,
the law thus deals with him : —

' He shall be deemed to have resigned any commission from
' the commonwealth that he may possess; and he shall be
' thereafter incapacitated from appearing as counsel or attorney
' in the courts of this commonwealth.'

Judges, too, who are sworn to support the Constitution of the
United States, and laws made under its authority, who may
issue a warrant under the Acts specified, are to be disposed of
in this manner : —

' It shall be considered as a violation of good behaviour, as

' well as a reason for loss of confidence, and as furnishing suffi-
' cient grounds, either for impeachment or removal by address.'

' And if any sheriff, gaoler, coroner, constable, or other officer
' of the commonwealth, including militia officers, who shall even
' aid in arresting, imprisoning, detaining, or returning any
' person, for the reason that he is claimed or adjudged to be a
' fugitive from service or labour, shall be punished by fine, not
' less than $1,000, and not exceeding $2,000, and imprisoned
' in the state prison for not less than one nor more than two
' years.'

Here, then, is the State of Massachusetts—and many others
are equally culpable—ignoring, in the most unscrupulous manner, a law that the Constitution expressly provided for. But
what can be thought of Pennsylvania, who has likewise been
guilty of the same misconduct? It was at the request of this
latter State for the return of a slave that had escaped from her
borders into Maryland, that Washington advised Congress to
enact the Fugitive Slave Law; and this, too, was thirteen years
after the passage of her Act of gradual abolition, which did not
free a single slave.

The Supreme Court of the United States has fully recognised
the constitutional protection to the right of property in slaves.
In the case of Prigg *v.* the Commonwealth of Pennsylvania, it
was asserted by every judge on the bench, that the design of
the clause in the Constitution above quoted was ' to secure to
' the citizens of the slave-holding states the complete right and
' title of ownership in the slaves, as property, in every State in
' the Union into which they might escape from the State where
' they were held in servitude.' These are the very words of
Mr. Justice Story, of Massachusetts, in delivering the opinion
of the Court. He added: ' The full recognition of this right
' and title was indispensable to the security of this species of
' property in all the slave-holding States; and, indeed, was so
' vital to the preservation of the domestic interests and institu-
' tions, that it cannot be doubted that it constituted a funda-
' mental article, without which the Constitution could not have
' been formed.' Judge McLean of Ohio said : ' It was designed
' to protect the rights of the master, and against whom ? Not
' against the State, nor the people of the State, in which he

' resides; but against the people and legislative action of other
' States, where the fugitive from labour might be found.
' Under the Confederation, the master had no legal means of
' enforcing his RIGHTS in a State opposed to slavery. A disregard
' of *rights* thus asserted was deeply felt in the South. It
' produced great excitement, and would have led to results
' destructive of the Union. To avoid this, the constitutional
' guarantee was essential. . . . . I cannot perceive how anyone
' can doubt that the remedy given in the Constitution, if, indeed,
' it give any remedy without legislation, was designed to be a
' powerful one—a remedy sanctioned by judicial authority—a
' remedy guarded by the forms of law. But the enquiry is
' reiterated, Is not the master entitled to his *property*? I
' answer that he is. *His right is guaranteed by the Constitu-*
' *tion*; and the most summary means for its enforcement is
' found in the Act of Congress. And neither the State nor its
' citizens can obstruct the prosecution of this right.'

THE DEPORTATION OF SLAVES.

With the exception of the edict of Mr. Lincoln, the only
emancipation decree ever issued in America was that by Lord
Dunmore, after all control over affairs in Virginia had passed
out of his hands. When the House of Burgesses of that colony
took the matter of the Boston Port Bill into consideration, and
appointed June 1, 1774, the day on which it was to go into
operation, to be observed as a fast, he dissolved the Assembly
(May 26); but most of its members met the next day, and
resolved that an attack upon one colony was an attack upon all,
threatening ruin to the rights of all, unless repelled by the
' united wisdom of the whole,' and a committee was appointed
to communicate with the other colonies on the expediency of a
general Congress. The Governor's oppressive measures brought
down upon him the indignation of the people, and he was eventually compelled to fly for refuge to a British man-of-war, then
lying in the James River, from which he some time afterwards
issued the following proclamation :—

' By his Excellency the Right Hon. John Earl of Dunmore,
  ' His Majesty's Lieutenant and Governor-General of the
  ' Colony and Dominion of Virginia, and Vice-Admiral of the
  ' same :—

' *A Proclamation.*

' As I have ever entertained hopes that an accommodation
' might have taken place between Great Britain and this colony
' without being compelled by my duty to this most disagreeable,
' but now absolutely necessary step, rendered so by a body of
' armed men, unlawfully assembled, firing on His Majesty's
' tenders; and the formation of an army now on their march to
' attack His Majesty's troops and destroy the well-disposed
' subjects of this colony; to defeat such treasonable purposes,
' and that all such traitors and their abettors may be brought
' to justice, and that the peace and good order of this colony
' may be again restored, which the ordinary course of the civil
' law is unable to effect, I have thought fit to issue this my
' proclamation, hereby declaring that until the aforesaid good
' purpose can be obtained, I do, in virtue of the power and
' authority to me given by His Majesty, determine to execute
' martial law, and cause the same to be executed throughout this
' colony.   And, to the end that peace and good order may the
' sooner be restored, I do require every person capable of bearing
' arms to resort to His Majesty's standard, or be looked upon as
' traitors to His Majesty's Crown and Government, and thereby
' become liable to the penalty the law inflicts upon such offences,
' such as forfeiture of life, confiscation of lands, &c.   *And I do*
' *hereby further declare all indentured servants, negroes, or*
' *others (appertaining to rebels) free, that are able and willing*
' *to bear arms, they joining His Majesty's troops as soon as*
' *may be, for the more speedily reducing this colony to a proper*
' *sense of their duty to His Majesty's Crown and dignity.*   I
' do further order and require all His Majesty's liege subjects
' to retain their quit rents, or any other taxes due, or that may
' become due, till such time as peace may be again restored
' to this at present most unhappy country; or till they may be
' demanded of them for their former salutary purposes by
' officers properly authorised to receive the same.

' Given under my hand, on board the ship William, off
' Norfolk, this 7th day of November, in the sixth year of his
' Majesty's reign (A.D. 1775).

' DUNMORE.

' God save the King.'

In accordance with this proclamation some 30,000 slaves
were carried off, or induced to leave their masters; but they
were not all employed in the military service. About 3,000
were shipped to the West Indies, and there sold into renewed
bondage—the average value being about 56l. sterling.
A large number died in Virginia of camp fever; many
others, labouring under disease, and afraid to return to the
plantations, wandered into the woods and perished. Those
negroes that remained with the army were sent to Nova Scotia,
and in 1792, they, then numbering 1,170, were removed to
Sierra Leone, that colony having been founded in 1787 by
clearing London of all its negro inhabitants, 470.

Although the American war was virtually brought to a close
by the surrender of Cornwallis at Yorktown, on the 19th of
October 1781, the provisional 'Articles agreed upon by and
' between Richard Oswald, Esq., the Commissioner of His
' Britannic Majesty, for treating of peace with the Commissioners
' of the United States of America [the States mentioned by name
' in the body of the document], in behalf of His said Majesty, on
' the one part, and John Adams, Benjamin Franklin, John Jay,
' and Henry Laurens, four of the Commissioners of the said
' States, for treating of peace with the Commissioner of His said
' Majesty, on their behalf, on the other part,' were not signed
at Paris until the 30th of November 1782; the ' Armistice de-
' claring a cessation of hostilities between the United States
' and Great Britain,' at Versailles, until the 30th of January
1783; and the ' definite treaty of peace between the United
' States of America and His Britannic Majesty,' until the
3rd of September 1783. The seventh article of the first and
last treaties reads :—

' There shall be a firm and perpetual peace between His
' Britannic Majesty and the said States, and between the
' subjects of the one and the citizens of the other; wherefore

' all the hostilities, by both sea and land shall ["then im-
' " mediately " in provisional, and "from henceforth " in the
' definite treaty] cease ; all prisoners on both sides shall be set
' at liberty, and His Britannic Majesty shall, with all convenient
' speed, and without causing any destruction, *or carrying
' away any negroes,* or other property of the American in-
' habitants, withdraw all his armies, garrisons, and fleets from
' the said United States, and from every ["port " in first, and
' " post " in last document] place and harbour within the same ;
' leaving in all fortifications the American artillery that may be
' therein ; and shall also order and cause all archives, records,
' deeds, and papers, belonging to any of the said States, or their
' citizens, which in the course of the war may have fallen into
' the hands of his officers, to be forthwith returned and delivered
' to the *proper States* and persons to whom they belong.'

Great Britain did not carry out her agreement in respect to
the negroes. Sir Guy Carleton, in reply to Washington's
demand, declared that British officers could not give up those
who had been invited to their standard, but reserved the point
for his Government to consider, and in the meantime allowed and
facilitated the taking of schedules of all the slaves, their names,
ages, sex, former owners, and States to which they belonged.
The British Government resisted demands for compensation to
the owners on the ground that, being taken in war, no matter
how, negroes became, like other plunder, the property of the
captors, who had a right to dispose of it as they pleased, and had
chosen to set it free ; that the slaves, having become free, belonged
to nobody, and consequently it was no breach of the treaty stipulation to carry them away.   It will be observed that the officers
declined to surrender the fugitives on one ground, and the Government on another.   But should not the case, according to the
latter construction, have been decided by a properly constituted
prize court ?   The matter was contested by the ' Congress of the
Confederation ' to the end of its existence, on the 3rd of March
1789, and afterwards resumed by the new Government under
the Constitution, which went into operation on the 30th of April
1789.   Washington, as President, in his first message to
Congress, presented the non-execution of the treaty in this
particular, among others, as one of the justly existing causes of

complaint against Great Britain ; and all the diplomacy of his administration was exerted to obtain redress, but in vain. The treaties of 1794 and 1796 made no allusion to the subject; and being left unprovided for, the claim sank into the class of obsolete demands; the stipulation remained a dead letter, although containing the precise words and the additional one ' negroes,' on which the Emperor Alexander, in quality of arbitor, subsequently took the stand, as will presently be seen, which commanded compensation, and dispensed with arguments founded on the laws of the war.

In the war of 1812-14, the British adopted the same system of warfare : they encouraged the slaves to desert from their owners, promising them freedom, and finally carrying them off. John Quincy Adams, Jonathan Russell, and Albert Gallatin from the Northern States, and James A. Bayard and Henry Clay from the Southern States, the United States' Commissioners at Ghent, being aware of this, inserted in the first article of the treaty concluded at that place on the 24th of December 1814, these words :—

' All territories, places, and possessions whatsoever taken by
' either party from the other, during the war, or which may be
' taken after the signing of this treaty, excepting only the islands
' hereinafter mentioned, shall be restored without delay, and
' without causing any destruction, or carrying away any of the
' artillery or other public property originally captured in the said
' forts or places and which shall remain therein upon the ex-
' change of the ratifications of the treaty, or *any slaves* or other
' private property.'

The British Government undertook to extend the limitation applying to public property to that which was private also ; and so to restore only such slaves as were within the forts, at the time of the exchange of ratification—a construction which would not have included the return of negroes that had been induced to run away, or those that left the forts before the confirmation of the treaty. She adhered to the construction which she gave to the parallel article in the treaty of 1783. The American Government, on the contrary, insisted upon the return of all the negroes, or compensation for those that were missing.

The point of difference was finally left to the arbitrament of the Emperor Alexander of Russia, the United States being represented by Mr. Henry Middleton, and Great Britain by Sir Charles Bagot—the Counts Nesselrode and Capo d'Istria receiving the arguments to be laid before the Czar. His Majesty's decision was peremptory : ' That the United States of ' America are entitled to a just indemnification from Great ' Britain for all private property carried away by the British ' forces; and as the question regards slaves more especially, for ' all such slaves as were carried away by the British forces ' from the places and territories of which the restitution was ' stipulated by the treaty, in quitting the said places and ' territories.' This was explicit; but the British Minister saw fit to understand it as not applying to slaves who *voluntarily* joined the army to free themselves from bondage, and who came from places never in possession of the British troops; and he submitted a note to that effect to the Russian Minister, Count Nesselrode, to be laid before the Emperor, to which he received the following reply :—' The Emperor having, ' by the mutual consent of the two plenipotentiaries, given ' an opinion founded solely upon the sense which results from ' the text of the article in dispute, does not think himself called ' upon to decide here any question relative to what the laws ' of war permit or forbid to the belligerents ; but always faith- ' ful to the grammatical interpretation, that, in quitting the ' places and territories of which the treaty of Ghent stipulates ' the restitution to the United States, His Britannic Majesty's ' forces had no right to carry away from the same places and ' territories absolutely any slave, by whatever means he had ' fallen or come into their power.' A convention was then formally drawn up for the purpose of putting the Emperor's decision into effect, by establishing a Board to ascertain the numbers and value of the disputed slaves; it was signed in triplicate by the Commissioners of the three Powers. Further misunderstandings arose, five years more were consumed in diplomatic notes, and then a new Convention was concluded at London, on the 13th of November 1826, between Albert Gallatin, on the part of the United States, and the Right Hon.

William Huskisson and Henry Unwin Addington, Esq. on the part of Great Britain.

It commenced thus :—

' Difficulties having arisen in the execution of the convention
' concluded at St. Petersburg on the 12th day of July 1822,
' under the mediation of His Majesty the Emperor of all the
' Russias, between the United States of America and Great
' Britain, for the purpose of carrying into effect the decision of
' His Imperial Majesty upon the differences which had arisen
' between the said United States and Great Britain as to the
' true construction and meaning of the first article of the
' treaty of peace and amity concluded at Ghent on the 24th
' day of December 1814, the said United States and His
' Britannic Majesty, being equally desirous to obviate such
' difficulties, have respectively named plenipotentiaries to treat
' and agree respecting the same.

' Article 1. His Majesty the King of the United Kingdom of
' Great Britain and Ireland agrees to pay, and the United States
' of America agree to receive, for the use of the persons entitled
' to indemnification and compensation, by virtue of the said
' decision and convention, the sum of twelve hundred and four
' thousand nine hundred and sixty dollars current money of the
' United States, in lieu of, and in full and complete satisfaction
' for, all sums claimed or claimable from Great Britain, by any
' person or persons whatsoever, under the said decision and
' convention.'

The sum named in this article was satisfactory to the claimants, and the United States received the money and paid it over to them in 1827. More important than the acquisition of money, the example and principle thus established was an advantage gained by the Americans.

It will be observed by the precedent furnished in this historical sketch that Mr. Lincoln's proclamation granting freedom to the slaves in the Confederate States becomes so much waste paper, and that the Northern States will have to restore all slaves taken, as well as those that may have escaped within the Federal lines, or make ample compensation to the owners for their loss.

THE POSITION OF SLAVES IN THE AMERICAN STATES.

Slaves are recognised as persons as well as property in America. Mr. Jay thus explained, in the 'Federalist,' their *status*:—

'We must deny the fact that slaves are considered merely as
'property, and in no respect whatever as persons. The true state
'of the case is, that they partake of both these qualities, being
'considered by our laws in some respects as persons, and in
'other respects as property. In being compelled to labour, not
'for himself, but for a master; in being vendible from one
'master to another master; and in being subject at all times
'to be restrained in his liberty and chastised in his body by the
'capricious will of his owner; the slave may appear to be
'degraded from the human rank, and classed with those
'irrational animals which fall under the legal denomination of
'property. In being protected, on the other hand, in his life
'and in his limb, against the violence of all others, even the
'master of his labour and his liberty; and in being punishable
'himself for all violence committed against others; the slave
'is no less evidently regarded by the law as a member of the
'society, not as a part of the irrational creation; as a moral
'person, not as a mere article of property. The Federal Con-
'stitution, therefore, decides with great propriety on the case of
'our slaves, when it views them in the mixed character of
'persons and property. This is, in fact, their true character;
'it is the character bestowed on them by the laws under which
'they live, and it will not be disputed that these are the proper
'criteria.'

Slavery, too, is recognised by international law. Mr. Bayard, of Delaware, speaking on this branch of the subject in the Federal Senate, March 1861, said:—

'The doctrine that slavery only exists by positive law means,
'that when the slave is carried beyond the jurisdiction of a
'State which sanctions and authorises slavery by its positive
'law, he becomes entitled to his freedom. If, then, the Federal
'Government does not recognise the right of property in slaves,
'what becomes of the property in a slave when, under the
'Federal flag, the vessel is more than a marine league from the

‘ shore? There is no State jurisdiction, there is no authority to
‘ keep him in a state of bondage, if the principle be sound, that
‘ the moment he gets beyond the jurisdiction of a State, which
‘ sanctions slavery, he is entitled to his freedom, unless the
‘ Federal Government recognises the right of property in
‘ slaves. If the vessel were forced, by stress of weather, to
‘ enter the port of a foreign power, and the slaves were declared
‘ free, the Federal Government could make no demand upon the
‘ foreign Government for compensation to the owner, if it does
‘ not recognise the right of property ; and in cases such as the
‘ Enterprise, the Comet, and the Creole, would be entirely
‘ abandoned by an administration holding this dogma of the
‘ republican party, that freedom is national, and slavery local,
‘ and that the Federal Government does not recognise property
‘ in slaves. In two of those cases, where the vessel was driven
‘ into harbour by stress of weather, the British Government at
‘ first resisted the claim for compensation, but subsequently
‘ paid the value of the slaves to the claimants. In the third,
‘ the Creole, they refused, notwithstanding the forcible argument
‘ of Mr. Webster, under the law of nations, in favour of the
‘ claimant ; but, ultimately, under the convention with Great
‘ Britain, when the case came before a commission, the umpire
‘ decided in favour of the American claimant, and the sum
‘ awarded as the value of the slaves was paid to him.

*　　　*　　　*　　　*　　　*

‘ But it has been said that slavery is the mere creature of
‘ positive law. All property is the creature of positive law.
‘ The true doctrine is, that though slavery exists by virtue of
‘ local law, as all property must, it was and is recognised by the
‘ law of nations ; and that, being property, it is entitled to pro-
‘ tection, unless voluntarily taken within the jurisdiction of a
‘ State or Nation where positive law, written or unwritten, pro-
‘ hibits the relation. I shall not trouble the Senate with an
‘ argument on this question, but barely refer to those authorities
‘ which I suppose to vindicate the position—the position I
‘ assume in relation to the right of property in a slave as exist-
‘ ing under the law of nations. These are the decisions of Lord
‘ Stowell, one of the ablest jurists and most commanding
‘ authorities on all questions connected with the law of nations

R

‘ that can be found in the history of jurisprudence, in the case
‘ of the Louis, in 2 Dodson; the decision of the Supreme
‘ Court of the United States, sanctioning that adjudication, and
‘ adopting its principles in the case of the Antelope; and the
‘ decision of the Court of King’s Bench in the case of Madrago
‘ against Wilks, to be found, if my recollection is right, in 3
‘ Barnewall and Alderson. Lord Mansfield himself explained,
‘ in 4 Douglas, that the extravagant *dictum* which is imputed
‘ to him in the case of Somersett, does not sustain the principle
‘ in support of which it has so often been relied upon. He
‘ said, in the case in 4 Douglas, that where a negro came to
‘ England as a slave, and lived with his master, if an action
‘ were brought for the value of the service, though the service
‘ might be rendered, he always non-suited the plaintiff, unless
‘ there was an express contract proved; and such never could
‘ have been his decision, unless he recognised the existence
‘ of the relation as continuing to that extent in England.

‘ But the doctrine that the Constitution of the United States
‘ does not recognise slavery, and that the Federal Government
‘ is not bound to protect it to the extent of its jurisdiction,
‘ limited as that jurisdiction is, involves an absurd conclusion.
‘ The primary object of all government is the protection of
‘ persons and property; and to argue that a right of property
‘ which existed in twelve States of this Union, when the
‘ Constitution was formed, was not intended to be within the
‘ protection, to the extent of its jurisdiction, of the common
‘ government formed by thirteen States, is irrational and absurd.
‘ It needs no refutation. The object of all government being
‘ the protection of person and property, it would follow
‘ necessarily, that when the States constituted a common
‘ government, this property existing at the time of its con-
‘ struction in twelve of the thirteen States, that government was
‘ as much bound to protect such property as any other species
‘ of property; and if the obligation of government existed then,
‘ I am at a loss to see how it has now ceased.

‘ In addition, I will quote the language of Mr. Webster, used
‘ in the argument addressed to Lord Ashburton, in reference to
the case of the Creole. This was the case of a mutiny in which
‘ the slaves took possession of the vessel, and carried her into

‘ one of the Bahama Islands, where they were set free by the
‘ local authorities, and a claim was made for damages, which
‘ was resisted by Great Britain; but, as I have stated, was
‘ ultimately decided in favour of the claimants, under the Con-
‘ vention of 1853, by the umpire. In the course of that letter,
‘ dated August 1, 1842, Mr. Webster said :—

‘ “ In the Southern States of this Union, slavery exists
‘ “ by the laws of the States and under the guarantee of the
‘ “ Constitution of the United States, and it has existed in them
‘ “ for a period long antecedent to the time when they ceased
‘ “ to be British Colonies.”

‘ Again, after instancing the case of marriages in one country
‘ held valid in another, though celebrated in a manner not
‘ lawful in that other, he said :—

‘ “ It may be said, that in such instances personal relations
‘ “ are founded in contract, and therefore to be respected ;
‘ “ but that the relation of master and slave is not founded in
‘ “ contract, and therefore is to be respected only by the law of
‘ “ the place which recognises it. Whoever so reasons, en-
‘ “ counters the whole body of public law, from Grotius
‘ “ down, because there are numerous instances in which the
‘ “ law itself presumes or implies contracts ; and prominent
‘ “ among those instances is the very relation which we are now
‘ “ considering, and which relation is holden by law to draw
‘ “ after it mutuality of obligation.”

‘ Considering the weight and authority of the whole body of
‘ jurists and publicists, though exceptional opinions may be
‘ found, the result is, that slavery was the universal practice of
‘ man for ages ; that the right to hold property in slaves became
‘ part of the law of nations by universal usage, originating in
‘ captivity in war ; and that being so established, unless
‘ abolished by all nations, it, of course, is a right of property
‘ still existent ; and when one nation chooses to retain it, the
‘ right rests not in others to alter the law of nations as it formerly
‘ existed, though each nation may prohibit the existence of the
‘ relation within its own jurisdiction.’

LAWS ADVERSE TO FREE NEGROES IN THE NORTH, AND FOR THE PROTECTION OF SLAVE NEGROES IN THE SOUTH.

The Northern States.

The Legislature of Massachusetts (then including Maine) enacted in 1788 the following law, revised the same in 1798, and again in 1802:—

'That no person, being an African or negro, other than a
' subject of the Emperor of Morocco, or a citizen of the United
' States, to be evidenced by a certificate, &c., shall tarry within
' this commonwealth for a longer time than two months; if he
' does, the justices have power to order such person to depart,
' &c., and if such person shall not depart within ten days, &c.,
' such person shall be committed to the prison or house of
' correction.   And for this offence, &c., he shall be whipped, &c.,
' and ordered again to depart in ten days; and if he does not, the
' same process and punishment to be inflicted, and so *toties*
' *quoties.*'

Marriage between the white and black races is prohibited in Massachusetts and by Maine, by the laws of 1705, 1786 and 1835.

Connecticut, by statute of 1792, declared:—

'That when an inhabitant of the United States (this state
' excepted) shall come to reside in any town in this state, the
' civil authorities, or major part of them, are authorised, upon
' the application of the select men, if they judge proper, by
' warrant under their hands, directed to either of the constables
' of said town, to order said person to be conveyed to the State
' from whence he or she came.'

'The select men of the town are to warn any person not an
' inhabitant of this State, to depart from such town; and the
' person so warned, if he does not depart, shall forfeit and pay
' to the treasurer of such town, one dollar and sixty-seven cents
' per week.   If such person refuse to depart or pay his fine,
' such person shall be whipped on the naked body, not exceeding
' ten stripes, unless such person depart in ten days.'

'If any such person return after warning, he is to be whipped
' again, and sent away, and as often as there is occasion.'

The statute of 1796 says:—

' Whatsoever negro, mulatto, or Indian servant, shall be
' found wandering out of the bounds of the town or place to
' which they belong, without a ticket or pass in writing, to be
' taken up,' &c.

' No free negro is to travel without a pass from the select men
' or judges.'

' Every free person shall be punished by fine, &c., for buying
' or receiving anything from a free negro, mulatto, or Indian
' servant.'

Vermont declared in 1801, that :—

' The select men shall have power to remove from the State
' any persons who come there to reside. And any person
' removed, and returning without permission of the select men,
' shall be whipped not exceeding ten stripes.'

The laws of Rhode Island are :—

' The town council shall, if any free negro or mulatto shall
' keep a disorderly house, or entertain any person or persons at
' unreasonable hours, break up his house and bind him out to
' service for two years.'

' That no white person, Indian, or mulatto, or negro, keeping
' house in any town, shall entertain any Indian, mulatto or negro,
' servant or slave ; if he does, to be punished by fine,' &c.

' That none (Indian, negroes, and mulatto servants) should
' be absent at night, after nine o'clock. If found out, to be
' taken up and committed to jail till morning, and then appear
' before a justice of the peace, who is ordered and directed to
' cause such servant or slave to be publicly whipped by the
' constable, ten stripes.'

' That whosoever is *suspected* of trading with a servant or
' slave, and shall refuse to purge himself by oath, shall be
' adjudged guilty, and sentence shall be given against him,' &c.

New York, in 1801, passed this statute :—

' If a stranger be entertained in the dwelling-house or out-
' house of any citizen for fifteen days, without giving notice to
' the overseers of the poor, he shall pay a fine of five dollars.'

' If such person continue above forty days, justices can call
' on the inhabitants of the town or city, and the person may
' be sent to jail, &c. And the justices may cause such stranger

' to be conveyed from constable to constable, until transported
' into any other State, if from thence he came.'

' If such person return, the justices, if they think proper,
' may direct him to be whipped by every constable into whose
' hands he shall come : to be whipped, if a man, not exceeding
' thirty-nine lashes; and if a woman, not exceeding twenty-five
' lashes; and so as often as such person shall return.'

In 1788, the Legislature enacted, that ' no person shall
' harbour or conceal a slave from his master, under the penalty
' of a fine of 5l. sterling; and if the slave died while thus
' harboured, the party was liable to the owner for the value of the
' slave; nor could anyone trade or traffic with slaves without the
' permission of the master, under the penalty of 5l. and three
' times the value of the article traded for.'   And it was further
enacted, that—

' If any slave shall strike a white person, it shall be lawful for
' any justice of the peace to commit such slave to prison ; and
' such slave shall be tried and punished therefor,' &c.

' That from and after the passing of this Act, no slave shall be
' admitted for or against any person in any matter, cause, or thing
' whatsoever, civil or criminal, except in criminal cases in which
' the evidence of one slave shall be admitted for or against
' another slave.'

The law of New Jersey, 1798, declares :—

' That no free negro or mulatto, of or belonging to this
' State, shall be permitted to travel or remain in any county
' in this State, other than in the county where his or her place
' of residence may lawfully be, without a certificate from the
' justices of the peace of the county in which he or she
' belonged, or from the clerk of the county, under the seal of
' the court, certifying that such negro or mulatto was set free,
' or deemed and taken to be free in such county.

' That no slave shall be admitted as a witness against any
' white person, or even a free negro, in any matter or cause
' whatsoever.'

Ohio, in 1841, enacted :—

' That no black or mulatto person or persons shall hereafter
' be permitted to be sworn or give evidence in any court of
' record, or elsewhere in this State, in any cause depending, or

' matter or controversy, where either party to the same is a
' white person, or in any prosecution which shall be instituted
' in behalf of this State, against any white person.'

In 1860, a law passed the Legislature of Ohio, entitled ' An
' Act to prevent the Amalgamation of the White and Coloured
' Races.' Its provisions forbid persons possessing a visible
admixture of African blood to intermarry with any person of
pure white blood; and if any person solemnize such a marriage,
he is liable to be fined not more than $100; or imprisoned
for a term not exceeding three months, at the discretion of the
court.

' No white person shall intermarry with a negro or mulatto;
' and any marriages between a white person and a negro or
' mulatto shall be absolutely void, without any legal proceed-
' ings; and all children born of such persons shall be declared
' illegitimate and bastards.'

' Every person who shall knowingly counsel, abet, or assist in
' any way or manner whatever, in any marriage between any
' negro and white person, or between any person having one-
' eighth part or more of negro blood and any white person,
' shall, upon conviction thereof, be fined in any sum not less
' than $100, nor more than $1,000.'

' No negro, mulatto, or Indian shall be a witness, except on
' pleas of the State, against negroes, mulattoes, or Indians;
' and, in civil causes, where negroes, mulattoes, or Indians alone
' are parties, every person other than a negro having one-fourth
' part negro blood or more, or any whose grandfathers or grand-
' mothers shall have been a negro, shall be deemed an incom-
' petent witness.'

The Constitution of Indiana, adopted in 1851, says:—

' Article XIII.—1. No negro or mulatto shall come into or
' settle in the State after the adoption of this Constitution.

' 2. All contracts made with any negro or mulatto coming
' into the State, contrary to the provision of the foregoing
' section, shall be void; and any person who shall employ such
' negro or mulatto, or otherwise encourage him to remain in the
' State, shall be fined in any sum not less than $10, nor more
' than $500.'   *   *   *

' 3. All fines which may be collected for a violation of the

' provisions of this Article, or of any law which may hereafter
' be passed for the purpose of carrying the same into execution,
' shall be set apart and appropriated for the colonization of such
' negroes and mulattoes, and their descendants, as may be in the
' State at the adoption of this Constitution, and may be willing
' to emigrate.'

' 4. The General Assembly shall pass laws to carry out the
' provisions of this Article.'

The Constitution of Illinois (1810) says :—

' No person of colour, negro or mulatto, of either sex, shall
' be joined in marriage with any white person, male or female,
' in this State; and all marriage or marriage contracts entered
' into between such coloured person and white person, shall be
' null and void in law; and any person marrying or contracting
' to marry shall be liable to pay a fine, be whipped in not
' exceeding thirty-nine lashes, and be imprisoned no less than
' one year.'

In the statutes of Illinois (revised in 1833) it is declared
by the Act of 1819 :—

' That it shall not be lawful for any person or persons to
' bring into this State any negro or mulatto who shall be a
' slave, or held to service at the time, for the purpose of eman-
' cipating or setting at liberty any such negro or mulatto; and
' any person or persons who shall bring in any such negro or
  mulatto for the purpose aforesaid, shall give a bond to the
' county commissioners where such slave or slaves are emanci-
' pated, in the penalty of $1,000, conditioned that such person
' emancipated by him shall not become a charge upon any
' county in the State; and every person neglecting or refusing
' to give such bond shall forfeit and pay the sum of $200 for
' each negro or mulatto so emancipated or set at liberty.'

It was likewise enacted in 1819 :

' That any such servant (free negro), being lazy, disorderly,
' or guilty of misbehaviour to his master, or master's family,
' shall be corrected by stripes,' &c.

' That no negro, mulatto, or Indian, shall at any time pur-
' chase any servant other than their own complexion.'

' All contracts between masters and servants during the time
' of service shall be void.'

In 1827, it was enacted that : —

' A negro, mulatto, or Indian, shall not be a witness in any
' court, or in any case against a white person.

' A person having one-fourth part negro blood shall be
' adjudged a mulatto.'

In 1829, it was further enacted that : —

' Any person who shall hereafter bring into this State any
' black or mulatto person, in order to free him or her from
' slavery, or shall, directly or indirectly, bring into this State,
' or aid or assist any such black or mulatto person to settle or
' reside therein, shall be fined $100 on conviction or indictment,
' or before any justice of the peace of the county.'

The statutes of 1833, state : —

' That if any person or persons shall permit or suffer any
' slave or slaves, servant or servants of colour, to the number of
' three or more, to assemble in his, her, or their outhouse, yard,
' or shed, for the purpose of dancing or revelling either by
' night or by day, the person or persons so offending shall
' forfeit and pay a fine of $20.' It was made ' the duty of all
' coroners, sheriffs, judges, and justices of the peace, who shall
' see or know of, or be informed of, any such assemblage of
' slaves or servants, immediately to commit such slaves or
' servants to the jail of the county, and on view or proof thereof,
' order each and every such slave or servant to be whipped, not
' exceeding thirty-nine stripes, on his or her bare back.'

In 1853, the following law was enacted : —

' If any negro or mulatto, bond or free, shall hereafter come
' into this State, with the intention of residing in the same,
' every such negro or mulatto shall be deemed guilty of a high
' misdemeanor, and for the first offence shall be fined the sum
' of $50, to be recovered before any justice of the peace in the
' county where the said negro or mulatto may be found. . . . . .
' If the said negro or mulatto shall be found guilty, and the
' fine assessed be not forthwith paid, it shall be the duty of the
' said justice to commit the said negro or mulatto to the custody
' of the sheriff of the said county, or otherwise keep him, her,
' or them in custody. . . . . The said justice shall, at public
' auction, proceed to sell the said negro or mulatto to any
' person that will pay the said fine and costs, for the shortest

' time; and the said purchaser shall have a right to compel
' the said negro or mulatto to work for and serve out the said
' time,' &c.

The law of Michigan declares that : —

' No white person shall intermarry with a negro or mulatto.'

The Constitution of Oregon (admitted into the Union in 1859)
says : —

' No negro, Chinaman, or mulatto, shall have the right of
' suffrage ; ' and further declares that : —

' No free negro, or mulatto, not residing in this State at the
' time of the adoption of this Constitution, shall ever come,
' reside, or be within this State, or hold any real estate, or make
' any contract, or maintain any suit therein ; and the Legislative
' Assembly shall provide by penal laws for the removal by public
' officers of all such free negroes and mulattoes, and for their
' effectual exclusion from the State, and for the punishment of
' persons who shall bring them into the State, or employ or
' harbour them therein.'

Free negroes cannot vote in Connecticut, New Jersey, Pennsylvania, Ohio, Illinois, Michigan, Iowa, Wisconsin, Minnesota,
California and Oregon. Maine, Massachusetts, New Hampshire,
Vermont, Rhode Island, and New York, permit them to vote:
but in some cases, with property qualification.

The Southern States.

The Constitutions of Delaware and Maryland make no restrictions concerning the continuance of free negroes within their
limits. The Constitution of Virginia authorises the Legislature
to ' pass laws for the relief of the State from the free negro
' population, by removal or otherwise.' But no laws appear to
have been passed to that effect; in 1860 there were 58,042 free
negroes within her limits, a greater number than in any State,
North or South, except Maryland.

The Constitution of North Carolina declares : —

' No free negro, free mulatto, or free person of mixed blood,
' descended from negro ancestors to the fourth generation in-
' clusive (though one ancestor of each generation may have
' been a white person), shall vote for members of the Senate or
' House of Commons.'

In all the Southern States there are very complete laws for
he protection of slaves. A few extracts will suffice to show
heir general character.

In South Carolina, in 1703, it was enacted, that :—

' Any slave killing an enemy in time of invasion, shall be
granted his freedom. Any slave that gets wounded in the
attempt to kill an enemy, shall be supported at the public
expense. In either case the master shall be paid for his slave
from the public treasury.'

Subsequently it was enacted, that —

' In case any person, &c., who shall be owner, or who shall
have the care, government or charge, of any slave or slaves,
shall deny, neglect, or refuse to allow such slave or slaves
under his or her charge, sufficient clothing, covering, or food,
it shall and may be lawful for any person, on behalf of the
said slave or slaves, to make complaint to the next neighbouring
justice in the parish where such slave or slaves live or be
employed; and the said justice shall summon the party
against whom such complaint shall be made, and shall enquire
of, hear, and determine the same; . . . . and shall make
such orders for the relief of such slave or slaves as he in his
discretion shall think fit; and shall and may set and impose a
fine or penalty on any person who may offend in the premises,
in any sum not exceeding twenty pounds current money, for
each offence, to be levied by warrant of distress, and the sale
of the offender's goods.'

' In case any slave or slaves who shall not appear to have been
fed and clothed according to the intent and meaning of this
Act, that is to say, to have been sufficiently clothed, and to
have constantly received from the preceding year an allowance
of not less than a quart of corn per day, shall be convicted of
stealing any corn, cattle, &c. &c., from any person not the
owner of said slave or slaves, such injured person shall and
may maintain an action of trespass against the master, owner,
or possessor of such slave, &c., and shall recover his or her
damages.'

The Statute of 1820 reads :—

' That if any person or persons shall hereafter bring, or cause
' to be brought into this State, any free negro or person of colour

' and shall hold the same as a slave, or sell or offer the same for
' sale, to any person or persons in this State, as a slave, every
' such person or persons shall pay for every such free negro, or
' free person of colour, the sum of $1,000 over and above
' the damages which may be recovered by such free negro.'

The Act of 1837 declares—

' That whoever shall hereafter be convicted of the forcible or
' fraudulent abduction of any free person of colour living within
' this State, with intent to deprive him or her of his or her liberty
' shall be fined not less than $1,000, and be imprisoned for
' not less than twelve months!'

' And whoever, in addition to such abduction, shall actually sell
' or assist in selling, or cause to be sold, such person or slave,
' shall, upon being convicted thereof, in addition to such fine and
' imprisonment, receive thirty-nine lashes on the bare back.'

Judge O'Neall, of South Carolina, remarked :—

' Although slaves, by the Act of 1740, are declared to be chattels
' personal, yet they are also, in our law, considered as persons
' with many rights and liabilities, civil and criminal. The
' right of protection which would belong to a slave, as a human
' being, is, by the law of slavery, transferred to his master. A
' master may protect the person of his slave from injury, by
' repelling force with force, or by action, and in some cases by
' indictment. Any injury done to the person of his slave, he
' may redress by action of trespass *vi et armis*, without laying
' the injury done, with a *per quod servitum amisit*, and this
' even though he may have hired the slave to another.'

' By the Act of 1821, the murder of a slave is declared to be
' felony, without the benefit of clergy; and by the same Act, to
' kill any slave, on sudden heat or passion, subjects the offender,
' on conviction, to a fine of not exceeding $500, and imprison-
' ment not exceeding six months. To constitute the murder
' of a slave, no other ingredients are necessary than such as
' enter into the offence of murder at common law. So the
' killing, on sudden heat and passion, is the same as man-
' slaughter, and a finding by the jury, on an indictment for the
' murder of a slave, if the verdict be guilty of manslaughter, it
' is good, and the offender is to receive judgment under the Act.
' An attempt to kill and murder a slave by shooting at him, was

' held to be a misdemeanor, and indictable as an assault with
' an intent to kill and murder. This was a consequence of
' making it murder to kill a slave.'

' The Act of 1841 makes the unlawful whipping or beating
' of any slave, without sufficient provocation by word or act, a
' misdemeanor; and subjects the offender, on conviction, to
' imprisonment not exceeding six months, and a fine not ex-
' ceeding $500.'

The Constitution of Kentucky says : —

' The General Assembly shall pass laws, providing that any
' free negro or mulatto hereafter immigrating to, and refusing
' to leave this State, or having left, shall return and settle
' within this State, shall be deemed guilty of felony, and be
' punished by confinement in the penitentiary thereof.'

The constitution of Tennessee declares that : —

' All men of colour shall be exempt from military tax in
' time of peace; and also from paying a free poll-tax.'

The laws of Georgia declare that —

' Any owner of a slave or slaves, who shall cruelly beat such
' slave or slaves by unnecessary or excessive whipping; by
' withholding proper food and nourishment; by requiring greater
' labour from such slave or slaves than he, or she, or they may
' be able to perform; by not affording proper clothing, whereby
' the health of such slave or slaves may be injured or impaired;
' every such owner or owners of slaves shall, upon sufficient
' information being laid before the grand jury, be by said grand
' jury presented; whereupon it shall be the duty of the attorney
' or solicitor-general to persecute such owner or owners for
' misdemeanor; who, on conviction, shall be sentenced to pay
' a fine, or imprisonment in the county jail, or both, at the
' discretion of the court.'

' From and after the passing of this Act (1815), it shall be
' the duty of the inferior courts of the several counties in this
' State, on receiving information on oath, of any infirm slave or
' slaves, in a suffering condition, from the neglect of the owner
' or owners of said slave or slaves, to make particular inquiries
' into the situation of such slave or slaves, and render such
' relief as they, in their discretion, shall think fit. The said
' courts may, and are hereby authorised to, sue for and recover

' from the owner or owners of such slave or slaves, in any court
' having jurisdiction of the same, any law, usage, or custom to
' the contrary notwithstanding.'

' Any person who shall maliciously dismember, or deprive a
' slave of his life, shall suffer such punishment as would be in-
' flicted in case the like offence had been committed on a free
' white person, and on the like proof, except in case of insurrec-
' tion by said slave, and unless such death should happen by
' accident in giving such slave moderate correction.'

Louisiana requires that:—

' Every owner shall be held to give his slaves the quantity of
' provisions hereinafter specified — to wit, one barrel of Indian
' corn, or the equivalent thereof in rice, beans, or other grain, and
' a pint of salt; and to deliver the same to the slaves in kind,
' every month, and never in money, under a penalty of a fine of
' ten dollars for every offence. The slave who shall not have,
' on the property of his owner, a lot of ground to cultivate on
' his own account, shall be entitled to receive from the said
' owner one linen shirt and pantaloons for the summer, and a
' linen and woollen great coat and pantaloons for the winter.'

' As for the hours of work and rest which are to be assigned
' to slaves in summer, the old usage of the territory shall be
' adhered to: to wit, the slave shall be allowed half an hour for
' breakfast during the whole year; from the first of May to the
' first day of November, they shall be allowed two hours for
' dinner; and from the first day of November to the first day of
' May, one hour and a half for dinner. *Provided*, however, that
' the owners who will themselves take the trouble of causing to
' be prepared the meals of their slaves, be, and they are hereby
' authorised to abridge, by half an hour per day, the time fixed
' for their rest.'

The Constitution of Missouri says :—

' Any person who shall maliciously deprive of life, or dis-
' member a slave, shall suffer such punishment as would be
' inflicted for the like offence if it were committed on a white
' person.' That is, he shall suffer death by hanging.

The Constitution of Texas reads —

' They (the Legislature) shall have full power to pass laws,
' which will oblige the owners of slaves to treat them with hu-

' manity, to provide for them necessary food and clothing, to
' abstain from all injuries to them, extending to life or limb;
' and, in case of their neglect or refusal to comply with the
' directions of such laws, to have such slave or slaves taken from
' their owner, and sold for the benefit of such owner or owners.
' They may pass laws to prevent slaves from being brought into
' this State as merchandise only.'

' In the prosecution of slaves for the crimes of a higher grade
' than petit larceny, the Legislature shall have no power to de-
' prive them of an impartial trial by jury.'

' Any person who shall maliciously dismember or deprive a
' slave of life, shall suffer such punishment as would be inflicted,
' in case the like offence had been committed upon a free white
' person, and on the like proof, except in case of insurrection of
' such slave.'.

The Constitution of Florida says : —

' The General Assembly shall have power to pass laws to
' prevent free negroes, mulattoes, and other persons of colour,
' from immigrating to this State; or from being discharged
' from on board any vessel in any of the ports of Florida.'

The Laws of South Carolina, Georgia, Alabama, Mississippi,
Louisiana, Texas, Missouri and Arkansas, do not permit the
ingress of free negroes.

THE ANTAGONISM OF THE RACES.

In the first chapter of this book reference was made to the
opinion of scientific gentlemen concerning the inferiority of the
negro race. It may be added that Professor Meckel (see vol.
iii. p. 69, Mem. Acad. Berlin) discovered that not only the
blood, but that the bile and cortical part of the brain are of a
darker colour in the negro than in the white race. In fact,
that he is not only a negro in the skin, but under the skin.

Nicholas Pecklin, in a work entitled *De Cute Æthiopum*,
and Albinus (*Diss. de Sede et Causa Coloris Æthiop.*) remarked that the muscles as well as the blood of the negro are
of a darker red than of the white man. These authors also state
that the membranes, tendons, and aponeuroses, so brilliantly

white in the Caucasian race, have a livid cloudiness in the African.
J. J. Virey says (*Dict. Med. Sci. Paris*, vol. xxxv. p. 388), that
the negro's flesh differs in colour from the white man's as much
as the flesh of the hare differs from the rabbit.   He speaks, also,
of the blood, the smaller size of the brain, and the larger size of
the nerves in the negro than in the white man.   Sœmmerring
and Ebel, Cuvier, Gall, and Spurzheim confirm all these views.
Dr. Samuel George Morton (*Observations of the Size of the
Brain in Various Races and Families of Man*, Philadelphia,
1849) says ' that the negro's brain is nine cubic inches less than
' that of the white man.'   The evidence of many other scientific
men might be adduced to prove that the negro by nature is an
inferior being to the white man.   But these should suffice to
show that the efforts of the Abolitionists to elevate him to the
condition of the superior race will be as futile in the future as
they have been in the past.

Mr. Bayard, in his speech before referred to, said :—

' I am perfectly aware that the senators who live in States
' where the negro is sparsely scattered cannot well understand
' this effect of the antagonism of race, arising from large relative
' numbers of both races placed on terms of equality under the
' law in the same community.   In the State of Delaware the
' negro has no such equality, although we have but few slaves,
' and a vast mass of free negroes.   Under the constitution of the
' State, the negro cannot vote.   Under the common law, the
' presumption of freedom is against him, because his original
' *status* was that of a slave when he came to the country.   He
' is not entitled to be a witness in a court of justice, under the
' decisions of our courts, made early in the history of the State.
' There is an exception where legislative action has given him
' the right of being a witness where he sustained personal
' injury.   Yet, if the attempt were made to give equal civil and
' political rights, in the State of Delaware, to a free negro, it
' would inevitably result in a collision of races.

' I have, in a forensic experience of more than thirty-five
' years, seen this effect of the antagonism of race too strongly
' exemplified to doubt its existence.   It is what the Roman
' lawyers called the primary law of nature, the instincts of
' mankind—such as natural affection, and the like.   The white

‘ men will not, where they exist in large relative numbers, admit
‘ the negro on terms of civil or political, much less social,
‘ equality with themselves; and if the equality of rights be
‘ given where they exist in such numbers, their assertion renders
‘ the collision inevitable. In Delaware, the antagonism exists
‘ now to such an extent, that in personal controversies between
‘ the negro and the white man, the negro being disqualified to
‘ sit on a jury, or be admitted as a witness, except in cases of
‘ injury to his person, from the effect of this prejudice, as you
‘ may call it—I call it the natural instincts of men—he has but
‘ little chance of justice on the same evidence which might be
‘ fairly weighed between one white man and another. If the
‘ doctrine of the equality of race be true, and is once admitted,
‘ the collision must come; but to us it is not so formidable, for
‘ this reason, that when the collision comes, the white race has
‘ sufficient power, and could drive the inferior race from the State
‘ without hazardous contest.

‘ I have before stated in this chamber, what I believe the
‘ records of history will authenticate, that where two races of
‘ men so dissonant in their organisation that amalgamation is
‘ out of the question, live in the same community in large
‘ relative numbers, there is but one of two results—the sub-
‘ jugation of the inferior race or its extermination. I do not
‘ desire the extermination of the negro race. I would weave
‘ into the law of slavery every possible guard against the abuse
‘ of the power of the master, but never strike at the subjection
‘ of the inferior to the superior race. Where the negro exists in
‘ large relative numbers, amalgamation being out of the question,
‘ the law of races requires that he should be kept in a state of
‘ subjection, both for his own welfare as well as that of the white
‘ race. It is his normal condition, and the instinct of race—the
‘ primary law of nature—demands his subjection. Any attempt
‘ to enforce a contrary doctrine will only end in the common
‘ destruction of both races, or else in the extinction of the
inferior race.

‘ Sir, this antagonism of race exists in the State of Delaware
‘ and other States as between the negro and the white man,
‘ only where there is a large free negro population; it never
‘ exists in relation to the slave. Where the inequality is admitted,

' and the inferior race is held in slavery, the antagonism does
' not arise.   The assertion of equality alone creates it.   It is not
' confined to the African.   In the State of California, where they
' have about sixty thousand Chinese—I make the statement on
' the information of the honourable senator from that State,
' whose term expired at the close of the last session, of whom I
' made the inquiry during the session—in the State of California,
' where there are about sixty thousand Chinese, composing about
' one-seventh of the population, what is the result of the antago-
' nism of race ?   The Chinese are a civilised people—though, I
' admit, an effete civilisation ; they are an industrious people
' beyond all question : but in California the Chinese cannot be
' naturalised ; the Chinese cannot exercise a single political right ;
' the Chinese are not permitted to be witnesses in a court of
' justice ; and, as that senator stated to me, a Chinaman might
' be murdered in the presence of five hundred other Chinese by
' an American, and the law would afford no redress, for no one of
' the five hundred could be admitted in a court of justice for the
' purpose of establishing the guilt of the murderer.   This is but
' an illustration of the antagonism of race which will always
' exist between dissonant races residing in the same communities
' in large relative numbers.   The law has grown up by judicial
' decision in their courts, as part of the unwritten law of the
' States, founded on the antagonism of race, which exists where-
' ever the dissonance of race is so great, and the relative number
' is so large in the same community.   You may play with the
' thing, and make it a political hobby in those States in which
' the negro is found in sparse numbers ; but your doctrine of
' equality of races becomes too gravely serious in its effects when
' asserted in those States where the relation of races exists, as it
' does in the small State of which I am one of the representatives
' on this floor.   I only wish senators could fully appreciate the
' results of this doctrine of equality when applied to commu-
' nities in which the relation of races does exist, and I think the
' doctrine would be entirely abandoned.'

The writer of these pages was born, and has resided nearly all
his life in Pennsylvania, where exists the largest community of
free negroes in the world, and he can testify to the gradual

decay in their health and morals as slavery disappeared from the neighbourhood. Neither the laws of the land, nor public societies for his benefit, prevent the African from degenerating: nothing but the controlling influence of a master will keep him from sinking to that barbarous condition which is his natural state. Notwithstanding the attentions and care bestowed upon them by the Quakers, the negroes congregate in certain districts of Philadelphia, live in hovels, and behave in the most disreputable manner.

APPENDIX.

SLAVERY AND ABOLITION IN AMERICA.

Mr. Robert J. Walker, the author of the subjoined remarks in reference to the institution of African slavery in the Confederate States, having held a prominent position in America, a sketch of his political life may not be out of place. He was born in Northumberland county, Pennsylvania, in 1801, and graduated at the University of Pennsylvania, Philadelphia, in 1819, when he removed to Pittsburgh in the same State. He soon took an active part in politics, and became Chairman of the Democratic State Central Committee in 1823, supporting General Jackson for the presidency in 1824. None of the candidates that were balloted for having the constitutional majority of the electoral votes, Mr. John Quincy Adams, the second in plurality, was chosen by the House of Representatives. Mr. Walker shortly after this, in 1826, removed to Mississippi, where he began the practice of the law. At that time the State could not have had over 55,000 white inhabitants (the census of 1820 records only 42,634), and he at once assumed a leading and influential position within its limits, taking active interest in its internal affairs. In 1834 he was the Democratic nominee to represent the state in the Federal Senate; but was defeated, owing to the Whigs having a majority in the Legislature; he, however, was successful the following year, and took his seat as one of the 'ambas-'sadors' from Mississippi in the Capitol at Washington in January 1836, which he continued to hold until March 3, 1845, when he was appointed Secretary of the Treasury by President Polk, which office he retained during the four years of his administration. Mr. Walker, in the whole course of his career in Mississippi, in Congress, and indeed up to the year 1858, was a strong State rights man, with extreme Southern sentiments. He began so early as 1826 to 'agitate' the annexation of Texas, repudiating the treaty of 1819 with Spain, and with persevering energy accomplished his wishes. It was not, however, until March 3, 1836, that Texas 'seceded' from the Mexican Union. This act was followed by the Battle of San Jacinto on

April 21, 1836, in which Santa Anna was taken prisoner, and on May 20, 1836, the Mexican Government passed a decree annulling all stipulations made between him and the 'rebels.' Prior to this date, on May 4, 1836, Mr. Preston in the United States Senate presented a petition from citizens of Philadelphia in favour of recognising the independence of Texas. That petition must have been signed within a week after the battle of San Jacinto, and the intelligence of the conflict could not have reached Pennsylvania at that time, as, in those days, there was no telegraphic communication, and the mails were conveyed in a most tedious manner. Mr. Walker, in an able and earnest speech on May 23, 1836, urged upon the Senate the propriety of recognising the independence of Texas; and on June 18, 1836, Mr. Clay, as chairman of the Committee of Foreign Relations, agreed to the same so soon as it should appear that Texas had in 'successful 'operation a civil government capable of performing and fulfilling the 'obligations of an independent power.' The matter lay over until the next session, when, on January 11, 1837, Mr. Walker introduced the following resolution, which was passed on March 1, 1837, and approved by President Jackson two days thereafter.

'Resolved that the state of Texas having established and maintained 'an independent government, capable of performing those duties, 'foreign and domestic, which appertain to independent governments, 'and it appearing there is no longer any reasonable prospect of the 'successful prosecution of the war by Mexico against said State, it is 'expedient and proper, and in perfect conformity with the law of 'nations, and the practice of this Government in like cases, that the 'independent political existence of said State be acknowledged by the 'Government of the United States.'

Mr. Walker having opposed, on March 2, 1839, the pretensions of England concerning the Maine boundary question, and likewise having taken part, on February 16, 1843, against the assumption by the Federal Government of the State debts (which idea he charged as being of 'British origin'), combined with his actions in regard to Texas, made him quite popular throughout the North; and in October 1843, he was put forward by the Democrats of his own State as an eligible candidate for the Vice-Presidency. On November 25, 1843, he was addressed by a number of the citizens of Kentucky, who requested his views on the topics of the day. His reply, dated January 8, 1844, was very long, extracts from which are subjoined, as noticed above. This letter, although Mr. Dallas was selected by the National Democratic Convention as a candidate for the Vice-Presidency, was used as an electioneering pamphlet, and induced Mr. Polk to invite Mr. Walker to a seat in his Cabinet.

Mr. Walker did not return to Mississippi, but, after his term of office of Secretary of the Treasury expired, March 1849, he commenced the practice of law at Washington. In 1851 he visited Europe, and while in London, January 12, 1852, addressed a communication to Mr. Arthur Davies, in which will be found the following strong Southern doctrines:—

' The United States of America are a Confederated Republic, formed
' by and composed of separate States, with a written constitution,
' limiting and designating the powers granted by the States to the
' general Government, all others being reserved to the States them-
' selves. . . . We think, also, that it has been confirmed by long
' experience in our country; and that all our presidents, chosen by the
' people, from Washington to Fillmore, all included, in moral worth, in
' exemplary deportment, public and private, in talents and patriotism,
' were very far superior to any monarchs who, during any period of the
' world, have, *for an equal period of time*, been placed by hereditary
' descent and accident at the head of any country.'

Mr. Walker, from the fact of having changed his residence from Mississippi to Washington in 1849, of course lost his influence in that State; but Mr. Jefferson Davis, who entered the political arena as late as November 6, 1843, did not allow his removal to interrupt the friendship that had for a long while existed between them. Mr. Davis, after having served in the campaign against Mexico, and in Congress, was selected as Secretary of War by President Pierce, and entered upon the duties of that office March 4, 1853. Through his influence in the Cabinet, Mr. Walker was appointed Commissioner to China. He received his outfit, but did not enter upon the mission, and returned the amount advanced him by the Government for that purpose. At Mr. Davis's request, President Buchanan selected Mr. Walker for the Governorship of the territory of Kansas, and, on May 25, 1857, he delivered his address to the people of that district, which had become invested with a band of lawless Abolitionists from Massachusetts.* In this document he said:—

---

* In order to exhibit the difficulties then existing in Kansas in a true light before the European reader, the following account is furnished, with extracts from the Report of the Committee on Territories of the Federal Senate, submitted on March 12, 1856. The Act of Congress for the organisation of the territories of Kansas and Nebraska was designed to conform to the spirit and letter of the Federal Constitution, by preserving and maintaining the fundamental principle of equality among all the States of the Union, notwithstanding the restriction contained in section 8 of the Act of March 6, 1820 [preparatory to the admission of Missouri into the Union], which assumed to deny to the people for ever the right to settle the question of slavery for themselves, provided they should make their homes and organise States north of 36 degrees and 30 minutes north latitude. Conforming to the cardinal principle of State equality and self-government, in

'Under our practice, the preliminary act of framing a State Constitu-
'tion is uniformly performed through the instrumentality of a convention

obedience to the Constitution, the Kansas-Nebraska Act declared, in the precise
language of the compromise measures of 1850, that, 'when admitted as a State,
'the said territory, or any portion of the same, shall be received into the Union,
'with or without slavery, as their Constitutions may prescribe at the time of their
'admission.' Again, after declaring the said section 8 of the Missouri Act [some-
times called the Missouri compromise, or Missouri restriction] inoperative and
void, as being repugnant to these principles, the purpose of Congress in passing the
Act is declared in these words: —

'It being the true intent and meaning of this Act not to legislate slavery into
'State or Territory, nor to exclude it therefrom, but to leave the people thereof per-
'fectly free to form and regulate their domestic institutions in their own way,
'subject only to the Constitution of the United States.'

The passage of the Kansas-Nebraska Act was strenuously resisted by all persons
who thought it a less evil to deprive the people of new States and Territories of the
right of State equality and self-government under the Constitution, than to allow
them to decide the slavery question for themselves, as every State in the Union
had done, and must retain the undeniable right to do, so long as the Constitution
of the United States shall be maintained as the supreme law of the land. Finding
opposition to the principles of the Act unavailing in the halls of Congress and
under the forms of the Constitution, combinations were immediately entered into
in some portions of the Union to control the political destinies, and form and
regulate the domestic institutions of those Territories and future States, through
the machinery of emigrant aid societies. In order to give consistency and
efficiency to the movement, and surround it with the colour of legal authority, an
Act of incorporation was procured from the Legislature of the State of Massachusetts, in which it was provided in section 1, that twenty persons therein
named, and their 'associates, successors, and assigns, are hereby made a cor-
'poration, by the name of the Massachusetts Emigrant Aid Company, for the
'purpose of assisting emigrants to settle in the West; and for this purpose they
'shall have all the powers and privileges, and be subject to all the duties, re-
'strictions, and liabilities set forth in the 38th and 44th chapters of the revised
'statutes' of Massachusetts.

The Committee here enter into a detail regarding the Massachusetts Emigrant
Aid Society, and remark: —

'When a powerful corporation, with a capital of five million of dollars invested
'in houses and lands, in merchandise and mills, in cannon and rifles, in powder
'and lead, in all the implements of art, agriculture and war, and employing a
'corresponding number of men, all under the management and control of non-
'resident directors and stockholders, who are authorised by their charter to
'vote by proxy to the extent of fifty shares each, enter a distant and sparsely
'settled Territory with the fixed purpose of wielding all its power to control the
'domestic institutions and political destinies of the Territory, it becomes a question
'of fearful import how far the operations of the company are compatible with the
'rights and liberties of the people. Whatever may be the extent or limit of Con-
'gressional authority over the Territories, it is clear that no individual State has
'the right to pass any law or authorise any Act concerning or affecting the Ter-
'ritories, which it might not enact in reference to any other State.'

'It is a well-settled principle of Constitutional law in this country, that while

' of delegates, chosen by the people themselves. That convention is
' now about to be elected by you, under the call of the Territorial Legis-
' lature, created and so recognised by the authority of Congress, and
' clothed by it in the comprehensive language of the organic law, with
' full power to make such an enactment. The Territorial Legislature,
' then, in assembling in Convention, were fully sustained by the act of
' Congress, and the authority of the Convention is distinctly recognised
' in my instructions from the President of the United States. Those
' who oppose this course cannot aver the alleged irregularity of the
' Territorial Legislature, whose laws, in town and city elections, in corpo-
' rate franchises, and all other subjects but slavery, they acknowledge
' by their votes and acquiescence. If that Legislature was invalid,
' then are we without law or order in Kansas; without town, city, or
' county organisation ; all legal and judicial transactions are void ; all
' titles null, and anarchy reigns throughout our borders.

*　*　*　*　*　*　*

' The people of Kansas, then, are invited by the highest authority
' known to the Constitution to participate freely and fairly in the elec-
' tion of delegates to frame a Constitution and State Government. The
' law has performed its entire appropriate function when it extends to the
' people the right of suffrage ; but it cannot compel the performance
' of that duty. Throughout the whole Union, however, and wherever
' free government prevails, those who abstain from the exercise of the
' right of suffrage authorise those who do vote to act for them in that
' contingency ; and the absentees are as much bound under the law and
' constitution, where there is no fraud or violence, by the majority of
' those who do vote, as although all had participated in the election.
' Otherwise, as voting must be voluntary, self-government would be
' impossible, and monarchy or despotism would remain as the only
' alternative.

*　*　*　*　*　*　*

' Those who oppose slavery in Kansas, do not base their opposition
' upon any philanthropic principles, or any sympathy for the African
' race. For their so-called constitution, framed at Topeka, they deem

' all the States of the Union are united in one for certain purposes, yet each State,
' in respect to everything which affects its domestic policy and internal concerns,
' stands in the relation of a foreign power to every other State.'

Hence no State has a right to pass any law or do or authorise any Act, with a
view to influence or change the domestic policy of any other State or Territory in
the Union, more than it would with reference to France or England, or any other
foreign State with which we are at peace. Indeed, every State of this Union is
under higher obligations to observe a friendly forbearance and generous amity
towards each other member of the Confederacy than the laws of nations can impose
on Foreign States.

' that entire race so inferior and degraded as to exclude them all for
' ever from Kansas; yet such a clause, inserted in the Topeka constitu-
' tion, was submitted by the Convention for the vote of the people, and
' ratified by an overwhelming majority of the anti-slavery party. The
' party here, therefore, has in the most positive manner affirmed the
' constitutionality of that portion of the recent decision of the Supreme
' Court of the United States, declaring that Africans are not citizens of
' the United States.

' This is the more important, inasmuch as this Topeka Constitution
' was ratified with this clause, inserted by the entire Republican party
' in Congress; thus distinctly affirming the recent decision of the
' Supreme Court of the Union, that Africans are not citizens of the
' United States, for, if citizens, they may be elected to all offices, State
' and national, including the Presidency itself; they must be placed
' upon a basis of perfect equality with the whites, serve with them in
' the militia, on the bench, the legislature, the jury-box, vote in all
' elections, meet us in social intercourse, and intermarry freely with the
' whites.' *

* The decision of the Supreme Court was in the celebrated Dred Scott case
(1854). The Chief Justice Taney said: ' The question is simply this :—can a negro,
' whose ancestors were imported into this country, and sold as slaves, become a
' member of the political community formed and brought into existence by the Con-
' stitution of the United States, and as such become entitled to all the rights, and
' privileges, and immunities, guaranteed by that instrument to the citizen—one of
' which rights is the privilege of suing in a Court of the United States in the cases
' specified in the Constitution? . . . . It becomes necessary, therefore, to determine
' who were citizens of the several States when the Constitution was adopted. And
' in order to do this, we must recur to the governments and institutions of the thir-
' teen colonies, when they separated from Great Britain and formed new sovereign-
' ties, and took their places in the family of independent nations. We must enquir
' who, at that time, were recognised as the people or citizens of a State, whose
' rights and liberties had been outraged by the English Government; and who de-
' clared their independence, and assumed the power of government to defend their
' rights by force of arms. In the opinion of the Court, the legislation and histories
' of the times, and the language used in the Declaration of Independence, show
' that neither the class of persons who had been imported as slaves, nor their
' descendants, whether they had become free or not, were then acknowledged as a
' part of the people, nor intended to be· included in the general words in that
' memorable instrument.' After referring to a number of historical facts, Judge
Taney continues :—' The language of the Declaration of Independence is equally
' conclusive: it begins by declaring that, " when in the course of human events it
' " becomes necessary for one people to dissolve the political bands which have
' " connected them with another, and to assume among the powers of the earth the
' " separate and equal station to which the laws of nature and nature's God entitle
' " them, a decent respect for the opinions of manhood requires that they should
' " declare the causes which impel them to the separation." It then proceeds to
' say :—" We hold these truths to be self-evident: that all men are created equal;
' " that they are endowed by their Creator with certain unalienable rights: that

Governor Walker, in his first despatch to the Federal Secretary of State, under date of June 2, 1857, alluded to the efforts of the Abolitionists to disregard the law; and on the 14th he called for troops to defend the Territory from their actions. The next day, July 15, he writes ' that this movement at Lawrence was the beginning of a ' plan, originating in that city, to organise insurrection throughout the ' Territory; and especially in all towns, cities, or counties where the ' Republican party have a majority. Lawrence is the hot-bed of all ' the Abolition movements in the Territory. It is the town established ' by the Abolition Societies of the east, and whilst there are respectable ' people there, it is filled by a considerable number of mercenaries, who ' are paid by Abolition Societies to perpetuate and diffuse agitation ' throughout Kansas, and prevent a peaceful settlement of this question. ' Having failed in inducing their own so-called Topeka State Legisla- ' ture to organise this insurrection, Lawrence has committed it herself, ' and, if not arrested, the rebellion will extend throughout the Territory. ' .... In order to send this communication immediately by mail, ' I must close by assuring you that the spirit of rebellion pervades the ' great mass of the Republican party of this Territory, instigated, as I ' entertain no doubt they are, by eastern Societies.'

Yet notwithstanding these declarations, Mr. Walker finally ' sym- ' pathised' with the very desperadoes that he complains of, and was in consequence removed from his position by President Buchanan, when he united himself with the fortunes of Stephen A. Douglas, one of the greatest political demagogues America ever produced. Mr. Walker ceased from that moment to have any influence, but taking advantage of the crusade against the South, he delivered two violent Northern ' spread-eagle' speeches at Brooklyn and New York, after the fall of Fort Sumter in 1861, on April 23 and May 30; and he has since been more or less connected with the Lincoln administration. It is said in the newspapers that he has been the chief adviser of Mr. Chase, the

' " among them is life, liberty, and the pursuit of happiness; that to secure these ' " rights, governments are instituted, deriving their just powers from the consent ' " of the governed."

' The general words above quoted,' Judge Taney remarks, ' would seem to em- ' brace the whole human family, and if they were used in a similar instrument at ' this day, would be so understood. But it is too clear for dispute that the en- ' slaved African race were not intended to be included, and formed no part of the ' people who framed and adopted this declaration; for if the language, as under- ' stood in that day, would embrace them, the conduct of the distinguished men who ' framed this Declaration of Independence would have been utterly and flagrantly ' inconsistent with the principles they asserted; and instead of the sympathy of ' mankind, to which they so confidently appealed, they would have deserved and ' received universal rebuke and reprobation.'

Federal Secretary of the Treasury; and it is alleged that he is now in Europe as the representative of that department.

Mr. Walker has recently published two pamphlets, in which he opposes the recognition by England of the Confederate States, and affects to be an Abolitionist on philanthropic grounds, thus abandoning the principles he advocated so zealously when the question of the recognition of Texas was under discussion.

In the same pamphlets which he calls 'letters,' although they have neither superscription nor address, he makes a most virulent attack upon Mr. Jefferson Davis, and endeavours to fasten upon him the responsibility of Mississippi repudiation, an affair in which he was in no manner concerned, and which took place some years before his entrance into public life. It was only at the request of the editor of the *Washington Union* that Mr. Davis furnished the particulars connected with the Mississippi bonds for publication in that journal, May 25, 1849. On being subsequently attacked by a Whig newspaper in his own State, he explained the transaction with still greater detail in an article addressed to the editors of the *Mississippian.*

Although Mississippi did not receive one dollar for the bonds, Mr. Davis personally has been in favour of arranging the affair in question by a private subscription of the property owners in that state. He has never been Governor of Mississippi, as is supposed, nor did he ever hold office within its limits, excepting the unimportant one of Presidential Elector in 1844; and whatever influence that position conferred upon him with the incoming administration, was employed in urging Mr. Polk to invite Mr. Walker to a seat in his cabinet. During the 'repudiation' excitement, Mr. Walker was the leading politician in Mississippi, and Mr. Davis at that time was not a politician at all. Mr. Walker was a resident of Washington when Mr. Davis's letter appeared. Why did he not then reply to it? why does he wait for fourteen or fifteen years, in which interval he has been on terms of friendly association with, and has been the recipient of repeated favours from, the man he now seeks to defame?

He, however, does not deny the accuracy of Mr. Davis's statements, but endeavours by some ingenious use of terms to make him appear as the head and front of all offending.

It may not be out of place to add that, upon the formation of the Provisional Government of the Confederate States, and just after the intelligence reached this country that Mr. Davis had been selected as their President, some parties in London addressed a somewhat threat-

* A history of the repudiation of these Mississippi bonds will be found in Chapters II. & III. of the preceding work on the Cotton Trade.

ening letter to him, intimating that they would take measures to prevent the bonds of his Government being placed on the Stock Exchange until this Mississippi affair was settled to their satisfaction. The letter was despatched by the Arago on April 24, 1861, before the news of the fall of Fort Sumter came to hand, but the person conveying it was arrested by the authorities at New York, and returned to Europe. Whether the communication has ever been received by Mr. Davis, is not known. But whatever the ethical merits of the case may be, such a procedure, at such a time, cannot be too strongly condemned. It was a pusillanimous attempt to extort from the necessities of a government struggling for existence money that it was in no manner liable for. No similar demand or threat was made to the Federal power when Mississippi was a member of that Confederacy.

Extract from a Letter of the Hon. Robert J. Walker, Jan. 8, 1844, in favour of the Annexation of Texas.

THE only remaining objection is the question of Slavery. And have we a question which is to curtail the limits of the Republic—to threaten its existence—to aim a deadly blow at all its great and vital interests—to court alliances with foreign and hostile powers—to recall our commerce and expel our manufactures from bays and rivers that once were all our own—to strike down the flag of the Union, as it advances towards our ancient boundary—to resurrender a mighty Territory, and invite to its occupancy the deadliest (in truth, the only) foes this Government has ever encountered? Is anti-slavery to do all this? And is it so to endanger New Orleans, and the valley and commerce and outlet of the West, that we would hold them, not by our own strength, but by the slender tenure of the will and of the mercy of Great Britain? If anti-slavery can effect all this, may God, in His infinite mercy, save and perpetuate this Union—for the efforts of man would be feeble and impotent. The avowed object of this party is the immediate abolition of slavery. For this they traverse sea and land; for this they hold conventions in the capital of England; and there they brood over schemes of abolition in association with British Societies; there they join in denunciations of their countrymen, until their hearts are filled with treason; and they return home, Americans in name, but Englishmen in feelings and principles. Let us all, then, feel and know, whether we live North or South, that this party, if not vanquished, must overthrow the Government and dissolve the Union. This party propose the immediate abolition of slavery throughout the Union. If this were practicable, let us look at the consequences. By the returns of the last census, the products of the slaveholding States, in 1840, amounted in value to $404,429,368. These products, then, of the South must have alone enabled it to furnish a home market for all the surplus manufactures of the North, as also a market for the product of its forests and fisheries—and giving a mighty impulse to all its commercial and navigating interests. Now, nearly all these agricultural products of the South which accomplish all these great purposes, are the result of slave-labour; and, strike down these products by the immediate abolition of slavery, and the markets of the South, for want of the means to purchase, will be lost to the people of the North; and North and South will be involved in one common ruin. Yes, in the harbours of the North (at Philadelphia, New York, and Boston) the vessels would rot at their wharves for want of exchangeable products to carry; the building of ships would cease, and the grass would grow in many a street now enlivened by an active and progressive industry. In the interior, the railroads and canals would languish for want of business; and the factories and manufacturing towns and cities, decaying and deserted, would stand as blasted monuments of the folly of man. One universal bankruptcy would overspread the country, together with all the demoralisation and crime which ever accompany such a catastrophe; and the notices at every corner would point only to sales on execution, by the constable, the sheriff, the marshal, and the auctioneer; whilst the beggars would ask us in the streets, not for money, but for bread. Dark as the picture may be, it could not exceed the gloomy reality. Such would be the effects in the North, whilst in the South no human heart can conceive, nor pen describe, the dreadful consequences. Let us look at another result to the North. The slaves being emancipated, not by the South, but by the North, would fly there for safety and protection; and three millions of free blacks would be thrown at once, as if by a convulsion of nature, upon the States of the North. They would come there, to their friends of the North who had given them freedom, to give them also habitation, food, and clothing; and not having it to give, many of them would perish from want and exposure; whilst the wretched remainder would be left to live as they could, by theft or charity: they would still be a degraded caste, free only in name, without the reality of freedom. A few might earn a wretched and precarious subsistence by competing with the white labourers of the North, and reducing their wages to the lowest point in the sliding scale of starvation and misery; whilst the poor-house and the jail, the asylums of the deaf and dumb, the blind, the idiot, and insane, would be filled to overflowing, if indeed any asylum could be afforded to the millions of the negro race whom wretchedness and crime would drive to despair and madness.

That these are sad realities is proved by the census of 1840. I annex in an appendix a table marked No. 1, compiled by me entirely from the official returns of the census of 1840, except as to prisons and paupers which are obtained from city and State returns, and the results are as follows :—

1st. The number of deaf and dumb, blind, idiots, and insane, of the negroes in the non-slaveholding States, is 1 out of every 96; in the slaveholding States, it is 1 out of every 672, or 7 to 1 in favour of the slaves in this respect, as compared with the free blacks.

2nd. The number of whites, deaf and dumb, blind, idiots, and insane, in the non-slaveholding States, is 1 in every 561, being nearly 6 to 1 against the free blacks in the same States.

3rd. The number of negroes, who are deaf and dumb, blind, idiots, and insane, paupers, and in prison in the non-slaveholding States, is 1 out of every 6, and in the slaveholding States, 1 out of every 154, or 22 to 1 against the free blacks, as compared with the slaves.

4th. Taking the two extremes of North and South, in Maine, the number of negroes returned as deaf and dumb, blind, insane, and idiots, by the census of 1840, is 1 out of every 12, and in slaveholding Florida, by the same returns, is 1 of every 1,105; or 92 to 1 in favour of the slaves of Florida as compared with the free blacks of Maine.

By the report of the Secretary of State of Massachusetts (of November 1, 1843) to the Legislature, there were then in the county jails and houses of correction in that State 4,020 whites, and 364 negroes; and adding the previous returns of the State prison, 255 whites and 32 blacks, making in all 4,275 whites, and 396 free blacks; being 1 out of every 170 of the white, and 1 out of every 21 of the free black population; and by the official returns of the census of 1840, and their own official returns to their own Legislature, 1 out of every 13 of the free blacks of Massachusetts was either deaf and dumb, blind, idiot, or insane, or in prison—thus proving a degree of debasement and misery on the part of the coloured race in that truly great State which is appalling. In the last official report to the Legislature of the warden of the penitentiary of Eastern Pennsylvania, he says: ' The ' whole number of prisoners received from the opening of the insti- ' tution (October 25, 1829), to January 1, 1843, is 1,622; of these ' 1,004 were white males, 533 coloured males; 27 white females, ' and 58 coloured females ! ' or 1 out of every 847 of the white, and 1 out of every 64 of the negro population; and of the white female convicts, 1 out of every 16,288; and of the coloured female convicts, 1 out of every 349 *in one prison*, showing a degree of guilt and debasement, on the part of the coloured females, revolting and un-

paralleled. When such is the debasement of the coloured females, far
exceeding even that of the white females in the most corrupt cities of
Europe, extending, too, throughout one-half the limits of a great State,
we may begin to form some idea of the dreadful condition of the free
blacks, and how much worse it is than that of the slaves, whom we are
asked to liberate and consign to a similar condition of guilt and
misery. Where, too, are these examples? The first is in the great
State of Massachusetts, that, for 64 years, has never had a slave, and
whose free black population, being 5,463 in 1790, and but 8,669 at
present, is nearly the same free negro population, and their descendants,
whom for more than half a century she has strived, but strived in vain,
to elevate in rank and comfort and morals. The other example is the
eastern half of the great State of Pennsylvania, including Philadelphia,
and the Quakers of the State, who, with an industry and humanity that
never tired, and a charity that spared not time or money, have exerted
every effort to improve the morals and better the condition of their
free black population. But where are the great results? Let the
census and the reports of the prisons answer. Worse—incomparably
worse, than the condition of the slaves, and demonstrating that the free
black, in the midst of his friends in the North, is sinking lower every
day in the scale of want and misery. The *Regular Physicians' Report
and Review*, published in 1840, says, ' the facts, then, show an *increasing*
' disproportionate number of coloured prisoners in the eastern peniten-
' tiary.' In contrasting the condition, for the same year, of the peni-
tentiaries of all the non-slaveholding States, as compared with all the
slaveholding States in which returns are made, I find the number of
free blacks is 54 to 1, as compared with the slaves, in proportion to
population, who are incarcerated in these prisons. There are no
paupers among the slaves, whilst, in the non-slaveholding States, great
is the number of coloured paupers.

From the Belgian statistics, compiled by Mr. Quetelet, the distinguished secretary of the Royal Academy of Brussels, it appears that in
Belgium the number of deaf and dumb was 1 out of every 2,180
persons: in Great Britain, 1 out of every 1,539; in Italy, 1 out of
every 1,539; and in Europe, 1 out of every 1,474. Of the blind,
1 out of every 1,009 in Belgium; 1 out of every 800 in Prussia;
1 out of every 1,600 in France; and 1 out of every 1,666 in Saxony;
and no further returns as to the blind are given. [*Belgian Annuaire*,
1836, *pages* 213, 215, 217.] But the table shows an average in
Europe of 1 out of every 1,474 of deaf and dumb, and of about 1 out of
every 1,000 of blind; whereas our census shows, of the deaf and
dumb whites of the Union, 1 out of every 2,193; and of the blacks in
the non-slaveholding States, 1 out of every 656; also, of the blind,
1 out of every 2,821 of the whites of the Union, and 1 out of every

516 of the blacks in the non-slaveholding States. Thus we have not only shown the condition of the blacks of the non-slaveholding States to be far worse than that of the slaves of the South, but also far worse than that of the condition of the people of Europe, deplorable as that may be. It has been heretofore shown that the free blacks in the non-slaveholding States were becoming, in an *augmented* proportion, more debased in morals as they increased in numbers; and the same proposition is true in other respects. Thus, by the census of 1830, the number of deaf and dumb of the free blacks of the non-slaveholding States, was 1 out of every 996; and of blind, 1 out of 893; whereas we have seen, by the census of 1840, the number of free blacks, deaf and dumb, in the non-slaveholding States was 1 out of every 656; and of blind, 1 out of every 516. In the last ten years, then, the alarming fact is proved, that the *proportionate* number of free black deaf and dumb, and also of blind, *has increased about fifty per cent.* No statements as to the insane or idiots is given in the census of 1830.

Let us now examine the future increase of free blacks in the States adjoining the slaveholding States, if Texas is not reannexed to the Union. By the census of 1790 the number of free blacks in the States (adding New York) adjoining slaveholding States was 13,953. In the States (adding New York) adjacent to the slaveholding States, the number of free blacks by the census of 1840 was 148,107, being an aggregate increase of nearly 11 to 2 in New York, New Jersey, Pennsylvania, Ohio, Indiana, and Illinois. Now by the census and table above given, the aggregate number of free blacks who were deaf and dumb, blind, idiot or insane, paupers, or in prisons, in the non-slaveholding States was 26,342, or 1 in every 6 of the whole number. Now if the free black population should increase in the same ratio in the aggregate in New York, New Jersey, Pennsylvania, Ohio, Indiana, and Illinois, from 1840 to 1890, as it did from 1790 to 1840, the aggregate free black population in these six States would be, in 1890, 1,600,000; in 1865, 800,000; * in 1853, 400,000: and the aggregate number in these

* The African race does not flourish north of Mason and Dixon's line. Instead of 800,000, as Mr. Walker supposed there would be by this time, making his calculations on their former increase, there were not, according to the census of 1860, notwithstanding the 20,000 manumitted slaves from the South, one-fourth that number of blacks in the six States. Here are the figures:—

New York	49,005
New Jersey	25,318
Pennsylvania	56,849
Ohio	36,673
Indiana	11,428
Illinois	7,628
Total	186,901.

six States of free blacks, according to the present proportion, who would then be deaf and dumb, blind, idiot or insane, paupers or in prison, would be in 1890, 266,666 ; in 1865, 133,333 ; and in 1853, 66,666 ; being, as we have seen, one-sixth of the whole number. Now if the annual cost of supporting these free blacks in these asylums, and other houses, including the interest on the sums expended in their erection, and for annual repairs, and the money disbursed for the arrest, trial, conviction, and transportation of the criminals, amounted to $50 for each, the annual tax on the people of these six States, on account of these free blacks, would be in 1890, $13,333,200 ; in 1865, $6,666,600 ; and in 1853, $3,333,300.

Does, then, humanity require that we should render the blacks more debased and miserable by this process of abolition, with greater temptations to crime, with more of real guilt and less of actual comforts ? As the free blacks are thrown more and more upon the cities of the North, and compete more there with the white labourer, the condition of the blacks becomes worse and more perilous every day, until we have already seen the masses of Cincinnati and Philadelphia rise to expel the negro race beyond their limits. Immediate abolition, whilst it deprived the South of the means to purchase the products and manufactures of the North and West, would fill those States with an inundation of free black population, that would be absolutely intolerable. Immediate abolition, then, has but few advocates ; but if emancipation

---

The census says: 'When viewed apart from the liberations or manumission in the 'Southern States, the aggregate free coloured in this country must nearly represent ' " a stationary population," characterised by an equality of the current of births 'and deaths.'

The city registrar of Boston observes: 'The number of coloured births in this city for the five years ending in 1859, was one less than the number of marriages, and the deaths exceeded the births in the proportion of nearly two to one. In Providence, Rhode Island, in 1860, the deaths are one out of every twenty-four of the coloured, and in Philadelphia during the last six months of the census year, there were 184 births and 306 deaths among the negroes. In the State registries of Rhode Island and Connecticut, where the distinction of colour has been specified, the yearly deaths of the blacks and mulattoes have generally, though not uniformly, exceeded the yearly births — a high rate of mortality, chiefly ascribed to consumption and other diseases of the respiratory system. The free coloured population shows an actual decrease in the ten years, 1850 to 1860, in Maine, New Hampshire, Vermont, New York, and Oregon, and their increase in the other free States was very trifling. The total number of coloured emigrants sent to Liberia from 1820 to 1856 was 9,502, of whom 3,676 were free born. So the decline in population was not owing to that outlet. In 1850, 1,011 slaves escaped from their masters, or 1 out of every 3,165, while in 1860 there were only 803, being about 1 to every 5,000. This proves conclusively that the negroes have discovered the deceitful practices of the Northerns, and that they prefer to remain at home, where they are well taken care of.'

were not immediate, but only gradual, whilst slavery existed to any great extent in the slaveholding States bordering upon the States of the North and West, this expulsion, by gradual abolition, of the free blacks into the States immediately north of them would be very considerable, and rapidly augmenting every year. If this process of gradual abolition only doubled the number of free blacks to be thrown upon the States of the North and West, then a reference to the tables before presented proves that the number of free blacks in New York, Pennsylvania, New Jersey, Ohio, Indiana, and Illinois would be, in 1890, 3,200,000; in 1865, 1,600,000; and in 1853, 800,000; and that the annual expenses of the people of these six States on account of free blacks would be, in 1890, $26,666,400; in 1865, $13,333,200; and in 1853, $6,666,600.

It was in view, no doubt, of these facts that Mr. Davis, of New York, declared upon the floor of Congress on December 29, 1843, that ' the abolition of slavery in the Southern States must be followed by a ' *deluge of black population to the North*, filling our *jails* and *poor* ' *houses*, and bringing *destruction* upon the *labouring portion of our* ' *people*.' Dr. Duncan also, of Cincinnati, Ohio, in his speech in Congress on January 6, 1844, declared the result of abolition would be to inundate the North with free blacks, described by him as ' paupers, ' beggars, thieves, assassins, and desperadoes, all, or nearly all, penni- ' less and destitute, without skill, means, industry, or perseverance to ' obtain a livelihood, each possessing and cherishing revenge for sup- ' posed or real wrongs. No man's fireside, person, family, or property ' would be safe by day or night. It *now requires* the whole energies of ' the law and the whole vigilance of the police of all our principal cities ' to restrain and keep in subordination the few straggling *free negroes* ' which now infest them.' If such be the case now, what will be the result when by abolition, gradual or immediate, the number of these free negroes shall be doubled, and quadrupled, and decupled in the more northern of the slaveholding States, before slavery had receded from their limits, and nearly the whole of which free black population would be thrown on the adjacent non-slaveholding States? Much, if not all, of this great evil will be prevented by the reannexation of Texas. Since the purchase of Louisiana and Florida, and the settlement of Alabama and Mississippi, there have been carried into this region, as the census demonstrates, from the States of Delaware, Maryland, Virginia, and Kentucky, half a million of slaves, including their descendants, that otherwise would now be within the limits of those four States. Such has been the result as to have diminished, in two of these States nearest to the North, the number of their slaves far below what they were at the census of 1790, and to have reduced them at the census of 1840 in Delaware to the small number of 2,605. Now if we double the rate of diminution, as we certainly will by the reannexation of Texas, slavery will disappear from Delaware in ten years, and from Maryland in twenty, and have greatly diminished in Virginia and Kentucky. As, then, by reannexation slavery advances in Texas, it must recede to the *same extent* from the more Northern of the slaveholding States; and consequently the evil to the Northern States, from the expulsion into them of free blacks, by abolition, gradual or immediate, would thereby be greatly mitigated, if not entirely prevented. In the district of Columbia, by the drain to the new States and Territories of the South and South-west, the slaves have been reduced from 6,119, in 1830, to 4,694, in 1840; and if, by the reannexation, slavery receded in a double ratio, then it would disappear altogether from the district in twelve years; and that question, which now occupies so much of the time of Congress, and threatens so seriously the harmony, if not the existence of the Union, would be put at rest by the reannexation of Texas. This reannexation, then, would only change the locality of the slaves and of the slaveholding States, without augmenting their number. And is Texas to be lost to the Union, not by the question of the existence of slavery, but of its locality only? If slavery be considered by the States of the North as an evil, why should they prefer that its location should be continued in States on their borders, rather than in the more distant portions of the Union? It is clear that as slavery advances in Texas, it would recede from the States bordering on the free States of the North and West; and thus they would be released from the actual contact with what they consider an evil, and also from an influx from those States of a large and constantly augmenting population. As regards the slaves, the African being from a tropical climate, and from the regions of the burning sands and sun, his comfort and condition would be greatly improved by a transfer from northern latitudes to the genial and most salubrious climate of Texas. There he would never suffer from that exposure to cold and frost which he feels so much more severely than any other race; and there also, from the great fertility of the soil, and exuberance of its products, his supply of food would be abundant. If a desire to improve the condition and increase the comforts of the slave really animated the anti-slavery party, they would be the warmest advocates of the reannexation of Texas. Nor can it be disguised that, by the reannexation, as the number of free blacks augmented in the slaveholding States, they would be diffused gradually through Texas into Mexico, and Central and South America, where nine-tenths of their present population are already of the coloured races, and where, from their vast preponderance in number, they are not a degraded caste, but upon a footing not merely of legal, but, what is far more important, of actual, equality with the rest of the population. Here, then, if Texas is reannexed throughout the vast region and salubrious and delicious climate of Mexico, and of Central and Southern America, a large and rapidly increasing portion of the African race will disappear from the limits of the Union. The process will be gradual and progressive, without a shock, and without a convulsion; whereas, by the loss of Texas, and the imprisonment of the slave population of the Union within its present limits, slavery would *increase* in nearly all the slaveholding States, and a change in their condition would become impossible; or if it did take place by sudden or gradual abolition, the result would as certainly be the sudden or gradual introduction of hundreds of thousands of free blacks into the States of the North ; and if their condition there is already deplorable, how would it be when their number there should be augmented tenfold, and the burden become intolerable? Then, indeed, by the loss of the markets of Texas, by the taxation imposed by an immense free black population, depressing the value of all property—then also from the competition for employment of the free black with the white labourer of the North—his wages would be reduced until they would fall to ten or twenty cents a day, and starvation and misery would be introduced among the white labouring population. There is but one way in which the North can escape these evils, and that is the reannexation of Texas, which is the only safety-valve for the whole Union, and the only practicable outlet for the African population, through Texas into Mexico, and Central and Southern America. There is a congenial climate for the African race ; there cold, and want, and hunger will not drive the African, as we see it does in the North, into the poor-house and the jail, and the asylums of the idiot and insane. There the boundless and almost unpeopled territory of Mexico, and of Central and Southern America, with its delicious climate and most prolific soil, renders most easy the means of subsistence; and there they would not be a degraded caste, but equals among equals, not only by law, but by feeling and association.

The medical writers all say (and experience confirms the assertion) that ill-treatment, over-work, neglect in infancy and sickness, drunkenness, want, and crime, are the chief causes of idiotcy, blindness, and lunacy ; whilst none will deny that want and guilt fill the poor-house and the jail. Why is it, then, that the free black is (as the census proves) much more wretched in condition and debased in morals than the slave? These free blacks are among the people of the North, and their condition is most deplorable in the two great States of Maine and

Massachusetts, where, since 1780, slavery never existed.* Now the people of the North are eminently humane, religious, and intelligent. What, then, is the cause of the misery and debasement of their free black population ? It is chiefly in the fact that the free blacks, among their real superiors—our own white population—are, and ever will be, a degraded caste, free only in name, without any of the blessings of freedom. Here they can have no pride, no aspirations, no spirit of industry or emulation; and, in most cases, to live, to vegetate, is their only desire. Hence the efforts to improve their condition, so long made, in Massachusetts, Pennsylvania, and many other States, have proved utterly unavailing; and it grows worse every year as that population augments in numbers. In vain do many of the States give the negro the right of suffrage, and all the legal privileges of the whites; the colour marks the dreadful difference which here, at least, ages cannot obliterate. The negroes, however equal in law, are not equal in fact. They are nowhere found in the colleges or universities, upon the bench or at the bar, in the muster or the jury-box, in legislative or executive stations; nor does marriage, the great bond of society, unite the white with the negro, except a rare occurrence of such unnatural alliance as to call forth the scorn or disgust of the whole community.

Indeed, I could truly say, if passing into the immediate presence of

---

* It would appear from this remark that Mr. Walker is labouring under a very common misconception, arising from the fact that, when the census of 1790 was taken, it was found that there were no slaves within the limits of Massachusetts, at which date Maine formed part of the territory of that State, not having been admitted into the Union as an independent commonwealth until March 15, 1820. By an official census taken in 1754, Massachusetts possessed 4,896 slaves, about one-half of whom were over sixteen years of age, and their owners were not permitted to manumit them without giving security that they should not become a burden upon the parish; the greater portion were, however, sent to the other colonies; and the advertisements in the Boston newspapers of the time prove that the young negroes were given away during infancy to the neighbouring colonies, who would take them as slaves, so that the labour of the mothers might not be lost. Neither Massachusetts nor Maine passed any abolition or emancipation laws, slavery having died out from natural causes within their borders. On the contrary, Massachusetts, and of course Maine, demanded through their delegates in the Convention that framed the Constitution, in 1787, that the Federal Congress should not have the power of prohibiting the African slave trade until after the year 1808, and the people of these two States, one then being a territory, continued the traffic until that year, which shows very clearly that they recognised the institution. There is not to this day to be found in the statute books of either State any law adverse to slavery. The 'Bill of Rights' of 1780, to be sure, says that 'all men 'are born free and equal,' but then that language was copied from the Constitution of the State of Virginia formed in 1776, and the Declaration of Independence promulgated to the world the same year; and we all know that the clause referred only to white men, and it has been so decided by the Supreme Court.

the Most High, that, in morals and comforts, the free black is far below the slave; and that, while the condition of the slave has been greatly ameliorated, and is improving every year, that of the free blacks (as the official tables demonstrate) is sinking in misery and debasement at every census, as, from time to time, by emancipation and other causes, they are augmented in number. Can it, then, be sinful to refuse to change the condition of the slaves to a position of far greater wretchedness and debasement, by reducing them to the level of the free negro race, to occupy the asylums of the deaf and dumb, the blind, the idiot and insane; to wander as mendicants; to live in pestilent alleys and hovels, by theft or charity; or to prolong a miserable existence in the poor-house or the jail? All history proves that no people on earth are more deeply imbued with the love of freedom, and of its diffusion everywhere, among all who can appreciate and enjoy its blessings, than the people of the South; and if the negro slave were improved in morals and comforts, and rendered capable of self-government, by emancipation, it would not be gradual, but immediate, if the profits of slavery were tenfold greater than they are. Is slavery, then, never to disappear from the Union? If confined within its present limits, I do not perceive when or how it is to terminate. It is true Mr. George Tucker, the distinguished Virginian, and professor in their great university, has demonstrated that, in a period not exceeding eighty years, and probably less, from the density of population in all the slaveholding States, hired labour would be as abundant and cheap as slave labour, and that all *pecuniary* motive for the continuance of slavery would then have ceased. But would it, *therefore*, then disappear? No, it certainly would not; for, at the lowest ratio, the slaves would then number at least ten millions. Could such a mass be emancipated? And if so, what would be the result? We have seen, by the census and other proof, that one-sixth of the free blacks must be supported at the public expense, and that, at the low rate of $50 each, it would cost $80,000,000 per annum, to be raised by taxation, to support the free blacks then in the South requiring support—namely 1,666,666, if manumission were permitted; but as such a tax could not be collected, emancipation would be as it now is, *prohibited by law,** and slavery could not disappear in this

---

* MANUMISSION OF SLAVES.—The following is an extract from the preliminary report of the Eighth Federal Census (p. 11):—'With regard to manumission, it 'appears from the returns that during the census year they numbered a little more 'than 3,000, being more than double the number who were liberated in 1850, or at 'the rate of 1 each to 1,309; whereas, during 1850, the manumissions were as '1 to every 2,181 slaves. Great irregularity, as might naturally be expected,

manner, even when it became unprofitable. No, ten millions of free blacks, permitted to roam at large in the limits of the South, could never be tolerated. Again, then, the question is asked, Is slavery never to disappear from the Union? This is a startling and momentous question, but the answer is easy, and the proof is clear; *it will certainly disappear if Texas is reannexed to the Union*; not by abolition, but against and in spite of all its frenzy, slowly, and gradually, by diffusion, as it has already thus nearly receded from several of the more northern of the slaveholding States, and as it will continue thus more rapidly to recede by the reannexation of Texas, and finally, in the distant future, without a shock, without abolition, without a convulsion, disappear into and through Texas, into Mexico and Central and Southern America. Thus, that same overruling Providence that watched over the landing of the emigrants and pilgrims at Jamestown and Plymouth—that gave us the victory in our struggle for independence—that guided by His inspiration the framers of our wonderful Constitution—that has thus far preserved this great Union from damages so many and imminent, and is now shielding it from abolition, its most dangerous and internal foe—will open Texas as a safety-valve, into and through which slavery will slowly and gradually recede, and finally disappear into the boundless regions of Mexico and Central and Southern America. Beyond the Del Norte slavery will not pass; not only because it is forbidden by law, but because the coloured races there preponderate in the ratio of ten to one over the whites; and holding, as they do, the Government, and most of the offices, in their own possession, they will never permit the enslavement of any portion of the coloured race which makes and executes the laws of the country. In Bradford's Atlas the facts are given as follows :—

Mexico—area, 1,690,000 square miles; population 8,000,000—one-sixth white, and all the rest Indians, Africans, mulattoes, Zambos, and other coloured races.

Central America—area, 186,000 square miles; population nearly 2,000,000—one-sixth white, and the rest negroes, Zambos, and other coloured races.

South America—area, 6,500,000 square miles; population, 14,000,000

' appears to exist for the two periods whereof we have the returns on this subject. ' By the Eighth Census, 1860, it appears that manumissions have greatly increased ' in number in Alabama, Georgia, Louisiana, Maryland, Mississippi, North Carolina, ' and Tennessee, while they have decreased in Delaware and Florida, and varied ' but little in Kentucky, Missouri, South Carolina, and Virginia, and other slave- ' holding States not mentioned.' Manumission is not ' prohibited by law ;' the freed negroes in many of the States have, however, without special acts of their Legislatures, to be removed from within their borders. In several of the Northern States there are stringent laws against the admission of any blacks.

— 1,000,000 white, 4,000,000 Indians, and the remainder, being 9,000,000, blacks and other coloured races.

The outlet for our negro race, through this vast region, can never be opened but by the reannexation of Texas; but in that event, there, in that extensive country, bordering upon our negro population, and four times greater in area than the whole Union, with a sparse population of but three to the square mile, where nine-tenths of the population is of the coloured races—there, upon that fertile soil, and in that delicious climate, so admirably adapted to the negro race, as all experience has now clearly proved—the free black would find a home. There, also, as slaves, in the lapse of time, from the density of population and other causes, are emancipated, they will disappear from time to time west of the Del Norte, and beyond the limits of the Union, among a race of their own colour; will be diffused throughout this vast region, where they will not be a degraded caste, and where, as to climate, and social and moral condition, and all the hopes and comforts of life, they can occupy, among equals, a position they can never attain in any part of this Union.

Since the foregoing pages were in type, Mr. Walker has issued another pamphlet or ' letter,' headed ' American finances and resources,' and to which he, as in the former productions, affixes with his name various titles—a somewhat anti-American way of making himself known to the British public. This, however, would be an innocent indulgence of vanity did he not 'parade' one to which he has not a proper claim. He never was ' Commissioner to China,' nor is it customary on the other side of the Atlantic, or even proper here, for an ex-secretary of the treasury to make use of the European expression, ' Minister of Finance,' as it is the chairman of the Committee of Ways and Means in the House of Representatives that holds the position equivalent to that occupied by the Chancellor of the Exchequer. Mr. Walker might be pardoned for these little bits of assumption, which are, no doubt, adduced in order to give weight to the unfortunate cause which he at present represents; but he has no right to attempt to mislead the capitalists of Europe by endorsing Mr. Chase's statements of the indebtedness of the Federal States, when he knows that they are utterly false. Mr. Chase, however, takes the precaution to add to his totals the saving clause, ' as appears by the books of the Treasury department.' If he would furnish the amounts due by the war, navy, state, and other branches of the Washington Government, full light might be thrown upon the subject. The fact is, that the entire indebtedness of the United States is $3,000,000,000, and it is complete folly in the Federal authorities to attempt to hide it from view, as it must soon appear, now that the shipments of breadstuffs, which have given to the North nearly $200,000,000 of specie funds, since the election of Mr. Lincoln, will cease. That large sum, with the aid of the credit system that has so long existed in the Northern States, which he has completely monopolised, directly and indirectly, has enabled him 'to go through' up to the present time : but his downfall is now imminent. It is probable that the several departments of the Government have not 'settled,' or rather issued, paper of the various kinds, for over $2,000,000,000. This huge amount has been floated by 'currency' to the extent of $500,000,000 ; the wants of the community from that source having, by the inflation, been increased from $350,000,000 ; and, by contractors consuming the former mercantile credit of the country, which was $900,000,000 in time of peace, but has now been augmented to $1,500,000,000, owing to the 'bubble' state of affairs that at present exist. The 'unsettled' portion of the Federal debt is about equal to the profits of the war and navy contractors, and those of the host of Government employés.

Mr. Walker does not act on the principle that 'self-praise is no commendation.' He boasts that, under *his* system, Federal securities were advanced to five per cent. premium. He avoids stating that at the time he took his seat as Secretary of the Treasury, March 4, 1845, the States had fully and fairly recovered from the panic of 1837 ; that the moderate tariff of 1846 increased their prosperity ; that the shipments of grain and provisions, with the high freights thereon, to supply the European deficiencies of that year, threw into the hands of the Americans about $100,000,000 ; that the military successes in Mexico, the acquisition of California, and the discovery of gold in that territory in 1848, as well as the revolution in Europe, and augmented cotton crops, all taking place prior to the end of his term of office, March 3, 1849, were a combination of favourable circumstances for the American States that had never before existed within any period of four years.

Mr. Walker's praise of Mr. Chase's system of finance, which of course is *not* meant to flatter the latter gentleman, is very absurd, and it is practising a piece of cruelty upon history—in fact, torturing it—to give him the *credit* (for dear knows he has enough of *that* already) for the invention. 'Let honour be given to whom honour is due.' Mr. John Law established a 'paper' system in Paris in 1715 ; after similar 'success' to that of Mr. Chase, it exploded in three years, shaking the foundations of the French Government, from which they never fairly recovered. At that period, the same 'system' was in operation in the New England States, and shared a like fate. The continental money of the American and the assignats of the French revolutions were both of the 'same pattern,' and met with the same result. It is, therefore, simply trifling with the good sense of his readers for Mr. Walker to say that Mr. Chase's system ' is without a precedent in history.'

He, Walker, becomes quite a joker when he calls 'greenbacks' a 'legal tender;' he means that they are issued 'according to (John) *Law*.'

Ridiculous as are Mr. Walker's other assertions, it is very ungrateful in him to attack Mr. Buchanan's administration, which he, by another able pamphlet on the slavery question, helped to place in power. In that pamphlet he stated, that in the event of the success of the Fremont party—the black republicans of 1856—the Southern States ought to secede. Indeed, the documents savoured so strongly of State rights, that Mr. Jefferson Davis, and a number of leading Southerners, urged upon Mr. Buchanan the appointment of Mr. Walker, as Secretary of State. But their efforts were outweighed by Mr. Howell Cobb and other (then) Union men of the South, ' now in the traitor army,' and General Cass was selected for the post. Mr. Walker accepted office (Kansas) under Mr. Buchanan's administration, and this was *after* the Ostend manifesto, and other horrible things of which he now complains. Mr. Walker is inconsistent as well as insincere.

Mr. Walker, in charging bad financial management upon Mr. Buchanan's administration purposely (because he was in confidential intercourse with it at the time) overlooks the fact, that so soon as Mr. Cobb took charge of the Treasury department, March 4, 1857, he, in accordance with the instruction of the old Congress, paid off a large portion of the Federal debt; that a commercial panic occurred in the latter part of that year, and continued throughout his whole term of office; and that the receipts from customs and sales of public lands, the chief sources of revenue, declined fifty per cent. below those of the previous administration.

Mr. Walker promises another pamphlet. In the meanwhile, his knowledge of finances might be improved by a perusal of a paper entitled ' Principles of Credit,' by Charles Francis Adams, which will be found in Hunt's 'Merchants' Magazine,' New York, vol. ii. p. 185, 1840. It might also be well for him to read that clause in the constitution which states that nothing ' but gold and silver coin' can be made a legal tender, and his own ' reports' when Secretary of the Treasury.

Mr. Walker is very reckless as to titles; even that of his last production assumes to give an account of the ' resources' of America. But not a word is said on the subject. His letter of January 6, 1844, the extract from which is prefixed, states in substance that the North has no ' resources' whatever, and that the Federal States will be ruined, without slavery, and the slave productions of the South. He, too, draws a very graphic picture of their downfall.

THE CONDITION OF THE NEGROES IN HAYTI.

Robert M. Walsh, Esq., of Pennsylvania, who was a commissioner from the United States to Hayti, wrote as follows to Mr. Webster while Secretary of State :—

' I trust you will pardon me, if I sometimes wander from the serious ' tone appropriate to a despatch ; but it is difficult to preserve one's ' gravity with so absurd a caricature of civilisation before one's eyes ' as is here exhibited in every shape.

' Nothing saves these people from being infinitely ridiculous but the ' circumstance of their being often supremely disgusting by their ' fearful atrocities. The change from a ludicrous farce to a bloody ' tragedy is here as frequent as it is terrible ; and the smiles which the ' former irresistibly provoke, can only be repressed by the sickening ' sensations occasioned by the latter.

' It is a conviction which has been forced upon me by what I have ' learned here, that negroes only cease to be children when they dege- ' nerate into savages. As long as they happen to be in a genial mood, ' it is the rattle and the straw by which they are tickled and pleased ; ' and when their passions are once aroused, the most potent weapons ' of subjugation can alone prevent the most horrible evils. A resi- ' dence here, however brief, must cause the most determined philan- ' thropist to entertain serious doubts of the possibility of their ever ' attaining the full stature of intellectual and civilised manhood, unless ' some miraculous interposition is vouchsafed in their behalf. In ' proportion as the recollections and traditions of the old colonial ' civilisation are fading away, and the imitative propensity, which is ' so strong a characteristic of the African, is losing its opportunities of ' exercise, the black inhabitants of Hayti are reverting to the primitive ' state from which they were elevated by contact with the whites, a ' race whose innate superiority would seem to be abundantly proved by ' the mere fact that it is approaching the goal of mental progress, while ' the other has scarcely made a step in advance of the position in ' which it was originally placed. It is among the mulattoes alone, as ' a general rule, that intelligence and education are to be found ; but ' they are neither sufficiently numerous, nor virtuous, nor enlightened, ' to do more than diminish the rapidity of the nation's descent, and ' every day accelerates the inevitable consequence by lessening their ' influence and strength.

' The contrast between the picture which is now presented to this
' country, and that which it exhibited when under the dominion of the
' French, affords a melancholy confirmation of what I have said. It
' was then, indeed, an " exulting and abounding " land, a land literally
' flowing with milk and honey; now, it might be affirmed, without
' extravagance, that where it is not an arid and desolate waste, it is
' flooded with the waters of bitterness, or covered with noisome and
' poisonous weeds.

' The Government, in spite of its constitutional forms, is a despotism
' of the most ignorant, corrupt, and vicious description, with a military
' establishment so enormous that, while it absorbs the largest portion
' of the revenue for its support, it dries up the very sources of natural
' prosperity, by depriving the fields of their necessary labourers to fill
' the town with pestilent hordes of depraved and irreclaimable idlers.
' The treasury is bankrupt, and every species of profligate and ruinous
' expedient is resorted to, for the purpose of obtaining the means of
' gratifying an insane passion for frivolous expenditure. A great
' portion of the public revenue is wasted upon the personal vanities of
' the Emperor, and his ridiculous efforts to surround himself with a
' splendour which he fancies to be pre-eminently imperial. It is a
' fact, that the same legislature which voted him several hundreds of
' thousands of francs for some absurd costume, refused an appro-
' priation of 25,000 francs for public schools. The population, for the
' most part, is immersed in Cimmerian darkness, that can never be
' pierced by the few and feeble rays which emanate from the higher
' portions of the social system, while there is a constant fermentation
' of jealousies and antipathies between the great majority and the only
' class at all capable of guiding the destinies of the land which threaten
' at every moment to shatter the political vessel in which they are so
' perilously working. As to the refining and elevating influences of
' civilised life—the influences of religion, of literature, of science, of
' art—they do not exert the least practical sway, even if they can be
' said to exist at all. The priests of the altar set the worst examples of
' every kind of vice, and are universally mere adventurers, disarmed
' by the Church, who alone can come here in consequence of the
' assumption by the Emperor of ecclesiastical authority which militates
' with that of the Roman pontiff.

' The press is shackled to such a degree as to prevent the least
' freedom of opinion, and people are afraid to give utterance, even in
' confidential conversation, to aught that may be tortured into the
' slightest criticism upon the action of the Government.

' In short, the combination of evil and destructive elements is such,

' that the ultimate regeneration of the Haytians seems to me to be the
' wildest of Utopian dreams. Dismal as this picture may appear, its
' colouring is not exaggerated. It is as faithful a representation as
' I can sketch of the general aspect of this miserable country, a
' country where God has done everything to make his creature happy,
' and where the creature is doing everything to mar the work of
' God.'

THE COMMERCE BETWEEN THE UNITED KINGDOM OF GREAT BRITAIN AND IRELAND AND THE UNITED STATES OF AMERICA, FOR THE YEAR 1860.

IMPORTATIONS FROM THE STATES.

Southern produce.

Cotton	£30,069,306
Flour, wheat, and maize .	2,366,147
Tobacco	1,181,182
Bacon	224,556
Lard	188,004
Beef	117,439
Pork	50,000
Rice	81,602
Hams	15,300
Tallow	47,345
Oil seed cake . . .	64,319
Hides	33,763
Timber	414,052
Spirits of turpentine .	213,917
Turpentine . . .	85,868
Resin	178,990
Tar	19,178
Bark	24,841

£35,405,809

Northern produce.

Flour, wheat, and maize .	£4,000,000
Cheese	532,143
Bacon	200,000
Lard	200,000
Butter	347,459
Beef	200,000
Pork	58,584
Hams	40,000
Tallow	300,000
Hides	150,000
Hops	254,865
Oil seed cake . . .	250,000

Carried forward £6,533,351

Southern produce—brought forward . . £35,405,809

          Brought forward £6,533,351

Clover seed . . .	196,788	
Wool	92,211	
Clocks	64,888	
Pot and pearl ashes .	84,344	
		6,921,582

Foreign produce.

Skins and furs . .	263,686	
Caoutchouc . . .	92,732	
Cigars	62,687	
Tea	45,325	
Logwood . . .	41,481	
Whale fins . . .	34,244	
Peruvian bark . .	13,921	
		554,076
		£42,881,467

EXPORTATIONS TO THE STATES.

Cotton manufacturers .	£4,534,136
Woollen ,, . .	4,084,693
Iron	3,136,340
Linen	2,084,165
Apparel, slops, &c. .	1,417,262
Hardwares and cutlery .	1,054,908
Tin plates . . .	1,018,536
Earthenware . . .	654,283
Soda	526,806
Silk manufactures . .	463,420
Coals, &c. . . .	192,779
Printed books . .	140,941
Drugs	125,627
Leather . . .	123,777
Salt	119,993
Empty bags . . .	104,873
Beer and ale . . .	100,375
Lead and shot . .	88,531
Plate and jewellery .	83,839
Painter's colours . .	75,351
Linseed oil . . .	7,477
Glass manufactures .	67,078
Spirits	66,322
Copper (wrought) . .	64,342
Stationery . . .	44,053 .

      Carried forward £20,379,907

Brought forward	20,379,907
Machinery . .	42,238
Tin (wrought) .	23,185
Wool . . .	206,274
Indigo . . .	154,678
Gums, lac, dye, &c.	94,486
Raw silk . .	72,856
Peruvian bark .	56,252
Hides . . .	47,169
Cochineal . .	35,930
Iron in bars . .	34,466
Opium .	30,893
Brandy . .	24,204
Wines .	26,233
Argol .	18,070
Bristles	16,793
Sundries	1,644,047
	£22,907,681

Recapitulation (1860).

Imports from the States	£42,881,467	
Exports to „ .	22,907,681	
		19,973,786
Gold and silver imported from the States . .	4,792,582	
Gold and silver exported to the States .	1,724,008	3,068,574
		£23,042,360

The balance of trade with the Continent of Europe, the East Indies, China, and South America, was against the States, and in favour of the United Kingdom; the differences were settled by bankers' credits.

Tonnage employed in conducting the commerce between the United Kingdom and the American States (1860).

Country	Entered		Cleared		Total	
	Ships	Tonnage	Ships	Tonnage	Ships	Tonnage
British . .	613	488,181	629	522,678	1,242	1,010,859
American . .	1,174	1,174,991	1,178	1,164,991	2,352	2,339,101
Other nations .	145	60,876	193	117,258	339	178,134
Total . .	1,932	1,724,048	2,000	1,804,046	3,932	3,528,094

A large portion of the commerce between the United Kingdom, India, and China is carried on by Northern American vessels.

The value of Gold and Silver Bullion and Coin supposed to be in the American States, 1800 to 1861.

1800	.	. $17,500,000	1831	.	. $34,000,000
1801	.	. 17,000,000	1832	.	. 38,000,000
1802	.	. 16,500,000	1833	.	. 45,000,000
1803	.	. 16,000,000	1834	.	. 49,000,000
1804	.	. 17,500,000	1835	.	. 55,000,000
1805	.	. 18,000,000	1836	.	. 65,000,000
1806	.	. 18,500,000	1837	.	. 73,000,000
1807	.	. 20,000,000	1838	.	. 87,500,000
1808	.	. 20,000,000	1839	.	. 87,000,000
1809	.	. 27,000,000	1840	.	. 83,000,000
1810	.	. 25,000,000	1841	.	. 75,000,000
1811	.	. 26,000,000	1842	.	. 76,000,000
1812	.	. 24,000,000	1843	.	. 96,000,000
1813	.	. 20,000,000	1844	.	. 100,000,000
1814	.	. 18,000,000	1845	.	. 96,000,000
1815	.	. 22,000,000	1846	.	. 97,000,000
1816	.	. 26,500,000	1847	.	. 120,000,000
1817	.	. 27,000,000	1848	.	. 112,000,000
1818	.	. 25,000,000	1849	.	. 120,000,000
1819	.	. 25,000,000	1850	.	. 154,000,000
1820	.	. 24,000,000	1851	.	. 186,000,000
1821	.	. 24,000,000	1852	.	. 204,000,000
1822	.	. 25,000,000	1853	.	. 236,000,000
1823	.	. 26,000,000	1854	.	. 250,000,000
1824	.	. 27,000,000	1855	.	. 260,000,000
1825	.	. 28,000,000	1856	.	. 280,000,000
1826	.	. 29,000,000	1857	.	. 290,000,000
1827	.	. 30,000,000	1858	.	. 320,000,000
1828	.	. 31,000,000	1859	.	. 330,000,000
1829	.	. 31,000,000	1860	.	. 350,000,000
1830	.	. 32,000,000	1861	.	. 375,000,000

Bank Note Circulation in the American States (1800 to 1861).

Year	Amount		Year	Amount
1800	$10,500,000		1831	$67,000,000
1801	11,000,000		1832	72,000,000
1802	10,000,000		1833	80,000,000
1803	11,000,000		1834	94,000,000
1804	14,000,000		1835	103,000,000
1805	15,000,000		1836	140,000,000
1806	17,000,000		1837	149,000,000
1807	18,000,000		1838	116,000,000
1808	22,500,000		1839	135,000,000
1809	20,500,000		1840	107,000,000
1810	25,000,000		1841	75,000,000
1811	28,000,000		1842	80,000,000
1812	40,000,000		1843	90,000,000
1813	62,000,000		1844	100,000,000
1814	99,000,000		1845	96,000,000
1815	53,000,000		1846	97,000,000
1816	69,000,000		1847	120,000,000
1817	45,000,000		1848	112,000,000
1818	45,000,000		1849	120,000,000
1819	46,000,000		1850	155,000,000
1820	45,000,000		1851	186,000,000
1821	46,000,000		1852	204,000,000
1822	47,000,000		1853	236,000,000
1823	48,000,000		1854	205,000,000
1824	50,000,000		1855	187,000,000
1825	53,000,000		1856	198,000,000
1826	54,000,000		1857	215,000,000
1827	56,000,000		1858	155,000,000
1828	58,000,000		1859	193,000,000
1829	60,000,000		1860	207,000,000
1830	61,000,000		1861	202,000,000

www.ingramcontent.com/pod-product-compliance
Lightning Source LLC
Chambersburg PA
CBHW021726110726
47902CB00005B/1364